Rainbow
Milk
Paul
Mendez

dialogue
books

DIALOGUE BOOKS

First published in Great Britain in 2020 by Dialogue Books
This paperback edition published in 2021 by Dialogue Books

1 3 5 7 9 10 8 6 4 2

A CIP catalogue record for this book
is available from the British Library.

ISBN 978-0-349-70058-8

Typeset in Berling by M Rules
Printed and bound in Great Britain by
Clays Ltd, Elcograf S.p.A.

Papers used by Dialogue Books are from well-managed forests
and other responsible sources.

Dialogue Books
An imprint of
Little, Brown Book Group
Carmelite House
50 Victoria Embankment
London EC4Y 0DZ

An Hachette UK Company
www.hachette.co.uk

www.littlebrown.co.uk

Paul Mendez was born and raised in the Black Country, and is a novelist, essayist and screenwriter. He now lives in London and is studying for an MA in Black British Literature at Goldsmiths, University of London. He has been a performing member of two theatre companies, and worked as a voice actor, appearing on audiobooks by Andrea Levy, Paul Theroux and Ben Okri. As a writer, he has contributed to *Esquire*, *The Face*, *Vogue*, *Times Literary Supplement*, *London Review of Books* and *Brixton Review of Books*. *Rainbow Milk* is his debut novel.

'This debut cements Mendez as a stunning new voice in fiction. Semi-autobiographical, this gripping coming-of-age story set in the Black Country in the 1950s follows 19-year-old Jesse as he comes to terms with his racial and sexual identity against the backdrop of his repressive religious upbringing ... An original addition to the queer fiction canon' *Cosmopolitan*

'Exquisite descriptions of the body, of longing and lust, set against the recent history of the nation. Proof once more there can be no discussion of English history that isn't also a discussion of blackness, queerness and class' Andrew McMillan

'Sensuous and thrillingly well written' *Observer*

'Eye-poppingly frank, urgent and fresh' Suzi Feay, *Financial Times*

'Moving and memorable, *Rainbow Milk* heralds Mendez as an original new voice in queer fiction' *AnOther* magazine

'This book is marvellous. It is beautifully written, balancing fine observation and pathos, sexuality and high culture, struggle with triumph. It's pacy, witty and gentle. I loved every minute of reading this, and I am excited for its future readers' Okechukwu Nzelu, author of *The Private Joys of Nnenna Maloney*

'Mendez's powerful coming-of-age story tackles subjects from immigration and religion to sex and race as nineteen-year-old Jesse struggles to make sense of the world' the *i*

'When did you last read a novel about a young, black, gay, Jehovah's Witness man from Wolverhampton who flees his community to make his way in London as a prostitute? This might be a debut, but Mendez is an exciting, accomplished and daring storyteller with a great ear for dialogue. Graphic Erotica Alert! Don't read this book if you like your fiction cosy and middle-of-the-road' Bernardine Evaristo

'*Rainbow Milk* is a rich, beautifully-crafted story, uncompromising in its exploration of identity and privilege. The characters are portrayed with such tenderness and honesty – I know that I'll be thinking about them for years to come' Angela Chadwick

'The kind of novel you never knew you were waiting for. An explosive work that reels from sex, to sin, to salvation all the while grappling with what it means to black, gay, British, a son, a father, a lover, even a man. A remarkable debut' Marlon James

'Vivid, moving and packs a visceral punch' Lisa Appignanesi

'This is a debut novel but it reads like a pro ... His prose is cool, slippery and cuts clean to the quick. He takes you places unfamiliar and confusing and with a sentence connects you to the core of the character's mind. It's a fast ride in an astonishingly cool car ... His sensual explorations of desire are mixed together with withering condemnations of British imperialist ideology, folded in with tender reflections on parenting, and what it means to be young, queer and black in the UK today' GScene

'One of the most widely anticipated books of 2020 (the *Observer* named Mendez as one to watch), *Rainbow Milk* is a coming-of-age story that touches on racism, the Windrush generation, sexual identity and love. Beautifully written, this is a must for your reading list this month' *Stylist*

'[*Rainbow Milk*] is more real and generous than most contemporary novels. Ultimately, this is a searing account of the human need for physical connection. Mendez never shies away from the melodrama of sex, the cymbal-crashing opera of desire. He is a unique new voice in the British novel' Johanna Thomas-Corr, *Sunday Times*

'A novel that does what great debuts do – bringing an originality of voice and vision to the form, refreshing our ideas of what is possible in fiction . . . a novel of huge power and emotional impact, written in language that is sharp, distinctive and often beautiful. 2020 has been a year of superb debuts and *Rainbow Milk* is among the best' Alex Preston, *Observer*

'Urgent, original and heartbreaking' *Irish Times*

'A debut novel set to make a name for its author, *Rainbow Milk* is a tightly-written but wide-ranging exploration of race, sexuality, class and religion' *New European*

'Daring, dexterous, exciting and accomplished, Mendez is a writer with plenty to say' *Attitude*

'The prose is muscular, the sex graphic, the dialogue sharp . . . *Rainbow Milk* is a complex and intersectional treatment of race, class, sexuality and sex work and a powerful, thrilling and accomplished debut novel' *The Skinny*

'A fearlessly groundbreaking debut' Colin Grant, *Guardian*

'A state of the nation novel ... extraordinary ... the voice of the character is so strong ... Paul Mendez is now a significant new figure in the literary world ... James Baldwin would be very proud of this book' BBC Radio 4 *Front Row*

'Exhilarating ... *Rainbow Milk* is an important and ambitious book ... a bravura piece of writing, with echoes of Andrea Levy's *Small Island* ... think Barry Jenkins's *Moonlight* but set in the West Midlands, with Bibles instead of crack ... if *Rainbow Milk* is anything to go by, Mendez looks set to shake up the literary establishment in the most thrilling way' the *i*

'A fearless and hopeful account of one black man's entry into adulthood that explores identity, family and sexuality against the backdrop of the Windrush legacy ... this is a wonderful read from an exciting new voice in British fiction' *Independent*

'A very beautifully and tenderly written account of what it was like to come to the "mother country", expecting a welcome and finding prejudice' Stephen Hough, *Telegraph*

'*Rainbow Milk* is a bold and raw novel ... memorable and affecting' Nadifa Mohamed, *New Statesman*

For James and Bertie

SWAN VILLAGE

July 20, 1959

This the best summer since we come to England three year ago. It hot, not hot like Jamaica but I don't feel a cloud pass the sun today, and no rain has fall for a long time now. I stand on my front lawn and breathe. The bush are strong with plenty of fragrant rose. My son Robert love to totter round with the watering can, that almost as big as him. I can hear how much water he is pouring on each root. I don't know how he can't feel the cold water dribbling on his foot. Strong little man. He is going to be tall; already he is quite up to my knee. Glorie want to help but she is too small, and I have to listen for her all the time in case I trip up on her or she scratch herself on the thorn.

'Not too much, son,' I say to Robert when I can hear the water start to puddle. 'Move to the next one.'

'Allo, little man, am you helpin' ya dad water the garden?' Mr Pearce, my neighbour, make me jump as he walk up his path.

'Say hello to Mr Pearce, Robert.'

'Hello,' he say, all quiet.

I say, 'Good afternoon, Mr Pearce. How are you today?', knowing he will just go on and on about his ailment.

'Oh, I int too bad, you know. Same old aches and pains. Me arthritis 'as been playin' me up summat rotten but I can't complain. Ethel int well herself, with her legs. Cor wait til your lad's big enough to run down the shops for we. Anyway, it's a bit hot for me in this heat. It's alright for you, coming from the West Indies.'

'Not really,' I say. 'My body used to the cold, now.' I have hardly any sight left but I know Mr Pearce never leave his door without his flat cap, old work coat and boot, though he must have retired from the gas work ten year ago.

'You must've heard all that that's been happenin' down London with all them White Defence League rallies. We was ever so sorry to see they'd painted them Keep England White or whatever it is on your door. Me and Ethel was talking about it the other night and we both agreed that *we* don't mind you being here at all. We'm all the same, int we, white or coloured or not.'

I should not be still here in the sun, like what the doctor said, because my head start to throb and darkness falling on my eye, so I step closer to the house, into the shade.

'Well, that is very kind of you, Mr Pearce. Your bag must be heavy. Why don't you take them inside and we'll talk later on. Robert, where are you?'

'Here, Daddy,' he say, still watering the rose and singing to himself. He love the new Cliff Richard song 'Living Doll', and he don't know the word, but he can sing the melody in his nice little voice.

'Remember to water the soil not the flower. Where is your sister?'

'There with the block,' he say, like I'm stupid cos I can't see what right in front of me. Cha. True, now I see the blur of her white gown in the middle of the lawn, and hear the crack-crack of the block as she bash one on another.

'Gerrin' big, ay they. How old am they, now?'

'Robert soon three, Glorie ten months.'

'He's ever so clever, int he!'

Clever but every time I hear one engine pass I fear he will dash into the road and dead under the wheel of a truck, or run and hide in the gas work. I don't have eyesight but that is the vision I have.

'Yes, he is a good help to we, especially with his sister.'

'And what about your Claudette? Ethel was saying she never sees her now. She thought you might've locked her up in the basement or summat,' him laugh.

I force myself to laugh a little bit with him, even though it hurt my head.

'No, no. She is fine. She just work a lot, at the factory and the hospital.'

'It's a shame, int it, in your culture, for the wife to be out doin' all the work while the 'usband's at home?'

'That not the same in every country?' I know I have to be careful the way I speak sometime. 'Nothing we can do about it anyway, for she is healthy and I am sick.' I wish this man can just mind his business so I can take my children inside and rest my head.

'You finish with the water, Robert?'

'Yes, Daddy,' Robert say.

'Good boy. Go play with your sister, then,' I tell him, and like any child told their work is done he throw down the can with a thud.

'Pick it up properly and put it by the door,' I say to him, and nobody talk until he do as him told.

'Bet you wish you could see them roses more clear. They look absolutely beautiful against your white fence.'

I sigh, the way this man torment me. 'I can't lie to you, Mr Pearce. I do wish I did have back my sight.'

'How much can you see?'

Not my children face, is the pity. 'Nothing, really. Everything is a blur. All I can see is colour, spread out and mix up together.'

'Such a shame. Fit young lad like you. Well, I can tell you, your garden's looking grand. Sometimes I see people trying to take cuttings, you know, and I always chase 'em off. Oh. Alright am ya!'

He is speaking to someone across the street who did call *Coowee!* Sound like Mrs Philpott from number three. I don't mind being blind in front of her.

'Good afternoon, Mrs Philpott,' I say.

'Afternoon,' she call, and I can hear her upturn nose. She always jealous of my rose, like so many people who have nice garden but who not an expert like me.

'Who came to steal my rose?' I ask Mr Pearce.

'It was, er, a woman. It happened just last week. I was sitting waiting for the postman and I seen her through me winder. Brazen cow her was, come right up your path in broad daylight with her clippers to take a cuttin' o' them ones right behind you there, the dark red'uns with the white tips. I knocked on me winder and she ran off. I int seen her before or since.'

'The Girod de l'Ain?'

'Ay?'

'Baron Girod de l'Ain. A French lawyer and politician who did help conquer Napoleon. The rose name after him.'

'Yo've been readin' your history books, then,' he say, like it a crime. 'I thought you was bloind.'

'I use to work as a gardener in Jamaica for a very high-class Englishman. He teach me about all the variation and their history. It why I know exactly which rose to plant and where. I did want rose that smell beautiful and fragrant, some for the shade, some for the sun, some for climb, all for repeat.'

'Is that so? Oh well. I'd better get all this in before the milk spoils. Alright, young Norman.'

'Thank you, Mr Pearce, and do send my regard to Ethel. Don't worry yourself when people want to take from me, for their conscience will burn them. The rose will grow back anyway. I'll see you, Mr Pearce.'

His front door shut. He's not so bad, really. When we first come here, he and Ethel don't talk to we for must be the first six month. Then I hear at work somebody say that most English people don't like to live next door to a West Indian family, for they don't like the smell of we food. Well. I write a little coupon from the newspaper to Mr Austin, the nurseryman of Wolverhampton. I choose the Baron, the pink Souvenir de la

Malmaison, the white Boule de Neige, the Honorine de Brabant, which light pink with a streak of blood red, and Kronprinzessin Viktoria, white, with a hint of yellow. And so I plant them in the spring, bountiful. I give them space to grow but build them up, and water them, and this is what we have now. Finally the Garden of Eden we come for, and not a sniff of Jamaican food will reach a white man nostril through these bush. Must be the most fragrant garden on the whole estate. I don't know if it would grow so strong if I did still working all day at the gas work. Jasmine at we back door, to stop the smell of coal burning coming into the kitchen.

'You want toto, baby?'

'Yes!'

'What you say?'

'Yes, please!'

'Good boy. Pick up Glorie block for me and come inside.'

I wonder who it is who try to take cutting from my rose bush. When you blind, it seem like anybody can come and do anything to you, and there is nothing you can do, like when Claudette did come home from work bawling to me, asking me how I did not hear somebody come up to we door to paint KBW – *Keep Britain White* – on it, when I was in the front room asleep with my children.

Back home I did use to work full-time for one American hotel in St Ann's Bay. Claudette work as waitress in the restaurant and I work outside. The white American love Claudette because she pretty and light-skin with long, wavy hair, but she wasn't charm by their fat white American money. Plenty time she find me to cry about some badmind drunk white man who think brown skin girl easy. We know one another from a long time ago, for we come from the same part of the parish, where Marcus Garvey born. Claudette visit me sometime in my little shack at the back of the ground; one morning she come and the biggest, most beautiful black-and-yellow Jamaican swallowtail butterfly follow behind she, like it give us it little blessing. When I was a boy, I used to watch them flutter round the forest all the time, but must be in hurricane most of them dead.

Then one day I hear that the owner plan to clear the garden to build a ballroom and car park. Next morning digger crush down the whole place; I hear a hum that get louder from dawn till I reach the hotel. When I see my shack gone the manager tell me to start work on the other side of the ground or he will take back my job. So I wish him all the best to find a better gardener than me and walk back home.

'Careful you don't make too much mess, Robert. You must pick up any crumb you leave on the floor before your mother come from work, you hear?'

'Yes, Daddy.'

They did help me make the toto this morning. I have to shut them up in the front room while I take time to wipe down the whole kitchen, and then when I finish I let them lick the cake bowl clean. The toto eat good. Soft and sweet. It a quarter to two, and *Listen With Mother* come on the radio. *This is the BBC, for mothers and children at home*, the announcer say. We don't get show like this for entertain we as children back home; we did outside a play. And what about the father – we not at home too, sometime? No. Not really. Only if something wrong with we. I can't see my daughter face and I don't want my children to see me cry.

'You want to dance to the music, Glorie, sweetie? The toto nice, eh? Soon you will meet your grandmother who pass me down the recipe.'

Pussycat, pussycat, where have you been? I've been up to London to look at the Queen.

I can imagine if Claudette was here she would tell me off for dancing Glorie on my knee while she eat in case she choke. 'One day I will take you both to London. You want to go to London with Daddy, Mommy and Robert? We can look at the Queen too, if you want. We can ride on the bus to Buckingham Palace, the House of Parliament, Westminster Abbey and St Paul Cathedral, and watch the marching band play "God Save the Queen". Whatever you want, we can do, you see?'

But she can't talk yet, just wah wah wah and make mess, and Robert must be in his own little dream world. The flower in the vase smell like the water want change.

It did me that take over the gardening back home after my father dead. I learn how to grow from seed or cutting everything from *lignum vitae*, the national tree of Jamaica, to more unusual shrub like crab claw and bird of paradise. Can't say my gardening skill was that good then, for I was young and I don't know anything, really, for Daddy did die quick of a heart attack and he don't teach me to that. I see that I can help my mother by keeping the garden clean. I pick up a spade and trowel and that was that; the rest I learn at the hotel. The day after I leave that job, one rich white Englishman stop by we house in his long-bonnet Bentley to ask who is we gardener, for some of the flower we grow he did not see before. I hear the engine roar up from where I was, at the bottom of the garden, clearing up the leaf beneath the blue jacaranda.

'Norman!' she bawl. Mommy voice strong. Can bet she don't even turn away from his face when she shout so. 'Norman!'

A prince standing there when I come around the side to see what all the noise about. With a strong handshake and his blue eye resting on mine, he introduce himself as Henry Chambers, owner of a big old plantation house outside St Ann's Bay. He compliment my work and ask me if I want to work for him in his garden. Never yet did such a man step toward we house. All my little picky-hair niece and nephew congregate round their grandmother feet at the door, quiet and good like it Bustamante himself show up. Mommy bow her head and ask him in for tea. She sit him down in the front room in the best armchair, with the same antimacassar on it back since the day my daddy bury. She blow out the dust from the best cup and saucer and shoo the children off to run and play somewhere else. She come back into the front room – in a green dress with her hair comb back and lipstick on her teeth – with pot of tea, milk, sugar and two piece of toto on her best wicker tray. She stretch out her vowel and talk slow and loud, as if Mr Chambers deaf, and in what she must think sound like an English accent. She even tell me to sit down on the settee, opposite Mr Chambers, a privilege I never yet grant in the front room, where nobody even go except on a special occasion. I know she will run her mouth to me after, for sitting in her good settee in my outside clothes.

'Now, I shall leave you two to chat,' she say. It feel like I am on a date. My hands too big for these delicate little cup and saucer. I fill up the cup too high with milk and tea after I watch what Mr Chambers do, and I'm fraid it will spill as I tremble it up to my lip. The room is silent apart from the tick of the clock on the mantelpiece. I wonder where Mommy get these pretty cup and saucer from, with hibiscus flower paint on them; which cupboard in the kitchen they stay. A vision pass my eye where in the still of night she clear out some big house abandon by English people gone to the war, but this was '54. The war done long time.

My first brother Philip, an engineer, volunteer with the Royal Air Force, training to become a wireless operator gunner. He become a gentleman, mixing with white people from Canada, Australia and New Zealand. He first have to train for sixteen week on a lathe and grinder, somewhere in the north of England, and learn blueprint, slide rule, and all the technicality of the British strategy. He write to tell we about his plan to marry one white girl from the switchboard, and settle in England, where it cold and depress from the war, but where most people seem grateful for his help in the fight, though some tell him he must come back a Jamaica when the war finish. He could have done great things, but he dead in a plane crash in '43.

The next year, Jamaica lick by a hurricane that can only come from the bottom of the Lord own belly. We don't suffer to that, for Daddy was a builder and he construct his house well, but the island mash up bad. The wind tear out the whole crop. The coconut, banana, pimento and sugar cane all kill off for five year at least. Bird, bee and butterfly lose their home and each other. Overnight everybody job finish. I did work in the sugar cane field every summer since I turn fourteen, to help my mother dressmaking money. The bauxite mine not open yet, and the American shut off the seasonal work opportunity that the Jamaican always use to have. My second brother Ellery take over Daddy business, so I help him a lot with all the work that need to be done after the hurricane.

I tell Mr Chambers about the hotel, and how they clear it all out to build a ballroom and car park.

'That ghastly Lomax,' he say. 'These wealthy Americans I'm afraid have an appalling taste for the vulgar, and I dread to think what'll happen the more of this planet they colonise.'

But then I sip the tea, and it don't taste right. I look up at Mr Chambers, and he haven't sip it yet. He mix up the tea with milk and sugar, then leave it on the table in front of his knee. It then I realise that the milk sour. Can happen in this heat. But he can hear Mommy footstep creep back to see how we be, and quick as you like Mr Chambers throw the tea in the plant by his armchair and smile on her so bright and handsome she don't notice the steam rise up from the soil.

'It was me or the dracaena palm, dear,' he say to me some time later. 'But that coconut cake was *divine*, so soft and subtly sweet. I haven't been able to quite stop thinking about it.

Do you think Mrs Alonso might be prevailed upon to share her recipe?'

I think to myself, if we give you the recipe, who will make it? We don't give away recipe like that in Jamaica. They get pass down from mother to daughter to granddaughter. Women don't teach their son to cook, and they are too competitive to let anybody outside the family know their flavour secret. They did rather their son come trouble her for food every night than give their daughter-in-law their mix. Every christening, wedding, big birthday and funeral every one of the mother will bring her own pot of food and watch how quick it empty down till people scrape the bottom. Everything Mrs Alonso cook done first, every time. One time I see a big man pick up the whole dutchpot to lick out the bottom till the gravy all over his chin, which he wipe with his sleeve, then suck the juice out the sleeve! That how good is Mommy cooking. My three sister all beautiful and sweet but their husband did marry them up quick because them want to eat my mother cowfoot soup and Sunday mutton. She won't give it away.

'Daddy, I finish.'

'Good boy. Clean up everything now. Make sure nothing left on the table or on the chair. You have crumb on your shirt?'

Mr Chambers have one housekeeper, Mrs Dinkley, who cook all his food, mostly what he must eat in England: egg and fruit for breakfast, soup for lunch and a chicken dinner, might be. She won't go out her way to change his taste, or season or spice up his food to that. He never ask for Jamaican food, which Mrs Dinkley can cook as good as any woman who is not name Mrs Naomi Alonso. But God help the man who can go behind the Jamaican lady in his life back to ask for another woman recipe! Woy! Mrs Dinkley a hard-face woman. It take must be six month after I start work at Weymouth House before she even say *Hello* to me. As far as she concern, I'm just a field hand with big muscle and no mind. I think it would take a thousand year before Mommy let she know any of her recipe. But as soon as I get home that afternoon and mention that Mr Chambers did inquire about her toto, my mother chase a pickney to run bring her money box from her bedside table. 'Make haste, come quick before it close!' she say, and send me out to buy the best paper I can find. I get to the post office in St Ann's Bay. Mr Jeffrie step out from behind his counter to shake my hand and ask me *what can I do for you, Mr Alonso?* He must hear that I get hire by Mr Chambers, so I am almost like a gentleman myself, even as I stand there in Daddy old boot. Mr Jeffrie smile on me for the first time in my life – even though my mother did send me to the post office at least once a week since I was a child – and wrap up the paper good in a little red bow. Just as I am about to hand over the money, he ask me if he should charge it to Mr Chambers' account!

'Which part you get this paper from?' Mommy say when I reach back with it, holding it up to the light out the front porch. 'Might be the ink won't even write on it!'

'It's fine paper, eh?'

'And why you come back with the money? Boy, I don't raise thief!'

'Mr Jeffrie ask me if I should put it on Mr Chambers' account.'

She gasp like I cuss in her face, and whisper-shout: 'Suppose he find out and sack you! Why you want to lose another job for!'

'Well, Mr Chambers ask me for the recipe, and he must know that we want to give him the best, or else why you sit him down in the front room chair and give him the nice china for tea, which he said was better than in England, by the way.'

There is nothing that Mommy love more than flattery. Since Daddy dead she don't bother with herself, but after Mr Chambers show up unannounce she pin up her hair and wear small-heel shoe every day, in case he choose to stop by again. All her grandchildren them get their hair comb and oil every day, and they dress up and sit quiet like for photograph. The whole house make up like the front room.

'Just think how happy he will be when he see the recipe for your toto on beautiful paper like this,' I say to her, and I can see the little cog in her mind tick around. 'He will keep it forever, and when he die, they will find it and put it in a museum in London. Your recipe a go famous through all the world!'

She look me up and down.

'Ee-eeh? A so you stay, now? Which part you learn to talk like politician? Everything on Lord Chambers' expense? Mm-mmh! Norman nuh easy! You can write good? Come in your Daddy study and write down the recipe. Lord God me never see paper so thick in all my life. Sit down at the desk. Your hand clean? Nuh bother splash the ink all about. Take time with the pen.'

First she make me sit in the settee, now she let me sit at Daddy writing desk. I don't think this room open except by my brother Ellery to look for one or two paper, or by Mommy to dust around a little bit and water the plant, since Daddy dead two year before. I look up at all the picture on the wall. Mommy and Daddy, smiling, Daddy tall, brown and handsome with his moustache, Mommy still beautiful and elegant in her white glove and pearl earring. My two brother Philip and Ellery, my three sister Loretta, Marlene and Delfi, and me, the youngest by six year, all as baby, all in we little white gown. Woman seem to live long time but man just work and work till them dead. Granddad dead. Daddy dead. Philip dead. Nan strong. Mommy strong. And I sit and wait for Mommy, with the nib in my hand ready to dip in the inkwell, at Daddy desk, in his chair, with the precious paper beneath me, but she don't know what kind of oven he have, she don't know which kind of dish he will cook with, so she don't know which amount to tell him, and she don't measure anything out even once in her life because she just *know*, she just take the *right* amount every single time, mix it up, pour it into a tin and bake it in the oven until it nice and brown. Then she take it out, make it rest a little while and cut a piece for everybody who want it warm, then put what is left on a platter under a cloth with a little drip of water on it so that it don't dry out. That toto never last more than one or two day because it eat so nice and people come round to eat it because the baking smell like heaven when they pass by we house.

I see that she have a little tear in her eye, because Mommy realise she can't write down a recipe for Mr Chambers. She can't give it away like that. *Not to that ugly black-face Mrs Dinkley,* she say, and we laugh.

'Put down the pen and come,' she say. 'I will show you how to make it for him.'

My little niece Andrea and me get teach the same time, just like my grandmother would one day have shown my mother when she did ten or eleven. And now I think, my mother don't have any daughter left to give away to good man, and Andrea still too young. But she do have a son, twenty-six year old, tall, strong and hard-working. Every minute my mother ask me, 'But why such a handsome, tall, nice, rich Englishman don't have wife? What he is doing up there all by himself in such a big house with all them flower and no woman fe give them to? All he have is that black-face Dinkley woman and my Norman. How old is he, you think? He don't even have son fe leave it all to?' She put everything in place, but never look to put two and two together in her mind. Instead, she send me with the toto I bake when I go to work for him the next day. Mrs Dinkley don't say anything but she purse up her lip like fist and turn her eye away.

'Finish, Daddy.'

'You clean up good? If I stoop down my big self and find something on the floor me go take switch and beat you. That's it. Climb down there and make sure the floor clean. If your mother come home from work and find mess she will beat you as well. Talk, child; I can't see.'

'Finish.'

'Finish what?'

'Finish, Daddy.'

'You put them nuh your mouth or in the bin?'

I know exactly what he done but children always think they're smarter than you. Especially Jamaican children. He think because I can't see what he is doing properly that I have no sense of time or space.

'The bin?'

'But I nuh feel you walk round me to go to the bin in the pantry, which must mean either no crumb on the floor, and you lie, or you put the dutty crumb in your mouth, and you lie. Which one it is?'

'Me eat them,' him mumble.

'Speak up! What did you say?'

'Me eat them!'

'Don't shout at me! You narsy, and a lie you a lie. Go in the garden carry switch come me guh beat you.'

'No! I'm sorry!'

'I say to don't shout at me! What you sorry for? You sorry that you lie or that you eat the dutty crumb from the floor?'

'I'm sorry ... fe eat ... and nuh put it in the bin ... and fe liiiie,' he cry.

'Say you sorry to Daddy, Mommy, and Glorie that you lie and eat the dutty crumb off the floor!'

'I'm sorry, Daddy!' He turn to face the door and shout like his mommy will hear in the hospital: 'I'm sorry, Mommy!' and then him turn gentle again to his sister on my lap. 'I'm sorry, Glorie.'

'I tell you from long time now, you a big boy, and have to provide a good example to your sister so that she learn how to behave properly, you see?'

'Yes, Daddy.'

'You do the job me and Mommy ask you to do straight away and in the right way, a so me mean, and you don't lie bout it, because when we find out, the consequence a go *bad* for you, you hear?'

'Oh, Daddy . . .'

'Stop the cry! Stand up! You want tea?'

'No.'

'No what?' This boy never a go forget his manners round me.

'No thank you, Daddy.'

'You want water?'

He don't say anything, so either he shake or nod his head. We don't yet get to the day that my child don't answer me at all.

'I can't see. You have to tell me.'

'Sasprilla.'

What a way this boy can lie and still feisty enough to ask for his favourite drink.

'You want sarsaparilla?'

'Yes please, Daddy.'

I can't see his big eye upon me but I know all about them.

It was Claudette who insist we come to England. She want to get away from this nasty little island, she say, when I get a letter from my old schoolfriend Laury about how life so good in the Black Country. *So much real man job I can try a hundred things before I settle on one,* he say. *Doreen and me will look to buy house.* Claudette and I did court for must be six month; we marry, then we travel, then she find she pregnant with this little man. She love me, but she marry because she want to better herself. She dream that England like something out of one of the upperclass romance novel she love read. She say she want to give we children the education they can't get in Jamaica, because we not rich enough. She think that all English children must get good education.

Mr Chambers say Jamaica will gain independence while

Harold Macmillan prime minister. They already give the Gold
Coast it independence and call it Ghana. *Ghana live a Englan'*,
I say, and it take him a little while to get the joke but he laugh.
He tell me he will miss me, and that I must remember to
write him. I miss him, too. He value my knowledge and skill
as gardener. He don't take exception when I tell him what to
do, and it on his verandah that I drink little red wine from
France for the first time and listen classical music record, great
big Wagner and romantic Tchaikovsky. Sometime now when
I work in my own garden and the children asleep I listen the
Third Programme. I never, before him, see man dress with
such refine taste, who speak in such *elevated* way. He give me
book to read – *The Great Gatsby* and *Of Mice and Men* – and
my mother send him currygoat, rice and gungo pea to eat. It
him that make me expect everybody in England to be a fine
gentleman.

Laury is my friend, but I know I should not trust somebody
whose face make me happy to be blind.

It my beautiful son and daughter who make me miss my eye.

By the grace of God, Claudette and me, with two week and
eight thousand mile gone, set we eye first time on the Mother
Country, and what a wondrous sight we see. A bright cheer
rise up as she appear true on the horizon, still far away on that
warm, spring day. Already it seem like everything white; the
bird in the air, the rock formation that stand up so like a baby
first teeth. Claudette look beautiful in one nice blue dress with
her belly just show, her hat and glove. She smooth her hand
down my lapel; only the gardenia did missing from my wedding
outfit. We kiss, my hand on her belly, then round her waist. We

baby will be born in *England*, in time for Christmas, in the snow. We never see snow, yet. I can't wait. We will build snowman with we baby, in we garden, drink hot tea with rum and breathe the steam up in the air.

The ship did never quiet. Musician who never meet before the journey entertain we with mento song. Engineer trifle with nurse over pudding; single lady drinking tonic in hat and glove practise their finery front of mechanic and clerk; aunty going to look after their family sit in the corner and watch as if at a wedding, hoping a young man might ask them to dance, so the band play 'Old Lady You Mash Me Toe' and everybody there laugh; skill work-hand talk about a couple years to make money then home, same time they sip rum and smash domino on the table; playful boxing contest make Claudette both mad and proud when girl whistle down my physique. We even play little cricket match on the deck with the back of an upturn chair for stump.

A great crowd of we walk down the gangplank at Southampton, the bawl of the bird and boom of the engine on the water replace by the hiss of train pull in and out, and the babel of we under the iron beam. We make friend on the boat, but we all have different address write on piece of paper in we pocket, so we embrace, wish luck and depart, some of we for London, others for Liverpool, others, like Claudette and me, for Birmingham. We wait at custom and show we paper and passport, and the man, who don't smile, tell us to catch a train to Paddington then change; *the Birmingham line is closed for now. A man threw himself in front of a train*, he say. Claudette gasp: *Is he dead?* and the man say, *I should think so*, but we know that just as bad things happen in Jamaica, so we get it out of we mind with the excitement of going on the train.

It was the twenty-sixth of May, '56, and it really did feel like we start a new life, inside Claudette belly and outside, beneath the English sky, where fluffy little English cloud pass overhead, slow and gentle. I watch my wife looking out of the window, and think, she not Jamaican again, because she English now, a beautiful brown Englishwoman with sexy red lip I love to kiss. The mother of my English child. I look forward to my new house and garden, and I already start think about the rose, dahlia, jasmine, hibiscus, pear and lemon I will cultivate, and we look forward to move in with Laury and Doreen in a town call Bilston in the Black Country, and meet we new neighbour, cook Jamaican food, and them for we, English food, as we wind in and out of each other house like family, we children and their children playing together and learning together, growing together, black children and white children the same way. We children will learn to speak good like real English people, get good education, grow up good and not have to work in factory or in the hospital, for they will have better opportunity than we, to become teacher or engineer or real nurse, and meantime I would get job in factory or on railway just to settle we, and then I would work another couple year until I can afford start my own gardening business, for plenty rich people in England will be too busy or grand to look after their own.

We get off at Paddington – an iron cathedral – and can't believe we standing in London, breathing London air, watching London people walk by with their black suit, newspaper and briefcase. Claudette learn more about fashion in one minute looking all about at woman walking by than she did reading those magazines she used to steal from the hotel lobby. We think about going to visit the Queen, but we don't want to miss we train; we feel like we might get lost if we do. We don't know where to go, and we never see so many people in one place in all we life, so we have to be careful not to get separate and lose we luggage as people come up around us from every direction, almost knocking Claudette out of their way as she point that way and I point the other way – they don't care that she pregnant! – and bouncing off me, kissing their teeth as they run toward their platform. I don't know how many times we say *Sorry! Sorry! Sorry!* We ask an attendant, in a hat, who speak to us polite like we live there already, and he point us in the right direction. On the way is a florist truck, and I quickly pick up a bunch of pink rose for my sweetheart (first time me count out sterling to pay for something; I can't forget the jealous look on Mr Jeffries' face when me draw it out). She feel even more glamorous when a photographer man stop we and ask to take we picture. Dizzy, we walk down the platform to second class, past all the rich white people like government official in the first class carriage, and a porter take we luggage.

We drink English tea from the trolley (almost as nice as from back home), serve by a white man in a smart jacket and white glove, his hair part and comb, his teeth white and straight. We look out of the window as the train pull off and follow the curve of the station exit. We pass by apartment block, factory, warehouse and gas tank, under bridge and through tunnel. How fast and smooth this train feel. England in Maytime. The country green – except you can't see much of the distance because of the tree – not heavy-green like Jamaica but like the estate painting that hang above Mr Chambers's bed; I start to look for big house like that but can't find one. We pass through pretty town call Leamington Spa, with chimney and steeple. Claudette fall asleep on my shoulder. I wonder who driving the train, what view he must see out his window every day. More house, more bridge. House build up on top of bridge. Freight train, shipping container, industrial machinery of a kind I never see yet. This country so big. So much more opportunity than Jamaica. I understand now what Laury did mean, and I hope I can enjoy England like Philip did in his short life. The train stop for a minute and I get to look over the expanse of rooftops, factories all blowing up smoke in the air, a sure sign of industry and prosperity. I wake Claudette just as the train pull into Birmingham Snow Hill station.

Police officer stand on the platform, alert, and watch we. Claudette curtsy. At least that make the police officer smile, and he stand back little bit while the porter bring we luggage off the train. Then I step off; the police officer look on me and his mouth drop down like red carpet will roll out of it.

'Blow me, yo'm a big lad, int ya!'

I don't understand a word.

'He is a big man, yes, but gentle and nice,' my ever-smiling wife say.

A porter tell we to get another train to the address we have written down, for Bilston about five mile away. So we find the next train, a much smaller one, and we wait for someone to take we bag, but nobody come and the attendant blow his whistle, so we carry them on for weself.

When Bilston come we think it must be a mistake. We eye never fall on so much black in all we life. The building black. The sky black. The people black, and not because they come from where we come from. The dog black. The bird black. Everywhere we look the ground open and something in the middle of demolish. Must be still where the bomb did drop in the war. The war done more than ten year now and they don't fix it up yet? Plenty job must be here, then.

'Bloody 'ell, look how many there am!' bawl one old woman to her friend, her neck and batty check back like hen, her hand clasp together with black purse over her feathery little wrist, scarf over her head. We look both way on the platform; must be five of we at most step off in Bilston same time, and only we with luggage. The friend stop and look and say, 'They'm tekkin' over, ay they!' and her big daughter, chewing her finger, twist up her head and stare up on me so hard she start dribble.

Better we did stay in Jamaica and move we marriage bed in a bauxite mine. The smile drop from Claudette face when she see the neighbourhood where Laury and his wife Doreen buy, and I don't see it again for must be one week. Doreen house clean but the other house dark an' dirty, stack all together like domino except the window black, too. Plenty of them look more suitable to keep chicken than to settle with family. Nothing in Jamaica compare to Bilston. Not a single Bilston wall not line with black soot. Claudette white glove turn grey in a drawer. The street baby run round naked and shit where they squat. Their face blacker than mine, but they're white; they run up and down the road with nothing on their feet and rusty nail and broken glass in the gutter, but they see me and call out, *Nigger! Nigger! Look, Charlie! Nigger!* They stop kick tin can and stare up on me, mouth open with wonder like bomber plane land in we street. We leave the Garden of Eden for the Land of Milk and Honey and find Sodom and Gomorrah. Instead of rolling hill, mountain of trash. River of crude oil. Blast furnace for tree. Woman with six children under the age of ten, the oldest boy sent out to work, the oldest girl with her little sister on her hip. I use to box, and take some hit, yet nothing catch me off guard like a fearless little boy with hair like the sun, angelic blue eye and gun for tongue.

I start to get the headache right away. My head hurt, and I sick to my stomach. I fear that my little baby not born yet will have to go to school one day with these badmind child.

The Labour Exchange send me to a forge. I think to just take the first thing that come along to settle we down, and then we can see about to buy in a nice neighbourhood, maybe one of the white house with little garden. We did see, passing through on the train, that England have more to offer than this, so we keep hope. I don't trust Laury to get me a job because he say, *I'alright, you cya leave one job one day an get nother one the next.* And he follow that plan, if I can call it that. One day he work in a steel factory, next day he working on a scrap yard. I don't know why he don't stay in the same place for more than two week.

Claudette tell me about the problem Laury and Doreen have already in their marriage. They marry quick in Jamaica because Doreen want to come to England, but it seem that she don't want to have relation with Laury and she certain she don't want to have children. Laury is a good man and I know him since about six-year-old, but he not Clark Gable. Sometime a man can make a woman laugh and lie back when otherwise she might scream and run, but Laury is both ugly and a fool. Doreen herself is quite thick-set and vex-looking – though she have nice brown skin and plenty good hair – so they are a good match to marry and migrate. She work plenty hour in a factory, making brick, and he, of course, don't know what he is doing from one month to the next. He even join me in the forge for must be one week, before he burn his arm and he move on to a foundry.

It was summertime, yet I was melting metal at temperature hotter than the middle of hell that cook you inside and out, so hot you can't breathe, and what you do breathe full up of black dust. Some of the man laugh and suggest I must use to this kind of temperature, coming from the tropic. Then they ask me if I am not black enough already so I need to come to Bilston to get more black. I don't even trouble them to light my cigarette. I come up 12 o'clock from the confinement to the light, and once my eye adjust, which take some time, I strip down to my waist and eat the Jamaican bun Claudette have to catch bus all the way near to Birmingham to buy. White girl with pram and half-caste baby side of them walk past, and look on me like I should follow them to their house.

When I get home, Claudette complain that when she push herself to go out to buy food and yarn, too many ugly white face looking on her, and even the face that not looking on her aware that she there. Somebody did throw stone nearby her, and she already knit more clothes for the baby than it will need, with five month left till it even born, and we room, and the share bathroom, corridor and stairs, that not even for her to clean, cleaner than at any time must be since the house first build. There did no point in her trying to get a job, because nobody want a pregnant woman. She say she don't have anybody to talk to because Doreen out at work all day at the factory. I listen, but I can't talk back, because my head heavy and sick, and I lie down, and she shout on me not to lie down on her clean sheet in my dirty overall, and tell me I better must wash before she give me dinner, so I get up, and my brain lurch in my head, then my stomach lurch, and she understand right away that something wrong, because she never see her Norman throw up straight out in the sink.

'I am sorry, Claudette,' I say, bend double and breathe hard.

She put her arm around me and lead me out the door, across the landing to the toilet. Somebody in there. I feel another surge come but manage to hold it back. The sweat drip down from my brow, though I feel half cold, half hot. My brain feel like blast furnace raging in my head. I squint my eye tight then open them wide, but they can't focus.

'You're not going back to that horrible forge again,' Claudette say. 'I will stop by them in the morning to tell them you take sick. Tomorrow we will find a doctor, but darling, we have to get away from here and find a better place.'

I don't need a doctor tell me I need a different job. I sleep, and Claudette mop my brow. She feed me good hot soup with soft cowfoot and nice thick dumplin I have to chew good to stimulate my temple and muscle from the inside.

I get up seven o'clock next morning, drink tea and eat plantain. I go out to the shop, take five newspaper, set myself up in a phone booth. Plenty people when they hear my West Indian accent tell me rubbish about that the vacancy already gone, but I do get one interview, for a job as a municipal gardener with Sandwell Council.

Plenty door I get lead through behind the secretary woman, who always check behind her like she worry that I watching her little bottom in her high-waist skirt and heel, and everybody look up and watch me pass. Mr Parker seem nice from the

minute I see him. Tall, not as tall as me but I think that why he
respect me straight away. Grey hair, comb immaculate. Grey
suit, blue eye. Thick, dark eyebrow and moustache. And he get
up from his great big desk with bright window behind, take off
his spectacle and rush out to shake my hand. Never did I ever
sit in a chair so comfortable in all my life. He smile on me and
ask all these question about Jamaica, and tell me he always want
to go. I compliment him on the flower arrangement behind
him – peony, rose, lily, lisianthus, alstroemeria, amaryllis – and
he tell me that hardly anybody who come to interview for gardening job know anything about flowers. I tell him I use to be
a groundsman for a hotel in St Ann's Bay, then for Mr Henry
Chambers of Weymouth House. Mr Parker start to look on
me all confidential. He pace up and down with his hand in his
pocket in front of his window and think out loud to himself . . .
then he offer me the job! I don't say more than few word, but he
shake my hand and tell me, *We'll see you Monday!* just like that.
He say that there is a job for life at the council if I did want it,
that I can take exam and train to become horticulturalist. He
say I can be one of the new wave of coloured professional in the
UK. When I come home and tell Claudette she scream like I get
groundsman job for the Queen.

It easy to get a council house when I work for the council,
and we move into one on a nice estate in West Bromwich,
close to Swan Village Gas Works. Doreen sad to say goodbye
to Claudette but Claudette not sad to move in a much nicer
neighbourhood where there is more space between the house
and where there is a common across the road. The house come
with three bedroom and a big garden front and back. We try not
to look at the tall, big, grey gas tank that fill up the sky from we
back garden. She can walk not too far to Great Bridge, a good
market street with butcher, fishmonger, grocer, wallpaper shop,
coffee house, cinema, post office, chemist, Woolworth, Tesco,
anything she could want.

December come, and Claudette gone into labour. They rush her straight into the birthing room and out follow we firstborn, bawling up in the air, the strongest, hardest chest I ever hear come from a baby. Robert James Alonso is sitting on my foot, playing with his toy, still making plenty noise. He eat good and start walk early, talk early and do everything early. He will make all of we proud, make his Uncle Philip proud, make his grandfather Barrington proud, make his daddy Norman proud, make his own son proud.

I work with a white man name Peter, who wear dirty overall like factory man and stop every minute what he is doing to comb his hair back. He is what they call a Teddy Boy. He chat rubbish, tell me he love cricket and he don't mind Learie Constantine, but he think the government should stop the immigration of coloured people to England. He use England test victory against the West Indies as proof that the black don't have anything to offer white people. I don't listen to him. He don't listen to me, either. He did apply for a big job in the council, but he don't get it, for he is idle. He start rant and rave and lose his mind. He say how much he in debt, how he got three children already, that he twenty-six and need to make more money for his wife pregnant again. All the time his friend come by and he stop and chat to them half-an-hour leaning on his spade plant in the ground. He stand over me while I dig out weed and ask me what I know about English soil – I don't live in a tree? Then he say that coloured people who can't even speak English good are taking all the opportunity, because the politician can say Britain don't segregate like America, and that we must be better than them, but the common white man like himself can't rise up.

The gaffer – maybe he know it will rattle him – tell Peter *listen to Norman. Do what Norman do.* Peter must think that if he working alongside a nigger then he must be a nigger too, and if he taking order from a nigger then he must worse than a nigger. And what kind of white man worse than a nigger? He don't think about all the time he is late to start work because he did drunk the previous night. He don't think about how I am better than him at my job, how I work two time as hard and how I have so much more knowledge and experience. He smoke his cigarette and say:

'How d'ya get this job? Let that old queer suck your big black cock off in his office, did ya?' And then he dash his cigarette butt right where I am about to plant a bulb.

I don't say anything to Mr Parker, but Peter soon lose him job anyway.

Summer '57, I help Mr Parker in his own garden on a Saturday. He live in the most sweet little house I ever did see in my life – with weeping willow tree and hydrangea bush at the front, a little pond with goldfish and a rockery at the back – by himself, for his wife dead and his children grow up and gone. We strip down to we vest in the sun and drink lemonade, and he play Louis Armstrong from his gram, while we turn the bed and water everything with his hosepipe, prune bush and cut grass. He take me in his Rover for drive out of town and we come across one little cottage, deep in the field. People who see we together look shock that a gentleman like him can walk round with a black man but he don't seem to care. When they stop to talk to him they can hardly look me in the eye, and when he introduce me, they can hardly reach to shake my hand. He sit me down in the shadow of an old oak tree, run in the pub and come back with two beer. He is like Clark Gable. The light tint with orange and pink as the sun start to set. He talk about his family, and I talk about mine;

he ask me how I can leave two son in Jamaica to come to England.

I don't know why I tell him that. He seem like the sort of man you can tell your life story to. When he sit and listen, you talk. When he talk, you listen. He tell me I can call him Clifford. Lynval and Gregory born to Lerlene. When we split up, she keep them. I never love her; I hardly know how I come to be father to two children with her. Lynval the clever one, light skin, coolie hair, handsome, the girl dem sugar, good dancer. Gregory more sensitive, considerate, darker. Robert favour Gregory more than Lynval. I send them money, letter and photograph, but she have a new man now and they're happy, which is all that matter. And I am happy as well with Claudette, and we new family with Robert. If only Claudette can see me now, I think, lie down in a field in the hot sun, drinking beer with Clifford, talking private things, blue sky and cricket whistle like back-home country. We go back to his house and he play Elvis and Johnny Cash record, we drink whisky, smoke cigarette and dance. After, he drop me back at the station, and I go home to my wife.

Claudette and me spend Christmas at home with we baby in front of the fire, and Laury and Doreen come by we on Boxing Day. Back home we did dream of snow in the English winter, like on Christmas card, and think about build snowman – we even dream about which tie we will put on him, and Claudette did even knit one red and green wool one – but we don't realise how cold it get even without snow; none of we did pack good boot or heavy coat; we don't realise, when snow fall, if it rain first it don't stick; we don't realise, when the snow mix with rain and wind, how it chop up your face like blade and prickle your ears-hole like needle; we don't realise, when the snow stick hard, you can't leave your house without spade to cut out path; you can't walk down road without fall, you can't reach work on time, because somebody, if they see you with spade, is going to ask you to cut their path too. The television doesn't work, your children get sick, and you can't see doctor because everybody children sick; you get sick too but you still have to go to work, because nobody will pay your bill or rent or put food in your children belly if you can't. Your finger them want to drop off from sweeping up the leaves, from knocking the snow off the tops of trees. It take plenty money just to heat up the house, so you have to squeeze up, and you can't even make love with your wife because your children there in the bed with you, separating you like jealous dog. Your big pink lip jam up and make you talk like you're sick in the head; nothing come out right, and the white people, like Teddy Boy Peter, think you're simple, inferior, black, stupid.

Maurice, one Jamaican man who live round the corner, that I make friend with since we move here, tell me he did go to the Black Swan, and like we always do in Jamaica he knock his fist on the bar to get the attention of the bartender. Maurice, who work for one builder's merchant in Great Bridge, is the sort of man who always chewing something, toothpick or fingernail, chicken bone or bottle top, whatever he can find, and he make noise with it, so I understand why some people might not love him soon as they see him. But what a way one dart player did walk up to him – when the sound of Maurice ring and watch bracelet on the bar did trouble him – to tell him he can't behave in England *like he is still in the jungle!* No, sir, I say. I can't believe that! I tell Maurice he is a liar, that a lie he tell me, just like Laury lie through his teeth when he write letter to say England the best country in the world, and that we must all stop slave in Jamaica one time and move here. A lie he did tell!

So next time Maurice want to go for a drink, I go with him to the Black Swan, *me*, big like Goliath, fist like brick, and we walk right in to the saloon bar, him first, then me, and I feel their face change, I feel their back freeze up like cat. They stop playing snooker; the thud of the next dart take long time to come. The dog hide under the table and flick their tail. Tall as the gas tank in my grey suit, I walk up to the bar and we stand there, wait, and wait, while the bartender serve some man who come up after we, wash some glass, scratch his ball and wipe down the bar. *Mar twelve-year-old's gerrin a trial at the Albion / Tell im not to gerris opes up too much, he'll always a'the gas works. / Burry woe know if he doe troy though, will he? What's he got to lose? / Even Duncan Edwards trained to be a carpenter, day 'e. / Ar, and look wharrappened to im. / Terrible ay it. Rest in peace.* But we wait, quiet and patient, we breathe; we don't get frustrate, and I hold Maurice hand when I hear the jingle of his bracelet. It look like the bartender – a fat, round man with must be about three chin, his trouser pull up right underneath his chest, tie up with must be a three-yard-long belt – need to clean up his bar, fix up himself and take time to serve we, because we are *Black* gentlemen, this pub call the *Black* Swan, and this region call the *Black* Country.

Finally he nod to we, say, *next please* like he don't know. I look in his eye and smile and say, *good evening, sir,* and he say back to we, *good evening* but he don't smile. It seem like he did step up to we with cosh at his back, but I turn to Maurice and ask him what he want, and he say he want a beer. I say, *that is an* excellent *idea, Maurice,* and Maurice look at me funny under his pork pie hat, but I turn to the bartender and ask for two of his *finest pint of beer please, bartender,* and the bartender say, *Two pints of beer it is,* but he still don't smile. He take two glass, put down one then take the other one, pull the lever until the glass full, and place it down nice on one mat in front of Maurice. Then he take the other one, pull the lever until the glass full and place it careful on the mat in front of me. I watch every step – because I can still see good, then – to be certain he don't spit on my beer or perpetrate some other nastiness against black man in his pub, and he don't spill even one drop, not even *one drop* of anything but condensation did roll down the side of my glass. He stand back and say, *One and fourpence please*. I put my hand in my pocket and again his batty muscle tight up like I might pull machete out on him, but I keep smiling, hold my hand up to my face, count out the correct money and drop it in his hand. He take away his hand quick as I drop the coin so that he don't get touch by my dirty jungle finger, but I don't care about what he say and do, because then I turn to Maurice, smile on him and tell him in fast patois the bartender won't understand, *a so yuh reach a pub n'a country yuh nuh baan*. 'God bless you, sir!' I take a big long gulp at the bar and make sure everybody in the saloon can hear how refreshing it feel: *Ahhhhhhhh!*

We laugh and drink we pint, then drink another one then leave, because I can't take the smell of the pickle onion.

February '58, Claudette start to feel pregnant again; we don't plan for another baby but we don't not try. We deep in bed asleep when we startle up by crashin' sound. Robert wake and Claudette scream. I take the cricket bat from under the bed and run downstairs. I find the curtain blow in from the street. I turn on the front room light and the carpet cover in shatter glass, and in the middle, a brick wrap up in paper. I tell Claudette to shut up and call the police. They come round must be fifteen minute later. They ask me if I have trouble with somebody recently, and I say no. But then they start to search up the place, and they ask me what I do with all these sign cheque write by Councillor Clifford Parker in my house, and I tell them I don't know anything about them, and now Claudette screaming again, because they arrest me and lead me off to the police station. They leave we door open with one officer there. All the neighbour come out of their house to watch me arrest, and it take a long time to make them all know that I did nothing wrong.

'Take *that*,' Robert say, and the Indian must dead in the fireplace.
    'A good job the fire not on,' I warn him.

The forge cheque must plant there, because I never see them yet, and not because my eyesight spoil. I tell them to call Mr Parker. They wait until morning, then Clifford himself come to the police station to vouch for me and convince them not to prosecute. It plain to me, for I read plenty Sherlock Holmes and Edgar Allan Poe story back home, that it Teddy Boy Peter who organise it. Maybe he have a friend in the police who he give the cheque to plant in my house because I am just a big nigger who nobody will believe, and he can punish me easy like that because he is too idle and he lose his job. We can't have brick fly through we window every night. We don't have relative to stay with. We thirty-two and twenty-three. It is me one who have to take care of my pregnant wife and son, and I can't have my life control by some mash-up white idiot like Peter. If people are jealous of my friendship with Clifford, I decide to finish it.

    I thank him and tell him I can't work for him again if it put my wife and son in danger. He disappoint but he accept my resignation, and send the council to come fix up we house. When he drop me home, he tell me to call him whenever I need anything. *Anything*, he say, and squeeze my leg.

It can't do me good to rely on people who don't know how to handle me. They put you front a themself and control you like game. I apply for the same kind of job but nobody want to know; again, they all say the vacancy fill when they hear my West Indian accent. I realise I did lucky to get through to Clifford, but I know I'm too proud to turn back. After two week of unemployment I take a job at the gas works, shovelling coal in the retort to burn at a thousand degree, surround by young man like Peter and old man who do the same job all them life. That is the life I can handle, if I can keep to my own business. We have we own garden to make beautiful. I remember the flower truck at Paddington station and think, maybe, if we good with we money, one day we can set up we own flower truck, Claudette and me, and send we children to a good school.

'Take *that*!' Robert say again.

'Robert, gimme them.'

He must think I wan' play with him, because he gimme them straight away. I take them in the kitchen an' put them in the bin. I come back in the front room and sit down. Seem like he a try to get up to find them.

'Sit down. I don't play game with you.'

'What happen?' he say. His voice sound like panic.

'I put them away. Plenty other toy you have,' I say.

He don't know what I mean. He start to cry. I pick him up and cuddle him. I forget sometime he just two.

'Shut up cry and listen. When you a play with cowboy a'Indian, you a take the role of the white man and kill the brown man, when in real life, you not the white man, you the brown man, and the white man want kill *you*. A so me mean. You haffi learn that.'

At no point should my need come before that of a white man, so man like Teddy Boy Peter think. Clifford a good friend, but when he not by my side, how I can walk in his world? I am too big, too black. My boy scream to learn that there lesson.

Soon as I start at the gas work it make me wonder why I bother move to England at all if this my level. I also start to wonder whether, if God did ask me which way I did want to fall down, I would choose to be blind or hard-of-hearing. The shit I hear talk every day make me think I did sooner go without ear than eye. Without ear, I can still see Claudette and my children and read book but I don't have to listen the workmate language, if I can call it that.

I don't know this about England when I did back in Jamaica, but they have this whole spread, thick like lard pon bread, of people who can't read, can't talk good, scratch themselves up like dog with flea, don't understand a thing about life outside their own head, but think they can call me *nigger, darkie, coon, gorilla*, tell me to go back to my own country where I belong and stop steal their sunlight – I don't have enough back in the jungle? I don't melt, like chocolate? The ignorance, the way they talk about their *missus* like she a bucket with hole, or they can't talk about anything more than which football team better, Albion, Villa, City or Wolves.

Seven, eight month I did keep my cool and fasten up my mouth among these men. They chase me and I walk away, head down. It feel like everything happening same time. The football World Cup, and the first black man I ever see who better than every white man, just like Jesse Owens with the Nazi. The workmate start to talk nice and tell me I'm good-looking and should model underpant in the catalogue or box professional, and they ask me why I don't join their boxing syndicate, because I could make some money out of it. I ask back how much and they say ten per cent of the takings go to the winner. I kiss my teeth and shake my head, and then they take a different turn, because they can never understand, never mind that it none of their business, how I did walk good and talk good, as if I should be making inarticulate sound and dragging my knuckle along the ground; they want to know how I sometime can use word they never hear, because I read, and most of them did go to school but, as Mommy would say, *they nuh go fe learn, they go fe rude*, and they think because we all work in the same industry, that we must all have the same mind. They don't like it that me, a black man, can think I am better than them, even if I can't say that I am better than them. It seem I can't go anywhere and not be an outsider. Too black for the council and too educated for the gas work. Any man can shovel up coal and feed retort. Not everybody can be Norman Alonso.

What the workmate can't understand, is that I am a Jamaican. I am a Jamaican man, and therefore, a British man. I did born British, so will be a British man all my life. We serve the Queen, and before her, the King, in the same way. Any time you walk down the main street in downtown Kingston you can hear one marching band play 'God Save the Queen'. We fight for we country. We help build this country. We help make rich this country. Without we, they might not have such a big army, such a big navy. They might not have been able to conquer the world. Might be they did lose the war against Hitler.

The littlest one, McCarthy, with his curly hair and boy-face that still look rude from school, come up to my chest and tip his head back like Claudette do when she want a kiss, and ask me what black woman cunt taste like because he imagine it like gravy, and what my wife like best for dinner, and I tell him, slow and deliberate, to remove himself up from out of my face before I crush him down, and some other man come up and tell me, *Leave him alone. He's just yampy*, but I say if he is ignorant then like we say in Jamaica, *If you cyah hear you mus' feel*, and all of a sudden I am surrounded, and my blur eye can't see everything, but I push McCarthy little way from me because his mouth stink, and next thing one other man step in front of him and throw punch. I take one step back and kick him out my face, and his eye don't leave mine as he fly back and skittle down the two man behind. McCarthy scream to lose his tooth. The workmate stop and back away. I stand there midst of them like hand grenade with the pin about to pull out.

You can't blame them. Colliery. Ironwork. Brickwork. Chainmaking. Work with their back and their arm, and not their brain. Metal is the work of their hand and the material of their mind. What produce grease and black smoke is good. That the history of this part of the country. Skilled labour. Their father did the same and their grandfather and great-grandfather before them. They work all day every day, go home to pie, mash, gravy and peas, then take their retirement in one of the English pub. There is a typical kind of man in the corner every afternoon, waiting to die, with no teeth, smoking cigarette after cigarette, drinking pint after pint, going to the toilet every twenty minute, too thin, his pale yellow skin drooping off his skeleton, his eye sunk back in his head, his white hair slick back, the same clothes he did wear when he was thirty hanging off his bones and secure with a belt.

The government don't talk to poor white people, just in case they give them too much information. Nobody tell them that immigrant come because the government invite we as free British citizen, because after the war so much get knock down to rubble and so many man get kill. They think we come in to get free money from their system and take over their liveli-hood, and put we own woman on street corner same time for make the little extra we need to buy we house. The establishment afraid we might take their perfect English landscape and strip it down to bush and savannah, exchange all their cow for goat and coal for sand. They fear we black people might run up in the parliament with spear and hand to we mouth, throw Macmillan on fire with English apple in his teeth, and take the Queen money to pay back the West Indian? They fear we might rape them dry like they did rape we for century, except we king cocky bigger than for their struggle cocky? Poor white people don't get the right information, because the establishment afraid they might join we. Because they are ignorant, they take out their frustration and unfulfilment on peaceful, willing immigrant like Claudette, me and the rest of we from the West Indies. All of we work hard, all of we face persecution. They can't understand that they get forsake just like we get forsake, that we both get raised by downtrodden mother and neglectful father.

I work hard, day in day out, sometime half-day Saturday, then Glorie born in August, same birthday as Claudette mother, and we name her after my grandmother. Claudette say she favour me with the eyebrow and her with the lip. Straight away she ask me why I hold Glorie face up to mine so close, but I have to study her face because my eye blurry and cloudy. Claudette worry that her husband losing his sight and that she might have to go out to look for job. She tell me, *Go to the doctor go to the doctor go to the doctor* but I don't take the time off work. She start to think about all the relative she can send for from back home to come and help we.

Few days pass and nobody say anything to me at the work.

The coal come in by rail. We pulverise and blend the coal and feed it into the retort, where it heat it up for thirteen hour at a thousand degree, which make coke residue. Sometime we poke the retort with long rod to quench the coke. Then we pump the gas through a purifier, full of wood shavings to soak up the impurity. It also make ammonium sulphate, to use as fertiliser, and water gas. Every five-and-a-half minute you get a blow-off that show that a certain amount of gas been made. It all very clever. Tar, mothball also produce. The coke then quench in the water tower. The steam everywhere. The steam from the train, the smoke from the coal burning. Fifty hour I do this job, handle the machine, some day shift some night. It dirty and loud but I love it. In it ugliness it beautiful. A different kind of heat than Jamaica.

That was when the headache really start to get worse and worse, while we watch on the news all the Teddy Boy running up and down terrorising the black people in Notting Hill. I find Peter sneer in the face of every man and woman there; the hatred, the feistiness, the badmindedness, just like the little blond boy in Bilston. McCarthy turn out alright; he did just an ignorant man goaded by ignorant man. I'm sorry that I lose my temper with him.

Talk turn to the upcoming boxing tournament. One of the foreman, Grime, take time come up to me gently to tell me I always remind him of Joe Louis, that I have great reaction and strength and can make a lot of money as a fighter. I did see him around sometime but he never talk to me yet. In his pleasant, quiet voice, he ask me if I ever did box bare-knuckle and I say yes, in Jamaica from must be about fourteen to nineteen, when Lynval born and I start to work full-time as a gardener. I never lose. I did amateur champion in the district. Some of the promoter want me to turn professional but my mother say no, and even if I did old enough to take my own decision by then I know that she did right; she say me too soft and peaceful even if big. Ten years pass and my life not different from then. I still have woman to look after and children to raise, and we live in a country where everything you don't want cheap and everything you do want dear.

I tell him I'm out of condition and too old to start learn to box again like adolescent. *It's like riding a bike*, Grime say. He even offer to train me himself. It don't matter how many hour I put in at the gas work; the money did less than the council, and Claudette go from celebration to botheration when I give it up, for she host tea party in pretty dress in we garden and tell one jealous friend, *Look how my Norman a march inna this country not even two year yet and already get a job for life and the friendship of a government official. Where for your husband, deh? Pon building site or sweep road or what?* and she even write boasty letter to her mother about how her son-in-law she never like – because I am nine years older than her daughter with two son already – make a success of we in England, and now she is planning to set up a business to help West Indian immigrant find good job and fair accommodation when they come, only for me to spend less than two year in that job, and the friend that come by the tea party walk past we window to see we curtain blow inside because somebody throw a brick through it, that we were lucky was not a burning bottle. I think that this could be the way to make me favour in her eye again, if I can come home as boxing champion, with the winnings.

Long time now since we make love. I feel like she is unhappy with me, at the moment. Last night she sleep far from me; at night is the only time we see the same. I listen to her breathe in and out. She smell of her face cream and the oil in her hair. She must smell better than anyone else in that factory where she work. This new face cream she using since we move to England so sweet, but she say it dry her skin.

Glorie start to wake. She don't sleep all night yet; still she wake around one. Sometime she cry a little bit then forget what she is crying for and fall back to sleep, but other time she is determine one of we get up to see to her, and normally she want Claudette breast, so I can't help with that. I feel sorry for Claudette. She work so hard. Glorie only seven-month-old when she lose her mother to the working world. Claudette have to get up every morning come rain or shine to work in the factory, and she only get that job because Doreen there too. Plenty women there making brick. Claudette couldn't find a job in a restaurant or hotel. They turn her away because she is a black woman; they don't care about her experience in Jamaica. They must think a black face will put their guest off their food, never mind that black people did cook for and serve white people for century. It is sad that she could not find anybody like I found Clifford, who see the black but also the skill.

Claudette startle, must be from a dream. Her breast heavy with milk that her baby should be drinking so she grateful to come home from work and feed Glorie. Still, she mutter about how she fed up and have to get up and work, get up when pickney wake, get up and get up and get up, and she think about them all the time and send people to check on we during the daytime when she at work, and if we want more than just fry fish and dumplin she have to cook enough to eat dinner then overnight food for the next day; she is tired, and no mother should have to lift brick seven months after giving birth. Once Glorie quiet on her breast, she say:

'I don't know how long I can live like this, Norman.'

Normally, we speak patois together and try to speak good English outside the home, so I don't know why she is addressing me in this way.

'Like what?' I say.

Her voice turn to me across the darkness.

'I'm tired, Norman. Woman don't get the same money as

man. I can't look after you, look after the children and work two job, when I fear every minute somebody will come knock down the door and take cosh to we head. I can't cope with the worry in my brain.'

'But it won't stay this way,' I say.

'What is going to change and when?'

She and her mother have been writing letters to each other. Claudette want to prove to her mother she made the right decision but it is hard. She was always her mother's favourite. The middle daughter. The prettiest, the lightest skin. The one she expected would marry a good middle-class Jamaican man, an accountant or some other professional, not a field hand. It is difficult for her to show her mother she made the right choice when her life has turned out like this. I understand, but nothing was supposed to happen this way. My mother did write to me too. On very nice paper, to tell me to *come home Norman. Come me look after you.* Claudette have to read it out to me, and she don't like it, but now, maybe, she think that might be for the best.

'Soon, love. Soon we will settle as a family. It take time. Remember when we first start court and your mother did against me, but she soon see that I am a good man and love her daughter more than anything? We both know that the longer time go on, that everybody who try to stop we would change their mind, and let us be together and free. We both know that the longer that time go on, the better we adapt to our way of life.'

She kiss her teeth, and laugh.

'I don't want to get better at suffering, Norman. I want to be happy. Me pray day and night and still we nuh see light!'

'A me nuh see light. You can see everything good.'

Glorie little mouth suck nipple. I wonder if she can understand that her mother is in pain.

'Mek we go back a Jamaica,' I say. 'If you cyah happy de yah, mek we go back home. You nuh miss the banana, that nuh taste the same when them ship across the world? The breadfruit, the cassava, the mango? We nuh say we fail. We say we get the experience and done.'

She don't say anything again. When Glorie asleep and down, she come back to bed, and I try to cuddle her up and love her but she push me away and slap me off. She get up and leave me to lie down with Robert, in his little bed.

I tell Grime I want thirty per cent of the takings. He come back by me after we stop for lunch, and say, *Deal*.

Hot weather training on Saturday with Grime in his shirtsleeve, on the common. We lunge with bar and sprint up and down. My muscle remember how to box more than my eye. I feel where is the pad before I see it, and I hit it clean every time, till one time he stop but continue to count out loud in the same rhythm, and I thrash forward and almost throw myself to the ground.

'Real power, aggression and instinct,' Grime say. But I hear him take off one pad. 'How many fingers am I holding up?'

'Four,' I say, and laugh.

'And now?'

'Ah. Six?'

He did silent a moment.

'Am ya blind, Norman?'

Of course, it cross my mind that my eye not as good as they use to be, but to hear that word from somebody else mouth, I could have dead from stroke on the spot. To hear it from a stranger, somebody who don't know me, somebody who need me to be at my best so we can make money, somebody who not even teasing me or trying to bring me down, it did shock me right in my heart. I have to accept now that the condition of my eye bad, that I have to see a doctor. Grime one of my boss, too. My boss can see that I can't see good and work on his factory floor, with heavy and dangerous machine that need to be operate by somebody with good eye.

'We'll finish here for today,' he say. 'I'll see you in work on Monday.'

I win the first fight in a straight knockout, but the second one start and the headache lurch and I feel weak, and just as I open my mouth to retire the Trini man lick me down. I work through the winter with the headache but one day, in April, one alarm did start ring inside my head like the air raid siren in a war film. I drop the spade, lie down and beg somebody to bring me water. The sun come out bright, bright after the rain.

'A rainbow! Two rainbows!' McCarthy shout.

Robert and Glorie watching television. The curtain are draw. My head still hurt, but I must start cook soon. Claudette will be home from work; it must be gone five. Every time I get up to cook I am afraid to drop hot oil on my children head.

Three month now, I don't work. The doctor we see tell me that I get the headache, and my eyesight spoil ... *because I am too tall*, because it is a different kind of sunlight in England.

'Daddy a laugh!' Robert say when I slap down me hand on my leg.

'Lord, if me nuh laugh, me wi' cry,' I say to him.

He must already think his daddy mad. But tell me what the doctor go to big English school such a long time for to chat so much rubbish? More than one hour I wait for less than five minute. They don't even check my eye properly. Claudette smile in her white glove and hat and say, *Yes doctor, yes doctor*, like she fear to inconvenience them. For some reason I can't talk. Plenty rest, they say, give me prescription for Panadol, tell me to stay out the light and to see one optician.

I still don't know how they can conclude, with all their big education, that a man born and raised in Jamaica can fraid a the lickle chink a light a come out the cloud a Englan'!

What a way the boy don't know his own business and ask me question about what I am laughing about every minute.

'Watch *Mother Rabbit Family* or I turn it off and listen classical music!'

You have your whole life ahead of you fe listen, bwai. Mek your eye eat nuff now case dem nuh hungry again.

A cruel God it is that stop me to see my beautiful children and the rose I plant to his salvation.

'Daddy, you a cry?'

This boy.

'Robert, what you want to watch? Wheh Glorie deh?'

'Nuh worry, Daddy, she asleep.'

My little man come up to hold his hand around mine like a priest and rest his head between my leg. I pick him up and stroke his cheek, nose, lip and eye, for I can't bother to try to look on his face good again. If you can't *see*, you must feel.

'Me read in the paper them fret bout mussi forty thousand West Indian already make the trip a Englan' fe live,' say Laury, when he and Maurice come by my house one evening after I stop work. 'But me also read that Englan' have population quite up to fifty million. Fifty million rahtid Englishman did win world war and them bawl bout lickle forty t'ousand black man in them yard! More German them deh yah than we! Cha!'

'Sometime if me deh pon bus top deck through the town centre me lucky if me see one black face mid all the sea a white,' say Maurice. 'How that one black face them cyah ev'n find room fa fe take over, eeh? Tell me that! Me give them mi raasclaat for take over!'

'You nuh worry them a go say you ah live off yuh woman?' say Laury, to me.

'No, sah. People say that don't know me and Claudette.'

'You going through the war, man,' say Maurice. 'Me sorry for you. Nobody nuh have it easy. Plenty worry a trouble black man ya so. Look wha happen last night with the black man a London. From Antigua, them say. Him bruck fe him arm a work so him go hospital, and them bandage it up, so him a walk home to him yard when mussi five white man him never see in him raasclaat life set pon him with knife. Them kill him dead!'

'A lie y'a lie,' I say.

'No sah, me nuh lie! Them tab him up an lef' him pon the pavement fe dead!'

'Lord Jesus! Wha' make man bad so?' say Laury.

'Them bad, yes! And them a riot, black man against teddy bwai white, tab up each other nuh the road with car burn and shop loot. Rahtid! We nuh come a Englan fe dis!'

'May he rest in peace,' I say.

'Kelso Cochrane, him name,' say Maurice.

Doreen did in the kitchen with Claudette. Even though I am blind I know Doreen not right. She don't hug me the way she did usually. When they gone Claudette tell me that Doreen got a black eye and say it was an accident at work. And Claudette too lovely for the botheration these badmind man she have to work with subject her to. She come home the other night to tell me she push a trolley onto one ward to wash the sick man face, and even as she reach them, with a big smile, one of them say to one other one, *I don't trust these darkies. They'll steal the milk out your tea if you take your eyes off 'em*, and they laugh. Even as she put the rag in the water to squeeze it, she did feel the strength withdraw from her hand as if her blood did turn to lead, but she bite her lip and wash the man face round, and he fidget and resist, but she do what she need do to this man, wheel back out the trolley, and soon as she leave the ward she drop down on her knee and cry. That is not the Claudette I know; the back-a-yard Claudette I know would take her nail, scratch corner in the man forrid and peel off his face, make him feel every nerve tear from his skin. So hard she work, with two job, then she have to deal with these bad mind man talking rubbish to her, casual like she is deaf and can't read lip.

They rub your hair and your skin to see if the black might come off. They say your hair like Brillo pad. Woman come from the West Indies for *Pride* and find *Prejudice*. No good morning, no good evening. *Keep Britain White*, they all say. We are a colony of stray cat at everybody gate, creep up in their house when they left their door open, to tuck up in their bed, sometime, as Maurice like to, with their wife. Darkie. The look they give. They say we smell. Or they don't tell we, they tell each other, because we put oil in we hair and cream we face against the British element, the element of the northern hemisphere, where the sun don't hardly shine but make me blind, where the people turn their back against we island. We surround. We feel like criminal. We feel like foreigner, not like British citizen. We feel like the headache.

I am a black man. A tall, big, strong black man. In slave time, I would fetch a lot of money, because of my ability to work, my eye, my mind, my obedience, my consciousness, my fertility, my desire for peace, to be happy, to keep everybody happy. Take away just one component, and what is he worth? Nothing. I am a back. I am a mule to load with sacks of sand. I should be out there at work, not sitting at home, stepping careful around two small children I can't see. Four children. How I did get four children? How is the mother of two of them out at work, and the other two the other side of the world, a call another man Daddy? How I did get so far from home? When was the last time I did read a book, or even one newspaper article? Why I did not go to college? Why I did not go to the University of the West Indies? Why I did not fight more to get an education? Why I did leave Henry? Why, oh why, does black man die?

Robert head on my chest, like he is asleep, and he don't answer me again. So my children both asleep leaving me to watch their kiddy show and I can't even get up to switch off the television. But now I can cry, because I love them so. But I don't feel good at all. I don't like this world. I can't go to church when God make me humiliate so, when he give me so much hope to bring up my children in a better place, only to take way the tool I did need to make that life for them. Lahd God. Merciless. Like Bedasse a seh, *Depression gwine guh kill me dead!*

GREAT BRIDGE

Chapter 1

August 2, 2002

He got off the 35 at Brixton station and waited at the same stop for the number 3. Two evangelists, both mic'ed up, competed with each other over dub basslines at the station's mouth. Facing it, a bespectacled, middle-aged man in a white shirt and high-waisted black trousers said the words 'sex before marriage' into his headset. Closer to Jesse, accompanied by a wheeled amp, a woman dressed completely in white from her synthetic hair to her Doc Marten boots was screaming, *Jesus died for you!* into her mic, pointing right into the faces of startled passers-by. A group of black girls with iron-straight weaves, crop tops and combats passed her in silence with their lips around McDonald's straws. Crowds of white people dressed in leather, skinny black denim and band T-shirts, some carrying pint glasses and bottles, were dispersing onto buses and into takeaways. A police car waited until it had crept into Jesse's personal space before deploying its siren, making him jump and swear before it escaped through the traffic. Men with dreadlocks stuffed into yellow, red and green knitted hats sold posters of black legends and incense from trestle tables. The smells of skunk, Southern-fried chicken, raw meat, fresh fish, green bananas and yams commingled in the cooling air, while debris from the day's market trade littered the gutters. A tall boy with thick lips and a durag crossed near and muttered the word *skunk* into his ear, but the number 3 came and Jesse jumped straight on it.

He sat at a window seat two forward from the back, not directly in front of the sleeping man in the black hoodie threatening to spill the lager from his can. The chaos of Brixton Road soon gave way to quieter neighbourhoods. A couple of stops in, three young people sharing a bottle of rosé – a blonde, a brunette, and a tanned boy, perhaps his age or a year or two older – threw themselves around him, in front and beside, and continued their conversation as if he wasn't there.

I just wouldn't mind doing a day trip somewhere, you know what I mean? I wouldn't have to spend loads of money just like, you know. When we went last year ... / What, to Brighton? / We just sat on the beach and got pissed and it was a really lovely afternoon. / Summer in Berlin's so nice though. / We've got a roof terrace now. So we don't have to mix with all and sundry. There's chairs out there, a bit fucked but we're gonna have to get some new stuff. We were thinking of just getting some fold-up stuff ... / There's a big storage thing in the middle of our flat. / It might be getting a tad extreme. / Where can you store turf? If you can find me some turf ... / On the roof and roll it out like a big garden, or you can get fake stuff. / You don't want to irritate the neighbours. / She's looking to move out by the end of the month. I doubt she'll have time to sort it. / What, this month? You'd have to meet the person first. / When are you moving in?

Jesse looked down out of the window, at a drunk man pissing under an archway next to a closed garden centre, wondering what these perfect white people must be thinking about him and whether it was obvious he was rent on his way to have sex with a client. Might they be able to smell it on him? He was apprehensive; he'd been advertising for a couple of months now and the good clients already seemed to be drying up. He cringed, thinking about his most recent, 'Dave', who answered the door of his Bayswater flat, sweating and out of breath, in a very tight pair of white Adidas shorts with green trim, a studded leather collar and dirty white socks. The smile dropped from his face; Jesse could see in his eyes that he was high.

'I thought you were tall,' 'Dave' had said, looking Jesse up and down as he stepped out of his doorway to let him in.

It was explicit on Jesse's Gaydar profile that his height was five feet eight, and his recent pictures were not deceptive in showing him to be of slim build. Jesse had quickly learned that sometimes, when these men see black skin, they believe King Kong's coming to see to them.

'Straight through,' 'Dave' said, as if annoyed. Jesse arrived in a dark front room, more like a den. It was early evening but the curtains were drawn and the room was lit by floor lamps and candles burning among all the scattered flammable articles. The heating was on and it was stiflingly hot, prickling sweat out onto Jesse's forehead.

'Doesn't it say six two on your profile?' 'Dave' had said, twitchily.

'Do you want me to go?' Jesse said, surprising himself with his aggression.

'At least you're on time,' 'Dave' said, snidely, then changed his tone. 'Drink? I've got beer, wine, whisky, vodka, rum, Coke, Diet Coke, Red Bull ... ' He rocked his head from side to side as if reading the name of each product from the ceiling, while a thick white foam started to collect at the corners of his mouth. Jesse wondered why 'Dave', who probably wouldn't look so bad with naturally grey hair, had bothered to dye it such an ugly orangey-brown. His body odour, in the intense heat, quickly began to sicken Jesse.

'Water's fine,' he said, taking off his rucksack, his upper lip tightening with disgust.

'Get your clothes off, then,' 'Dave' said as he turned out of the room.

The red sofa cushions had been arranged on the floor to

make a bed over which was spread a clear plastic sheet, and a frameless mirror lay flat on a wooden footstool to the side in front of the closed curtains, with two lines of what looked like cocaine racked up ready. There was a smoky smell about the place, underneath the stale sweat, from something other than cigarettes and weed; a blackened glass pipe and a lighter rested on a small box underneath the table. 'Dave' had looked perfectly normal in his pictures, but there were warning signs, Jesse was beginning to realise, in his overcomplicated phone directions ('Last flat on the ground floor' would have sufficed).

From the sitting-room doorway Jesse watched 'Dave' take a pint glass down from a cupboard and fill it with cloudy water straight from the tap without running it first; he came back in and spilled some down Jesse's fingers as he handed it over. Jesse put it down on the floor while he removed his trainers and tracksuit. 'Dave' stepped onto the middle of the makeshift bed in front of him, as if it was a stage.

'Now, I've got some coke, do you want some coke? I've got some G, some T, as well, and some grass as well, if you want some. Poppers, obviously. You can do whatever you want, or you don't have to do anything just, make yourself at home. Over there in that bag are some paddles, belts, canes, whatever you think. Have you ever caned someone before? Can't remember if I asked you. Well, I want you to cane me if you want. Then you can fuck me. Do you want some Viagra? I've got some Viagra, if you need anything just say. Fuck me, your cock looks *much* more massive than in your pictures! How big is it? Nine? Ten? Does it stay hard? You should get some better pictures done, mate. Do you want me to take you some pictures? I've got a camera ... Anyway, later. Do you want me to do anything? Where do you want me? Do you want me to suck you off first or do you just want to go straight in and fuck me? Do you want me naked? You can fuck me bareback and come in me if you want. I really want you to come in me, actually.'

He was fidgeting and gurning, and kept trying to shove fingers up his own arse. Before Jesse could answer, he just peeled the shorts off altogether, almost falling over, got on all fours in front of him, pressed his face into the plastic sheet and spread his arse cheeks. 'Please! Please!' was his muffled cry, and Jesse felt relieved he'd decided *not* to stop off at McDonald's for a super-size Double Quarter Pounder Cheese Meal with nine chicken nuggets and a strawberry milkshake on the way.

He said, 'Sorry, I can't do this,' and started putting his track-suit back on.

'Dave' flipped himself over like a beetle and stared up at Jesse in shock.

'What? Why? What's wrong?'

'I'm not feeling well,' Jesse said, which wasn't a lie. 'I feel sick, actually. I have to go.'

'No! Why? What happened? Is it me? What did I do? Don't go!' He got up and Jesse shot him a *don't touch me* look. 'We can just relax and take it slow! Do you want a line and just sit and watch some porn? I've got ghetto guys fucking white daddies if you want, I know you like that! Please! What can I do?'

But as soon as he'd slipped his trainers back on, he grabbed the rest of his things in his arms and left 'Dave' shouting after him, calling him a time-waster and threatening to write him a career-ending, blacklisting review.

Yeah, don't do what we did. We went to Thailand last year and she really, really wanted to stay. That was weird but I said, no, sorry I can't. / Oh. / I said to her, when we booked Brazil ... / I was trying to say to her ... / She didn't get it ... / Why don't you sublet your room? / ... She could've saved all that money ... / ... Is that what you really want?

''Scuse me,' said Jesse, getting up.

'Oh, sorry,' said the brunette, as if she'd only just seen him.

He got off the bus where instructed in the text, crossed the road, found the three-digit number and crunched along the driveway with the silver Audi on it. His client, Thurston, lived in a gold-brick semi on a quiet Dulwich street lined with sticky lime trees. There were accessibility bars drilled into the walls, either side of the black front door with its stained-glass inserts. Jesse took a deep breath as he pressed the bell, lit in orange, which trilled high, and for a stupid second, he panicked that he didn't have copies of the *Watchtower* and *Awake!* with him ready to present to the householder, and that he wasn't wearing a tie. Don't fuck this up, he thought to himself, mindful of the £18.33 he had left to his name, and hungry for that next gram of coke. A big-sounding dog barked twice, but didn't seem to be coming to the door, as if it understood its job was merely to chime with the ring. Even the dogs here are restrained, Jesse thought, unlike the feral Alsatians back home that would sprint barking from the bottom of the garden straight through the house and smash themselves against the inside of the door until their owners appeared and locked them away.

The hallway light came on. They'd exchanged lots of messages on Gaydar. Jesse had wanted to close the deal straight away but Thurston slowed him down with his respectful tone. He was looking for someone to get to know and see for *some periodic, safe and sensual attention*. He was fifty-one, tall, slim and passive. His pictures were all of him smiling, with paintings behind him in a gallery, or in a fancy restaurant or bar, where someone else had been cropped out. They found that they were both born in the Black Country, Thurston in the semi-rural village of Tettenhall, outside Wolverhampton; Jesse in the industrial village of Wordsley, outside Dudley. Both had been honest about their real names. Thurston had a partner of thirty years, his senior, with advanced multiple sclerosis, and they couldn't have sex like they used to. As Jesse's heartbeat escalated, Thurston approached behind the coloured glass, opened the door and slipped Jesse in, smiling almost coyly in white and grey linen, barefoot on the black-and-white mosaic floor, looking as if he'd just showered, shaved and neatly combed his hair, a little bit older than his pictures suggested but not dishonestly so, as were too many desperate men, ten or twenty years older – wrinklier, looser and fatter – the lie, not the age, being the turn-off. The cackle of a TV gameshow audience came from behind one of the closed white interior doors. Jesse could smell fresh flowers, clean laundry, a clean body – talc, which he'd not smelled since swimming lessons at his infant school, where the teachers were reluctant to put it on him because of its chalky effect on black skin.

Jesse took off his rucksack and hung it on the corner of the bannister behind him. Long arms slid around his body, reeling him in. Thurston was even lovelier and more handsome in the flesh than in his photos and clearly getting better with age. Slow, full-lipped kisses tickled Jesse's forehead, moved down his nose and found his mouth. As Thurston held him closer and tighter, Jesse filled his hands with Thurston's firm arse and felt the nudge of a growing erection against him. Painted portraits hung on the walls, leaning in like an expectant audience.

'Hello,' said Thurston, still dotting Jesse's lips with kisses.

'Hello,' said Jesse. They took to each other immediately, smiled and laughed discreetly. Straight away, it felt, to Jesse, different from other clients. Thurston led the way upstairs, allowing Jesse a second to kick off his trainers to join those lined up against the wall, his socked feet sinking half a luxurious inch into the near-white carpet. He watched Thurston's arse and feet as he climbed, copying the exactness of his gait, already hard and excited to taste him. As the staircase veered right, a painting was revealed of a black male nude, his dick lazing across his thigh, clutching a large blood-red flower in his hand, the red paint dripping down his forearm as if he'd stigmatised himself on a thorn. It stung Jesse immediately, as if he had driven a pin right into the centre of his own palm. He thought about that picture of Jesus and the thief in *The Greatest Man Who Ever*

Lived, their ribs showing, blood draining down their stretched-up arms, thick pins driven through their palms into stakes. It looked like the man in the painting was falling back through the sky, grey-blue like Thurston's eyes.

Jesse followed Thurston into a lamp-lit room the blue of a midsummer evening, with a four-poster bed dressed in white and wine-red, the walls completely covered, from floor to ceiling, with paintings, photographic portraits and drawings, all, from what he could see, of men of various ages and colours in states of undress. With his back to Jesse, Thurston took off his top, and the waistband of his trousers sat perfectly under what Jesse saw as the most beautiful part of any man, the flat, tender patch right at the base of the spine. He thought of Graham, his white adoptive father, standing at the bathroom sink with the door open, shaving with his towel low round his waist.

Quickly Jesse and Thurston were naked, their clothes on the floor, Thurston's dick, neither big nor small, with an upward curve, straight into Jesse's mouth as they met on the bed. Jesse pushed the foreskin back with his lips, making Thurston's knob swell against the soft flesh at the back of his mouth, pushing his tongue down the piss-hole, licking up every flavour, rolling his balls around in his hand, his nutsack shaven, loose and thick-skinned. The murmur of a string quartet rose from the Bose clock radio. Incense burning, condoms, lube, poppers, bottles of water and Coca-Cola on the bedside table. The moment Jesse came up to breathe, Thurston pushed him round onto his back and took him in his mouth in turn, bending his arse right out for the triptych of mirrors on the dressing table opposite the bed. Jesse sat up, resting on his palms, watching himself being serviced.

Thurston tried to suck Jesse's dick the way Jesse had sucked his, but couldn't deal with Jesse's extra length and girth and repeatedly gagged. Soon he came back up to the bedhead – out of breath, blushing and with a wet, pink mouth – and rolled Jesse round on top of him. Jesse crept his fingers lightly over the contours of Thurston's collarbone, neck and shoulders, and nibbled his nipples, which stood up prominently. There wasn't a hair on his body until a fine, almost adolescent trail from just beneath his navel that spread to his trimmed pubes. As Thurston's dick pulsed in his mouth, Jesse began to worry he might come too quickly, so he lifted Thurston's legs over his shoulders to draw him more comfortably to the middle of the bed, and spread him open. He felt fresh guilt and ecstasy to observe such a man from that angle, where it had become boring and commonplace with more obvious, sluttier men. The underside of his tongue was still sore from the last guy. Thurston's hole puckered, opened and closed. Jesse swirled around it, circling closer and closer until he touched the heart. He closed his eyes and concentrated, making Thurston gasp, levered up by the backs of his knees inside the crooks of his elbows, rotating his ankles and flexing his toes, open and vulnerable as Jesse reached in as far as he could go, then further. This was the best part about his new life. He looked up along Thurston's body, at his hairless pink scrotum, at his dick twitching against his belly, then at the veins that were showing on his neck, his bottom lip caught between his teeth, eyes closed, voicing little gasps of satisfaction.

Jesse came up for a moment and stared in, making the little fine hairs tremble with his breath. Thurston opened his eyes; the trust with which he was looking up at Jesse from his pillow aroused Jesse all the more, and he felt the notice of an orgasm pass through his body. *This* was the best part about his new life. He lifted himself up, anchored his feet in the bed and pushed himself inside.

'Please, lube!' Thurston said, wincing as he stiffened and pushed Jesse out with his hands.

'Sorry,' said Jesse, curling his tongue under and consoling the nip of rawness. He reached over to the bedside table and squirted some Liquid Silk onto his palm.

'Condom?' Thurston's elbows were locked open, keeping Jesse out.

So Jesse reached for the packet of condoms on the side table, taking care not to spill the lube from his palm, but Thurston freed his legs and pulled himself up to sitting.

'Sorry,' Jesse said, as Thurston dragged down one of the two small hand towels folded over the brass bedhead and gave it to Jesse to wipe his hands with, using the other to dab the droplets of sweat on his forehead and neck.

'It's okay. You were in the moment,' Thurston said as he used his towel to dry his slick arse, then in a mildly chastising tone: 'You did say you practise safe sex.'

'I do, usually,' Jesse said, unable now to make eye contact.

'How many times have you had unprotected sex?'

Jesse dried his hand of all the sticky lube and sat on his feet, watching his dick go down. He ogled the drinks on the bedside table.

'Help yourself to whatever you want,' said Thurston.

Jesse took down the bottle of Coca-Cola. He didn't know how thirsty he was until he drank half of it in one go. He drank it so quickly the fizziness burned his throat. Some of it dribbled down his face and belly, and onto the bedcover.

'Sorry,' he said, rubbing it into the towel.

'Don't worry,' said Thurston, now sitting up against the bedhead, with one leg bent and the other hanging over the edge of the mattress. His dick had retreated back within his thick foreskin, relaxed against the pink drape of his scrotum. His eyes searched Jesse. 'Do your clients make you fuck them without a condom?'

Jesse glanced at Thurston's face, just to see if he might be judging. He saw concern.

'Have any of your clients ever fucked you without a condom?'

Jesse looked over his shoulder, as if he wanted to leave the room.

'You're a beautiful boy, and you have your whole life ahead of you. Have you been safe?'

'Not always,' said Jesse, quietly. He drank another three gulps of Coca-Cola, which again, burned his throat.

'Have you been tested?' asked Thurston.

Jesse shook his head tightly, as if his neck was seized in lime-scale, and looked down at his dick, twitching up again as all the men and all the ways went through his mind.

'Do you know where to go?'

Jesse, again, shook his head.

Chapter 2

'Have we entered the Great Tribulation?'

Brother Thomas Woodall, the congregation's presiding over-seer, a tall, broad, blue-eyed painter and decorator with dimples, white teeth and thick golden hair, spoke with a soft, low voice that refused to compete with a baby mythering, or an elderly Sister unwrapping a boiled sweet. A special meeting had been convened to deal with the congregation's needs after watching the fall of the Twin Towers, and the deaths of three thousand people, live on TV. Tipton Kingdom Hall – hand-built by members of the congregation to a basic single-storey architectural model – was packed full of beatific smiles, white with black, old with young. Two extra rows of seats had been added. Fringe and erstwhile members came in and sat on the back row, and were welcomed further forward. Disfellowshipped persons, shunned by the organisation for their unrepented sins, slipped in at the last and sat by the door, ready to disappear at the end of the closing prayer. Jesse's mother, sullenly pulling her cardigan tighter and folding her arms over her chest, was in attendance for the first time in weeks. A group of Sisters, concerned by her latest bout of depression, had coddled her as soon as she'd arrived, telling her how well she looked and asking her if she'd lost weight.

In the navy blue suit he'd bought for his son's recent wedding, Brother Woodall introduced from the rostrum Mark 13:1-8, holding his bible up and out on the palm of his hand, broadening his chest like the bearded Christ on the board illustrating the scripture of the year. In the gentlest of Tipton accents, Brother Woodall read slowly and deliberately, looking up to address a different member of the congregation with each phrase.

'As he was going out of the temple one of his disciples said to him: "Teacher, see! What sort of stones and what sort of buildings!" However Jesus said to him: "Do you behold these great buildings? By no means will a stone be left upon a stone and not be thrown down."

'And as he was sitting on the Mount of Olives with the temple in view, Peter and James and John and Andrew began to ask him privately: "Tell us, When will these things be, and what will be the sign when all these things are destined to come to a conclusion?" So Jesus started to say to them: "Look out that nobody misleads you. Many will come on the basis of my name saying 'I am he,' and will mislead many. Moreover, when you hear of wars and reports of wars, do not be terrified; these things must take place, but the end is not yet."

'For nation will rise against nation and kingdom against kingdom, there will be earthquakes in one place after another, there will be food shortages. These are a beginning of pangs of distress.'

Jesse kept glancing at Fraser Hammond on the front row between his mother and brothers, to see if he was paying attention. It was hard to tell. His head was always down as if in study, yet when the speaker – trying to get Fraser involved more – picked him out to read a verse aloud, Fraser simply shook his head, leaving the speaker to look awkwardly elsewhere. He'd graffitied his bible with band logos, right across the holy scriptures, and his parents – arty types who'd moved up from South London when Ian Hammond accepted a placement at a Dudley GP surgery – didn't seem to mind or care. Fraser had revealed to Jesse that he was dyslexic, and had trouble reading, especially out loud. Jesse was flattered that Fraser would share such information with him. Fraser liked to do things with his hands, and found the ideal professional home in the Black Country, working as a fabricator.

'So what do we learn, from Jesus's words, to his apostles?' asked Brother Woodall, rhetorically. 'If we expect to put a date on God's coming day of judgement, perhaps we should say, Remember September 1975.'

Sister Doreen Charles, sitting on an end seat in the middle, her black beehive wig blocking the view of the Brother behind her, nodded her head in agreement then shook her head at the memory. Jesse had heard her story many times, of how she had finally run out on her abusive, non-believing husband, she was so convinced, as most Witnesses then were, of the imminence of Jehovah's Day of Judgement.

'We all thought, then, that the world was going to end on that specific date,' said Brother Woodall. 'We sold our houses and left our jobs. We thought we were clever, with our mathematics' – Jesse glanced at Fraser's brother, Duncan, a recent Maths graduate, who was unmoved – 'and assumed *we* could predict when Jehovah God would act. Even before that, we thought that the Great Tribulation began in 1914, with the Great War. Not so. That was just the *beginning, of pangs, of distress*. The Bible tells us of five situations we'll face, that will come together to announce we are *in* the Great Tribulation. The first of those five will be an attack on false religion, as described in Revelation, chapter seventeen.'

Jesse knew it all already. He didn't have to listen. He was the darling boy of the congregation. Baptised for three years now, about to become a ministerial servant, halfway to elderdom, at nineteen. He manned the roving mics. Gave important talks from the platform, encouraging and admonishing the congregation, scripturally. Was considered to be a Brother of quite high standing, whilst remaining, almost shockingly, youthful.

Brothers and Sisters saw in him the power of Jehovah's love. They saw in him what a relationship with Jehovah can do for a young man: give him direction, make him satisfied, happy even, with his lot. A suitable wife was being sought for him: a mixed-race girl who had been introduced to him from another congregation, and when she stuck around him, shy and smily in her cream mohair turtleneck, moist little curls hanging from her forehead, he knew what was happening. She was pretty. They got on, but through no fault of hers he felt uncomfortable. He went home and scratched at his body as if he wanted to break out of his own skin. He prayed to Jehovah, but it was no use. He didn't feel as if he was actually speaking to anyone. His words, as he spoke them in his head, died. He knew that something was wrong, and hoped to God his real truth would not find its way out.

Jesse didn't know, when he went out to preach from house to house on September 11, 2001, that a different option, a different way of thinking, was waiting for him in the front room of an unassuming Victorian two-up, two-down. It began on a simple Tuesday afternoon, and despite his inexperience, he conducted the field service briefing because Sisters weren't allowed to if there was a baptised Brother present (in the absence of a senior male, they could ask a prayer, covering their heads). Unprepared, he read 1 Corinthians 7:29-31 for the Sisters – mostly single, childless women in their late twenties who like him had dedicated their lives to the full-time ministry:

'Moreover, this I say, brothers, the time left is reduced. Henceforth let those who have wives be as those who had none, and also those who weep be as those who do not weep, and those who rejoice be as those who do not rejoice, and those who buy as those not possessing, and those making use of the world as those not using it to the full; for the scene of this world is changing.'

They must have been wondering where he was going, but it

all made sense by the end. They were an odd number, so the Sisters paired off and Jesse worked alone, one of those estates of terraced houses whose front doors opened into a staircase and sitting room. The first he knocked on was answered abruptly by a skinny young man, topless in jogging bottoms and with a face like he'd just seen something life-changing. Jesse was about to go straight into his spiel with the current issues of the *Watchtower* (Can Anything Really Unite People?) and *Awake!* (Depression – A Generation at Risk) when the young man interrupted him to say back into the house, *It's just a Jova*, then turned to Jesse and said, *You int sin the news av ya, mate! A plane's crashed into a skyscraper in New York!*

The young man left his front door open and went back to his seat next to a stubbly South Asian man in a polo shirt with the collar up, sitting awestruck in his slippers on the edge of a sofa, smoking what smelt immediately like a spliff and drinking a mug of tea, so Jesse, hesitantly, stepped in, closed the door and crossed in front of them to sit in the matching armchair. True enough, a cloud of grey smoke poured out from a great crater near the top of a New York skyscraper, as if from the mouth of an active volcano, obscuring the crown of its identical twin, a gruesome sight against the pure blue sky. Joypads, DVD video games and their cases were strewn across the floor in front of the TV.

'What's actually 'appened?' said Jesse.

'They doe know, yet,' said the South Asian man, through his cigarette smoke. 'We just turned on the telly to play a game, then the . . .'

'The announcer,' said the skinny man.

'Yeah, the announcer said we're gonna interrupt the program-ming schedule . . .'

'To bring a special news report,' said the skinny man, trem-bling with nervous energy.

Jesse's heart thumped as if he had been caught stealing. He had always imagined, that when the Great Tribulation began with the global banning, by the United Nations, of all false religion – executing Jehovah's will – it would be announced, like this, by a news report interrupting the regular scheduling. The Asian man passed his spliff to the skinny man, who dragged on it desperately as they both stared at the screen in widening horror. A camera at ground level, watching the building on fire, immediately switched its gaze up to the sky. A man screamed *Oh shit!* as another plane careered stupidly over their heads and smacked right into the second tower with the sound of an empty can being crushed underfoot. The whole world gasped at once, and then for a tiny, frozen moment there was utter silence, as air rushed into the cavity of the building before a fireball boomed out from the wound.

'Fuck! Fuck! Fuckin' hell, man! What the fuck's gooin' on!'

The skinny man sprang up from his seat, ash flying everywhere, his dick lolloping around in his joggers.

'We are awaiting confirmation from the White House that the American government is now treating this incident as a coordinated attack,' said the reporter.

'Hundreds of people am dying, Carl, right there,' said the Asian man, as the skinny man backed onto his seat in shock.

'Jesus foretold,' Brother Woodall reasoned, 'that the broad attacks, by the United Nations, on false religion, will not go so far as to destroy our *true* religion. What, then, does Jesus tell us we should do? Let's turn to Matthew, chapter twenty-five, verse thirteen. One of the shortest verses in the Bible. Brother Jesse McCarthy, would you like to read that out for us?'

Jesse was suddenly nervous. He had a hard-on. The soft, loving tone with which Brother Woodall said his name didn't help. An attendant, with a roving mic, hung it in front of Jesse's face. Jesse kept his bible on his lap.

'*Keep on the watch, therefore,*' he read, '*because you know neither the day nor the hour.*'

*

Jesse stayed with Carl and Abdul as long as he could without being feared missing, all three transfixed by the news – and he left them a copy of *Awake!*, which at least offered more practical answers to life's questions than the dogmatic *Watchtower*. He drank their tea and breathed in their weed smoke, dreamed of being forced to suck their dicks. They shook their heads and thought silently of those who had lost their lives, even as they watched their bodies burn. Armageddon was coming, someday, but if he'd been on that plane or in that building he would already be dead. What kind of God lets people die so horribly? He was shocked at himself, at that thought, but more than anything, confused by something he'd never previously questioned.

He found the Sisters – who themselves had all been invited in by householders to watch the events unfold – similarly shock-faced in the next street, but still almost felt he had to lie when they asked him where he'd been and prayed they couldn't smell anything on him. *I was invited in by a couple*, he said. *Nice people, but I don't think we should call on 'em again*. Abdul had described how members of his family had threatened to kill him. He and Carl lived far enough away from their childhood homes to feel safe but not so as to become isolated. They lived together in that little house as a couple. Two men. They ran a window-cleaning business together and had finished for the day. Various sexual configurations went through Jesse's mind. They were both masculine; he thought he might be able to understand it better if one of them was like a girl, but these two – *men* – lived together. They seemed so free. They spent afternoons in their slippers and jogging bottoms, playing computer games, drinking tea and smoking weed. They had a kitchen and a garden, and upstairs, probably two bedrooms – plenty of privacy – and a bathroom. Jesse used their downstairs toilet and thought to himself, *I'm having a wee in the house of two men who live together like man and wife*. Lived together. Two men. In such a cute little house with a red door, one sash window at the bottom and one at the top. All they needed. Carl was a skinny white man, like the skinny white boys Jesse went to school with who said racist things to South Asian men like Abdul, calling them *dirty fuckin' Pakis*, but now, this skinny white man, and this South Asian man, probably in their mid-twenties, had found love, with each other. It was the first time Jesse had ever met a gay couple, and he didn't run away from them in disgust. Perhaps he would've done if they had not experienced together, he and them, the unfolding of such a cataclysmic event.

The way Carl and Abdul looked at each other, the way they held hands, Jesse found electrifying. They sat next to each other, watching something far more destructive to the world than their love. He left with a foretaste of Armageddon, and wondered whom he would want to experience it with. *These are a beginning of pangs of distress.*

'Did Jehovah God intervene,' Brother Woodall concluded, 'to bring things to a conclusion, after the Great War and Spanish flu killed twenty-five million people, between 1914 and 1919? Did Jehovah God intervene, to bring things to a conclusion, after World War Two, and the Holocaust, killed an estimated seventy-five million, people across the world? Will Jehovah God intervene, because three thousand people just died in New York and Washington, DC? We cannot say no, but nor can we say yes, because the time Jehovah God will act is known only to Him, and all we can do, is keep our faith, go out there on the ministry, and comfort those who need the support only we, as God's servants, and His voice on the Earth, can give. It could happen tomorrow, it could happen in a hundred years. In the meantime, mankind will continue to do what mankind has constantly done since it broke away from God's favour, and that is, to divide itself into tribes, and go to war.'

Chapter 3

September 16, 2001

All the pubs in Great Bridge were closed, so Jesse and Fraser met outside the off-licence on Whitehall Road, Jesse in his best going-out clothes – a pair of corduroys, a grey bomber jacket, black polo shirt and Adidas Sambas. Fraser was wearing his Rockports, a Barbour waxed jacket zipped up to the top, with the cuff of a blue gingham shirt just visible over his watch.

'What do you drink?' he said, to the window of the beer fridge.

'Same as you, I suppose.' Jesse, at nineteen, had still not quite acquired the taste for lager, but Graham drank Foster's, so Jesse was glad when Fraser picked out a six-pack. He put his hand in his pocket.

'Don't worry, they're on me,' Fraser grinned, taking out his Visa.

'You have any ID?' said the young Indian guy serving.

Fraser, twenty, got out his driving licence and asked for a pack of ten B&H Silver.

'Fags?' Jesse said, looking round to see if anyone else in the shop might recognise them.

Fraser winked at Jesse over his shoulder. It was a chilly, damp night, and as soon as they were out on the street, Fraser unwrapped the cellophane. A gassy smell entered Jesse's nostrils. With smoke rising from the cigarette on his lip, Fraser put one in Jesse's mouth and lit it, sheltering the flame from the wind. 'Take it down gently,' he said, assuming Jesse had never smoked before. He sprang back and laughed as Jesse coughed and spluttered till tears came to his eyes.

The council estate up the road was awaiting demolition, and the empty block next to the library, lackadaisically fenced off, appeared the perfect hideout. Fraser squeezed through a gap and made space enough for Jesse. They scaled the debris of crumbling breezeblocks, sheets of plaster and abandoned furniture, climbed two flights of damp stairs over broken glass and joints of weather-rotten window-surround, and found a room, lit by a streetlamp, stripped back all the way to the brick, with the front wall of the building missing, facing Great Bridge. In the middle there were two piles of breezeblocks, arranged, as if just for them, to resemble sofas at right angles to each other in a sitting room. They each sat down on a pile and cracked open a can.

'Have you heard *The Blueprint* yet?' Fraser said. 'Jay-Z's new album. It's only out in America so far, but I just ripped it off Napster.'

'You ripped it off wha?'

'Napster,' he said, as if Jesse was years behind the times. 'It's an online file sharing website, so people in like America or wherever upload tracks or albums as MP3s to Napster, which you can then download anywhere in the world. You can burn them to CD if you want.'

Jesse didn't understand any of it. 'That's cool,' he said. 'I wish I 'ad a computer.'

'You can just come round mine and download anything you want,' Fraser said, as he blew smoke rings. 'It's a sweet shop.'

Why aren't we at yours now? Jesse thought. 'Cool. So is it good?' he asked.

'It's wicked. I've been listening to it over and over. You wanna hear some?'

'Goo on then.' Fraser presented his Discman from one of the very practical large outer pockets of his Barbour, and unwound the earbuds, handing Jesse one. The music started straight away. Jesse was into glitchy electronic pop-R&B produced by Timbaland and the Neptunes. He was building quite the collection of singles, cheaper than albums and more immediate. Albums were for grown-ups; maybe it was time for him to come of age. Fraser was an albums man. Jesse felt pretty cool, sitting in a dark, wet, derelict room drinking a can of Foster's and taking an earbud to listen to a new Jay-Z album that wasn't even out yet. It still stung him, though, every time he heard a rapper swear.

'This runnin' this rap-*ish* tune's good,' he said, nevertheless.

He knew he could steal a march on the ruder boys at McDonald's if he had a copy of this before them and could learn some of the lyrics. His mother had never allowed him to listen to rap, so he'd been blocked all his life from hearing black men talk about the world on their own terms. White boys, who considered themselves to know more than he did about 'the struggle', made fun of him. He remembered the first time he'd ever heard the word *nigger* on record, listening to The Notorious B.I.G.'s *Ready to Die* with the three Hammond brothers in Fraser's bedroom, hearing them pronounce every word of the lyrics without missing a syllable, getting rowdy with their gun fingers: *I've been robbin' muthafuckers since the slaaaave ships!*

Fraser drained the last of his first can and threw it in the corner with a tinny echo, cracking open his second, the strong middle finger of his right hand keeping his earbud pressed into his ear. Jesse imagined sucking that middle finger, the trimmed nail scraping down his tongue. *A wise man told me don't argue with fools, cos people from a distance can't tell who's who.* Must remember that, Jesse thought. Fraser just nodded his head to the music, listening hard to the lyrics. The pop single Jesse already knew well came on next.

'Izzo's a tune,' he said. The samples generally, so far, had impressed him. This track made use of 'I Want You Back' by The Jackson 5. It reminded him of his childhood, when his mother used to play her vinyl loud in the front room when other Witness couples came round for dinner, all her soul classics like Stevie Wonder, Marvin Gaye and Roberta Flack. She'd recently given it all away in boxes to a Brother – indeed, a *brother* – from another congregation. She'd stopped listening to them years ago, buying only CDs now. 'Wha, Jay-Z used to sell drugs? Crack? Int he gonna be arrested, mekkin' that confession on record?'

'Dunno.' Fraser lit another cigarette, then offered Jesse one, which, against himself, he took. Here he was, smoking and drinking, the very acts he'd so long looked down on others for defiling their bodies with. He was enjoying the music, but craved Timbaland beats. He still hadn't quite got over Aaliyah's death, just a few weeks before, and was secretly slightly disappointed by her last album. The sound was great but wasn't *Timbaland* enough. He'd wanted a whole album of 'Are You That Somebody?' – impossible-to-dance-to machine-gun beats that dropped when they wanted to, surprising with their placement; baby-crying and teeth-grinding samples. Her self-titled album was slicker, more soulful, more emotional, more grown-up.

Jay-Z namechecked the Fugees. I need another album by Lauryn Hill, Jesse thought. I need her voice in my life. He thought of her performing 'Killing Me Softly' with The Fugees on *Top of the Pops*. No one in that crowd, surely, had ever heard a voice like hers, much less live. That song embarrassed him, when he first heard it coming out of the speakers one morning. It sounded like a Gospel song; what was it doing on Radio 1? He thought the idiots at school would take the piss out of him, knowing he was a Christian. But then it went straight to the top of the charts and sold over a million copies, and everyone loved it. It became his sacred song, and The Fugees came back to give an even better performance of it for the *Top of the Pops* Christmas Special. This is such a romantic song, he thought, of the slow-jam now playing. There'd been bedroom rap songs, but never, to his mind, had a six-foot-four black rapper sounded so tender about another man. It was like Jay-Z was speaking to Jesse. It was like Jehovah was speaking to him. That plaintive *nigga?* at the end, where his voice cracked? This is a love song, Jesse thought, and was almost embarrassed; a song about love between Brothers. He glanced at Fraser, who didn't look back, but smiled slightly, and nodded. He let his knee touch Jesse's. Jesse's instinct was to move his own, to make himself smaller and allow the white boy his space, but he kept his knee where it was. An electric pulse ran through his whole body. Another slow soul song. Was this the most emotion any serious rapper had ever shown on record? Smiling, Fraser lit up, dragged deep and puffed out a strong, sweet-smelling cloud. Weed? The boys at McDonald's smoked it but Jesse had never known a Witness to. Fraser took another toke and the smoke rolled sexily up from his bottom lip, up his nostrils before disappearing with an intake of breath. His eyes locked on Jesse's as he passed it to him. Jesse put the spliff to his lips; it was already moist. He put his lips to the thing a man had put his lips to, and sucked. He felt the difference immediately from the cigarette, that he would cough and choke if he wasn't gentle. He opened his throat to it. Breathed it right down. He let the smoke come back out through his nostrils – two white jets like plane trails against a blue sky. The air felt less cold, stiller. His eyelids dropped down by a millimetre. He felt a degree or two warmer. An inch or two closer to Fraser. The volumes and balances of the music evened out. He could *see* the music. This is so much better than that Dr Dre album everyone loves, he thought. What rappers usually peddle is the idea that black men lack emotion.

Fraser held out his left hand, his fingers splayed to accept the spliff. 'Puff-puff-pass, puff-puff-pass,' he said.

Jesse passed it to him, giving him a kiss with his eyes. 'There's something I don't like about this beat,' he said. 'It's too 'arsh for Jay-Z's voice. Them drums are too tinny. Er, Eminem? I'm so bored of him.'

'Why, because he's white?'

You hit the nail on the head, nigga, Jesse thought, startling himself. 'Are you trying to say I'm racist?' he said.

'He's got the best flow on the whole album,' said Fraser. 'Black men invented rap but you have to say the best rapper's white.'

Like Jesse, Jay-Z wasn't raised by a black man. Jay-Z's mother wasn't at home, sitting on the sofa all day in her nightie watching TV, like Jesse's mother was. She was out there at work, making money to raise her family. Jay-Z didn't have a useless white adoptive father who kept himself to himself and didn't care. If he had a computer, Jesse thought, and wasn't a Jehovah's Witness, he would write a book about his childhood. Jehovah's Witnesses don't write books. It's not about them, as individuals, but about Jehovah's salvation only. His only vocation would be to promote and uphold Jehovah's Will.

The best song came on last, a remix of 'Girls, Girls, Girls', with a cheeky soul sample and Motown-style beat underpinned with bouncy hip-hop drums.

'There's nothing better than just smoking a spliff and listening to a good album,' said Fraser, when it was finished but still echoing around in Jesse's head. Fraser took back Jesse's earbud, wound the cord around his Discman and put it back in his pocket. 'Well, apart from sex maybe.'

'I wunt know,' Jesse said, sadly. It was the subject he most, and least, wanted to talk about with Fraser.

Fraser passed him the spliff. 'Are you still a virgin?'

'Of course I am. I'm a baptised Brother. I can't,' said Jesse, trying not to sound judgemental.

Fraser sucked his teeth, or at least attempted to. 'You need to get into that pussy, bredrin, literally. Anyway, I'm not baptised, so I can do whatever I want, and there's nothing they can tell me.'

'Who ya seein'? Someone in the truth?'

'The truth. Isn't it funny that they call it the truth!' He laughed. Jesse found him beautiful, and even more so when he laughed. Fraser leaned back, with his legs wide open. 'No, she's not in the truth. She works across the road from me. We go round her house, in her car, round the back of my work, all the time.'

'I suppose, if you need to and your conscience is okay with it,' said Jesse, mesmerised, his dick as hard as a hammer, but trying to sound like an upbuilding Brother.

'Not with the state of the women in the truth, with their long skirts and blank smiles. Actually, it wouldn't surprise me if they were absolute beasts once you broke them open. The truth though, Jess. The fucking truth. Bullshit.'

He finished his second can, and chucked it the way of the first. Dry from the spliff, Jesse impressed himself with how easily he was able to copy Fraser. His heart was thumping; he'd never heard a Witness swear before.

'You know what?' Fraser said, taking another can out of the blue plastic bag and opening it with a spritz of foam that he caught quickly in his mouth. 'That Brother Woodall, he's an alright guy, I like him, but he asked me to go out with him on the ministry, so I asked him about the dinosaurs. I said, if God created the Heavens and the Earth, how long ago what was it they say?'

'Six thousand years ago?'

'Exactly. What about the dinosaurs? Sixty-five-plus-million-year-old fossils I can go to the Natural History Museum in London and touch with my own hands? How do they explain those?'

'What did he say?' asked Jesse. He'd never thought about it before, even when *Jurassic Park* was out. It was just another, though very good, monster film.

'He said dinosaur fossils are fabrications by world

governments to discredit Jehovah as Creator, bredrin,' Fraser said, looking at Jesse and gesturing with a pointed finger. 'That's why I won't get baptised. I don't believe it. I go to the meetings because of my mum, but I don't believe a single fucking word that comes out of their mouths. And they think I shouldn't fuck that girl who works across the road from me? Whose fucking business is that, but mine?' He got up to pee.

'I suppose they can't expect us to stay virgins until we're married, in today's world,' Jesse said, surprised at where his mouth was going but unable to do anything to stop it. He was almost drooling, and shocked by Fraser's new candour. The dinosaur thing was real, but he couldn't comprehend six thousand years, never mind sixty-five million. He listened to Fraser pissing loudly. So many times he'd stood at a urinal in a public toilet, facing straight in front, bringing himself on a headache looking too far in the corner of his eye for the source of that jet washing the ceramic and making such a noise, afraid to turn his head even a degree for fear of having his forehead cracked up against the tiles. Maybe, still, he could be tempted; then usually, someone else came down the stairs – a child, a cleaner, an unattractive or otherwise sexually uninteresting human – so he'd shake the last of the pee from his dick, put himself away, zip up, wash his hands in predictably ice-cold water and leave dripping because the hand-dryer was out of order.

Cars glided past on the wet road. It started to rain again but the weed had made Jesse feel warm and calm. Fraser turned round from peeing high up the back wall, still putting himself away, looking like he was deep in thought. Jesse took another toke on the spliff. Fraser stood in front of him, blocking out the light, taking the spliff from him and putting it straight to his lips. White smoke danced there then rushed down his throat, the ends of his gelled hair backlit by the streetlamp. He wasn't baptised, but Jesse was. There was temptation, and then there was need. Fraser took another drag of the spliff, and looked past Jesse at the dark empty rooms. Jesse realised why they were in the derelict flats; Fraser must've been scoping out locations. He thought of how deliberate it felt, when Fraser lingered a hand on his arse at the meeting. He'd been planning this. They were alone. Nobody was going to come to disturb them. They couldn't do this at his house, not with his parents and brothers there. This area was normally so noisy with the workings of the ironfounders across the road and trucks coming up and down with scaffolding poles on their beds; now it was noisy with the sound of his heart thumping and the rain falling. He looked at Fraser's crotch in his jeans and thought, even in the darkness, he could make out the contours of a hard-on. Jesse allowed himself sometime looking at it, rolling it around the mouth of his inner life. Abdul and Carl were nodding at him, encouraging him into their world. The muscles in his left arm were ready to contract, lifting his hand.

He couldn't believe what was happening; he couldn't believe what was no longer happening as Fraser sat down next to him and gave him back the spliff.

'Another beer?' he said.

'Yes, please,' Jesse said, taking the last can from him, pulling off the plastic ring and throwing it behind him. He felt out of breath. There would always be next time. He didn't usually litter but reasoned the whole place was trash. What they said, and did, would be crushed to dust and wiped away forever.

The smoke filled his head and thickened in his sinuses, narrowing his eyes, distorting his vision, slurring and drying his mouth. Jesse took another, deeper drag, puffed out and burst out laughing.

'Nice, isn't it,' said Fraser.

'Where d'ya gerrit from?'

'A mate from work.'

'You're bad, man.'

'You probably don't know this,' Fraser said, 'but I had a sister, who died. It would have been her birthday yesterday.'

This came out of nowhere. Jesse was almost overcome with sympathy and love for Fraser, and did well not to choke.

'I'm so sorry. When? How?'

'Leukaemia. The only way she would've survived was if she'd have been given a blood transfusion, but my parents couldn't because of their beliefs, and she died.'

'That's horrible, but it's God's Will,' Jesse said after a pause, tapping and rubbing Fraser's back, unable to stop the inadequacy coming out of his mouth.

'It's fucking bullshit,' said Fraser, sharply, leaning away from Jesse's rubbing hand. 'It killed my mum.'

'Sorry,' Jesse said.

'After my sister died Mum stopped coming to the meetings. She hardly ever left the house. She couldn't understand which God would want her daughter to die. Which God would make a rule that said her daughter couldn't have the one thing that would keep her alive.'

'I doe know if it's that simple.'

''Course it fucking is.'

Jesse held out the spliff for Fraser to take, and he did.

'I dint know that your family had to go through that. I'm sorry. How old were ya?'

'It happened before I was born,' he said. 'She was a year younger than Duncan. I never knew her at all, just had to live with the grief, but when I got older and found out it explained everything. Mum agreed to start coming back to the meetings if we moved somewhere else, she didn't care where. So when the job came up in Dudley my dad took it. We could've moved anywhere in the country, but we're here at random.'

'Well, if you ever need someone to talk to, just like this,' Jesse said, 'you know where I am.'

'Cheers, Jess.'

The whole time they had been talking, Fraser was looking out into the street and Jesse wished he would look at him. He did now, almost making him jump. They clinked cans and Fraser passed back the spliff. Jesse took in the fact that they were sitting in the living room of a flat.

'Why do you stay at home?' Jesse said, as he felt the spliff take him into a perfect world.

'Huh?'

'Why doe ya move out and gerra flat a your own?'

'No, I can't do that yet,' Fraser laughed, leaning his elbows on his open thighs.

'Why not?'

'It's just a thing. In my family you don't leave your mum's house until you're married.'

'Int that the way wi' Witnesses in general? Are all your dad's brothers Witnesses?'

'Most of them. A couple of them have fallen away over the years.'

'Do you ever think about leaving?'

'Sometimes. Not sure where I'd go, though. You?'

'Never. I look at the world out there, all the wars, all the stupidity. The organisation int perfect, but it's better than out there, and I can stay in it wi' people like you in it.'

Fraser laughed through his nose. 'I don't know why you'd say that. I'm just a bum.'

Jesse looked at Fraser.

'Why dunt we gerra flat together?'

'What?'

'We'm best friends, we enjoy each other's company. We can keep each other on the straight and narra.'

'I don't know about that,' Fraser said, as he pressed a button on his Casio G-Shock watch.

'I'd be like your girlfriend, or summat. I'd look after ya.'

Fraser's brow tightened. He looked Jesse up and down and Jesse started laughing, idiotically. 'You know wharra mean.'

'Suppose I'd better head home,' said Fraser, standing up and taking a great gulp from his can. 'Working tomorrow.'

'Yeah,' Jesse said. It had only just occurred to him how cold and damp his arse felt. 'Ministry.'

They drained and chucked their cans. A mild sense of panic came over Jesse, as his brain lolled around drunkenly in his head, that if the police saw him he'd be arrested, taken to a police station and thrown in prison when they found out he'd had a spliff. Why else would he be hanging out in a derelict block of flats, if not for criminality and drugs? News would get out and the whole congregation would know. It might even get in the local papers. *Young, baptised Brother caught trespassing and smoking weed*. He followed Fraser down the stairs, the sorts of stairs he'd been up and down for years, ringing doorbells and tapping letterboxes, trying to find people in to preach to, posting copies of the *Watchtower* and *Awake!*. He'd worked that actual block before, many times. It all felt a world away as they stumbled through the site yard back to the fence.

'You alright, mate?'

'Yeh, just a bit . . .'

'Stoned?'

'If that's what you call it.'

'Mate, that was a weak one. I only had a tiny bit of weed left.'

'I suppose I just int used to it.'

They hugged in that way drunk boys who don't understand their love hug, in that slap-each-other's-backs-really-hard-and-suddenly-doubt-ourselves kind of way. But in that short moment Jesse could smell the damp of Fraser's waxed Barbour and feel the slip of its fabric against his cheek. He could feel Fraser's heart beating, quickly, against his chest. Fraser stood away from him, but for a full second their mouths hung close, breathing hot boozy steam into each other's. It was the most beautiful second of Jesse's life. *Strumming my pain* ... Fraser took a step back, smiled, said goodnight, tapped Jesse on the arm and walked away as Jesse hung back to pee. He closed his eyes and his mind spun around like he was in a fairground; his solar plexus glowed.

When he'd finished peeing, he staggered back out onto Great Bridge. A car approached him, pipping its horn and pulling over, its passenger winding the window down.

'It *is* him! Brother McCarthy! Jess?' she said, smiling. 'Alright, am ya? What yer up to? Do you wanna lift somewhere?'

It was Sister Tammy Winstanley, an athletic black woman from the neighbouring congregation, who worked as a bricklayer. 'Oh, alright, Tam?' He didn't want to see or speak to anyone. He could feel his speech slurring and he didn't want to come down from the glorious place he'd been in. 'I'm alright, just walkin' 'ome.'

'Jump in! Me and Ness'll tek ya!' She leaped out and pulled her seat forward.

Sister Vanessa Marriott, a plain, short white woman, waved to him from behind her wheel. It was only a seven-minute walk home at most but it was cold and drizzly.

'Alright,' he said, and contorted himself into the back of Vanessa's green Metro, shifting over behind the driver's seat because of Tammy's long legs.

'Wharrave *you* been up to tonight, then?' Tammy asked, looking over her shoulder sceptically at him as Vanessa pulled away and over the not-so-great Great Bridge. He realised they must be able to smell the weed, beer and cigarettes on him.

'Oh, nothing,' Jesse said. 'Just hung out with a mate for a beer.'

'Am they in the truth?' asked Vanessa, questioning him in her interior mirror as they bore right where the road forks at the Limerick pub. He was careful not to draw attention to Fraser bearing left, towards Horseley Heath, on foot.

'Nah, just someone I know from work.'

'Well, you know what they say, doe ya? Bad associations spoil useful habits!' said Tammy. They had been to a party thrown by friends of theirs from a congregation in West Bromwich, and likely themselves had enjoyed a glass of red. There is nowhere in the Bible that actually says you shouldn't smoke or drink; it was addiction that was considered the sin, because to use the body for anything other than Jehovah's salvation constituted the worship of false idols. They took a right at the island. McDonald's was quiet and about to close. He saw through its windows some of his colleagues assembling Drive-Thru orders – bleached-blonde Lisa; indie-boy Masood, who wore his cap tipped back; ginger Craig, who once summoned heavily and gobbed right in a customer's burger after he'd dared to claim he'd been short-changed, forcing the manager to cash up a till at the height of a manic Saturday afternoon. They watched the customer sit at a table and nosh down every last bite. The till had been correct.

Down the road to the left was the landfill site where Graham used to work, but they went straight on, past the new ASDA, and turned left up Carlton Street, by the Cash & Carry where Graham was now employed as a hand at Goods Inward. Jesse had half-planned to go into McDonald's with Fraser, just to show him off. Why had he freaked out like that when Jesse asked him if he fancied moving in together? Wouldn't it make sense for them both to get out of unhappy homes? Jesse was dreaming about finally learning to drive, getting their weekly shopping in. Did Fraser find what Jesse had suggested in any way sinister? *I'd be like your girlfriend. I'd look after ya*, he'd said. That was the one moment of the evening he regretted, like a heavy dash of cinnamon that could be tasted above everything else. He supposed it was the start of a new working week tomorrow; it was late.

The curtain flickered in his parents' bedroom as the car door shut, the gate whined and Tammy, in her loud Tipton voice, shouted, *Love to your mum and dad!* He hovered the key miserably about the lock before he finally found the slot. Tammy and Vanessa bipped their horn and drove away. There was light beneath the front room door, and in the kitchen, through the dining room. He tried to be as quiet as possible, toeing off his muddy trainers in the hallway. He climbed the stairs to bed and undressed in the dark. Drunk and stoned, he lay back on his bed and thought of Fraser, of Brother Thomas Woodall in his white work dungarees, and of Graham, downstairs in his white underwear, watching TV.

Chapter 4

September 19, 2001

Graham had never learned how to be a father to Jesse. For a long time he worked on a landfill site with tattooed men, and once allowed Jesse, then thirteen, to go to work with him in the school holidays. The site kitchen was from Hell, its walls filthy and blackened with dust. Early that morning Graham made Jesse a cup of tea in there, boiled from a kettle crusted in scum. The calendar girl for August was a knickerless redhead with a black lacy bra pulled down under her breasts, black stockings and suspenders, and parted red lips. Jesse drank the tea quick as his mouth could take as the first quavers of daylight started to sound.

'Mornin', Macca!' A tanned man with receding golden hair side-parted and slickly swept back crunched in along the gritty, muddy floor and stopped still with the stamp of a boot, his eyes popping out of his head. A plume of thick hair puffed out from the cleft of his chest; his nipples stood erect within his vest. He wore his overalls – down which dwelt a searching hand – open to the waist, the arms dangling loose. Jesse, still prisoner to adolescent sleep, wondered how this man could be so jolly.

'Mornin', Johnny,' said Graham. 'Jess, this is Johnny, one o' the gaffers.'

'Alright, Johnny,' Jesse said.

Johnny stared at Jesse with a wide-eyed, open-mouthed

fascination, stooped across the table – the St Christopher around his neck swinging forth and back – and extended the same hand with which he'd been adjusting his person, warm and tight as a boxing glove.

'This ya missus's lad?' Johnny said to Graham but all the while looking at Jesse. He stood back with his hands on his hips. Jesse looked at his hand then worried about what Graham might think of him thinking about where it had vicariously been, so he dutifully, though discreetly, wiped it on his trousers.

'Yeh, from before she met me,' Graham replied, without a hint of suspicion.

'Fuck me, he's a beauty, int he!' Johnny said, slapping the same hand comically across his mouth, in recognition either of the fact that Jesse was a minor in front of whom he shouldn't curse, or a Jehovah's Witness as such. 'Come out for a day on the soit with ya dad, 'ave ya?' he asked Jesse, as if he was hard of hearing.

Jesse nodded.

'Well, I'm sure ya'll a'fun, mate. People throw things away all the toim that ya moit dig out and think ya could use.'

'One man's trash is another man's treasure, int it?' Graham smiled.

'How's he at school? Is he clever, loik? Bet ya'm an arty type, ay ya!'

'I like music,' Jesse said, finally sniffing his hand as he pretended to wipe his nose. It smelled like his own balls but sweeter, and made his eyes lose focus for a second.

There was something strange in how Johnny walked away, looking Graham in the eye, to the corner of the kitchen, scanning all the cups. Jesse had washed the one he'd drunk from, with the West Bromwich Albion FC crest on it, and put it upturned to dry on the side of the sink, which was caked in mud, chips of plaster and brick dust. Johnny picked it up and held it up to the light.

'Someone bin using mar cup?' he said, almost threateningly.

'Oh, is that yours, Johnny?' said Graham. 'I dint know. I med tea for Jess in it. Sorry.'

Johnny looked at Graham over his shoulder, then at Jesse, with some degree of *what the fuck d'ya think ya doin'!* etched on his face; perhaps correcting himself, he smiled, flicked his eyes once more between them, and clearly despite himself, burst out laughing.

'That's alroit!' he said. 'I'll just wash it!'

There was a soap dispenser drilled into the wall next to the taps above the sink, full of a grainy gel scrub for industrial use; Johnny squirted *seven* loads one after the other into his cup and began to scrub away furiously at it, all the while grinning, telling Graham with great wide-eyed animation, ducking and diving and surfing through his knees, the story of his journey home in the traffic the night before, through the early after-math of an accident out of which the driver was being cut as he himself cruised past, the police closing the road and figuring out what to do with the traffic that had nowhere else to go for fear of clotting the vein of an important through-road, ambulance crews arriving to scrape up the mangled body of a – *ya know, black* – kid twenty yards away from the wreckage, the car presumably having kissed the child dead and swerved off the road and into the side of a building. As he was talking, Jesse was thinking, how could Graham, a Christian, work in a place like this? Johnny was scrubbing his cup as if an alien's tongue had rimmed it, his forearms and biceps flexing, a dark mark of sweat spreading on the front of his vest, his face remaining as jolly and animated as a ventriloquist's puppet. Finally, he turned on the hot tap full-blast and scalded off the bitty, gluey soap, drying his now-pink hands down his legs and across the flesh of his backside, flicking on the same abysmal kettle to make himself a cup of tea with two bags – 'Ar loik it strung'n *black*, ar do!' he said – using the dirty teaspoon left casually on the draining board.

'I suppose we'd berra get gooin',' said Graham, flashing Jesse a look to suggest that Johnny was best left well alone.

Out on the road, truck drivers with thick hairy forearms resting on their window ledges nodded and raised their hands as they drew up next to them at traffic lights, making Jesse wonder whether they would scrub their mugs too, if he'd used them. Graham put the radio on – CeCe *Penis*ton; *Wet, Wet, Wet*; Radio*head* – just as they passed a billboard for a local radio station, featuring a boombox with Photoshopped speakers meant to resemble a woman's breasts, with the tagline *Always First for the Biggest Hits!*

They didn't talk. Jesse didn't dare open his mouth.

Now, he sat quietly on the settee in the front room. There were three two-seaters. His parents sat together on the one next to the patio doors, where, most non-meeting nights, they would watch TV, but it was off. The fire, though, was on, and Jesse's mother had stretched her ashy feet out on the rug in front of it. She hadn't showered or washed her face, and was sitting in her head wrap and nightie, her breasts down in her lap. She would never normally allow herself to be seen by anyone outside immediate family like that, but Jesse didn't allow himself the thought that she was not in her right mind. The third settee, with its back to the front bay window, was waiting for Brother Frank Grimes, who was coming with another elder to discuss something about Jesse. The little carriage clock on the mantelpiece read two minutes to seven.

Of course, Jesse knew it was going to be about the drinking and smoking. He expected to be counselled, for the elders to sit and reason with him from the scriptures. He deserved it; he didn't know what he'd been thinking, as a baptised Brother. He felt awful the next day, groggy and slow, and flat on his back in bed, had to call Sister Doreen Charles – with whom he was scheduled to work on the ministry – to cancel. Sister Doreen

Charles doted on him like he was her grandson. She'd never had children of her own and was nearly seventy now. She was steadfast in the ministry and a bit of a handful for the elders. As a Sister, she was supposed to be quiet and acquiescent, but she often challenged them on aspects of how the congregation was run. She thought she had all the answers. An elder, knowing of Jesse's closeness to her, once asked him to *have a word*. He said he would, but knew he could do no such thing.

Sister Doreen Charles was her own man. She sang louder than anyone else in the congregation, constantly criticised the elders and often lamented that the one thing she did not like about being a Witness was having to be in subjection to *shchupid man*. She had been faithful to Jehovah since the Sixties, when a black woman and a white woman, working together, knocked on her door and preached about God's Word, and brought her into a congregation where white and black mixed freely as equals under God. She believed beyond any doubt that when she died she would be resurrected into a new world restored to its paradisiacal glory, and into the body she had when she came from Jamaica in 1954. She had seen off a husband who used to beat her, telling him: *If yuh hever lif up hev'n one finger fe touch me hagain, so elp me God, me ha go wait till you sleep han pour ot hoil down your hears'ole dem!*

Jesse felt terribly guilty to let her down, but couldn't go out in that state. Of course, it would be fine, another couple would break up so that an older Sister was not left pacing the mean streets alone. She accused him of working too many hours at McDonald's, told him to rest and that she hoped he'd feel better soon. She'd been such a comfort to him, through the long and draining, head-banging years of his adolescence. Often working on the ministry together, he'd told her all about how things were at home, how he and his mother didn't speak to each other, could barely exist in the same room, how he made her feel like he was upsetting her with his mere presence, how he barely spent any time in the house even though she was charging him rent allegedly for his use of the hot water, gas and electric, when actually, she'd more than once turned off the power at the mains when he'd spent longer than five minutes in the shower, leaving him barely able to rinse the shampoo out of his hair in the freezing cold. Sister Doreen Charles told him to be patient and trust in Jehovah. She told him she had never been a friend of his mother's. *The truth always come out*, she told him. He always wondered what she meant.

All he wanted to do was sleep and forget. He kept replaying in his mind what he'd said to Fraser. *I could be like your girlfriend. I'd look after ya.* He bit into his pillow and groaned in frustration. What was he thinking? It was Fraser's own fault for giving him weed. Jesse sent him a text to say he enjoyed last night, that he was going to buy *The Blueprint* as soon as it came out and sorry if there was any weirdness. He pressed send before he thought maybe he was reading too much into it and that there was no weirdness to speak of. In any case, Fraser, who normally responded at once to texts, didn't reply all day. It had now been two days. It was the meeting tomorrow night. He hoped to see him then.

The doorknocker tapped, twice; a ring in the mouth of a lion. It felt like they had been sitting in silence for hours, when really, it had only been a few minutes. Jesse was about to get up when Graham jumped to his feet and said, *No, you stay there.* The room had begun to smell embarrassingly frowzy, as if his mother, who had not brushed her teeth or said a word all day as far as he was aware, had opened her mouth and breathed into the fire to spread the foul smell.

Brother Frank Grimes and Brother Thomas Woodall walked in – Jesse was desperate to remain, in Brother Woodall's eyes at least, *whiter than white* – making quiet greetings that finally elicited an audible response from his mother, the heels of their polished Oxford shoes sounding funereal on the wooden floor.

Jesse's sisters, he could hear, had assembled at the top of the stairs. The elders didn't offer their hands to him, as they normally would, and he didn't get up. They barely even looked at him, just pulled up the fronts of their trousers near the pockets and lowered themselves down. Jesse's eyes immediately dropped down to their crotches before he could think to not look. Brother Woodall looked gravely at his stripy new tie while Brother Grimes, owner of a stationery firm, his expensive-looking suit reflecting his relative wealth, began, after a brief solemn prayer, addressing Jesse's parents:

'We asked you if we could come round this evening to discuss some matters you've brought to our attention about your son Jesse. Shall I just outline what we know so far?' Jesse felt as if he was being spoken about like a failing pupil at parents' evening. 'On Monday night, Brother Thomas Woodall received a phone call from yourself, Graham, to express concern about certain behaviours you believe your son might be engaging in, that would be in danger of compromising his faith, you felt, if allowed to continue unchecked. I understand you, Val, received a phone call on Monday afternoon from Sister Tammy Winstanley from our neighbouring congregation, to ask if Jesse was okay, because she found him staggering up Great Bridge on Sunday evening in a state, she suspected, of inebriation, and when they offered him a lift and got him into their car, they said that the smell of cigarettes and marijuana coming from his person was overpowering, and that it was difficult to hold him down to a coherent conversation. They drove him home, and it was once he was in and upstairs that you, Brother Graham McCarthy, still awake watching TV, opened your living room door and smelled the same kind of smell. When you got home from work the next day, Val told you, Graham, about the telephone conversation she'd had with Sister Winstanley, and that was when you felt that the situation was no longer one that should be dealt with in the home but by your elders. We appreciate and agree with your assessment. We're here, of course, to serve our congregation's needs in such a way, so Brother Woodall and I would like to commend you on your decision. Does that tally with what you know so far, Graham and Val?'

Jesse's parents nodded their heads. Graham voiced a small *yes*.

'Jesse,' Brother Grimes continued. 'You have been a credit to this congregation. The youngsters look up to you and older members find your youthful enthusiasm refreshing. You know your Bible, and publicly made a stand, when you finished school, to eschew further education for the sake of dedicating your life to the full-time ministry, making everyone proud, as you've continued to do until now. I'm pretty sure you know, though, without turning to your Bible, what 1 Corinthians 15:33 says.'

'*Do not be misled. Bad associations spoil useful habits,*' said Jesse, nervously, wary of the praise he was receiving.

'That's of course correct. Your Bible knowledge is exemplary.' Brother Grimes licked his lips and changed his tone. 'Can you tell us what your movements were on Sunday, September 16? I mean, in the evening, after the meeting?'

Jesse took a deep breath. He had no idea what he was going to say. He spoke as he would from the rostrum, in one of his bible readings:

'I went out with a friend, someone I work with, who'd told me he'd been having problems at home. I think he's really struggling, and knew that as a Witness I'd be able to give him counsel.' He saw here an opportunity to found his actions scripturally, using the hand gestures, pausing, facial expressions and modulation he'd been taught to use in the Witnesses' Theocratic Ministry School. 'The apostle Paul tells us to be all things to all people, so I thought it'd be best to speak to him on his own terms, as Matthew chapter seven, is it verse twelve? says – *All things you want men to do to you, you also must likewise do to them.* So we just had a few beers, and he told me if I wanted him to listen to me I had to listen to him, and that meant enjoying what he was enjoying, as in, a cigarette, and a spliff.'

'And where did this take place?' Brother Grimes asked. Brother Woodall was still silent, serious, listening.

'Well, we couldn't go to his house, cos that's the source of his problems, so, there's these derelict flats on Whitehall Road which we just chanced upon, 'n we just went in there.'

'And that's where you went?'

'Yeh.' The only other sound in the room was the occasional gust of wind scuttling down through the fire grille.

'It was a pretty chilly and miserable night, Sunday. Were you okay?'

'Yeah, it was fine.'

'Booze kept you warm. What were you drinking?'

'Just Foster's.'

'Where did you get them from?'

'Just the off-licence on Whitehall Road.'

'And he had the cigarettes and marijuana already, your friend from work?' Brother Grimes's eyes were narrow and implacable, but Jesse refused to acknowledge this as he looked into them. At this point he was telling the truth.

''E bought the cigarettes at the shop,' Jesse said, recalling his surprise when Fraser asked for them, and his complete willingness to go along with anything Fraser did. He spoke against the memory of Fraser tipping the joint filter-end-down and tapping it twice on his thigh as they listened to the most emotionally raw rap song he'd ever heard. He remembered the smell of it, when he lit it, and the fact that he never thought to prepare himself to say no. He wanted that moment back. The fire was warm, but he wanted to be cold, sharing time and breath with Fraser. 'He must've already pre-rolled the spliffs because he just took 'em out his pocket.'

'Had you ever smoked marijuana before?' Brother Grimes asked, burning his eyes into Jesse's.

'No.' He had, once, had a drag of someone's spliff out the back of McDonald's, just out of curiosity. It was a hash joint, and a hot rock dropped out of it and burnt a hole in his work tie.

'So you both work at McDonald's? How long have you worked together?'

'About two years, now.'

'And what sorts of problems is he facing?'

'A violent father, his girlfriend's pregnant, his brother's in prison.' These were all true things about Craig.

'Sounds unfortunate. What guidance were you able to give him?'

'I didn't have my bible with me, so we just talked as friends. I tried to give advice where I could, just in terms of what I know from the Bible, as a friend.' He shook his head as he said this, to suggest anyone else would do the same, and that Witnesses always do this sort of thing, apart from the smoking bit, which he was waiting for the opportunity to apologise for. 'I told him it'd be best if he refrained from drinking and smoking cos they're just a waste of time and money and damaging, both to himself, to his girlfriend and their unborn baby. I told him their baby doesn't deserve to have its life compromised before it's even born.'

Jesse compulsively flashed a look here at his mother, who was staring at her own ashy feet, her lips scrunched as if she was poised to jump up and punch him in the face.

'But he must have thought you a hypocrite if he saw you doing the same as him,' said Brother Woodall, who, even in this situation, spoke to Jesse in his usual cossetting, fatherly tone. Jesse conceded this and nodded.

Brother Frank Grimes continued: 'How much did you both have to drink?'

'Three cans of Foster's each.'

'And how much did you smoke?'

'A couple of spliffs, a couple of cigarettes.'

'So you went toe-to-toe?'

'I suppose I did.'

'Over what kind of time period?'

'We met at seven, so a couple of hours.'

'And that's when Sister Winstanley and Sister Marriott picked you up in their car.'

'Yeh.'

'How was he, when you left him? What's his name? Shall we give him a name?'

'Craig. He seemed more positive. He was a bit drunk, and a bit stoned obviously, but that's the way he always is. He usually smokes a big fat spliff before work. It's the only way he can get through.'

A strange, cynical grin broke onto Brother Grimes's face that Jesse had seen before; the photograph was probably still among those folders in the sideboard cupboard right next to Brother Grimes, aka Uncle Frank, who led a black-and-white minstrel troupe as the surprise entertainment at Jesse's parents' wedding reception, in full blackface, tails, top hats, afro wigs, white gloves and canes. Jesse, aged four, was dressed as a negro page in a cream satin suit, pop socks and buckled shoes. He found the minstrels terrifying and screamed throughout their performance. Fresh off the stage, Brother Grimes had tried to console Jesse, grabbing him to pose for the photo, pulling his sinister, white-lipped minstrel grin while Jesse squirmed, trying to escape. The bride was in the background watching on, with a facial expression as if to say *watch ya doe get shoe polish on his outfit!*

'Does he have ginger hair?'

It took Jesse's breath away. That feeling, again, of having been caught stealing. All moisture seemed to evacuate his mouth and dampen the palms of his hands. The back of his neck froze. The longer he delayed his answer, the more obvious it was that he was lying. His parents both shuffled in their seats. It wasn't possible for Brother Grimes to know Craig Tillman.

'Answer the question, Jesse,' Brother Grimes said, looking at his notes, like a lawyer would, rather than at Jesse, and searching in the inside pocket of his suit jacket for a pen – a Parker Jotter, obviously – clicked it on and wrote down the name, Jesse supposed, *Craig*.

'Yeh.'

'That's funny,' Brother Grimes continued, 'because I went through that McDonald's Drive-Thru with my youngest on Sunday night at about eight, I think it was, and was served at the first window by someone with ginger hair with Craig on his name badge. Has he got four stars? Working hard for a fifth? Jesse?'

Jesse clenched his jaw and stared at the flickering orange and blue flames.

'It's extraordinary that he was in two places at once. Or do you work with two people named Craig with ginger hair? Or does he have a twin and forgot to take his own name badge to work and posed as his brother? My two eldest are identical, as you know, and so could probably stand in for each other all the time if they wanted to, if they were liars.

'Who were you really with, Jesse?' asked Brother Grimes, with a tone in his voice as if to warn him to tell the truth.

'Just. You don't need to know.' Was this a genuine shock to them, or were they discovering him to be the unreachable black teenage boy they'd suspected him to be all along?

'Well, actually, really, we do, because if you're lying about something, and you're implicating others in your lie, that is really quite a serious accusation.'

'Who were you with, Jesse? Just tell us the truth,' said Brother Woodall, pleadingly.

Jesse breathed in, as if he was going to talk, then breathed out, and didn't.

'If you're not going to answer us, or you've forgotten, then perhaps we can fill you in. Sister Winstanley and Sister Marriott, after they dropped you off, drove back towards where they both live in Tipton, and said they saw Fraser Hammond crossing the road, walking slowly and looking deep in thought. They stopped him, just to say hello, and asked him where he'd been. He said he'd just been having a drink with a friend. They thought, oh, that sounds familiar, so when they asked who that friend was, he said, Jesse . . . *McCarthy*! When they said they'd just dropped him off at home, and he'd said he'd been out for a drink with someone who wasn't in the truth, he said, they quote, *he's probably right about that*, wished them goodnight and walked away. So this is why Sister Winstanley rang your mother on Monday, Jesse, to see if you and he were both alright, because both she and your mother care about your spiritual well-being.'

'My so-called mother doesn't care about my well-being at all,' Jesse said, under his breath but loud enough.

'Oh Frank, I can't cope! It's slowly killing me, I know it, I'm so depressed! I cor do nothin right! He meks me feel like I'm worthless! I know he's always comparing us to other people like you who've got more money! I've had enough! I can't live like this! He meks us feel like nothin's ever good enough for him! All we've ever done, all we've *ever done* is do our best, and it just could *never*' (his mother stabbed her finger into the arm of the sofa) 'be enough for *him*' (she stabbed the same finger at Jesse) 'because he's so high and mighty!' (she rocked her neck; she was shouting at the top of her voice). 'He makes me feel stupid. Do you know what it's like to be made to feel stupid, old, fat, ugly and worthless and not good enough by your own child? No, you wunt know, because you int got kids like him! I've seen the way both your kids are and them golden! Why have I got *him*?'

'Val,' Graham said, as if to calm her, but he put his hand on her thigh. Tears were streaming down her face and white scum had formed at the corners of her mouth. The smell of her breath thickened in the warm room.

'I cor deal with it no more. We've tried our best to give him

everything we could. We've tried our *best*, to provide for him
so that he can go on the ministry. We've shown him nothin
but support, and what's he do? He throws it back in our faces!
I've never been treated so badly by anybody! Me own son! He's
disrespectful, a liar, a cheat and a thief, and I cor live with him,
but I cor throw him out either cos I just doe know what the
world'd do to him, me own son! He'll learn his lesson. He'll
gerris comeuppance! He'll be crushed out there! Go and look
in his room! If you need any proof about what I'm saying, go
and look in his room! Exemplary to the youth of the congregation? Go and look in his room! That's the real Jesse! He
lives in a dungeon! I've told him, and told him, and told him,
burr'e refuses to listen! We've tried beating sense into him,
we int spared the rod, but that dunt work either! It's almost
like he enjoys it, and he does things to spite Graham so he'll
be disciplined! He's mental! You think you know *im*, but you
doe, and now the real truth's coming out! You have to gerrim
away from me!'

She turned her head into Graham's chest and he cradled her
as she cried. She had swallowed the room. They were all thrashing about in her stomach, her acid burning their flesh away.
There was no air to breathe. Brother Grimes called out, *Oh,
oh!* He tried to calm her down. He told her it was okay, to go in
the kitchen, make herself a cup of tea and calm herself down,
that they would sort it. Brother Woodall looked disturbed, as
if he wanted to put his hand over his nose but knew it would
appear rude. Jesse worried that those new frown lines would
become scars and never disappear from his handsome face.
Jesse's mother got up, whimpering, left the room and closed the
door behind her. A sister, probably Ruth, the favourite, crept
down to ask her if she was alright. 'I'm alright, I'm okay, just go
back upstairs and leave me alone for a bit. Look wharre's done
to me!' Jesse watched her as she opened the door, and thought
he could detect a sneer on her top lip where she could have

burst out laughing at her own triumph. She had exposed him, so that everyone could now see what a walking lie her son was, and it was obvious to the elders the depth of depression living with such a person had brought on her. Graham sat staring at his feet.

'Shall we do this quickly, and truthfully?' Brother Grimes, after a moment to let the air clear, said.

'What happened with Fraser?' Brother Woodall said.

'Nothing. The same as I said happened with Craig, we just talked about different things.'

'Such as?' said Brother Grimes.

Jesse shrugged his shoulders. 'You'll have to ask him that. I believe that whatever conversation two adults have should stay between those two adults.'

'Well, we did ask Fraser,' said Brother Grimes, 'and he said that he left because you made homosexual overtures towards him.'

'What? No I didn't!' The walls of Jericho are coming down. He is buried in the rubble.

'He said, quote, *that you leaned into him, and told him that you could be like his girlfriend, and that you would look after him.* Is this true?' Babylon the Great is slain riding on the back of the many-headed monster.

Would he dob Fraser in, over his girlfriend? Was it worth it? He had nothing to lose if Fraser didn't want to be in the truth any more. He remembered the Hammond brothers' hands all over him, feeling to see how big his dick was, how tight his arse was. The stray hand left on his arse at the Kingdom Hall. The way Fraser stood in front of him with a hard-on, smoking his weed, and looking past Jesse into the empty derelict rooms as if Jesse could do whatever he wanted and it would've been nothing to do with him. Fraser had probably ratted on him because he *didn't* get a blowjob. *I'm not baptised, so they can't say anything to me.* Jesse said nothing. He couldn't bring himself to be disloyal.

'Turn to 2 Timothy 3:15-17,' Brother Grimes said. 'Graham, please will you read it out?'

Their pages rustled. Graham, with a voice lacking in any modulation or colour, read: *'And that from infancy you have known the holy writings, which are able to make you wise for salvation through the faith in connection with Christ Jesus. All Scripture is inspired of God and beneficial for teaching, for reproving, for setting things straight, for disciplining in righteousness, that the man of God may be fully competent, completely equipped for every good work.'*

'Thank you, Graham. Now let's turn to Titus 1:15-16,' Brother Grimes said. 'You'll know from your extensive studies, of course, that it's on the facing page! Will you read it out?'

Jesse looked up to see that Brother Grimes was talking to him, with undisguised contempt. With a barely open throat, he read, *'All things are clean to clean persons.'*

'Nice and clear and loud like you do from the platform,' Brother Grimes said.

Jesse, startled, obeyed. *'But to persons defiled and faithless nothing is clean, but both their minds and consequences are defiled. They publicly declare they know God, but they disown him by their works, because they are detestable and disobedient and not approved for good work of any sort.'*

'This is why you have to be disfellowshipped,' Brother Grimes said, shutting his bible with a thud.

The words *this announcement is to inform the congregation that Jesse McCarthy has been disfellowshipped* would've entered the Kingdom Hall like a shooter.

Jesse McCarthy. Not Brother Jesse McCarthy. Not even Young Brother Jesse McCarthy. Just Jesse McCarthy. Jesse, as named after the outlaw Jesse James, rather than King Jesse, the sinless father of David, or even Jesse Owens, the laughing disarranger of white supremacy. *Inform the congregation.* Nobody was allowed to know why he had been disfellowshipped. He could have been an unrepentant thief, a sex offender, a fraudster, a drug addict; he might've been in an accident, or diagnosed with a terrible illness, and chosen to accept a blood transfusion.

Disfellowshipped. Witnesses avoided people who'd been disfellowshipped as if they had leprosy or AIDS. There would have been gasps. More than one middle-aged Sister would have slapped a hand against her own chest, as if to stop her heart bursting out. The elderly would have asked for repeats, questioning their hearing. Sister Doreen Charles might have wailed in grief. Multiple heads would have spun to see if he was sitting at the back, next to the door, then their gaze would have turned to his family, particularly his mother. All of a sudden, she was the pitiable mother of an unreachable, now lost, black teenage boy. It would be clear to them what was the source of his long-suffering mother's depressions. There was nothing that could be done about unreachable black teenage boys, except deliver them the punishment unreachable black teenage boys get. He'd never considered himself to be an unreachable black teenage boy before. Perhaps *that* was the problem. He was no longer allowed to communicate with or attempt in any way to engage anyone from his loving congregation.

Fraser texted him *Sorry*, but Jesse didn't reply, and deleted his number from his phone. In fact, he threw his phone smashing against a wall in the bins area at McDonald's and had to get a new one. He went full-time. He gave no reason to the manager, after he'd spent two years refusing to work Tuesday evenings, Thursday evenings or Sundays because of his meeting commitments. His teammates circled him, challenging him to become harder, more aggressive, their idea of *black*. They were his only friends now. He smoked their weed, went out clubbing with them, listened to rap albums on his Discman, tested swear words in his mouth. They were mostly white and Asian boys who acted like black boys. He tried to change his accent so that he sounded more black. One of his colleagues joked that Jesse was like a black boy trying to be a white boy trying to be a black boy. Craig remained ignorant of his pivotal role in changing Jesse's life.

At home, he confined himself to his tiny room. He took his clothes to the launderette on Hill Top and mainly ate at work. One day, traipsing home up Carlton Street after working a breakfast shift, a car stopped next to him. It was Brother Thomas Woodall in his painting and decorating clothes. He was often to be seen, driving up and down as he worked on several projects at once, from a shopfront in Great Bridge to the home of a Brother and Sister in a neighbouring territory. Brother Woodall silently reached over to the passenger door of his minivan and with his neck, beckoned Jesse in. Jesse obeyed, got in the car and shut the door, even though he was only five minutes' walk from his house. The Escort van was filthy inside, incommensurate with Brother Woodall's usually impeccable presentation as presiding overseer of the congregation, but of course, being a white man, Brother Woodall's filth was cleaner than Jesse's squeaky-clean black. He drove up almost to the top of Burton Lane, just to take a longer route to drop Jesse off at home. They didn't say a word to each other; and when Jesse, fighting back tears, tried to say thank you, Brother Woodall turned his head away. Jesse got out of the car and stood grieving on the pavement as Brother Woodall drove away.

Christmas, he stayed in his room with crisps and snacks, craving a spliff, even a cigarette. His parents and the children watched TV downstairs all day. He was not invited to eat with them. He'd bought *Giovanni's Room* by James Baldwin, finally, which his GCSE English teacher had encouraged him to read. It dawned on him that the novel depicted a gay relationship; he panicked to think she might have recommended it to him because he was a black gay like Baldwin. Still, he managed it, in one day, from cover to cover. He thought it striking that a black man could, in the first paragraph, have his main character look himself in the mirror and see a tall, blond white man standing there in his dressing-gown holding a tumbler of whisky – and it brought a tear to his eye, because he recognised that if he was a tall, blond white boy, everything would have been different.

He recognised that he had thought of himself as a blond white boy all his life. He'd never thought of himself as a black boy, or compared himself to other black people. He'd known so few black people, and those his mother knew she often derided for being *too black*, doing things in *too black* a way, being late because they were *too black*, being disorganised because they were *too black*, being rough and uneducated because they were *too black*. He wouldn't have been treated so harshly if he wasn't *too black*. He wouldn't be cooped up in a prison cell, an exile within the family home, too embarrassed to accept any of his workmates' invitations to spend Christmas with them and their families, if he wasn't *too black*. He knew he would have to spend the rest of his life convincing people that he wasn't *too black*.

He managed to keep himself together until Easter, when the Witnesses, separately from the main branches of Christendom, mark the Passover, which Jesse refused to attend. He came home from work that night, stoned, just as Graham was closing down the house to go to bed. They looked at each other. Jesse, unexpectedly to himself, started to cry. *Sorry*, he said. *I'm sorry*. He kept saying *I'm sorry*. He moved towards Graham and put his head on his shoulder. Graham remained unmoved, hands by his sides. All Jesse wanted was some love. He hugged him, squeezed him, grabbed handfuls of his flesh, smelled his neck, kissed him, leaked tears into him. Graham, firmly, grabbed Jesse by both arms and held him away from himself. Through his teeth, he said, *You have to get out of this house*.

Chapter 5

May 3, 2002

Jesse's alarm went off at seven, but he'd barely slept. He was excited, if nervous; he'd been scared of London all his life but he was a man now and after a few months saving up, he was ready to do it. He'd found a hostel on the Internet, in Earl's Court, for twelve pounds a night. He had three hundred pounds in his bank account and no responsibilities to anyone; he packed only what he absolutely needed – his best clothes, some underwear, ten or so CDs, his Discman, the James Baldwin novel *Another Country*. He left his key and bible on his pillow. The Bible was supposed to have an answer for everything but did not have guidance for sons whose families had betrayed them and turned them out. He wanted to tuck its ribbon at a verse that would show his parents what they had done. The New World Translation's *fathers, do not be irritating your children* did not go far enough, and he eventually decided he didn't want to waste any more time inside a book that had made him literate but told him everything he did and stood for was wrong. He stared at it, closed, leather-bound and gold-leaf-trimmed, for an indecisive moment before he ran downstairs and out of the front door without leaving a note. He ran until he'd turned the corner. His mother wouldn't have been quick enough out of bed to see which direction he'd gone in. Perhaps, actually, she was sleeping easy. He'd been to the Carphone Warehouse to change his phone number again. He intended it to be a dramatic disappearance, that would leave even his McDonald's colleagues wondering where he had gone.

He pounded through the estate, already forgetting the scruffy dark-brick semi-detached houses with mattresses and wheel-less cars on their driveways, that kids he went to school with, or householders who'd accepted his literature, lived in, and caught the 74 from Swan Village bound for Birmingham. He looked out of the window but saw nothing. There were clock towers and fancy buildings in London, much greater than these, he thought. He did not care if he never saw this part of the world again.

Birmingham was big. It had tall buildings and busy roads, a national train station and a shopping centre with all the top brands. Though he'd grown up with a Birmingham postcode, he hadn't visited the city centre that often; usually, when he was a kid, shopping with his mother and aunts, waiting around hungrily, thirstily, needily while they tried on a hundred dresses, jeans, coats, boots, coming home a little fatter and frustrated having been all the way on the bus and bought only a Kentucky Family Bucket, leaving him the boniest bits (which had the crispiest, tastiest, best-seasoned crumb).

But Birmingham was not his destination. It wasn't far away enough. He'd only been to London twice, on the Witness trips to the British Museum, but he knew it was for him; he knew from the length of the coach journey, the size of the place, the variety in every direction he looked. He saw black girls with long braids; African women in wrappers; young punks and old dandies; city men with their briefcases; model-like white girls with cute little dogs; feminine-looking men walking, outrageously, frighteningly, hand-in-hand; black boys wearing trainers that weren't for sale anywhere in the Midlands.

Maybe now he could go to college after all. He felt it a shame that his disfellowshipping happened just weeks too late for that academic year. There was so much he could now put right. He wished he hadn't listened to Sister Doreen Charles, whom he'd treated as an elder, an authority, even though she was a woman and women weren't allowed to be considered elders or authorities. He could still hear her words:

'*Nuh bodda go college when you kyan preach di good news of God Kindam from 'ouse to 'ouse han daah to daah, servin' di need of di canregiashan! Hif me did your hiage han a man, dat what me would do!*

'*What you need from your hedukiashan other than fe read good ah write ah count ah praise Jeoviah, for you a go get heverlastin life fe look up at di star ah hundastan all dem ting bout the huni-verse an dat?*

'*Council flat dem kyan rent fe fifty pound a month, so why you nuh jain your daddy pan di rubbish tip? Fe God imself a go sustain you wid heverytin y'a guh need!*

'*We in di last day, now sah! Mi bet you nuh reach twenty-one fore Harmageddon appen when you fass hasleep inna yuh bed!*

'*Nuh bodda go college, Jeoviah him wah you!*'

At New Street station, he baulked at the cost of a train ticket but the attendant explained it would be cheaper if he waited until ten o'clock when Super Off-Peak kicked in. So he bought himself a McDonald's breakfast, with a cup of coffee, and ate it on a bench to the sound of constant tannoyed announce-ments. He went into WHSmith and bought a London *A-Z* and a large pack of Duracell AA-size batteries for his Discman, as well as *The Face*, with Eminem on the cover wearing a pink vest and lip balm, looking quite gay. There was an article in it about the Sugababes and their new member. He'd already bought their new single, 'Freak Like Me', hoping it was going to Number One, and had been listening on repeat to the 'We Don't Give A Damn' Mix – a mash-up between Adina Howard's lewd 'Freak Like Me' and Gary Numan's dystopian

'Are Friends Electric' – sung by three girls who could've been his schoolfriends.

There were men everywhere. Would any of them do what Fraser had not, and let him suck their dick? Businessmen, construction men, security men. Black, white, brown, in suits, tracksuits, workwear, wearing flat caps, baseball caps, helmets. All seemed to be heading – the interesting ones anyway – to the station toilets.

There were eight cubicles, and he ducked nervously into the sixth and locked the door. He was already hard, so had to bend his knees and tip his body forward to piss straight into the pan. He noticed movement to his left-hand side. There was a puddle on the floor, in between the two cubicles, and in it he could clearly see the reflection of a man wanking, and in a manner that meant the puddle wasn't coincidental, the result of a leak, but was a kind of mirror, created by the man pissing on the floor to make the two occupants visible to one other.

His neighbour's dick emerged from his clenched fist long, thick and upward-curving. Unsure as to whether this man would see his reflection in return, Jesse shook his dick of piss and started wanking himself over the puddle. In acknowledgement, this man knocked twice on the thin cubicle wall between them. Jesse knocked twice back. He heard his neighbour unlock his door, and knock twice again. Buttoning his hard-on back in his jeans, Jesse unlocked his, peeped out into the corridor to make sure there was no one standing at the sinks opposite, or that no one at the adjacent wall of urinals would notice, and made his move, completely unable to believe what he was doing; right away the man stepped back to give him space, and Jesse shut and locked the door behind him.

The man was probably in his late thirties, stocky, with dark brown, receding hair; he wore construction worker's boots, jeans and a pair of Calvin Klein trunks suspended around his knees, a light blue office shirt with the sleeves rolled up revealing meaty, furry forearms, and a thick silver watch. He smiled and nodded, and kissed Jesse wholly on the lips, his stubble grazing his fine skin. Jesse clutched the man's dick in his hand – a dick! The heat and weight of it thrilled him – and drew his thumb over its slippery contours, which made the man grab and wank Jesse in return. *Nice cock*, he said, looking down in a manner that forced Jesse to crouch down before him. The man's dick was intimidating, urinous and pungent, twitching up and down in front of his face; he smarted a little at the strength of its smell.

The man put his hand over the top of Jesse's head and for the very first time in his life, Jesse took a dick into his mouth, held it and felt it pulsing, and sucked, helped by the man's pelvic thrusts, until he could feel the tickle of pubic hair in his nostrils. He was hard, thick and heavy, catching on the soft flesh just where dry lip became wet mouth. Jesse pulled his head back, licked his lips and took the man back in as deeply as he could. He felt invaded, taken over. The man put his warm, clammy hands around Jesse's ears, pushed into the back of Jesse's head and whispered, *Oh my God, you've got no fucking gag reflex*. Jesse felt the man's nuts on his chin, held onto his arse, pulling him in deeper, feeling him stretch his throat and the back of his nose.

He'd been waiting for this all his life, and when the man pulled all the way back out, Jesse licked his balls, reaching his hand up his stomach and tweaking his nipples, making sure the whole man was all there, before the man pushed his knob back between Jesse's lips and fucked his head. Jesse closed his eyes and imagined any one of those men from the landfill site, the ironworks or the warehouses in their dirty jeans and muddy boots, fucking his mouth like this man was, giving him no time to breathe or wipe his streaming eyes, grabbing his head and fucking it any old way; he thought his left eye might pop out; somehow Jesse knew that he should try as best as he could to keep his teeth out of the way, unless he liked it? Some people did, didn't they, *like* pain?

Not long enough a time seemed to pass until the man's eyes scrunched shut and his face reddened as he grabbed Jesse's head in both hands and spunked six or seven jets in the back of his throat. Letting out a controlled, discreet hiss, he pulled out, and held Jesse's face in front of himself; he pulled his eyeballs down from the back of his head; he was almost laughing, puffing; a rope of spit hung between the underside of his knob and the inside of Jesse's bottom lip; a new pearl sprang forth inside his pisshole; the man's arms weakened, and Jesse plunged back down on him to get it, making the man shrink back; *Stop!* he whispered. He quickly pulled up his pants and jeans, and ended the moment with the hasty buckling of his belt.

'Can I 'ave ya number?' Jesse whispered, shuffling up from his crouching position, his thighs and knees aching.

'Nah, mate,' the man said, and showed Jesse his wedding ring. With that, he kissed him on the mouth, said, 'Lock it behind me and give it a minute,' squeezed himself around the door and disappeared right out of the toilets without washing his hands.

Jesse, as instructed, locked the cubicle door, still trying to swallow the cum in his throat, as if he'd caught a slight cold, the man's nether sweat all over his face. He licked his lips, inhaled through his nose, closed his eyes and imagined the man still inside him. He swallowed, and swallowed, as his train was announced.

EARL'S COURT

EARLS COURT

Chapter 1

May 4, 2002

His jeans were too tight, constricting his gait, and sat low on his hips. It was the first time he'd ever walked down a street without underwear. Sightings of gay-looking men were more frequent round here, and one or two of them looked him up and down as they passed by, but Jesse kept walking and listening to his music, becoming more nervous with every step.

Every time he'd been to a rave with the McDonald's lot, he wished he'd had the space and freedom to peel away from them and go to a gay bar. Even so, he made the most of those pumping UK garage and R&B sound systems, the scene still buzzing from the moment it tangibly crossed over into the mainstream. So Solid Crew had performed their Number One hit '21 Seconds' in sweatbands and wolverine contact lenses on *Top of the Pops*, scaring the life out of the producers, who must've feared a riot would break out on national television and swallow up the white girls at the front singing along with Lisa Maffia. In the clubs, he enjoyed the dancing, the boys, on a couple of Bacardi and cokes and maybe half an E, showing their tender sides, flirting with the girls. He applauded the PAs from the boyband Damage, performing 'Ghetto Romance', and Mis-Teeq, performing the 'Ignorants Remix' of 'All I Want'. Everyone went to see Destiny's Child perform in pink bikinis and rhinestones at the National Indoor Arena, just as 'Independent Women' was about to be released, with a rare line-up of Beyoncé, Michelle and Kelly – who had sprained her ankle and sat singing on a stool – completed by Solange, performing Kelly's dance moves.

But none of those nights was ever going to end with the taste and feel of a dick in his mouth, maybe only a fist or a foot if he ever tried it on. Now, he happened to be walking behind a red-haired boy in too-pristine sportswear – looking as if he didn't usually dress that way and the transformation wasn't working for him – who kept looking over his shoulder, at Jesse, nervously. *I'm not actively following you*, Jesse wanted to call out. He was simply walking in the same direction, having left the hostel and turned the corner onto the Earl's Court Road perhaps a few seconds too late as far as this pert-arsed stranger was concerned. He considered and rejected the idea of crossing the road, as if to turn left, only to then turn right (it would look like a distraction tactic) or of quickening his pace to overtake the boy (an aggression). He looked down at his own feet as he walked so as to not be caught checking out the boy's inviting arse, and wondered whether, if he had been looking up as usual, he would have skidded through the smudge of dog shit he consequently missed. The boy stopped, watched Jesse pass by, and when Jesse peeked round a moment later, he saw the boy had swung round and was walking back the other way.

Jesse hooked a right onto the Old Brompton Road and jogged between passing cars to the other side. With his hands in his pockets, he pulled his jacket tighter round himself as the undulating rainbow flag that advertised his destination – more confidently than he was prepared for – confirmed the change of pace the weather had taken. A shaven-headed doorman with a wide stance and clasped hands blocking his crotch stood at the corner door. Jesse looked up at the building, 'The Coleherne Arms 1866' inscribed high on its façade. He couldn't see through the reflective window panes, but a group of men drinking and smoking on the pavement acknowledged his arrival with expressions ranging from winks of approval to nudging smirks and blinks of fear or indifference. The odd blast of strident house music – chopping and twisting the music in his earbuds – let out by the opening and closing door hyped the atmosphere within. He pulled down his baseball cap, flicked an instinctive final glance round to make sure he was unseen by anyone from the hostel, and smiled guardedly at the doorman, who took a step to his right, blocking the door.

'Pardon?' said Jesse.

The doorman gestured he remove his earbuds and stared out into the distance.

'See some ID, please, mate.'

Jesse squeezed a hand into his back pocket and pulled out his provisional driving licence, bent and slightly softened against the football curve of his arse. He looked young, even at nineteen. The doorman studied it with interest. Jesse looked down. The front of the doorman's trousers was completely flat, unlike Graham's in his grey tracksuit bottoms. Disappointing.

'You do know this is a gay venue, don't you?' he said, rubbing Jesse's picture card between his thick, dry fingers and thumbs, with a hint of a sneer, before handing it back.

'Yeh,' said Jesse, indignantly. He hadn't come this far to have his hard-earned self-acceptance questioned at the door of an actual gay bar.

'Thank you. Enjoy,' said the doorman, as he stood out of the way.

A tall, blond man with blue eyes, whom Jesse felt he'd seen before – on TV or in a film, perhaps – hung over him, coming out as he was going in. He stepped back to watch Jesse pass. *Aww, cute!* he said, but then another man, darker and with a less friendly, somewhat cynical face, followed him and pulled him away. The blond man smiled over his shoulder as if to say, *See you later*, making Jesse's mouth start to water, but the doorman said, *Keep the door closed, please. Local residents.*

The bar was packed, full of rotating light beams and middle-aged men in jeans and T-shirts, football and rugby shirts, baseball caps and leather hats, leather jackets, studded wrist-cuffs and chaps over jeans, drinking pints and shouting over each other, the warm beats, thick bass and effortless female vocalist. Feeling exposed, he thought he would pop his earbuds back in, for now.

He wanted to feel like Mutya in the video for the 'We Don't Give A Damn' Mix, as she sang in his ears, strutting noncha-lantly through the club as everyone turned round to notice her. Here, some men wore moustaches like Graham's in the Eighties; some had beards, some were clean-shaven; some had hair, some were bald, some were voluntary skinheads like the doorman; some didn't look gay at all; some looked straight, at a glance, but made effeminate gestures as they spoke; others wore har-nesses that reminded Jesse of a toddler's reins; some men had handkerchiefs hanging out of their back pockets – what sort of trend was that? The room smelled of beer, piss and aftershave, and sounded, beneath both layers of music, like laughter, clinked glasses and heartbeats.

There were men with perfectly trimmed silver, grey or black beards who were old enough to be his grandfather; there were men five to ten years older than him with gym-toned bodies, whom he thought he might want to emulate. The only boy he could see around his age, tiny and swarthy with green eyes, was squeezing through the bar with a stack of used pint glasses and giggling while being groped all the way through. Jesse sup-pressed the urge to touch the steeply curved lower back of a black giant in a skin-tight T-shirt, stonewashed jeans and bovver boots as he made his way past behind him, but allowed himself a quick sniff of his fresh sweat. There were men with average bodies and friendly faces who looked like they were married with children, men who looked like accountants or schoolteachers. Men like Graham, six feet tall, normal-looking, going a little bit grey, broad and muscular from a lifetime of manual labour. Those were the men that he wanted.

More men squeezed into the bar behind him, pushing him further in. A bearded man across the bar with a tuft of hair peeking out from underneath his rugby shirt clocked him and smiled, but Jesse looked away when he saw he was cross-eyed. A tall, bearded, Nordic-looking man with tattoos and glowering eyes, who stared into his face as they came together, kept moving as Jesse took too long to react. *I'm packin' all the flavours you need*, sang Keisha. He realised how nervous he felt; his mouth was dry, and his stomach felt sore, as if there was a wound in it.

There were several black men dotted around, all looking natural, one of them wearing make-up, with finger-waves in his hair and a black leather harness over his white T-shirt, lip-syncing with his arms crossed over his chest like Naomi Campbell in the 'Freedom '90' video. He wondered if he should just go over and introduce himself but space opened at the bar next to a broad-shouldered, stocky man with dark blond, slightly curly hair, wearing a charcoal suit jacket, jeans and brown brogues. He was reading a gay circular and drinking a pint of bitter, so Jesse stood there and waited for attention from the bartenders. The man in the suit jacket was wearing a nice aftershave, and Jesse worried that he stank in comparison. The shower on his floor at the hostel had a blocked drain, and he couldn't bring himself to stand for more than a minute in the grey backed-up water.

After two good-looking, muscular men who had come to the bar after him were both served first, he caught the eye of a bartender, a chubby guy in glasses and a white polo shirt with the round Coleherne logo, and ordered a pint of Foster's. He nodded his head nervously as he waited. A tall, slim man with grey mutton-chop sideburns stood drinking his pint with one foot up against the wall behind him. Jesse began to harden as the man tapped his thigh with one hand, drawing attention to the dick clearly defined down his standing leg. His boyfriend, Jesse guessed, because they looked the same but ten years apart in age, came up from the toilets and claimed him with a full, hard, lip-sucking kiss. Jesse mourned him as the 'We Don't Give A Damn' Mix played out its heavy, jubilant coda.

The man in the suit jacket seemed to be in his own little zone. He was wearing a crisp, high-collared white shirt, unbuttoned to mid-chest; he had a bit of a belly, and smooth cheeks. Jesse enjoyed being close enough to smell him. He wasn't dressed like anyone else in the bar, and nor was Jesse, so because they both seemed to be outsiders, perhaps they could share common ground. Jesse was aware that he was being looked at. The man stood up to full height as Jesse turned to face him, their eyes met, he took out his earbuds and reached inside his jacket to switch off his Discman.

'I thought you were going to pull out a knife,' said the man, laughing and showing a narrow gap between his front teeth. His voice was low and quiet, but clear and discernible over the thumping music. 'What were you listening to?'

He spoke as if they were already acquainted and Jesse had just arrived late for their date.

'A song called "Freak Like Me" by the Sugababes,' said Jesse.

'Just Sugababes, no article,' the man said, enjoying the stunned reaction on Jesse's face. 'Which version?'

'The "We Don't Give A Damn Mix"?' Twenty-four hours living with Aussies and Jesse was already copying their rising intonation.

'Ah, the record of the moment,' said the man, as he leaned in to talk into Jesse's ear, which was quickly moist from his breath. 'Probably the best pop single released in this country since "West End Girls". Did you see them on *Top of the Pops* last night?'

*

He had checked into the hostel and was given a bottom-bunk bed in a quad room overlooking a beautiful Victorian street. Most of the tenants were in their late teens or early twenties, largely from Australia, South Africa or New Zealand, with one or two from France and Spain, on short- or long-term stays. The only English he'd met were contractors or long-distance drivers staying overnight. He certainly wasn't going to stay at the hostel for long, with its matted red carpets and shoddy MDF wardrobes. There was woodchip underneath the textured wallpaper, and he imagined the loud, rude, farty sound it would make as it was torn away from the plaster underneath. No wonder the hostel manager Greg, a bald, tanned, muscled and oddly flirtatious Australian, said that most people only stayed there for a couple of weeks while they were looking for somewhere more permanent, or as a pit-stop on their travels.

The crowd drinking and watching television in the common room later in the evening greeted him with friendly curiosity. He gratefully accepted the offer of an oozy slice of pepperoni pizza and a can of Foster's. One or two girls started to fawn over him, patting his hair until it sprang back, telling him he was *soy hendsome!* and that they were jealous of his big, wide eyes and long, curled-up lashes. *D'ya wear muscara?* one of them asked. When he burst out laughing in denial, she said, *I don't believe you!* and poked him in the eye with her greasy finger whilst trying to touch them. It had finally stopped watering by the time *Top of the Pops* came on, and Sugababes, complete with incongruously smiling new member, glared at their audience, posed, tapped their pockets, nodded their heads and gave a flawless rendition of the 'We Don't Give a Damn' Mix, drawing emphatic cheers at the end with a harmonious *a cappella*. Mutya looked like she didn't give a shit but sounded incredible. The speakers were so bassy it was almost like being there.

The drinking went on, and a core group stayed while

others went out to pubs and clubs. Jesse had not encountered Australian people before outside *Neighbours* and *Home and Away*, and nobody in those shows had ever held an unlit spliff between their fingers and said, *Dude, fency camun out with us for a mull on the stips?*

'Yeh,' Jesse had said, and followed two men wearing check shirts and vests (what the Australians called 'singlets') out into the mild evening air, just as a souped-up, purple Vauxhall Corsa slowed down and lowered its windows, its driver turning down Nelly's 'Country Grammar' just for a moment to sing *because I got high / because I got high / because I got high*, the refrain from the song by the American one-hit-wonder Afroman, before thrusting off with his mates in a screech of giggles and skinny tyre tracks. Jesse hadn't had his hair cut for a couple of months but it wasn't *that* long.

'Cunts,' said Jeff as he lit up, pulling several times as the end glowed robustly. He was tall, hairy-chested and bearded. 'Bit ya git thet a lot, roight?'

'No,' Jesse sniggered.

'Hay, look at 'im,' said Tod, less discreetly than he might have wanted. He was shorter and fairer than Jeff but just as stocky. A portly, suited middle-aged man descended the steps to a basement flat across the road.

'Someone's lookin'a get laid,' said Jeff, as he blew a rich, fragrant plume into the night air. He had the thickest eyebrows Jesse thought he had ever seen, and dark red, pouty lips.

'Who lives there?' asked Jesse.

'It's a boy brothel,' said Tod.

Jesse looked confused. 'Right there?'

'Yih,' said Tod, taking the spliff from Jeff. 'That's where closet queers who can't face goin' to the Coleherne go.'

'The Coleherne?' said Jesse.

'Thet pab reownd the corner?' said Tod. 'Where all the queers go?'

'Mate,' said Jeff. 'Ya can't use thet wurd any more. Thay prefur gay.'

Tod shrugged, holding his beer out in front of him. 'I stend corrictud.'

Jesse took the spliff and looked across the road at the basement flat, shrouded by a black fence and some overgrown shrubs. He made a mental note to look up the Coleherne on the Internet the next day. He took a deep pull and burst into a cough.

'Thought you guys were s'posed to know what you're doin,' laughed Tod.

'Dude,' said Jeff, as he tapped Jesse manfully on the back.

'They were *amazing*,' said Jesse.

'The only current girl group who can actually sing live,' the man said. 'British girl group, I mean. Of course there are a plethora of American groups with pitch-perfect harmonies, but we don't seem to produce them to any great quantity or quality here. I wonder why that is.'

He stood back and waited for Jesse's next move as if he might magically produce a couple of sisters or girlfriends whose voices were perfectly matched. Ruth and Esther did sound good together – especially when harmonising early Sugababes songs – but, alas, were nowhere to be seen.

'I doe know,' said Jesse, bewildered, though not entirely unprepared for this conversation. 'There's more black people in America, int there.'

'But what about the gospel scene? America has Destiny's Child, SWV, Brownstone, En Vogue. We had Eternal, who were terrific, but it's difficult to think beyond them. It's terribly compelling, the use of soulful black female vocals over a secular white male backing track, *à la* "Freak Like Me". Of course, it all comes round and round. There'd have been none of the lo-fi isolationist post-punk Gary Numan traded on without the Lee "Scratch" Perry-produced dub reggae sounds of the Seventies, or without Kraftwerk, for that matter. I'm Rufus, by the way.'

He stood back and held out an enormous, plump hand.

'Arm Jesse,' he said, accepting it. It was preternaturally soft, as if Rufus hadn't worked a day in his life. 'Are you a record label boss or something?'

'No,' he laughed. 'Why?'

'Cause o'what ya just said,' said Jesse. 'I thought you must be a music journalist or something.'

'We're gay,' Rufus said, unsurely. 'I'm assuming?'

'Yeh,' said Jesse, indignantly, recalling the doorman having also questioned him.

'Well, we do everything to pop music,' said Rufus. 'Dance, sing along, kiss, fuck. Know what I mean?'

He forced a laugh as Jesse smiled and sipped his pint.

'I've not seen you in here before,' Rufus said, with a different tone, perhaps feeling he had passed a stage in the pull and found it okay to proceed.

'It's my first time. I just moved to London.'

'How much?' said Rufus, bluntly, taking Jesse by surprise.

'Wha?' The music being damagingly loud, Jesse leaned in to hear him better.

'Do you charge? Are you rent?'

'I don't know what you mean,' Jesse cringed.

'Oh, well, congratulations,' said Rufus, picking up his glass and offering it to Jesse to clink his against.

'For wha?'

Rufus rolled his eyes. 'Moving to London! Keep up!' he said, and offered his glass to toast.

'Cheers.'

Rufus was into the last third of his pint. Despite the fact that there were other men waiting to be served, he simply pointed and nodded, and the bartender started pulling another for him. Other men were trying to squeeze in at the bar so Jesse came away from it and Rufus, abandoning his old pint for the fresh one, closed his magazine and turned around to face him. Jesse's eyes shot straight down to the right-leaning bulge in Rufus's jeans.

'Bloody hell, he'll have someone's eye out,' Rufus said, looking over Jesse's shoulder.

Jesse turned round, indiscreetly. It was a man with a spiked-up mohawk, wearing a kilt, turning his head this way and that as he and an older South Asian man in a bowtie and scarf hooked up with another group, including the immovable force that was the black giant with the beautiful, muscled back and enormous, hard arse. It became clear from their facial expressions and hand gestures that they were all deaf and signing at each other.

'It's cool 'ere,' said Jesse. ''Ow often d'you come?'

Rufus grinned, as if there was a joke in the air. His eyes were dark blue and sharp. Jesse wondered if he might be a lawyer or something.

'Every Friday and Saturday night for the last five years, unless I've been away.'

'So you'm part o' the furniture, then?'

'The squashy old sofa. Or the vintage slot machine, take your pick,' Rufus said as he put pint glass to mouth.

They sipped. Jesse watched two men angle their heads together as if for a kiss, holding something up against each other's noses to sniff and each standing back slightly flushed. Other men looked on, wanting to join in, and soon the bottle, Jesse could now see, was being passed around.

'Do you live locally?' Rufus asked, as if worried the conversation was over.

'I'm staying at an 'ostel round the corner till I find somewhere more permanent.'

'The Aussie one?'

'Yeh.'

'How is it?'

'It's alright, nothin special,' said Jesse, as a pierced, shaven-headed black man with a thick beard walked past, making knowing eye contact with both before sharply averting his eyes.

'Sounds great,' said Rufus, quickly. 'Do you share a room?'

'Wi'three other blokes.'

'What's that like?'

'Ask me in a couple a weeks,' said Jesse. 'It's alright for now, just to settle in.'

'Gay?'

'One definitely is. One definitely int. One I int sure about.'

'Cute?'

Jesse laughed. He had spent the morning in bed playing a high-level game of Snake on his phone, distracted by his roommate's conspicuous nakedness as he paraded himself around, letting his towel fall away as he dried his hair, then staring statuesquely out of the window as if Jesse wasn't there. Blaise was slightly taller than Jesse and had a broad-shouldered, slim-hipped body, hairless apart from a dark frizz of pubes around his uncut dick and low-hanging balls. He wore his hair in long, loose curls. Jesse stayed in bed pretending not to be looking out of the corner of his eye, and trying not to become aroused. He was relieved to have the room back to himself when the roommate who, despite his silence, might have been expecting a reaction to his generous display, quickly got dressed and left, with a rucksack and a quiet *Bye*.

'Maybe in a few years,' said Jesse, meaningfully.

'I see,' Rufus said. He smiled broadly and Jesse anticipated pushing his tongue through the gap in between his teeth.

'You know there's a boy brothel across the road from there, don't you?'

'Yer, I heard,' Jesse said, realising why Rufus had asked him if he charged.

'So what *are* you doing in London?'

'Startin' again,' Jesse said, newly self-assured and defiant.

Rufus burst out laughing. 'How old are you?'

'Nineteen,' Jesse said, and immediately regretted how foolish he sounded. 'And you?'

'Old enough to be your dad,' said Rufus. 'Forty-seven.'

'Ya doe look i',' said Jesse, whose mouth had begun to water again.

'Flatterer,' said Rufus, and he kept his eyes on Jesse's as he took an almighty gulp of his pint. The DJ had been impressively smooth in his mixing, and a song with an ear-catching bassline and key-change, and the lyrics *Love will set you free*, was playing. Rufus stepped in closer so that their bodies were touching. The last man he'd been this close to was in the toilets at New Street station.

'What are you up to tonight?' Rufus asked, making Jesse's heart thump faster.

He shrugged his shoulders and turned down the corners of his mouth.

'Just 'angin' out.'

He'd begun to tire of the itchy tickling caused by the restriction. He needed a piss, but knew it would be a struggle to get his dick back into his jeans.

'Would you like to come to my place?'

'Where d'ya live?'

'Literally down the road.'

They threw back their drinks and Jesse followed as Rufus shouldered his way through the crowd, and they were out of the door before the last of the foam hit the bottom of the glass.

Chapter 2

Jesse suavely thanked the doorman, who wished them an antic-
ipatory goodnight as he winked and Rufus set off down the Old
Brompton Road in the direction he'd come from. The soulful
house beat faded with each step even as the singer seemed to
scream for them to stay. There had been a smile of recognition
on the doorman's part, as if having taken note of Jesse's sexual
preferences for his own future use.

Rufus kept his distance, staring straight ahead and led by
his chest and arms, letting regular people who just happened
to be out at that time on a Saturday night pass between them,
so that they wouldn't assume he and Jesse were together. They
all looked at them: two thirtysomething gays in jeans and worn
leather jackets heading to the Coleherne; a tough-looking tattooed woman in vest and shorts, dangling a busy bunch of keys
by her side, with a bottle of Smirnoff clutched to her chest; a
guy in a Von Dutch cap walking his dog. Perhaps they thought
Jesse was a drug runner about to do an exchange around the
corner with the monied-looking man in the suit jacket.

Jesse accepted Rufus's lack of engagement. He could be
himself in the bar, and would hopefully return to being so in
the comfort of his own flat, but the shared streets were clearly
a less convivial place. They were a middle-aged white man and
a teenage black boy, although, Jesse – a black boy with a white
father – had known the curiosity and confusion of strangers all
his life. Most people had thought Graham sweet for deigning to

take on a young black boy, when they saw them together alone, but when they were with the rest of the family – a white man, a black woman and three mixed-race girls – Jesse always looked the odd one out, the adoptee.

He thought about his colleagues at McDonald's, three days into his never seeing them again, and had the sudden urge to text one of them to tell them where he was going and who he was with, but remembered with a pang that he'd changed his number and deleted all his contacts. Rufus led him past the lights and they crossed the quiet road. Jesse stood well back as Rufus pulled out his keys to a side door next to the main entrance of a public library – Brompton Library – so as, again, not to appear threatening. He looked past his reflection in the main doors along the darkened bookshelves and wondered about all the books Rufus was lucky to have such easy access to. Rufus directed him in and up a couple of floors of clean, brightly lit stairs, making Jesse nervous; Rufus's words, uttered with the rim of a pint glass in his mouth – *squashy old sofa. Or the vintage slot machine, take your pick* – went through his mind. Rufus explained that, as they were directly above the closed library, they need not worry too much about noise, once inside; *he'd not heard a peep from the next-door flat*, he said, *so they must be away*. His manner, now, was cool and matter-of-fact, as if he would need to be warmed up again. He stopped Jesse in front of flat 8, unlocked it with a single Yale key and invited Jesse straight through into the lounge at the end of the hallway. He had left all the lights and his stereo on; this is a man who's really into his black music, Jesse thought – like Graham, who often, on Saturday evenings when he was back from work and the weekly grocery shop had been done, danced with his daughters in the living room to CDs or tracks Jesse's mother had taped off the radio.

The piercing violins and guttural funk guitars of 'Forget Me Nots' by Patrice Rushen – sampled by George Michael not long after he'd been caught and arrested for cruising a policeman – could just be heard making way for the portentous synths of 'Just Be Good To Me' by The S.O.S. Band, which he recalled his mother, still in her nightgown and headscarf, playing loud on her turntable in the front room one dark afternoon between the soaps and the kids' TV shows. Jesse and his twin half-sisters sang along in their exile upstairs, pretending to perform it live on stage. He hoped it was the long version, that seemed to go on forever without threatening to outstay its welcome, not the radio edit she also had on cassette, that was cut halfway through as if at random by bored, suited white male executives in big glasses. There were no breaks in the music; it was a subtle, insistent groove. Every component of it kept rotating.

Rufus's hallway was a gallery of framed black-and-white photographs of himself smiling and posing with women, some of whom Jesse was astonished to recognise.

'Is this Farrah Franklin from Destiny's Child?' he almost squealed.

'Yes,' said Rufus, standing over his shoulder. 'They'd been on *Top of the Pops* with "Say My Name". She was sacked within days.'

'What do you do?'

'I manage a jeweller's,' he said, almost ruefully, and went into his bedroom.

There was Su-Elise from Mis-Teeq, Lisa Maffia from So Solid Crew, solo singers Michelle Gayle, Beverley Knight, Mica Paris and Gabrielle. More of these pictures led him into a lamplit open-plan room, with parquet floors and a plumply cushioned settee facing the window to the street. To his right was a good-sized kitchen, and a dining booth with seating for six. It was tempting to kick off his Adidas and slide around on the shiny floor behind the settee, lashing his hips against the beat. Tall plants in heavy-bottomed pots huddled in a corner like girls in a club.

The lyrics of 'Just Be Good To Me' read differently coming

from the sound system of a stranger he was about to have sex with. He now couldn't imagine how his Christian mother found refuge in the sentiments of a woman openly permitting her boyfriend to be unfaithful, just as long as he was good to her. Back then, the door knocked loudly, causing his mother to get up and turn down the music. Jesse ran down to answer it to Brother Frank Grimes, who said he'd happened to be driving by and thought he'd pop in for a cuppa. He was wearing a tan blazer and brown trousers and shoes, with a stripy tie and tinted glasses. Lately, Jesse's mother had missed a couple of meetings and told other Sisters she'd been feeling depressed, so Brother Grimes counselled her, as Jesse and his sisters sat at the top of the stairs listening to their conversation. *What message does that send to your daughters, Val? Is that the treatment they should expect? Or to your son? Is that how he should treat women? How about that nice Patti LaBelle and Michael McDonald song, 'On My Own'? Have you got that instead?*

Rufus's music, of a volume just above background level, wasn't coming from a stereo but from speakers connected to an iMac with a turquoise plastic insert. He'd not seen one in real life before. He approached it and ran his hand over its warm rear curve, a paraboloid, or so he remembered from GCSE Maths chit-chat, his being the top-*top* set. With everyone expected to get at least an A, he – having taken on the role of class clown – had been the one the jowly teacher warned would let down the set by getting a B, but actually, he succeeded; the one to fall short was Aiden Phillips, born in 1981 when his parents could not have predicted his peers would call him AIDS for short. The paraboloid was warm in his hand. He wondered how long it had been left on; how long Rufus had been in the bar waiting for someone like Jesse to walk in, because he was certainly decisive when he did.

'Just Be Good To Me' was partway down a list of songs burned on to a CD called *Soul Divas*. There were some masterpieces, classics from his early childhood, the mere titles of which brought back the smell of the Sof'N'Free products his mother used to keep her curly perm wet, before she relaxed her hair into leaf-like fronds and switched to Dark & Lovely. He wondered where Rufus was, back then. If he was forty-seven now, he would have been in his late twenties when 'Just Be Good To Me' was big in the charts and the clubs. He would have been in his late twenties when Jesse was still a toddler not even at school.

Jesse wondered if Rufus had always been attracted to black men, and whether the muscular guy with the nose ring who had clocked them both in the Coleherne was a former conquest. He took off his jacket and crossed the room to fold it over the back of a dining chair.

'You've got great taste in music,' he told Rufus as he walked in in his shirt sleeves.

'Inside every gay man is a fabulous black woman,' he smiled coolly, gesturing to the settee. 'Sit down, if you like. Beer?'

'Yes please,' Jesse said, crossing behind the coffee table and carefully perching where he wouldn't disturb the perfectly fluffed-up pink and green damask cushions. *Inside every gay man is a fabulous black woman.* Did he really believe that? Jesse finally kicked off his trainers. He could now see the size and shape of Rufus as he pottered around, particularly his thick arse and thighs, bigger than Graham, whose weight was concentrated around his shoulders and chest. He wore his jeans high and belted to give himself a waist, with his shirt tucked in, and moved in an officious manner around the longweave rug, twisting shut the Venetian blinds in front and turning back into the kitchen, opening the fridge door, taking out two bottles of Beck's and flipping off the tops with a bottle opener. *Poor man's champagne*, as Graham used to greet the popping sound.

'Glass?'

'No thank you,' Jesse replied instinctively; his mother always told Graham off for dirtying glasses. *Drink out the bottle*, she'd say, laughing into her glass of Babycham.

'Sure?'

'Ar, goo on then,' he said, tipsily sliding into real Black Country-speak.

'You haven't told me where in the Midlands you're from,' Rufus said, placing Jesse's beer and glass on coasters in front of him before going back to fetch his own.

'The Black Country,' Jesse said as he filled his glass too quickly. It foamed up, so he rushed to drink the head back before it spilled over.

'Whereabouts?' Rufus filled a bowl with some nuts and brought them, along with his glass of beer, to the coffee table.

'I was born in Dudley'n grew up in West Bromwich. D'ya know the Black Country?'

'Dudley,' Rufus laughed, sitting down, watching keenly as Jesse took off his hat and unknotted his hair with his fingers. It was the *la-la-la-laaaaaaa!-laaa-laaa-la-la* bit of the song and he closed his eyes and nodded along. 'Never been, but it is quite a famous town. Lenny Henry's from there, isn't he? You've got the castle, haven't you, and the zoo? It used to be quite important. Sue Lawley's from there, of course.'

'Wha? Sue Lawley the newsreader?'

'Yes,' said Rufus, pinching a handful of nuts.

'Never! *Sue Lawley* int from Dudley!'

'I read an interview of hers,' Rufus muttered, before swallowing, 'in which she talked about what it was like when she first moved to London to work for the BBC. She was standing waiting at a bus stop one cold winter morning, and when she said, *Cum on, buzz!* in her accent, and the lady next to her gave her a look as if to say, *Where on earth are you from?*, she realised she'd have to change it if she wanted to present the *Six O'clock News*.'

'It's a dump now,' Jesse said, crunching down some nuts, impressed by Rufus's ability with the accent but unable to digest the fact that Sue Lawley was from *Dudley*, a ghost town where the area around the central bus station was almost completely derelict, and the high street had been routed by the Merry Hill complex a ten-minute drive out, all the key retailers replaced with pawnbrokers and betting shops.

'I can see why someone like you would want to leave. There wouldn't be much hope of getting anywhere in life, I suppose, staying there. You must have *some* ambition.'

'I went to school wi' girls whose ambition was to get pregnant so they could gerra council flat,' said Jesse. 'One's got four kids at twenty, last I heard. Started when she was thirteen and got took out o' school. This is a tune, this is.'

He glared at Rufus, who grinned back, glad his musical choices were not lost on his young guest. The gospel handclaps closing 'Just Be Good To Me' had given way to the finger clicks and 808s of Gwen Guthrie's 'Ain't Nothin' Goin' On But the Rent', which Jesse and his mother used to freak out to on full-blast at their flat when he was very small. He remembered his aunties being round, babysitting him while his mother went out on a date with Graham before they were married, bending their knees to the descending bassline, crouching until their backsides almost touched the floor, pointing to the missing jewels at their ears, necks and wrists, and laughing, saying they would never, ever go out with a white man, unless he was very rich. He missed his aunties, but they had children of their own now and had never been able to help. His mother was their big sister, whom they loved more than anyone. Their big sister had picked them up from school and cooked for them while their parents were still working at the factories. They couldn't see her ugliness like he could. She had been quite pretty before she started wearing glasses, and until the twins were born, when the weight gain became irreversible. She wore her Afro thick, side-parted and scooped up-and-over, with big earrings. She pouted in pictures because she hated her teeth (there was nothing wrong with them), and covered her mouth with her hand when she laughed. There was one of her and Jesse together, gold around the edges like lost time, him sitting on her lap, next to his aunts, on the settee at his grandparents' house. He was looking and smiling at his uncle behind the camera, while his mother, who had a forearm around his waist, propped her cheek on her fist on the arm of the settee, watching him dotingly. He was probably only two or three. It was as if he was right there, even though he was sitting next to Rufus.

'Wait. You can't remember this. Were you even born when this was released?'

'When'd it come out?'

''Eighty-six?'

'I was four.'

Rufus grimaced. 'You're not supposed to make me feel so old.'

'Wharrif I like *old*?'

'Do you always go for older men?'

Jesse nodded and clicked his fingers, dancing sitting down like his mother did, aware of Rufus watching his mouth as he sipped his beer with a kissing sound, having forgotten to drink from the glass. He had what his old colleagues at McDonald's used to describe, on girls, as *shiner's lips*. They used to cause him embarrassment, not least when kids at school called him *rubber lips* or tried to mimic him by trying to touch their noses with their tongues whilst folding down their bottom lips, but they were his pride and joy now. White women were rushing out with fat wads of cash to get their pouts pumped up; the kids who used to tease him chatted shit through papercuts and smiled skeletally. Rufus had pretty, full lips with a Cupid's bow, in a surprisingly lurid shade, like strawberry-flavoured chews. Jesse wondered about the colouring elsewhere on Rufus's body.

'Why?' Rufus asked.

'I just fancy ya more,' Jesse said, his voice high and defensive.

'More money,' said Rufus, as if he'd heard it all before.

'I s'pose,' said Jesse, trying to sound like he hadn't thought about it and cringing at the song's lyrics, in which Guthrie was asking the universe for nothing less than a man who could afford to keep her financially secure.

'I'm not rich, by any means,' said Rufus, wryly.

'Good job I int here for ya money, then,' said Jesse.

'So what *are* you here for?' said Rufus, smoothly.

'Because you invited me,' said Jesse. 'After talking to me, a stranger, in ya local pub for five minutes. I might be an axe murderer.' Graham always said silly things like that. Rufus gave him a look as if to say, *So might I*, but Jesse decided to trust his instincts, which had been fine so far.

'I thought you were cute and somebody I wouldn't mind getting to know,' said Rufus.

'Past tense?' said Jesse, hoping Rufus might've clocked that there was more to this scrawny, doe-eyed black child than met the eye.

'I *think* you *are* cute.' Rufus laughed, and caressed Jesse's cheek with a forefinger. 'Clever, funny, sexy, and someone I'd like to get to know.'

He opened the drawer under the coffee table.

The seat was warm where he had been. Jesse put the spliff down, took the yellow straw and met this curious new version of himself – the same but less pathetically innocent – in the mirror flat on the table as he leaned over the line. The cocaine was twinkly and iridescent. He put his finger over his right nostril, as Rufus instructed, hovered the straw in his left, closed his eyes and sniffed along. It stung immediately, so he pressed his nostril down hard to subdue the pain.

'Don't lose it,' said Rufus. 'Keep taking it in.'

Jesse continued to sniff as if he had a cold, and swallowed. The stinging slowly abated. The coke smelled bleachy inside him. The side of his face where he'd snorted felt numb.

'How is it?' asked Rufus.

'I doe know yet,' said Jesse, looking around the room and squinting his eyelids as if everything should have taken on a different shape or colour. The paradisiacal 'Hanging On A String' by Loose Ends came on with its cowbell-like drum effects. It tasted of tropical juice and dried his mouth. He took a sip of beer.

'Feel free to take your clothes off,' Rufus smiled. 'And give it time.'

Jesse stood up, stripped off his T-shirt and jeans and threw them on the floor. He kept sniffing and swallowing as if a tap had opened at the back of his throat, dispensing a fluid both milky and toxic, like the semen from the man at New Street station. Rufus draped a towel over the settee, picked up Jesse's clothes and put them with his jacket over the back of a chair, then sat down to unlace his high brown brogues. Jesse was naked but for the white Nike socks he was about to take off.

'You might leave those on,' Rufus said as he heaved off each boot and placed them next to the settee. Jesse felt sexy, his dick imposing its presence. 'Will you roll a nice, tight joint? You're probably better than me at it. My fingers are too fat. Bit like your cock.'

He stood up, unbuckled his belt and pushed down his jeans, revealing white Calvin Klein trunks. Rufus looked down at Jesse hungrily and stooped to kiss him deeply. This was Graham's favourite song; he and his mother used to sing the lyrics to each other as the sheets blew on the line outside with the patio door open. *You're a black man in a white man's body*, Graham's colleagues at the landfill site used to tell him. The white boys at McDonald's were the same. Jesse realised he'd spent much of his life learning what it was to be a black man from white men. *You're like a black boy trying to be a white boy trying to be a black boy.*

He was nineteen; twenty in less than three weeks. Freedom

wouldn't wait for twenty-one. He'd wanted out at fourteen. He was six when the twins were born and his overrun mother abandoned him to the Bible; one child was one, three might as well have been nine. He overheard his mother, when he was ten, asking Graham what Jesse was going to be like at fifteen, because she was already sick of him. Too clever by half. Attitude problem. *Misstra Know-It-All*, she called him. *Don't answer back*; *don't NO me*. At school he did everything right; at home, everything wrong. Graham would come home from work at six, and once he was out of his overalls he got his chest wet from tears she'd blamed her son for. *Nothing's ever good enough for him, Gray!* she would tell him, not that he'd won the house points contest, or the spelling test, or the multiplication test, or the division test, or how his art teacher had told him his painting made her happy, or how he'd been chosen to be the school's first ever black Head Boy, but of the tone with which he'd spoken to her when correcting her grammar, how he'd broken a toy he was too old to play with, how he'd muttered under his breath in complaint about the two bits of charred liver and lumpy gravy she'd given him for dinner. He leaped up the stairs two at a time but Graham had the strength to push his door open and Jesse couldn't help but count along to the belt straps; he could hear all the kids at school counting along. Sometimes, Graham got so worked up Jesse lost count. Ruth and Esther screamed in their room, in harmony with him as his voice started to break.

The orchestral opening chords of Anita Baker's 'Sweet Love' announced themselves. His parents' wedding reception was held in the assembly hall of a local secondary school for which one of the elders was a caretaker, so they were able to get a discount, and it was there that his mother and Graham enjoyed their first dance, as a married couple, to 'Sweet Love'.

Jesse, sitting, pulled down the waistband of Rufus's trunks. He weighed the heavy balls in his hand. He kissed and sniffed Rufus all around, looking in his eyes as if they were making an unspoken vow. He felt as if he could fall in love, and didn't know whether it was real or the cocaine working. Rufus looked so calm and serene, his eyes and skin so clear, his lips so full and pink. There was so much of him. Jesse felt an inner upsurge of desire, to open, to explore, to devour. Rufus's balls and pubes smelled of that sweet male tang unique to the crotch. What if they could live like man and wife? What would other people think? What would other people's opinions matter, if they were in love? He could feel his eye sockets pulling. He had never seen so clearly.

Rufus sat down and put his arm round Jesse as he pinched off the end of the joint and sparked up, hovering his hand over it out of habit, as he was used to smoking outdoors in dark, hidden places where the wind was his enemy. It was a slow burner that hung heavily from his lip, and the smoke he inhaled was opaque. Rufus crossed one leg over the other, and Jesse rested a hand on his thigh.

'Are you warm enough?' Rufus asked, opening his body.

'Yes,' said Jesse, but he leaned back into him anyway. Rufus's chest hair tickled his nostrils.

'Do you have anything to do tomorrow?' asked Rufus.

'No,' said Jesse. The innocent pop of 'When I Think of You' by Janet Jackson. He wanted him so much. To draw his finger down from the top of his spine all the way down then under and over and up until he found his lips. To kiss the soft skin inside his collarbone. To nibble his heavy pink earlobe. To watch the hairs grow from his chin and the little pulse in his neck flutter. To hover his nose over his open mouth, smelling his beery breath. To stare into his eyes until he had to stop, until his whole world changed with the batting of his eyelids. To feel his muscles: the traps of his shoulders all the way down the thickness of his forearms. To nestle in his chest and belly and wet them with his happy tears. To suck on his nipples as if they would draw milk. To be warm and cared for. To lift one great leg up, then the other, making his knee joints click. To sniff him all about like a dog. To get under the covers and live there. To feel him moving around in his throat. He rolled the lit end of the spliff along the inner rim of the ashtray and handed it to Rufus, and waited to hear the crackling of the end burning over his head as he combed his fingers through golden pubic hair and picked out his belly button fluff. Rufus had a hand in Jesse's hair, massaging down to his scalp.

Jesse slid forwards off the sofa, careful not to disturb the table, and knelt between Rufus's legs as he sat back smoking the spliff. He hoped he wasn't making too much noise, slurping and making fart sounds. He made Rufus grunt, stretch out his legs and tip back his head, looking up at Rufus as he grew in his mouth, watching his eyes move in and out of focus, only coming up when he could see that Rufus needed to use the ash-tray. Rufus leaned forward over Jesse's back to tamp the spliff, before wiping Jesse's mouth dry with one hand and holding the spliff in front of Jesse to let him take a couple of long tokes, white ribbons and rings of smoke dancing around his face. He admired Rufus's body, his paunchy belly, his spread pectorals, his hard nipples, the fine covering of blond hair. He went down again until he had to be stopped. 'I don't want to come yet,' Rufus said, as he cupped Jesse by the head in his huge warm hands, and lifted him; Jesse forgot the table was behind, almost upending it, and everything on it, including the beers, with his arse. There was a moment of terror before they both laughed and fell into a wet kiss.

'You're not getting cold, are you?' said Rufus.

'No,' said Jesse. He was restless, and the sweat glands in his armpits tingled. He hadn't eaten.

'Do you want some water? More beer?'

Rufus was speaking to him in an undertone, like they were a couple.

'Beer please,' he said, against himself.

Jesse followed Rufus into the kitchen. There could be nothing in a room so impudent as a naked middle-aged white male arse, shapely and comely, meaty and bouncy. There it was! Graham, without the almost-transparent underwear. Jesse pressed him up against the sink from behind, his dick so hard it was almost numb, Rufus grinding against him. He was about to give his first fuck and lose his virginity, and it was for this that he wished he had been disfellowshipped. He wanted to treat Rufus like other boys treated girls.

'I wanna fuck you right 'ere in the kitchen,' Jesse told him as he reached round to tweak his nipples, making him moan and whimper.

'No. Let's go next door,' Rufus laughed, pushing Jesse's hands away.

The lamplit bedroom was filled by the bed. Jesse paced around in the doorway sipping his beer, watching Rufus fold down the duvet, lay a towel, then climb across it on all fours to access a drawer in the bedside table, from which he produced a tube of lube and a small brown bottle with a skull-and-crossbones label, like the one being passed around at the Coleherne.

'What's that?' said Jesse, climbing onto the bed and reaching over to put his glass on the bedside table.

'The poppers?' Rufus asked. 'Have you never done poppers before?'

'No,' said Jesse, as he climbed on top of him and pushed his tongue in his mouth. Rufus was twice his size, and Jesse could sense he had the potential to crush him if he chose to. He closed a hand around Rufus's throat and licked the gap between his two front teeth. Rufus pulled himself up and took the poppers bottle down from the table, unscrewed the cap, covered a nostril with a thumb and inhaled the gas up the other, swapped round, then invited Jesse to do the same, and said 'Not too hard,' as Jesse felt a drop of fluid shoot up his nose and start to burn, but he was okay. Whatever poppers were went straight to his head, made him dizzy and his heart thump. They melted onto the bed top and tail and gargled each other's dicks as if it was normal, then Rufus lifted a leg over Jesse's head and twisted his body until he was on his front. Jesse took his time with that first taste, slightly peppery on the end of his tongue, then mushed his face in. Rufus took another sniff of the poppers, closed the bottle and lifted himself up onto all fours, reaching back between his legs to pass the bottle to Jesse, and he carefully opened the bottle, took a deep sniff up each nostril and kept his presence of mind long enough to secure the screw cap back on.

Jesse's head pounded like a bad hangover headache, but without pain. He contemplated the huge, wide open arse in front of him, and smashed his face into it, concentrating all his energy through his tongue. Rufus moaned like he was crying, his face squashed into a pillow; Jesse peered down Rufus's back, slanting to his silver temples. He saw in the corner of his eye his reflection in the mirrored wardrobe doors, and it was so strange, the sight of a small black boy with long eyelashes, who didn't look old enough to be doing what he was doing. He had to come up, to breathe, to let himself live in the moment. He liked what he saw; he *loved* it. This was what he wanted and had tried so hard to imagine. This was the truth, the whole truth and nothing but *the truth*.

'Fuck me until you come,' said Rufus, as he spun round, grabbed the poppers and sniffed, sniffed, sniffed until his lips turned blue.

Chapter 3

Jesse and his mother were at the wool shop in West Bromwich. The floor, the shelves and lights were bright white, and the walls and floor cases were stacked high with balls of wool in every colour. He ran around them with his vroom-vroom police car, pretending they were skyscrapers in America. His mother had banned him from revving up his vroom-vroom police car in public places, warning him he would lose it. Women smiled at him and told his mother how beautiful and handsome he was. It was strange when a man walked in, wearing bright colours and big glasses, but he smiled and looked nice and went straight for the pastels.

'Breakout' by Swing Out Sister came on the store radio. 'I love this song!' Jesse rejoiced, and all the women, and the man, turned around and laughed. His mother was being taught how to knit by Sister McCarthy. His mother liked yellow, green and orange, colours that would work for a boy or a girl, and white, for a big shawl. She wondered if a vivid magenta that matched her nail varnish might work for a cardigan pattern for herself that she'd found in *Prima* magazine, and she held a packet of gold triangular buttons up against it that a shop assistant said matched her earrings. The same shop assistant held open for Jesse a bag of Opal Fruits, his favourite sweets, and he took a purple one, his favourite flavour, but then she said, *Tek a couple if ya want, bab!*, so he put his vroom-vroom police car in his pocket and dug out all the purple ones. *Them mar favourite, too!*

beamed the shop assistant, who had lovely thick red hair like the lead singer from T'Pau and a green jumper with bobbles on. *Doe tek all of 'em!* said his mother. *He's alright!* said the shop assistant, kindly. *What d'ya say, then?* said his mother. *Thank you,* Jesse said, angelically. *Aww, he's ever so 'andsome, int 'e,* said the shop assistant. His mother had just told him that he might be getting a new little brother or sister, so he would have to be polite and show them a good example even though they weren't born yet. He was so excited. He hoped it would be a brother. He liked the boys at school, one in particular, a boy called Lee who went into the Wendy house with him and closed the door; they hugged and touched each other between the legs. The nice man paid for his balls of wool in baby pink, pale yellow, pale green, light grey and a bright electric blue, and smiled and waved at Jesse as he left.

Jesse revved up his vroom-vroom police car, hoping his mother wouldn't notice, as she stopped sharp and dropped her basket. It clattered on the floor and the balls of wool rolled out. The vroom-vroom police car crashed into one of the floor cases. It all went quiet apart from the music, for a second, before the gasps started. The bright red spots between his mother's feet stood out on the white tiles. She started to cry and clutch her stomach. The red-haired shop assistant ran over to put her hand on his mother's shoulder, then led her into the back, asking if she was pregnant; she nodded and burst into a wail. Jesse was left standing alone, chewing three purple Opal Fruits all at once until he felt pain in his temples. He thought he should leave his vroom-vroom police car exactly where it was. An ambulance took them to the hospital, where he was sent to play in a little nursery with other children whose brothers and sisters or parents were sick.

Deep inside Rufus, Jesse heard 'Breakout' for the first time since. *Your dick is so big your dick is so big your dick is so big . . .*

Rufus was in front of him digging his fists into the mattress, moaning, arse bouncing, craning his neck over his shoulder, watching himself in the mirrored doors, telling him, *Come in your daddy. Come in your daddy.* It felt so good. There was so much to fuck. Jesse held on to Rufus's waist, positioned himself at the right angle, got into a stride and hit top form just as Rufus let go of all the tension in his body. Jesse could've passed out from the height of his orgasm. Rufus slithered off him, spun round and made Jesse squirm as he cleaned everything off.

Flat on his back while he caught his breath, Jesse relit the spliff in the ashtray, thinking about how his mother always used to laugh at Yazz for being so tall, thin and light-skinned. 'The Only Way Is Up' was Number One in the charts when his twin half-sisters were born – Ruth and Esther, from the Bible, like Jesse, though she hadn't known that at the time. Rufus came back from the toilet.

'So what are you doing tomorrow?' he said, again, as he collapsed back on the bed, front first, then twisting his body and pulling himself up to the bedhead. It satisfied Jesse to see how much he had made Rufus sweat. He too was soaking wet and his stomach muscles were visible.

'Nothing,' said Jesse, watching the smoke rise on the still air. 'How about you?'

Rufus looked as if he had something on his mind.

'Nothing,' he said. He was lying on his back with one foot crossed over the other. 'Nothing.'

'You alright?'

'Yes, yes. Well, as a matter of fact, no. Something, er, something happened at work,' he said, pulling himself further up his pillow and headboard. His jaw was rocking around unnaturally. 'I – do you know what – I absolutely by mistake left with a piece of jewellery I'd been trying on and forgot to take off before I left, I mean, it happens. My assistant arrived stupidly early the next morning to – to – to do the inventory and, obviously, just, doing her fucking job reported the thing missing of course, I took it off here, and, forgot – to take it back to work with me, stupidly, so, yes I can see that, to all intents and purposes it looked like it had gone missing under my . . . watch, er, almost literally!'

He laughed maniacally at his own joke.

'So what's happ'nin'?' Jesse asked, just as he noticed his own jaw moving from side to side.

'Well, er, not good, er, head office have, er, suspended me. Pending further inquiries.'

'But did you try to steal it?' said Jesse, realising he would rather continue rocking his jaw than try to stop it.

'Of course not!'

'So why'nt ya just tek it back to work wi'ya?'

'You see I can't. I can't, because I'm not allowed on the premises. *You* could go down to the store! The CCTV cameras are on all day, obviously, but . . . no part of the store is ever under constant surveillance.' He shifted himself to sit up on his knees, facing Jesse, and worked it all out in his head as he spoke. 'You'll go down to the store. I'll tell you when the camera won't be looking and you can just pop it back and leave! Easy! Stuff's gone missing and then turned up in plain sight plenty of times.'

'Okay . . .' said Jesse, unsurely. 'What about the security guard'n that?'

'Oh, don't worry about S—, he's a friend of mine. I – I'll – I'll *pay* you, obviously,' he said, as an afterthought. 'A hundred quid on completion of the job? Another line? Spliff?'

He got back to the hostel just after eleven on Sunday. Blaise was in bed straining to read a short French paperback in natural light. They wished each other a cursory good morning, but next to no sound came from Jesse's throat.

'You are fine?' asked Blaise. His cynical features masked a more modest personality; Jesse saw that Blaise was new in

London too, and friendless, though that conversation would have to wait.

'Yeh, thanks,' he said, and managed a quick smile that discouraged further talk. Shattered and cold, he stripped off regardless and climbed into bed. He had breezed through the hostel door, past the weekend receptionist, straight up the stairs two at a time and into his room. His dick felt like the next-day muscles of a new gym goer who does too much too soon.

Rufus had awoken him from what was at most a couple of hours' sleep, and told him he had to go. Already showered and dressed and wearing glasses, he offered neither breakfast nor coffee. Before Jesse had fallen asleep, it had felt – in certain moments, especially in the five minutes after a line, above all in the thirty seconds after a hit of poppers – as if he and Rufus would be forever inseparable, but as Jesse left the flat Rufus shut the door immediately behind him. It had taken Jesse a disconcerting moment, as normal people walked past down the Old Brompton Road, to realise the street door only opened via a button on the adjacent wall; he felt like a rodent in a humane trap. There hadn't been a right moment to ask for Rufus's number, though Jesse at least knew where he lived.

Two black women had come out of McDonald's as he walked by, looked him up and down and stopped laughing. His jeans were too tight to be wearing on the Lord's big Sunday, and it might even have been apparent to their horror that he was without underwear. Their eyes withered him as if they had seen everything he had done. The bright morning, even if it wasn't sunny, pursued him like paparazzi. He hadn't seen himself in a mirror, or washed his face. His nose felt like a prosthesis. There was some tightness to his cheek, which he feared might be cum, so he licked his hand and rubbed it, and dried it with the sleeve of his baseball jacket. In bed at the hostel, he could still feel Rufus in his throat and around his dick, and smell the sweat from his balls and crack that clung in his nostrils and kept him intoxicated, even while his sinuses were so congested. His hands smelled horribly of lube, but once in bed he felt too exhausted to go to the bathroom and wash them.

Rufus might have said something like, *That was absolutely fucking mind-blowing, really the deepest, most intense fuck I've ever had in my life, but we can't see each other again. I'm not looking for a relationship.* Or, *You've shut me up for six months, at least. Honestly, I can barely even walk you to the door, and anyway, it's time to go back to the real world. Maybe we can see each other again. Let me take your number, and if and when the right time comes, I'll call you.* Even, *See you around at the Coleherne.* Instead, he sat in silence, with an open binder full of papers and a laptop, muttering a clipped goodbye as Jesse left.

The more cocaine Jesse snorted, the more weed he had smoked, the more paranoid he became that this operation Rufus was asking him to perform, going into a jewellery store to replace what had been reported stolen, was a bad idea. He saw himself surrounded by armed police and flashing blue lights – he saw them shine when he closed his eyes – trying, as a runaway black boy with cocaine in his blood, to explain how he had come across this very expensive piece of jewellery that Rufus hadn't even shown him, and what honesty and grace he was showing by putting it back. Is that what Rufus thought of him? Is that why he'd picked him up?

Jesse had gone to the Coleherne looking for a white daddy who could take care of him; whether he'd known it at the time or not, that had been his aim. A near-fifty-year-old man in a suit jacket looked like a wad of cash, tasted of roast beef, felt like velvet, smelled of success. To Rufus, he was just a *roughneck brotha that can satisfy me*. Was that all Jesse was, a black boy? He didn't want the £100 on offer on completion of the job. He wanted a contract: to move to London and land on his feet. He wanted to have slipped through his family's fingers right into the lap of a Rufus. Lit by cocaine, Jesse floated up like a party balloon. He cringed as he recalled his own words: *You should be my boyfriend, you'd get dick all the time. I could move in here and help you. You're never gonna wanna let me go. I'm the best you'll ever have. I can get any man I want, I can. You should take me on while you've got the chance.*

Rufus's mood changed as he realised Jesse would not be taking on the job he was asking him to. An anxious frown appeared on his forehead, ageing his formerly supple skin. They went back and sat down on the settee at the coffee table. Jesse rolled a shaky spliff and Rufus chopped up quiet lines. When Massive Attack's 'Unfinished Sympathy' came on, Jesse started to feel sick. He hadn't eaten since a KFC after the FA Cup Final the previous afternoon, since when he'd had four beers, four lines and two spliffs – 4-4-2, like Arsenal's winning formation against Chelsea. 'Unfinished Sympathy' would always remind him of the day he found out who his father was.

Really hurt me baby. Really hurt me baby. Jesse's mother had never told him his father's name, or shown him a picture, just explained, once and for all, that he died when Jesse was small, and to forget about him, because his father rejected Jehovah and would never be getting a resurrection. He stopped paying attention in Maths, a subject that came less easily to him than English, and was moved down a year. Everyone laughed at him, because he was supposed to be clever yet was just a *stupid nigger* after all.

When the kids at school called him *that, rubber lips, coon, blackie* and *paki*, he came home, stared at himself in the mirror until he was full of anger and hate, put the hot tap on until it ran scalding and set to scratching off the black; the face-cloth wouldn't work, nor would his nails, so he stole a Brillo pad from under the kitchen sink and rubbed and rubbed until the foam went pink, but that made his skin sore, red raw. It healed back to black. None of the teachers could work out what was wrong with him.

He was nine. It was a sunny weekday afternoon at home, with the patio door open to a cool summer breeze. His mother was in the garden pegging up washing, with the twins playing on the lawn, and Jesse took the chance to sneak into a cupboard in the front room wall unit to search through her old photographs. In one of the orange Kodak folders was a picture of a young black man in a white shirt, sitting on the floor against a wall, looking up at the light coming from the window. Jesse studied the picture very closely, squinting his eyes as if *they* were out of focus, rather than the photo itself. He wiped his thumb over it, clearing it of dust. It had that way about it that all old pictures did, of being golden and soft. He studied the shape of the man's eyes, large and wide, with whites as white as his irises were dark. He was barefoot, and handsome, with high cheekbones and thick eyebrows. Jesse also had thick eyebrows, similar-shaped eyes, and high cheekbones. He didn't look like his mother. If he could get to a mirror.

He felt her presence behind him in the doorway.

Hey, hey, hey, hey!

She slapped him around the head and snatched at the picture just as he gripped onto it, ripping it in two on the twist. She froze, retaining the half with his face on. He scrunched his eyes shut to make sure he would always retain it in his mind.

'Look what you've done!' she screamed. They fought; he knocked off her glasses; she scratched his neck, grabbing the other half of the photo away from him.

'Was that mar dad?' he said, defiantly, rubbing his ringing ear as he stood up and bit back tears.

'Mind your business, boy!' She showed her teeth, and raised the back of her hand again in warning.

'Fe me dad fe me business!' he shouted back, surprised at his angry patois, running up the stairs. On Radio 1, Simon Mayo cut to his *Confessions*. In his bedroom, with the door slammed shut and the chest of drawers pushed in front of it, Jesse got under the covers and pretended he was dead, as if his mother had miscarried him, as if he was a tiny dead baby and nobody had ever heard of him. He was waiting for her to come upstairs with the belt, the slipper, the hairbrush, the air freshener, the net curtain cord, anything to beat him with, but the girls were crying in the garden so she had to run to them.

He remembered, when she miscarried on the floor of the wool shop, how Graham rushed to the hospital from work and, for the first time, she didn't mind him tucking himself into bed next to her in his filthy work clothes. She cried into Graham as if Jesse had been no comfort at all. Graham looked after Jesse at home, that first night, just kept the television on and made him beans on toast. The day after that, he let Jesse lie against him, with his arm around him, while they watched television together until late into the night. He didn't bother to change out of his dirty work clothes. The next morning, Jesse woke up with an ache, a beautiful ache, unable to remember his dreams. Jesse's mother didn't seem to like it when they went to visit her and she asked what they'd been doing, and Graham said, 'We've just been cuddlin' up on the settee watchin' the telly, int we, lad?' After that, Jesse was sent to stay with Graham's parents.

Sister McCarthy hoped to train Jesse like a pet, giving him instructions and speaking in a firm tone, then saying, *Good boy!* when he'd done what she asked, rewarding him with lollipops. Brother McCarthy's disability didn't stop him hobbling out on field service, which was the only exercise he got. Otherwise he sat in his armchair watching cricket or horse racing (though as a man of God he didn't gamble any more). They had a big dog and Jesse was petrified of it. He was scared of the washing machine too, because – like its owner – one of its feet was broken so it clattered on spin within the confines of the kitchen, making Jesse fear it would explode.

They let his mother out of the hospital after a week. He remembered how all the Sisters in the congregation came round to comfort her, bringing cupcakes, doughnuts and Victoria Wood shows taped from the TV. He remembered how they prayed for her, brought her pink roses, white carnations and purple chrysanthemums, and babysat him. He remembered, when black Sisters came round, they laughed and tried to stay happy, but when white Sisters came round, they cried and stayed sad out of respect. They brought chocolates and flowers but forgot about basic needs like milk. So when his mother made him breakfast that first morning back from the hospital, when she still couldn't bring herself to wash, she knowingly poured milk that was off on to his cornflakes and threw his bowl down on the table so that some spilt. It tasted so horrible, he thought he'd made his mouth bleed somehow. He had to pinch his nose so that he couldn't smell or taste it. His breakfast tasted like a bag of Opal Fruits had been mixed together with the milk. *She feeds me rainbow milk*, he said to himself. *She wants me to die.*

That evening when Graham came home from work, Jesse could hear his mother downstairs, sobbing. *Sneaking about when my back's turned and going through my stuff! I've got no privacy, Gray!* Their babies were unsettled. Esther was struggling with her eczema. Jesse's stepfather came upstairs into his room and warned him never to speak to his mother like that again.

'Like wha'?' Jesse said.

His stepfather left the room as if he would otherwise lose control of himself. It was all very well, his mother marrying a white man who worked hard and loved to dance, but at the beginning at least, Graham McCarthy wasn't the type to beat his or anyone else's children. Only at his wife's nagging did he reluctantly apply his physical strength to Proverbs 13:24. *Whoever spares the rod hates their children, but the one who loves their children is careful to discipline them.* Thus he formally instructed his stepson to bend over the foot of his marital bed – there was no space for a man of his size to raise a belt in Jesse's room – and to take down his trousers and pants, removing his belt to lash Jesse half a dozen times, telling him, in a calm low voice, not to answer his mother back or upset her again, and to learn some respect for his elders, who loved him. Once he got used to the hard leather, Jesse bent out his back as he waited for each lash, clutching fistfuls of the bedcovers. No lash stung for more than a couple of seconds.

Unless Jesse was in trouble and needed to be punished, it seemed that Graham hid from his adoptive son. Jesse had heard the sorts of things his stepfather's work colleagues asked about his mother. It was as if Graham was ashamed to be seen with him, except on the field ministry, and those were the rare occasions they could be alone together, on Saturday mornings or Sunday afternoons, though Graham refused to talk about Jesse's mother. *She's my wife and I have to stick by her*, he said once, and that had been enough.

Jesse felt they might have been closer if Graham hadn't been kept away from him by his mother. They had never been allowed to do the things that fathers and sons regularly did, like going fishing on the River Tame, or going to the Albion to watch the football. Graham wasn't even really a football fan anyway, which put him in a minority of one among the Brothers of the congregation, who, even while they quoted scriptures warning against idolatry, were openly worshipful of the Baggies' Number 9.

Lukasz, the Polish builder in the bunk above him, turned in his sleep, making the slats beneath his mattress bow. Jesse lay still, waiting for them to snap and Lukasz to crash down. With Rufus, it had been his first time feeling a man's true weight on top of him. He had come in Jesse's mouth and fallen asleep, leaving him lying awake. He could still feel his residue in his throat. Every time he thought about it, he cringed, then wished he could lick Rufus right where he couldn't possibly have. He'd wanted to be right in the centre of London; right in the eye of the storm. He worried that it was the wrong time to leave his family for the unknown. He knew from the attacks on New

York and Washington that he could die at any time; that Jehovah could unleash his sovereignty, see that Jesse had rejected his faith and execute his most devastating wrath. He was having sex with men, the way men have sex with women, outside of marriage. Was this what he was going to be now? Would he be seen as a pagan and apostate? He had gone against everything that he had ever been taught.

He hadn't eaten in more than twenty-four hours, and wasn't sure what he was hungrier for: actual food; friendly, familiar faces; or, Rufus's now-withheld availability. It was too late to get up and bang around in the dark, or turn on the light. Would Lukasz wake up and try to kill him if he made a pass? It was as if he was still inside Rufus, when he wasn't. He *still* hadn't washed Rufus off himself, and wasn't sure that he ever could. He could *still* smell him in his nose hairs. He *still* closed his eyes and could see Rufus on all fours in front of him. He felt as if he'd eaten the tastiest plate of food in his life, only to be told he would never be served it again. Still, the *thought* of what they had done together was more than enough. He cleaned himself up in his dirty T-shirt, rolled over and shut his eyes tight.

She used to chop him with the handle of the comb when he answered back, or when he fidgeted too much when she was combing his hair through. When she was in a good mood, she would wet the comb first, and work a little oil through his hair; when she wasn't, she would drag the comb through the dry knots and cuss him for his flaky scalp.

Now she is chasing him through his school corridors, down from English past Drama and in front of the assembly hall, holding by its handle a McDonald's bun spatula, a wide, long sheet of aluminium the size of a tea service tray, designed to scrape the buns out of the flatbed toaster, curved at the edges so that employees would not think of it as a weapon. How can she run so fast in her nightie and slippers? Why is he running so slowly?

Her hair is long and straight, a weave worn in a high black pony-tail. She is wearing green eyeshadow and pink lipstick, baring her teeth. She is going to chop him on the arms, chop him in the head, chop him across the neck. She is chopping him on the arms, across his back, over his head, cracking his skull, drawing blood. Shards of bone are crashing to the floor at his feet; there are red splashes on the walls and all over her nightie.

Mum! Stop! Mum! Stop!

Just phone social services, a schoolfriend tells him as she calmly walks past.

Mum! Stop! You never used to be like this. She is chopping him in the neck. Chopping him down the middle of his spine. *You used to love me,* he tells her, sorrowfully. *We used to be together all the time. You used to stroke my head and tell me bedtime stories. You were patient with me when you were telling me the bible story about the beat-up man and I couldn't understand that the beat-up man wasn't the aggressor but the victim. That was before Graham came to live with us, and you changed! You forgot about me! Why did you start to hate me?*

He is on the floor. She is standing above him. *What happened to you? The weave doesn't suit you. Your hairline's too far back.* She raises up the bun spatula, in both hands, and the edge of it is blocking out the light. His eyes are falling out. He cannot see. Schoolfriends walk past. *Dunt Jesse's mum look pretty? I love 'er 'air.* The edge of the bun spatula comes down. His chest is open. He can see his lungs, his heart, his kidneys. Here he is. Here's Graham, dressed as Flash Gordon, come to save him.

What you doing, Val?

She is gone. Graham picks him up. They shoot up like a rocket, up through the ceiling, up into the sky, and Graham pushes Jesse's eyes back into their sockets. They look into each other's eyes. The ground they were standing on has come up with them, in a column. Into the stars. Up, up, and up, until Brother Frank Grimes watches them fall off the edge.

Chapter 4

Hunger focused his mind when he got up, just before ten. He quickly showered, brushed his teeth and put on fresh clothes. It was Monday and the hostel was quiet. He went down to the kitchen to eat cereals and drink coffee from the buffet. It was large, the size of a small canteen kitchen, with wall-to-wall cupboards, an American-style fridge and separate chest freezer. Every storage space was filled with someone's labelled Tupperware. He poured a bowl of Coco Pops, drew a cup of coffee and sat down in the adjacent dining room.

A tanned and tattooed, blue-eyed man in jeans and a grey T-shirt, probably about fifty, sat nearby drinking a cup of tea and reading the *Daily Express*, its front page dominated by the headline TOP TORY SACKED FOR RACE OUTRAGE; the jubilant Arsenal players on its back page screaming I DON'T CARE IF UNITED BEAT US 100-0. His forearms were as thick as legs of mutton. He caught Jesse looking at him, nodded, finished his mug of whatever he was drinking, quickly got up and left, taking his paper with him. Jesse wondered if he knew his button fly was undone.

He wondered what to do, physically, with himself. Where would he live? What would he do? What could he do? The idea of becoming a writer seemed fine, up to and not including the fact that he was a slim, young black man with a pretty face that should not be wasted at a desk. Writing could wait until he was old and had something to write about. Wouldn't he be better off, for now, doing something with his body? In any case, he couldn't do what James Baldwin was doing in *Another Country*, though he felt he had things in common with its main character – coincidentally called Rufus – a black jazz drummer on a downward spiral of poverty, prostitution and self-hatred. But he would never fall so low. He would always be in control, he thought to himself. He would never find himself, like Baldwin's Rufus, hungry, walking the streets of London looking for a man to take him in, fuck him and feed him, though from the perspective of this new time and place, Jesse couldn't yet imagine what a winter in such a big city might be like. Surely, by then, he would be settled, have made friends, and have a plan.

He walked down Earl's Court Road, checking himself out in shop windows, and stopped at an estate agent's. The rental prices of the flats on offer were astounding. He wanted to live by himself, and take hour-long showers if he wanted, just standing there, letting the hot water massage his shoulders and neck. He dreamed of cooking up a storm in his own kitchen, inviting friends round for dinner. Inside the estate agent's, beyond his reflection and the glossy photos of swanky apartments in the window, a man and a woman, both perhaps in their late twenties or early thirties, sat at their desks. In tandem they looked up at him through the window, then back down at their PC screens. They could tell he wasn't their kind of customer. She had straight dark blonde hair and wore a fitted purple dress under a grey blazer; he was a paler blond and wore a black suit with a red polka-dot tie. They spoke to each other without looking up; their mouths hardly moved, as though they had worked with each other for a long time and were attuned to each other's voices. Jesse looked down at his own outfit, at the jeans and bomber jacket that probably stank of weed, beer and sex. He wondered how these two had got their jobs, what their CVs looked like and what they'd worn to their interviews. The woman looked at him again, then snatched her glance away as if she could tell he was looking at them and not at the adverts in the window. The man clenched his jaw and picked up his phone, and Jesse hurried away.

He crossed the road and jogged up the stairs of the Internet café. He couldn't shake the feeling of being a runaway who should either find himself a reason to not be home, or go home. Home to him was jail-like. Despite somehow staying with his family until the age of nineteen he had never felt the freedom to get up and go to do whatever he wanted. He had left his family behind, but was not yet independent of mind; he could feel home, no matter where or how far he went, snatching him back, and he could feel the beating he was going to get. He walked with tight shoulders, as if expecting to be smashed on the back of the head. Everywhere around him were men who looked like Graham, and were of that strong, masculine, working-class type Jesse both fancied and feared. His instinct, even at the hostel, was to stay in bed until something outside of himself changed. He had to find a job, both for money and purpose. He knew he would be welcomed with open arms at any of the many branches of McDonald's, with his two and a half years' experience, but they would simply call up his previous branch – who would then find out where he was – for a reference. His former colleagues could not learn about his new life; it had to be a clean break.

McDonald's had kept him fed. He also made himself a regular at the Black Country Chippy in Great Bridge, where the local delicacy, battered chips, soaked up the salt and vinegar, but the dandelion and burdock was less sweet than he remembered from summer days on his infant school playground. He understood the benefits of working in a restaurant as far as keeping fed for free was concerned, but also knew that he couldn't live on fatty, fried food forever; it was thanks to his genes – clearly his father's rather than his mother's, a possible source of her resentment – that he stayed thin. He searched online for restaurant jobs in London, and Gilbert's, a French-style brasserie in Covent Garden, were advertising for a waiter with two years' experience in food and beverages. In the photographs, the staff wore immaculate white shirts and black ties, and looked like dancers, with straight backs, high chins, clear eyes and white smiles. The copy required him to be hard-working, and passionate about food and wine, for which *free staff meals* and *generous remuneration* were offered. His palate was amused by all the things he wanted to try – what was *foy-grass*? *Steak tar-tear*? What did oysters taste like?

He called the number, and a man named Richard answered. He sounded attractive, and as Jesse was still sitting in the Internet café he offered to go straight there for a chat. He emailed Richard his CV as requested and checked the Tube map on the back of his *A-Z*. Covent Garden was an easy journey, eight stops up the Piccadilly line, but the price of the ticket made his jaw drop. He paid the unsmiling, mute attendant and her nails an outrageous £6.20 for a one-day Travelcard, Zones 1-2, and took the lift down to the platform with a scared-looking little white woman and her muzzled black wolf-dog. The Cockfosters train clattered in straight away; he checked around to see if anyone else was laughing. He stepped into the carriage as several people got off, and a woman kissed her teeth at him for pushing on. He sat down and hung a strap of his rucksack over one knee. In front of him, a rolled-up copy of *The Times* was tucked in the gauze side pocket of a bag between tan Timberland boots and light blue jeans. A sleeping, silver-haired man, probably about fifty, couldn't close his legs because of the size of his packet. Rufus was still in Jesse's air – the rushes of the coke and poppers still occasionally moving through his body like a song stuck in the head – but the man with the big box woke up with red eyes at the next stop and got off.

*

Opposite the Albery Theatre, Gilbert's was grander than any restaurant he had ever walked into, brightly lit, with plants, mirrors and ceiling fans, and gold lettering on the window. He arrived on time and was approached at the door by a thin brunette with grey buck teeth, wearing a trouser suit. She looked him up and down and said, *Can I help you?* When he said he was there for an interview, she told him to sit at the bar, facing a wall of bottles, and offered him a glass of water with a choice of still or sparkling. He went for the latter and the bartender, a curt young man with a gelled quiff, asked him if he wanted ice, which sounded like a threat, while the receptionist spoke on the phone, presumably to Richard. The bartender placed a tumbler in front of him on the bar with a black square napkin and merely twitched an eyebrow when Jesse thanked him. Several waitresses – one of them black – were scuttling around setting up. The tables were dressed in immaculate white cloths, with perfectly folded linen napkins, sets of shiny silver cutlery and tall, globe-like wine glasses. The chairs were upholstered in burgundy velvet. Impressionistic paintings of moustachioed black-tie waiters with white cloths draped over their arms, and still lifes of fruit, cheeses, hams and wine, were picked out by spotlights. A flower arrangement stood in a ceramic blue vase on the corner of the marble-topped bar; he recognised the pink peonies and purple gladioli. In the background, a slow, vibrato-rich female jazz vocal simmered. There was a vinegary smell about the place, still an improvement on old shortening and McD cleaning products. The bartender polished champagne flutes, checking them through narrowed eyes under the hanging lamps. He and the receptionist were talking about someone.

'Poor fet bitch try to lose weight but she can't,' said the bartender, who tended to overenunciate the letters *d*, *t*, and *s*, and to gesture a lot; doing so in a confined space with thin-stemmed wine glasses in his hands made Jesse feel uncomfortable. 'Every day she nearly knock somebody drink off as she try to squiz around de taybows.'

'If I was a customer I'd be scared of 'er eatin' me dinner on 'er way upstairs,' said the receptionist, a slither of black bra visible underneath her shirt.

'And de hair? Babes. I keep say to her, is time!'

'Oh my God! Innit weird 'ow some people are completely bald and some others just have way too much of it?'

The phone rang, and the receptionist sauntered over to answer it, swinging her hair round her shoulder to clear her ear. Jesse couldn't tell whether it was damp or just greasy, and looking at the waitresses, thought how he immediately disliked the uniform; contrary to that suggested in the advert, it was a navy blue shirt with a tie the same colour but a different, slightly waffled texture; black trousers and shoes, and a white apron. They all had medium-length hair tied back primly in black bands and wore minimal make-up. He could tell the black girl knew he was there and was deliberately not looking at him. It seemed he would be the only boy-waiter. Sometimes he worked the breakfast shift at McDonald's with only girls, so he would have to take in the deliveries and pack the walk-in freezer full of boxes of burgers, buns and fries, because they were considered to be boys' jobs. He spun round on his stool with a smile as a paunchy, sleazy-looking man with stubble, gelled hair and thick-lensed spectacles approached and held out his hand.

'Jesse?'

'Yeh?' Jesse's smile faded quickly as he jumped down to accept the handshake.

'I'm Richard, thank you for coming. How are you?'

Jesse instinctively looked downwards. Richard's belt was too tight, his trousers were too low and his shirt had been hurriedly tucked in, so he was showing a triangle of hairy underbelly. Massive packet, though.

'I'm very well, thank you,' he said. 'How are you?'

'Ah, well. You know. Not bad,' Richard said, putting his hands on his hips and making Jesse wonder whether he should ask if he was sure. The bartender made some sort of snorting sound he didn't try hard enough to conceal.

First Richard introduced all the staff who were on, and oddly, where they were from: Gemma, the receptionist, from Croydon, who pretended to be busy flicking through some sort of diary at the front desk; Vitor, the bartender, from Porto, simmering like a soap-opera villain; then the waitresses, starting with Élodie, Marion and Claudia, all from Bordeaux. Élodie looked up, pouted and looked down again as she crouched down to adjust a wobbly table; Marion sort of flickered a cheek in Jesse's direction as she stocked up a station with freshly folded napkins; Claudia was polishing cutlery from a metal bucket, which was the source of the vinegary smell. They all looked young – even Gemma didn't look much older than twenty-one – but there was a certain choreographed aloofness about them as a group. Jinny (he assumed it must be spelt), who was from Brixton, seemed to be looking around for something to do. She caught his eye, shyly, as he turned to follow Richard, and before Élodie told her, quite sharply, to check that the customer toilets were well stocked with paper and hand soap. Richard led Jesse down some tricky service stairs, talking blandly about it being constantly busy, with never a quiet shift, interrupting himself to introduce the fire escape, where deliveries were dropped off, and outside which staff were allowed to smoke. Various storerooms and cupboards were stocked floor to ceiling with tablecloths, waiter pads and cleaning products. The poky staff changing room featured lockers, a full-length mirror and a side-toilet.

The kitchen already felt busy though there were no customers yet. Soggy cardboard boxes lay flat in front of the sink, and men dressed in whites were running around preparing their stations. The tall and thin head chef, called Farid, was trimming bloody meat on a red board and couldn't shake Jesse's hand; nor could the short and stout sous-chef, Reda, who was filleting fish on a blue one. They were both Algerian, with bad teeth and patchy beards. While most of the upstairs staff were white, everyone in the kitchen was brown or black, including the friendly, soaking wet, dark-skinned man washing pots; he and Jesse smiled at each other before Jesse followed Richard into a tiny office next to the kitchen, crammed with paperwork, coats, unpacked crockery and a fusebox of flashing coloured lights.

A printout of his CV lay in front of Richard on the desk. Jesse was disconcerted that the font was unaccountably different from the one he had designed it with. He took the worn-looking, crumby seat offered him, brushing it off with the back of a hand just before his bum fell on it. Half-eaten packets of various branded biscuits and a grab-bag of Cool Original Doritos were spread across the back of the desk, and the bin was full of empty Pepsi Max bottles. He could imagine Richard sitting at this desk for years, hitting company targets, forgetting about himself, getting fatter and fatter. Jesse was reminded of one particular, typical moment at McDonald's when an enormously obese woman chewing her own hair ordered a super-size Double Quarter Pounder with Cheese meal, nine chicken nuggets and a Dairy Milk McFlurry. *What drink would you like?* Jesse asked her. *Diet Coke*, she deadpanned, and when her order was ready, she sat by herself on a four-seater bench and smashed the lot in five minutes flat.

'So, you've just moved here, have you?' said Richard, as he clicked his mouse repeatedly and various spreadsheets flashed in and out of view.

'Yeh, just a few days ago.'

'Where are you living?'

'Earl's Court?'

'Nice area. Have you moved here on your own?'

'Yeh.'

'From?'

'The Black Country.'

'Yes, I thought so. How old are you?' He looked down at Jesse's CV. 'Nineteen eighty-two?'

'Nineteen.'

'So it'll be your birthday, soon?'

'In a couple a weeks, yeh.'

'It's a very brave thing to do, isn't it, moving here by yourself? Are you studying anything?'

'Norrat the moment.'

'So you're looking for a full-time job in the meantime? Save a bit of money?'

'Yeh.'

'It says here you've most recently been working at McDonald's?'

'Yeh, I was there for two years. I got five stars and was promoted to Training Squad,' Jesse said, sitting up straight. He recalled a teacher at junior school nodding at him as her choice for Head Boy, and all the other boys turning round and scowling at him.

'Surely it would be easier for you to get a job at one of the branches down here? This is a very different kind of restaurant, where grace, conviviality and politeness are bywords.' He spoke as if verbatim from a managerial handbook.

'But you said in the advert full trainin'd be provided,' Jesse said, worriedly.

'It is, but on the assumption the bare minimum is already in place,' Richard said. 'What hours are you available to work? Full- or part-time?'

'How many hours is full-time?'

'Forty-eight. And then I'd ask you to sign an agreement to opt out of the maximum forty-eight-hour week, because sometimes we'll need you to work fifty-five or sixty. Because we're so busy, I need my staff to be flexible and available,' he said. Sixty hours sounded like a lot of money. It also allowed a hundred and eight hours per week of freedom. 'A high-volume quality place like this has to be staffed by people who know what they're doing, and it's like that ten-thousand-hour rule – the more you do something, the better you become at it. It's a big menu, a long wine list, there's a lot to learn. It's all about speed, directness and lightness of touch. You need to be on the ball. It's great training for anything else you might want to do in life, to be able to think on the hoof and hold a lot of different scraps of information in your head. I hire girls because they're better at multi-tasking, and as long as they're blonde and smile every so often they'll be forgiven for being a bit matronly. Do you think you're up to all that?'

'Erm, yeh,' said Jesse, though he was aware he didn't quite know what he was saying yes to, and thought perhaps Richard saw this.

'Well, you're clearly not stupid,' Richard said, scanning Jesse's GCSE results. 'A-grades in English literature, Art, History. Sounds like you're the creative type. Why aren't you at university?'

Jesse thought about the day he received his GCSE results and took them home to show his mother, hoping she would be impressed. It could not have been a hotter or sunnier August day, yet she was in front of the fire with her nightie on, the door and windows shut tight. He knocked, and when she didn't answer, he invited himself in. The heat and smell almost knocked him back. He held out the envelope over her shoulder, and spoke to her calmly and politely, but she didn't take her eyes off the TV. As if she had been offered one of the last of a tin of chocolates, all the best ones gone, she plucked the envelope from his fingers apathetically, and taking out the papers, glanced at each with her nose and mouth scrunched up. When she was finished, she gathered them back up, threw them out across the floor and wordlessly refocused her attention on the TV. Jesse, heartbroken, got down on his knees and collected them as he looked up into her face, and watched her watching *Home and*

Away as if nothing had happened. He could see that she knew what she was doing. That there was a laugh in her eyes.

'I int decided wharra want to do yet. My parents are Jehovah's Witnesses, and they discourage 'igher education.'

Richard raised his eyebrows. 'Alright, look. I'm not sure whether this is the right thing for you or not, but why don't you come in for a trial shift tomorrow, just for a couple of hours, and we'll see how you get on. 11.45 for a midday start. Wear black shoes and trousers, the rest will be provided.'

'Thank you!' said Jesse, picking up his rucksack and rushing out of the muggy office.

He walked out into the warm sunshine, with a job all but secured and the rest of the day to himself. It was as if the whole of London was resting with its hands behind its head on a grassy bank. He switched CDs in his Discman, from 'Freak Like Me' to the N*E*R*D* album *In Search Of*. Artists drew with chalk on the pavement outside the National Gallery. Open-topped buses carried tourists in T-shirts and baseball caps, not really taking it all in but desperately twisting their bodies in every direction to get that picture they needed to show friends back home where they'd been. Red buses carried adverts saying BEAT THE QUEUE AT MADAME TUSSAUDS! Policemen walked in pairs with their hands tucked into their vests, as if protecting their nipples against irritation from the stiff Kevlar. He wasn't sure if he was expecting his mother and Graham to have reported him missing, but the two policemen showed no interest in him as he walked by thinking about an article he'd seen in a news-paper covering a May Day rally, where all kinds of cults seemed to converge on Trafalgar Square against capitalism and stirrings of war – SEX WORKERS ACROSS THE WORLD UNITE said one banner, danced around by cyberpunk milkmaids with shaved heads. According to his *A-Z*, he was very close to Buckingham Palace, so headed down The Mall to see if he might catch the

Queen talking on the phone in her bedroom window or coming back from the shops. He couldn't believe he was breathing the same air as her. A lot of people seemed to have had the same idea; families, and groups of tourists, speaking any kind of language – afraid to lose each other in a foreign city – posed for peace-sign pictures in front of her gates and her bearskin-capped guardsmen. Disappointingly, she was away on her Golden Jubilee tour, he overheard another policeman, also covering his nipples, say. He crossed through Green Park and up Piccadilly, a broad and spacious avenue of bookshops and boutiques, with double-height tea rooms and well-dressed doormen. He came out on Piccadilly Circus. Samsung. McDonald's. Carlsberg. TDK. *Imagine all the people living life in peace.* Boots. Gap. Burger King. Fountains. Camcorders. Polaroids. Ahead of him was the promised glitz of Leicester Square. He remembered what Rufus had told him about Sue Lawley, new in London, being shamed for her Black Country accent and realising she would have to change it in order to get by. He wondered how Rufus was, whether he was okay, whether he'd been able to find anyone else to do his dirty work, how stupid he must've assumed Jesse to be if he thought a good fuck would blind him to all sense and lead him to sacrifice his future.

Wear black shoes and trousers, Richard had said. Oxford Street, he'd heard, was the main shopping street, so he followed his *A-Z* down Regent Street, a beautiful curve of grand stone buildings and a Ferrari showroom, again, pestered by gaping tourists posing for pictures in front of the cars. He went into Topman at Oxford Circus, where, right on cue, the radio edit of 'Freak Like Me' came on. Everywhere he looked, his eye fell on handsome, effeminate, immaculately dressed shop assistants who sized him up then turned away. He bought a pair of basic black trousers in a size twenty-eight and a pair of cheap, smart black shoes, then headed north to Tottenham Court Road, another famous London address he'd heard of, that turned out to mainly comprise of electrical shops, so he turned back straight down Charing Cross Road, hovering by a side street full of musical instrument shops and specialist record shops, finding on the main road a huge two-floor Internet café.

He ate a burger and chips at a window table in All Bar One and watched single-sex couples turn on to the street opposite and start holding hands, as if they had reached their safe place, which was a revelation to him; he wondered whether he would ever feel comfortable enough to be so publicly engaged with a man, and who that man might eventually turn out to be. Every few seconds a man walked past the window and made eye contact with him. He had never in his life seen a black man hold hands with another man, white or otherwise, and had barely even seen a black man hold hands with a woman. He tried to remember if he'd seen a black man kiss someone on a TV show or in a film.

He left All Bar One, crossed onto the street where the gay couples were headed – Old Compton Street, it was called. On the corner was a bar called Molly Moggs, where he could see through the windows a tall blond man with very thin eyebrows reading a magazine on the bar, while several retired-looking men sat on stools drinking pints. Opposite, Ed's Easy Diner, styled after a classic American burger shack, was pumping The Four Tops' 'Reach Out (I'll Be There)' as good-looking foreign people sat outside in their sunglasses. He watched through the window of an amusement arcade a teenage boy clattering loudly in his cheap shoes on a dance-step machine. The Prince Edward Theatre was showing *The Full Monty*. He stopped by a place with a big purple-and-gold front, called G-A-Y, which had piles of free gay magazines stacked up in its entrance. He took one of each to put in his rucksack. A line of fruity-looking men drinking coffee outside Caffè Nero watched him walk by.

The Admiral Duncan, another bar decked with a rainbow

flag, was virtually empty; a ginger-haired man in a white vest was laughing and wiping his finger down the bar as if to check for dust. There was no one to tell him he couldn't walk into a bar and order a half-pint on a Monday afternoon. He crossed the road and walked into Comptons of Soho, the most inviting-looking of the bars with its window boxes and proud flag, where a couple of men in jeans were drinking and smoking outside, just like at the Coleherne.

There were only a few in, mostly older men, one of them a middle-aged punk dressed in neon, with too many studs, piercings and tattoos; another, businesslike in his suit, was perhaps on a lunch break from his office. The same kind of soulful dance music was playing as at the Coleherne, but at a lower volume. It was dark coming in from the sunlight, and Jesse leaned on the sticky bar, again horseshoe-shaped. The best-looking man in there was tall and stocky, perhaps a construction worker, standing the other side of the bar in a red hoodie, drinking a pint of Guinness. They made eye contact. Jesse showed his ID to the bartender, ordered half a lager and flicked through one of the free magazines. The back pages had been reserved for classified listings, mostly men looking for men. It excited Jesse that he could meet a man, anywhere at any time, just by calling a number. Some of the men seemed to be advertising themselves in exchange for money. They showed their arses, or the sizes of their dicks, in jockstraps or leather trousers. They were upfront about what they did and did not do, and how much they would cost – a hundred pounds an hour here, five hundred a weekend, there. There was even a plumber, his face marked with God-knows-what, clutching a U-bend in one hand, the other stuffed down his overalls. Jesse thought to himself, could he be paid for sex, like the boys in the basement across the road from the hostel? What difference would it make, if he was already having sex for pleasure with random men, to be paid for it?

He and the man in the red hoodie looked up at each other

again. There was one black man advertising in the magazine, with a ring through his nose, every single muscle defined and glistening, his enormous dick stuffed into a minuscule pouch, the whole thing resembling a tapir's nose. It looked like, and possibly was, the man who had nodded at him in the Coleherne when he was about to leave with Rufus.

'Where are the toilets, please?' he asked the bartender, who pointed towards the back of the bar.

There was a bleachy smell on top of the decades of bodily fluids soaked into the walls and floors. The man with the red hoodie drinking Guinness at the bar followed him in and stood next to him at the damp dripping urinal, his thick pink lips hanging open, his dick already hard in his freckled hand. After the bland bitterness of the beer it tasted like melted butter. They crashed through a cubicle door and slammed it behind them. The man pulled down his cargo pants and turned to face the door, spat on his hand and reached behind himself. Jesse pushed inside him – with some of his own spit, viscous from the beer – and fucked his squashy arse up against the door, reaching up under his clothes to find a sexy nipple ring; when Jesse was finished, the man said nothing, merely pulled up his trousers and walked out. He'd already left by the time Jesse came back into the bar to finish his pint. Everyone turned round to look at him, admiringly.

Chapter 5

May 7, 2002

He was to be trained by Marion. She had dirty blond hair and wore little make-up, and stood with her hands on the back of a chair at what she called table four, which was set for five people. Jesse clasped his hands behind his back as the other waitresses, Élodie, Claudia, Jinny and Patrizia (the runner), chatted among themselves getting everything ready for service. Vitor was stocking up his bottles; Gemma was on the phone. Jesse was trying to catch Jinny's eye but she was following Élodie around and wouldn't look at him.

'Rishar say you don't ave a lot of expérience so I ouill go froo everyfin wiv you,' Marion said, with a husky voice. 'Ouen ve guest arrive' – she said *guest* instead of *guests*, as a Jamaican would – 'Jhomma take vair coat and jackette and sit vem wiv ve menu and ouine list. She offair vem still, sparkling or ouatair from ve tap, and put froo ve till. You keep your eye on ve dispense bar, and if dair is ouatair dair, you fetch it and pour it at ve tâbl, alouays startin ouiv ve ouoman, clockouise, and ovair dair right shouldair.'

Jesse nodded, though he wasn't sure how much of this he would remember.

'Aftair you pour all of ve ouatair, or at ve same time if you feel confidon, you discrètely try to get ve tâbl attontion to tell vem ve spécial of ve day, and anyfin on ve menu vat is atty-six.'

'That's wha?' said Jesse, fretting that he'd missed something.

'Ouen somefin ouee don't ave on ve menu, vat finish, in restaurant ouee say is atty-six.'

She drew the numbers 8 and 6 in the air in front of him with an index finger.

'Eighty-six? Why's it called tha?'

She turned down the corners of her mouth and shrugged, holding out the palms of her hands and shaking her head.

'You offair ve tâbl an apéritif, but vey might not ave time to look at ve menu yet. Sometime vey ave a standard apéritif, for éxompl a Martini or a jhin and tonic, and ouee ave a lot of regulair customair so sometime you ouill learn ouat is vair fâvourite drink. You put ve apéritif ordair froo ve till, ven leave vem to contomplât ve menu until ve drink are ready at ve bar. You take a tré from ve bar and load ve drink ve ouay vey have been laid out on ve bar. Vat is vairy importon, because sometime vair is two drink on ve bar vat look exactly ve same and one of vem might be vodka and ve ovair jhin and we sairve bof of vem ouiv limon so ve only ouay to tell ve différence is to put vem on ve tray exactly as vey ave been laid out on ve bar, ouich should be accordin to ve tickette. You ven serve ve drink, again ve ouoman first, clockouise, ovair dair right shouldair. Ouen you finish you put ve tré on ve shelf on ve stassion, ven come back ouiv your pad and pen, and you should already ave written down ve nombair of ve pairson in a column in ve middle of ve pâge, wiv a circle around it for ve ouoman.'

She looked at him.

'Ouee ouork ouiv posission nombair. You don't ouork ouiv posission nombair before?'

'How you can be waiter if you can't open bottow of wine?' Vitor asked Jesse, loudly, in front of the customers, as Richard came up the stairs and on to the restaurant floor to see how he was doing. Jesse hadn't taken into account that this would be part of his job. He'd never even drunk wine; Graham drank lager, as did Jesse's mother, but with blackcurrant. Wine was partaken by the anointed during the Passover. Vitor held up his hands in consternation.

'I thought you had hospitality experience,' said Richard.

'I have, in McDonald's,' said Jesse, so Richard took him through how to open a bottle of house red, while Vitor paced up and down the bar with his jaw clenched. After Jesse crumbled one cork in half out of tentativeness, Vitor slammed a second bottle down on the bar, which Jesse popped clumsily and spilt all the way down his apron, cutting his thumb on the foil.

'Hahahai meu Deus!' Vitor turned away, shaking his head and laughing incredulously. Jesse had seen him topless in the changing room, and he was skinny, but ripped. He knew nothing of Portuguese, and so Vitor could've been saying anything, calling him a stupid nigger or a black bastard.

'Vitor, pipe down,' said Richard. 'There's a first-aid box behind the bar. I'll get you another apron.'

There was a spell, for an hour or more, when it felt like the whole of London was coming in. Some of the customers reminded him of hunting dogs, trotting in with their noses in the air. Marion directed him with incessant tasks, many of which she ended up performing herself, though he insisted on opening all the wine so that he could learn. He was left-handed but it felt more natural to operate the corkscrew with his right. The first glass he poured was almost to the brim when the customer, an older woman with big blow-dried hair, put out her hand and said, *Stopstopstopstopstop!* Marion rolled her eyes and marked with the stub of her finger where to pour to. Her nails were bitten down almost to the quick. She and Élodie, who was training Jinny, glanced at each other across the room, but Jinny seemed to be doing well, and now and then, smiled at Jesse encouragingly.

Marion sent him to new tables with menus, which he handed

out, taking it upon himself to say, *Allo, and welcome to Gilbert's*;
some of the customers appeared to find this funny. Every minute
he was being asked to reset a table, and was then told off when,
for example, the tablecloth was longer on one side than the
other. He was thirsty, and needed a piss, so asked to go to the
toilet, but was told *No*. He felt he was being pushed and pulled,
asked questions and then immediately told to shut up, poked in
the ribs then disciplined for laughing, but after Gemma passed
a message round to say they were *all in* – as in, everyone who
had booked was at their table – there seemed to be more time
to spend with the customers, which in his mind was the whole
point of the job. After all, this was a world of *grace, conviviality
and politeness*. The customers seemed to like him; one or two
asked him where his accent was from and what he was doing
in London. A woman with blonde hair bleached to the roots,
rouged cheeks, red lips and an enormous pink dress made a
gasping face as she beheld him.

'So beautiful!' she said in a high, airy voice, in front of her
guests, all men in suits, one or two of whom looked embarrassed, the others jealous. 'Come here, my darling! Oh, isn't
he just like a young Michael Jackson! What is your name?' She
took him by the hand, firmly pressing his fingers between hers.

'Jesse, madam.'

'Oh, just listen to his darling little accent! Where are
you from?'

'The Black Country, madam.'

'Where are your *parents* from?' she said, closing her eyes and
opening them again as if that was her original question.

'Me *grandparents* are from Jamaica, madam.'

'Of course, with your glowing skin and perfect teeth
and ...' – she looked him up and down – 'Oh, you're just
absolute perfection, aren't you, darling! Are you studying
something?'

'No, I've just moved here, madam, so I'm just settlin' in.'

'I just want to put him in my handbag!' she said to her men, who laughed with her, mechanically. He thought he could detect a glint in the eye of one of them, whose smile and eye contact lingered. She let go of Jesse's hand and turned away. Her handbag was next to her on the banquette. There was a dog in it, that he'd failed to notice before, a silent little terrier with a pink bow in its hair.

Marion shouted at him to run the drinks from the pass, more with her eyes than her voice. He didn't want to just rip himself away from this lovely woman, so even that took a beat longer than it needed to. The table numbers, which he had learned quickly, now eluded him. A too-thin young American with a too-short bob, a brace in her mouth and two little white pills next to her water glass screamed, *I didn't order that!* when he put a gin and tonic in front of her, and the whole room went quiet for a moment, the way it goes dark and still when the one cloud in the sky passes over the sun. The older man she was with scowled at Jesse as if he should be ashamed of himself, and put his hand on her shoulder to console her, but she flinched away. Marion redirected him with the drinks and told him not to go back to that table.

After two o'clock it slowed down a bit, as most of the suited customers had gone back to work, but Jesse was running, trying to win over the French girls, collecting glasses and clearing plates. Claudia told him off for taking away a man's plate while his guest was still eating. The woman with the silent little terrier had gone without saying goodbye, after spending most of her lunch talking on her rose-gold flip phone, drinking champagne rosé and feeding the dog scraps of smoked salmon from her plate with her pinky nail. He was disappointed she didn't seek him out before she left.

He went over to the service hatch to help Patrizia, who was swearing under her breath all the time in Italian, to run food but she told him, *No, I am fine! You don't understand, when you*

decide, you want to 'elp me, it make a problem for me! He wondered what he had done to upset her, but then a Nina Simone
song his mother used to play sometimes came on over the Bose
ceiling speakers, and he lip-synced and pirouetted around,
allowing his apron to float up like a dress. *Oh Lord, please don't
let me be misunderstooooooooooooooood.* The American with the
too-short bob turned and looked out of the window, but Jinny
was laughing quietly, and even the French girls, who had made
his ears burn all service, looked briefly enchanted.

'You're very much in your own little world, Jesse,' Richard
said in the office after Jesse's trial came to a close, 'and you'll
have to speed up – a lot – but I've seen that you are intelligent
enough to improve. You could be a breath of fresh air in here,
but you need to learn when you can entertain the customers and
when you need to knuckle down. Believe me, you don't want to
piss the Frenchies off.'

He saw Jinny on his way back to the changing room. She had
been sent to fetch a roll of blue paper from the store cupboard.

'How was your trial? Did you get the job?' Her voice
was high and childlike, and she spoke very quickly in her
London accent.

'Well, I've been asked to come back tomorra at 11.30, so I
suppose so,' he told her. She laughed. For the first time, with
the light shining down on her from upstairs, he saw how pretty
she was. She was very dark-skinned, with big white eyes, a flat
little nose, full, round lips and a tiny, doll-like chin. Where he
grew up, adults would say to children who pulled faces that if
the wind changed, they would be stuck like that forever, and
it was as if this had happened to Jinny while she was blowing
someone a kiss.

'What ya laughing for?' he said, smiling.

'Nothing,' she said, still laughing, and covering her mouth.
'Your accent's really sweet.'

'Thanks,' he said, bashfully.

She composed herself. 'Marion said to tell you if I saw you that you need to leave out of this door, because we're not allowed to walk back through the restaurant,' she said.

'Okay, I will, thanks. See ya tomorra.'

'Bye.'

She did that weird thing girls sometimes do, waving at him when he was still there.

He woke up in a panic, his hair flat on one side. He'd forgotten to set his alarm, and the weather had changed. Sometimes he liked the rain – in the spring and summer it made everything greener – but not when he didn't have protection, though if the city suit carrying the Dick Lovett-branded umbrella had offered theirs to him he wouldn't have taken it. Wet and out of breath, he got to work half an hour late after having to wait for a bathroom at the hostel, then enduring severe delays to the Piccadilly line due to the alarming circumstance of a *person under a train*. Nobody else in the carriage seemed to bat an eyelid as they sat in the tunnel for five minutes between Hyde Park Corner and Green Park.

Gemma, whose hair was still lank and greasy, told him as he walked through the front door, 'Go back out and use the staff entrance. Staff are not allowed to come in this way. And you're late.' He wanted to say, *I'm late because there was a person under a train*, but he thought she might say, *Yeah, yeah, black people are always late*.

He ran around to the side entrance, quickly changed into his uniform downstairs, and felt hungry; he'd left it too late to eat breakfast at the hostel. When he got back up to the restaurant floor everything was ready for service, the ceiling fans were on, some lazy old jazz music was playing – apparently for customer comfort, though he craved something more uptempo – and the French girls were speaking amongst themselves in their language at the front, waiting for the customers to start arriving for lunch. Jesse said *Good morning*, and they either didn't hear or were ignoring him. Gemma and Vitor were sharing their own conversation at the front of the bar, broken every so often as she answered the cordless phone to tell whoever was calling that it was fully booked.

'When do they serve the staff food here?' he asked Jinny, who was standing alone at the back of the restaurant like the new person at school no one wanted to talk to.

'Eleven o'clock,' she said.

'So why did Richard tell me to come in at half past?'

'That's when you get paid from,' she said. 'If you want to eat before, then it's up to you, but the food is served at eleven. It's like that in most places.'

'Why dint Richard tell me that? What was it?'

'Eggs, tomatoes and bread,' she said. 'And bare oil.'

He finished tying his tie. He could see now that her hair was not her own but a weave. She stared straight ahead, out at the rain coming down the front window behind GILBERT'S (backwards) in gold lettering, and seemed tense, as if she didn't want to be seen with him; he wondered whether the other staff had been cussing about him behind his back à la Vitor and Gemma and the *poor fet bitch*.

'How long have you been workin' 'ere?'

'Three days,' she said.

'Dunt ya like it?'

'It's a job.'

'Wharrelse d'ya wanna do?'

'I've applied to go to drama school in the autumn,' she said, brighter.

'Oh ar? Which one?'

'RADA, LAMDA and Central.'

He'd never heard of any of them. 'When'll ya know whether you've gorrin or not?'

'In the summer. I've got through to the workshop for all three, so here's hoping.'

'Which one d'ya most want to go to?'

'I'd be happy to get into any of them, but LAMDA's got the best reputation for developing young women in theatre,' she said, as if Jesse were interviewing her for the place.

'So you wanna be an actress? That's cool,' he said, his mind blank to that world. He had never been to the theatre, and wasn't allowed to watch much TV at home, so he really knew very little.

'How about you?' she said.

He thought about *Giovanni's Room*, the way David saw his own reflection, wearing only a dressing-gown and holding a tumbler.

'I think I wanna be a writer,' he said, out loud for the first time in his life. It made sense. He could write, to make sense of everything that had happened to him.

'That's great,' she said. She smiled, but didn't seem to Jesse all that impressed. 'What sort of writing?'

'I doe know,' he said. 'Poetry, fiction, novels.'

'Aww. Are you studying?'

'Norrat the moment,' he said. 'I'm just gonna work for a bit and settle into London.'

'Well, I hope you get what you want,' she said.

'And you too,' he said. He studied her smooth, dark brown skin. 'Where's ya family from?'

'Jamaica on my mum's side, Nigeria on my dad's. And you?'

'Fully Jamaican, I think. I never knew me dad.'

'Shame, me neither. He lives in Nigeria with his next wife.'

'Whereabouts?'

'Do you know Nigeria?'

'I know a bit about the history, like, the civil war and tha,' he said.

All the bodies in the school changing room were white or Asian.

'Black blokes am usually all stacked'n muscled, ay they,' Luke Reid said, 'but looka Jesse! *Skinny li'l Biafran.*'

Fifteen other boys looked Jesse up and down and dutifully laughed, even though a lot of them were obese or out of shape, but then Jesse took his pants off to shower – rejecting the towel he would usually hide behind so that the boys who had no dick at all, just a knob on balls, wouldn't feel bad about themselves – and the changing room fell silent. After that, instead of loafing around the school grounds with his classmates, some of whom had laughed at him, Jesse spent his lunch break in the school library, reading from the *Encyclopaedia Britannica* on hardly the most recent of African crises. It was a very specific insult, to be called a *skinny li'l Biafran*, one that showed knowledge, not ignorance. Jesse wondered how Luke Reid had learned about this corner of black history Jesse himself was completely ignorant of, and why he would then use it against him. Jesse asked himself if his real father had not died, whether he would have taught him about the black world, a history cruelly neglected by the GCSE curriculum. They said, *Go back to Jamaica then* when he told them he was Jamaican, not African.

His mother had married a white man, but how could a white man raise a black boy to be anything other than white, and to consider his blackness as a disability to endure? Graham had told him repeatedly to *just ignore'em*. Was it the duty of the white father or of the majority-white school to teach the black son about the facts of life and the order of things, how to see a world that will only look at him a certain way? Graham had taught him nothing about anything; he left Jesse, a black man's son, to the Bible, and doted instead on his pretty *half-caste* daughters.

Luke Reid was intelligent; he and Jesse were in all the same classes together. The two boys had in common the early deaths of their birth fathers. They could, and should, have been best friends. Perhaps, even lovers. There were rumours of Luke with other boys, but he could hide behind his girlfriend. He had thick red lips, a slim body and lived in a detached house; Jesse fancied him, and Luke probably knew it. There was no need for Luke – who was good-looking, the school's star striker, and going out with a popular girl Jesse was also friends with – to pick on Jesse, but Jesse began to understand, even then, that Luke was switching between personae in order to deflect unwanted attention from himself. In English class, Luke would say *are* and *aren't*, yet in the changing room said *am* and *ay*; he chose when and when not to speak properly, when other boys – who knew from a young age they were going to become panel-beaters or welders – spoke badly because they refused to learn how to speak well.

Their History class made no mention of Biafran secessionism or any other subject related to the lives and times of black people. It evangelised about the royal households and prime ministers, Britain's naval power, its empire, and all the good it did the world. The history of black people was not a mainstream subject, and would therefore become a weapon in the wrong mouth. Jesse felt it would not have been as bad if Luke had called him a *skinny li'l Ethiopian*, displacing him, as white kids had all his life, in the Live Aid-triggering famine of the mid-1980s, but Luke Reid had gone all the way back to the 1960s to humiliate Jesse. The only black people on TV were criminals, sportspeople or starving Africans; and it was with the latter that white bullies identified him.

'You should have punched him in the mouth,' said Jinny.

'It did mek me realise how white people assume we'm all the same,' said Jesse.

'I get stick from both sides,' she said. Jinny was not a skinny li'l Biafran. She was petite, with small, high breasts.

'What do you mean?' Jesse said.

'Nigerians are always saying Jamaicans are good-for-nothing but Jamaicans see themselves as being superior to Africans, as if they're not from there in the first place. Because we're not educated in black history, people don't know that. I was at my grandmother's house on the Jamaican side one day when I was about twelve, and we were watching some athletics on TV when a Nigerian guy came on to do the high jump, and my aunty said, *not bad-looking, for an African.* I told her she was African too and she told me to shut my mouth.'

'Do mix,' Richard said to them both as he came up the stairs and walked past the bar towards the reception desk. Jesse and Jinny both sneered at him.

'I applied for the job here under my proper name and didn't hear a thing,' she said, when Richard was out of earshot, talking to the French girls. 'Then when I applied as Jinny Redmond, with my mum's surname, he called me straight away.'

'What's your proper name?'

'Ginika Ndukwe,' she said.

'How do you spell that?' he asked.

'G-i-n-i-k-a, N-d-u-k-w-e,' she said, patiently.

'I bet you have to do that all the time. Nice to meet ya, Ginika. Arm Jesse McCarthy,' he said, and they shook hands. Hers was tiny, and delicate, and he held it loosely. One of the few things Graham had taught him was that he had to shake hands like a man.

'It's alright for you, Jesse McCarthy just sounds white, like you're Irish or something,' she said. 'I didn't change anything else about my CV, not even the font. I made myself sound less black, and he called me and said, *Hi! So you're gonna be a famous actress? You sound great! I'd love to meet you!* It was too late by the time I came in for the interview; he couldn't turn me away. Their shoulders must've dropped when another blackie turned up a day later, with an Afro!'

'I wonder who he thought was gonna turn up?' said Jesse, flattered that Ginika would say that about his small, uncombed mound of growth.

'Some blonde girl, like them, but English, importantly,' she said, subtly jutting her chin at the French girls. 'Whereas my full name sounds like an African queen who won't lift a finger!

I should have come to my interview topless with a headdress and a stick!'

They both laughed, and Jesse knew they would be friends.

'Which name did ya use on ya drama school forms?'

'My full name. In Igbo, Ginika means *God is the greatest*.' Then there was that pause, before the conversation took a more serious turn, which he knew only too well. 'Do you believe in God?'

'Okay, guys,' said Richard. 'Gather round for the briefing.'

There was the same immediate midday rush as the day before but this time the French girls seemed less willing to countenance his slowness. Customers barked instructions at him. He had learned the menu but not the ingredients. Vegetarians, and people with allergies, asked him questions and looked around for someone else when he couldn't answer. These were people who had an hour to eat their lunches and close their business deals. The waitresses were busy themselves and unwilling to help, so he ran quickly downstairs to the kitchen to ask Farid, who screamed at him: *Don't ask me any fuckin' question in the service I am fuckin' busy you fuckin' waiter need to learn fuckin' menu! Of course the egg they are not fuckin dairy! Cow they lay fuckin' egg? Fuckinell!*

Jesse was almost in tears when he got back to the restaurant floor to find Claudia pouring that table's wine, having already taken their order. Then he tried to carry a tray with dirty glasses on it to the bar, with one hand, like the French girls did and Ginika was now able to, and he could see that one of them was too close to another and making it tilt, and he thought he would get there, but he didn't, and couldn't save several glasses from toppling and smashing on the hard tiled floor. Just like the day before with the thin woman and the gin and tonic, the whole room went silent for a moment. Dutifully, and protectively, Ginika was right there with a dustpan and brush. She gave him a narrow smile, as if to say it was alright, that she, at least, was on his side.

Richard, who Jesse now knew spent most of his shifts down in the office stuffing his face and reading the Internet, came upstairs holding out a pair of very heavy-duty-looking black rubber gloves.

'Wilfred's had to leave us,' he said. It took Jesse a moment to realise who he meant. Wilfred was the kitchen porter, a Ugandan. 'We need someone in the pot-wash.'

All the girls turned quickly away and got on with their sections, except Ginika, still crouched down sweeping up glass, who looked up in concern. Gemma was at the desk, fetching jackets and umbrellas and grinning her grey buck teeth at departing guests. Vitor crouched down to check that the two glasses of red wine he was pouring were exactly the same. A snigger came from the nose of the very beautiful, flat-chested girl in a short black dress, with her legs crossed and her dangling foot tucked behind her calf, sitting at the table next to where he and Richard were standing.

'Pardon?' said Jesse.

'We need you to be our new kitchen porter. Temporarily,' said Richard. He had a blank look on his face as if to say, *You're doing this, or you don't have a job.* His nose was in the air like the guests who reminded Jesse of hunting dogs.

'I applied for the waiter job,' he said, his entire body hardening as if an ancient hormone had been released into his bloodstream. There was a sense of an old work horse being replaced, and Jesse didn't like it at all.

'Just until we replace Wilfred, then with a bit of training, you'll be back on the floor,' he said. 'Take the gloves, please. We need someone down there straight away.'

BRUCE GROVE

Chapter 1

December 25, 2002

He'd wriggled out of his T-shirt, socks and underwear during the night and kicked them down the bed. The weather had been disappointingly mild and sunny for several days, and pale yellow light leaked around the edges of the slatted blind behind him. Teased by the smell of frying bacon from downstairs, he sat against his headboard smoking a cigarette, pulling the duvet high up over one shoulder. He had been dreading Christmas. He stubbed out the cigarette, but found he couldn't remember how the last few drags had felt, and wondered if he might not light up another straight away.

One of his housemates, Owen, a late-to-bed, early-to-rise kind of man, was also home. They hadn't discussed spending Christmas *together*, but both knew neither had made other plans. Owen's polished black boots thumped dully on the timber floors downstairs, his two daughters' presents waiting, wrapped in blue and gold, by the front door since the night before. He had come to the house in August, and Jesse had first viewed the room in September. While Bryan, a Canadian jobbing actor with a blank smile, greeted Jesse in the hallway, Owen stood in the background smiling shyly. He was five eleven, with pale grey eyes and dark, almost black hair side-parted. He was effortlessly handsome, friendly and polite. Within ten seconds, Bryan had made the 'Jesse Owens' link, and Jesse decided he would take the room. They didn't seem to mind what he did for a job, and indeed found it exciting, unlike some of the others, whose dirtier, smaller, pricier house-shares he had viewed, and who assumed Jesse would prove unreliable.

In the first month or so of living together, Jesse and Owen ran into each other casually, often in the kitchen as Jesse arranged his bowl of beans with an egg, or his pork chops and spinach, while Owen cooked a stir-fry or risotto. Bryan was cast in a play in Manchester, the biggest job of his career so far, so Jesse and Owen were left alone.

Owen's smile, which Jesse never saw him without, always made him feel welcome, and they got to know each other a little, though Jesse shrunk away from him after *that man*.

Owen was from the Wirral, and had lived in London since graduating from Cambridge, but still spoke with a Scouse accent. He wrote poetry and taught creative writing at University College London. Jesse could tell Owen liked him, but he doubted anything could develop; Owen was eleven years older than him and led a complicated life, separated from his wife. He was a laugher and a talker, often drifting from subject to subject, keeping Jesse rapt. Both admitted to moving to Bruce Grove because the name sounded like someone they wanted to sleep with. Sometimes, Owen would get drunk while marking papers at the kitchen table. He said he needed to drink to have the confidence to talk to men, despite his looks, masculinity and intelligence. He'd catch guys on Gaydar back home from clubs in Soho or Vauxhall, and drive to see them in the early hours when there was less traffic. One afternoon in an Internet café, Jesse wondered whether Owen had come across his profile, and immediately removed his most explicit pictures, saving them to a private album instead.

They hadn't spoken in a while, not really, since *that man*. Jesse heard the front door close, got out of bed, put on his dressing-gown and the pair of socks from within his bedding, went for a pee then tiptoed down the stairs. He loved being alone in this house, with its wooden floors, high ceilings and mid-century coat stand in the hallway, as then he could pretend it was his own. He opened the fridge to the gold foils of six bottles of champagne, a joint of something, some mushrooms, a Christmas pudding and various cheeses. He had some chicken thighs in the freezer to roast and eat with spinach and boiled rice. The frying pan was still on the stove, and he picked out and ate the crispy titbits of bacon Owen left behind in the oil, habitually wiping his fingers on his dressing-gown. He pulled a bag of coffee beans down from the cupboard to fill the old grinder chamber, flicked the switch and held it down to the work surface.

A Barnett Newman exhibition guide, on top of a folded copy of *Socialist Worker*, lay where Owen's car keys usually were. It was a Wednesday, but felt like a Sunday, and might have been a nice *going to the Tate Modern* sort of day were it not Christmas. The Tate Modern had become his sanctuary, where he would go on a Sunday, or sometimes even a Thursday, if he felt the absence of the Kingdom Hall in his life, which was often. He could hardly believe it was free to just walk around at his leisure. He never bothered with the paid exhibitions. The first time he went, he was hoping the Andy Warhol show was still on – instead, there was a Matisse/Picasso, and a Norwegian artist whose name he wasn't sure how to pronounce. A steward gave him a printed guide, suggesting that, if it was his first time there, he might just appreciate the permanent collection, so he headed in, through the sculpture installation in the massive Turbine Hall, straight for the room called *Nude, Body, Action* and Steve McQueen's *Bear* – the first time he had ever seen two naked black men physically engaged. It shocked and amazed him. He tried not to show it, and had to keep his mouth closed, especially when, as the camera looked up from underneath, their dicks and balls swung, catching the light in slow motion. He couldn't understand how they didn't have erections. He did. He was mesmerised by the teeth-baring struggle on their faces, perhaps against themselves. The presences of others watching – white women in particular – made him feel uncomfortable, and he could feel their eyes on him as he left. But then he found the Rothko Room. He sat down on a bench and it was as if all his problems, his guilt, loneliness, isolation, sloped away from him, yet he burst into tears and had to cover his mouth and make an effort to stay silent. Other people must have thought he was having an intense spiritual experience with the art. He looked into those pink, red and scab-black paintings and knew he'd delivered himself into destruction, that he'd left behind his privilege of knowing the truth and that there was no way back. He had touched Graham's body up and down. He had propositioned Fraser Hammond. He had run away from home. He had sucked men's dicks until they nudged his tonsils, gumming up his sinuses with cum. He had talked with his tongue root-deep in arseholes, ached to push his whole head in. He was in love with Owen, who would not want someone damaged and pathetic like him. Maybe he should leap into the canvas before him with a splash and drown himself. It had only been three years since he got baptised, left school and decided to dedicate his life to Jehovah, and now here he was, with a wound in his rectum that in healing had probably sealed in the transmission of a deadly disease, all his own fault; he felt, now, like the man in that painting at Thurston's house, naked, bleeding and falling through the sky.

He returned with his coffee upstairs to his room, sat on the edge of his bed and crushed a skunk bud in his grinder – just enough for a small-sheeter – rolled his spliff and sparked up. He twisted the blind rod to let in more light. The sky was clear and blue. He couldn't remember the last time he'd changed his sheets. Was he allowed to do a load of washing on Christmas Day? Perhaps if he did it now, he thought, on fast, then it might be out of the machine and nearly dry by the time Owen came home to take over the kitchen. After taking a nice long draw on his spliff, he drew up his blind and opened the uPVC window to let in some fresh air that coolly licked him underneath his dressing-gown. He wondered if Owen, next door, ever smelt anything, whether it be a spliff or cigarette being smoked, an ashtray full of old butts, or the smell of Jesse's body when he couldn't be bothered to wash, which was most days, these days, unless he had something or someone in particular to get up for, which hadn't been for six weeks, since *that man*, and in any case, some clients had liked him to be dirty and smelly, but since *that man*, his money had run down and he didn't know when he might be able to work again.

He lay back, with his feet on the bed, and took a long drag. The wound must have healed, but still twinged inside him. He could see *that man*'s face looking down on him, astride him, lifting himself up to remove the condom before easing back on, whispering, *Is it in all the way to the hilt? You can come in me, if you want.* Jesse slapped himself across the face for becoming aroused at the thought; how could he still want to give him the satisfaction? But it did feel good, the way his hole fluttered and quivered around his dick, warm and solicitous. It was as if he could still feel the friction pushing back his foreskin. They hardly even needed lube. He was too stoned to care that the condom had been ripped off. *That man* had said he never hired escorts, so wouldn't be paying. *That man* kept begging Jesse to come in him, before he was ready. On top, *that man* wanked himself off until a rope of spunk leapt out of his dick and dribbled over his hand, which ended up between Jesse's legs, in his hole, fingering him until Jesse came, a little trail that didn't even pool on his belly. His own dick felt like a rubbery prosthesis in his hand. *That man* got up, went to the bathroom, got dressed, said, *Good luck with your writing*, and left. Jesse lit the rest of his spliff and stared at the ceiling.

Almost straight away the stinging started. Burning. He neither ate nor shat nor slept the whole night. He went to the clinic the next morning, where a doctor called him through straight away. An Indian woman with thick glasses stuck a lubricated, clear plastic tube in his hole, and shone in a torch.

'You've got a two-inch long wound in there, full of congealed blood.' She looked confused, and a little bit disgusted, not quite at Jesse, but *for* him. Health advisers fussed and tried to get him to report what had happened to the police as a sexual assault, but who would protect him? *He might have been trying to infect you with HIV*, they said. There was a widespread resurgence in new diagnoses, and the most common transmission zone was *the soft, absorbent, easily broken tissue of the rectum*, just where Jesse had been breached. *Who knows who else out there he might be targeting?* they said. *You must press charges. We can do it for you, but we need your permission*. He wanted nothing to do with it. All they could do was test, monitor, and test him again in three months, once the incubation period had expired. Now, he had another six weeks to wait.

If his result came back negative he would have to find legitimate work. He needed to settle down; he could not keep quitting and running away when he was out of goodwill. He thought, in the new year, he would get himself a regular job, even if it meant stacking shelves in the local Safeway, anywhere that would have him. But he didn't really want to do that. He wanted to be looked after, though he had ruined himself before he'd had the chance to prove himself. He'd never been on as much as a date in his life. He felt he would never be taken seriously as an object of romance. No man had ever taken him out for dinner at a restaurant. He'd been engaged by clients to visit them in hotels, but never had they been willing to be seen in public with him, for how would it look socially if a well-to-do white man took him out to dinner? How would they justify their acquaintance? This wouldn't be something, Jesse imagined, white escorts would have to think about so much; they could be explained away as young relatives or junior colleagues if they wished to keep their intimacy discreet. Nobody wanted to make love to him. He was a skinny, twenty-year-old black boy with a big dick, which was all anyone ever seemed to briefly want him for. He was just a fuck machine they could pay then get rid of. He had been fucked, but only by white men who wanted to use his body to demonstrate their own strength, power and supremacy, or black men who would cross the street if they saw him the next day.

Suddenly he jumped up from the bed, stripped it of its duvet cover, sheet and pillowcase, emptied his rucksack – *JUST DO IT* – and stuffed them in so that he could transfer them downstairs without offending the shared spaces of the house with their smell. He pulled his other set of bedding from the bottom of the chest of drawers and remade his bed. It was hot work, but the little wisps of cool air through the window that touched him every so often were refreshing. It was really more like Easter than Christmas.

He stepped in front of his mirror and opened his dressing-gown, letting it slip to the floor, and observed his nakedness as he stood in his dirty white socks. Didn't men like men with more meat on their bones? He didn't know that he had been pulling such a wretched facial expression, as if it was his new default. He held his dick in his hand, heavy and warm though unemployed. The reason he was sick, in mind, body and spirit, was his dick, which had developed a mind of its own. He was sick because he wasn't a woman. If he was a woman he could enjoy men – although, for God's sake, just one man – all he wanted. A man could come in her over and over and fill her womb with cum, and everyone would rejoice in her, even nuns and priests, because she would be married and having a baby. But because he had been born a man, his actions were a dereliction of his masculinity. He flexed an arm but was repulsed by the smell of his armpit, then scratched his balls and sniffed, and it was strong.

Turning on the shower, he made it hot, and stood under it until he could hardly breathe for the steam, letting the water pressure warm him up. He helped himself to Owen's products, washing and conditioning his hair with Head & Shoulders, and lathering up his body with Molton Brown. He dried himself with a fresh towel and after wiping the condensation from the mirror, shaved with one of Owen's disposable Gillettes. Back in his room, he dried his hair as best he could with the towel, remembering Ginika when he combed it out and saw that it now really qualified as an Afro.

Owen was back, pottering around downstairs, but Jesse couldn't tell what sort of mood he might be in, as can often be judged by the weight and metre of someone's footsteps and the way they close cupboard doors. It couldn't have felt great for him, Jesse thought, to have left his daughters behind who, he imagined, would've cried and thrown their arms around their father's waist, refusing to let him leave their grandparents' house. Jesse tucked a grey shirt into a pair of black jeans and padded around his room barefoot, smoking a cigarette, feeling clean. He wondered why he could not leave his room. It was almost one in the afternoon. Could he not go down to wish Owen a friendly Merry Christmas, like any other normal person would? But then he heard the pop of a champagne cork, and Owen's footsteps creak up the stairs. He wanted Owen to knock on his door, as much as he didn't, and was surprised when he did, expecting him to go to his own room.

'Hold on,' said Jesse, as if he wasn't yet decent. He stubbed out his cigarette in the ashtray and opened the door. Owen's smile was more guarded than normal, but seemed to brighten as he took in Jesse's refreshed state.

'Merry Christmas,' Owen said, as Jesse accepted the glass of champagne being held out to him.

'Merry Christmas,' Jesse repeated. It felt strange and shocking coming out of his mouth, Christmas greetings as forbidden as swear words once were. They clinked and took a sip. The bubbles dissolved crisply on Jesse's tongue.

'I haven't seen you for a bit,' said Owen. His smile had the capacity to convey every intention and emotion, and had faded slightly, transmitting concern. Jesse tucked his lips between his teeth. He did not know what to say. He was desperate to but could not tell Owen the truth; he wanted Owen to think of him as being strong and capable. Owen loved Jesse's stories. He had not long come out himself, and told Jesse he was living his gay youth vicariously through him. He said he wished he had been as brave, and Jesse wanted to remain his hero. 'How've you been keeping?' Owen said.

'I'm alright,' said Jesse, as brightly as he could manage. 'How are you?'

Owen's broad chest expanded and he breathed out hard through his nose. 'Either my daughters don't miss me at all, or they're taking our separation much more maturely than anyone should expect of a six- and four-year-old. Anyway, they seemed happy enough. They loved their presents.'

'What did you buy them?'

'I bought them both iPods,' he said, and laughed. 'I know. Is there anything wankier?'

'Did they like them?'

'It's what they've been asking for. I gather some of their schoolfriends already have them, so there would've been strife if I'd left it any longer. Their grandparents sneered at me as if I was trying to buy the girls' loyalty.'

'Did they give you a hard time?'

'Oh, I don't blame them, really I don't,' he said, with a smile of resignation. 'They're just being protective of their daughter, and grandkids, from someone they basically think is a sex offender. I only stayed for about twenty minutes. Gave the girls their main presents, told them I loved them, and left.'

Jesse was happy for Chloe, six, and Emma, four, but he had never received a Christmas present in his life, at least not since he was two.

'So, you really planned to spend Christmas by yourself?' Jesse asked Owen. Owen nodded, and smiled, sadly. 'What are you going to do?' They had both got comfortable, Owen leaning against the doorframe and Jesse against his bedroom wall. Owen shrugged, and turned down the corners of his mouth.

'Not much. Just treat it like any other day. Do a bit of work, listen to some music, have something to eat a bit later. How about you?'

'The same, I suppose. Just chill in my room and write, a bit.'

Owen beamed and stood straight. 'Cool! What are you writing?'

'Just a bit of silliness.'

'Of course it isn't.'

'It's nothing special. I just write to remember things and explain things to myself.'

'That's the best kind of writing.'

'But it's not poetry. It's not what you do. I don't even understand what you do.'

'Don't assume I do.'

'But you went to Cambridge. You got a proper education. You spent years learning all that. I just had the Bible.'

'The greatest piece of literature the world has ever known. You're just as privileged as I am for an education.'

'Except what was used to educate me is now used to judge me,' Jesse said.

'Well, I'm sure the life you're living, set against the way you were raised, is giving you plenty to think about, and writing is the best way to order one's thoughts, so keep it going.'

'It's just rubbish, really.'

'The important thing is to have something to say. You can be taught how to say it. If you ever want me to read anything, I'd be delighted to.'

'Thank you,' Jesse said, conscious of the pressure on him to produce something, now.

'Cheers to that.' They clinked again, and sipped, and stood awkwardly in the doorway.

'I've not seen your room, have I?' Owen said, looking past Jesse. 'Not since it was empty anyway, before you moved in.'

'Come in.' Jesse stepped back. He never liked anyone to see his room, especially not after his most recent visitor – *that man* – and was relieved he'd tidied and cleaned up, though he still darted his eyes around looking for missed traces of squalor.

'Wow, love your posters,' Owen said, nodding at the two centrefolds from *AnOther Magazine*, one of a muscled man in ballet pumps, tights and flesh-coloured bondage-wear from the John Galliano Archive, the other of a leaping Kate Moss in an Alexander McQueen tutu. The *VIBE* cover tribute to Aaliyah and Beyoncé's cover from *The Face* flanked the bedhead like guardian angels. The room seemed to shrink with Owen in it, as if they might be tipped into each other. 'So, is this where you make your living?'

'I almost never have anyone here,' Jesse said. 'It's my personal space. I come here to escape that.'

Owen sat down on the bed, and tested the mattress by gently bouncing up and down; Jesse leaned back on the radiator and watched him, unsure of what to do or say. 'Do you actually enjoy it?' Owen said.

'Yeah, it's alright,' Jesse shrugged.

Owen nodded his head, and insisted on maintaining eye contact. 'Are they ever completely disgusting?'

'Sometimes.' Jesse shuddered as bodies he wished he had never seen, smells he wished he had never breathed in, loads he wished he had never had to wash out of his hair, passed through his mind and still fed blood into his dick.

'But you fulfil the engagement anyway?'

'Yeah.' He didn't know whether Owen would be impressed by his steadfastness, or pity him for his desperation.

'Have you ever made arrangements with someone, then got there, and been unable to perform?'

Jesse thought about it for a second. 'Dave'. He remembered running to catch the bus, clutching the waistband of his trackies, with a hard-on. I should've fucked the fucking shit out of him anyway, he thought. It was exercise, as much as anything.

'No.'

'You've always managed to keep it up for everybody?'

'Yeah.'

'Wow,' Owen said, and laughed. Jesse began to wonder what might happen between them, spending at least the next twenty-four hours in the house together alone, undisturbed and emotional. Owen gulped down half his glass of champagne and stared into space for a moment, then said, 'I never met the guy who was in here before you but Bryan told me he was the dullest person he'd ever met, which nobody could ever say about you.'

'Thanks,' Jesse laughed, modestly. 'I'm quite boring, as far as prostitutes go!'

'You're much more than a prostitute, so stop thinking of yourself like that,' Owen said, and drained the rest of his glass. 'You're an intelligent young man with a world to discover.' He stood up and stretched, and his T-shirt rode up. The density of his body hair increased towards the waistband of his boxers, obliging Jesse to look at his crotch.

'Want a top-up?'

'Yeah. Shall I come down?'

'Or maybe you'd like to listen to some tunes in my room?' Owen said. 'Fuck it, it's Christmas. Bring your weed.'

*

Owen's room was much larger than Jesse's, clearly the master bedroom. Jesse sat on the settee in the bay window and started rolling a spliff. The walls were mauve-coloured and hung with prints, one of a woman in a dress and a hat, red shoes and no facial features, sitting in a deckchair; one of a Russian film featuring a woman in stockings and heels spiralling down through the air from the top of a skyscraper; another of a bunch of roses against a grey background, a promotional poster for the New Order album *Power, Corruption & Lies*. Jesse felt the warmth of being trusted to be alone – if only while Owen had popped downstairs for a moment – in his room, with all his things. Owen kept a little framed picture of his daughters on his bedside table, with a digital alarm clock. His vinyl was arranged in two boxes either side of the fireplace, though Jesse had never heard any loud music and suspected Owen rather listened on his headphones, attached by a long, coiled cable, as he worked on his laptop or sat marking papers. Owen came back with the champagne in an ice bucket – pleased to see Jesse already skinning up – which he placed on the coffee table, topping up their glasses with the aid of a napkin, then crouching down to flick through one of the record boxes. His T-shirt clung to the toned muscles of his back, and failed to cover the little patch of hair above the waist of his checked boxers.

'What do you fancy listening to? Nothing Christmassy.'

'What have you got?'

'Anything you like. Do you like hip-hop? The Roots? Or is that too obvious?' He began to talk to himself. 'Too obvious. Saint Etienne's new album . . .?'

'Did you see *Donnie Darko*?' said Jesse, as he watched Owen read down a list of track titles.

'Yeah, top film.'

'Do you remember the scene during the house party, when Donnie answered the door to Gretchen and took her upstairs to his room? What was that song?' And he hummed it.

'"Love Will Tear Us Apart"?' Owen laughed.

'Yeah, who's that?'

Owen gave Jesse a strange grin of unexpected brotherhood, then picked out several LPs from the front of the first box and presented them to Jesse on the coffee table – a white, a grey, a black and a blue.

'This is the one with "Love Will Tear Us Apart" on it,' he said, tapping a clean, trimmed nail on the grey sleeve printed with *Substance* in green and JOY DIVISION 1977–1980 in white. 'This is a really good place to start if you're looking to get a wider view of their best work. Well. All their work was their best work.'

'How many albums did they release?'

'Just two studio, then several posthumous compilations. I've got everything official.'

'Posthumous?'

Owen looked at Jesse, shook his head and laughed. 'Hurry up with that spliff.'

With great care, Owen unsheathed the vinyl from a black sleeve and placed it on the turntable, as Jesse licked the Rizla gum and smoothed the roll.

'This is where you start. Merry Christmas.' They held up their glasses and drank. Owen sat down next to him as Jesse sparked up.

Thin white jagged lines on a black background, like skin under a microscope. Jesse handled it as Owen had done, with a sense of deference. It was a piece of black card with only a little bit of writing on the back, the band name – JOY DIVISION – the album title – UNKNOWN PLEASURES – and underneath, FACT 10 • A FACTORY RECORDS PRODUCT. Even before the needle hit the disc, Jesse thought of his night with Fraser in the derelict flats, of the broken glass, rotting joints of window-surround, the cold, damp breezeblocks.

Owen closed the blinds behind them, though it was only lunchtime. The sound emerging from the floor-based speakers was like nothing Jesse had ever heard. Plosive drums at the beginning, pumping like the heart of a black boy being chased into a dark tunnel by white thugs, and before he had time to understand what he was hearing they were joined by little black dots of bass, high then low, high then low. A studio effect, like a car sinking in a canal with the radio on, weaved in and out. Jesse felt transported to the deserted foundries and factories of his childhood before they were demolished, cleared away and replaced with car showrooms and supermarkets; the cavities in walls you could climb through to run around the dead, black, oily waste of a century of industrial heft. He missed that world, the sooty, subsiding streets of his ministerial territory, the snotty-nosed children running round dirty-faced kicking battered footballs.

And then a man started singing in a low baritone, as reverberantly as the instruments around him. Jesse and Owen let their legs stretch out, their feet nestling in the rug underneath the coffee table. Jesse watched Owen blow a plume of smoke up towards the high ceiling above him and wondered what he was thinking. He wanted to ask who the singer was, but didn't want to spoil the depth of engagement. He also wanted Owen to touch him, put a hand on his knee, make some sort of concession – even if he would then have to reject him – but he just passed the spliff back, sipped his champagne and closed his eyes, letting the beats pop in the air and flood the floor. Jesse closed his eyes too. *I've got the spirit, lose the feeling, take the shock away.* There was no chorus, just a guitar line, then a new verse. The weed went to his head and it was as black as blindness. The rhythm, extruded from drums, bass, guitar, studio effects and untrained baritone, was perfectly balanced, nothing louder than anything else yet everything distinctly audible. It sounded different from 'Love Will Tear Us Apart,' but was a better match for his mood; there was light, but like the narrow beam of a headlamp in a mine shaft. A keyboard sound like the glow of white-hot metal. These were the echoes of his childhood; his mother might have been playing soul and R&B at home but this was the sound of the streets, the factories and warehouses, the canals, the ironworks, the steel works. *Blood on your fingers, brought on by fear.*

He wondered how *that man* was spending Christmas. He hadn't told Owen, and wondered how he would feel, whether he would want to protect him, whether he would take Jesse as his own and wish to avenge his honour; whether he would tell him he was just being silly and should grow some balls. What had *that man* done? Was it deliberate? It would take some audacity to come into a black man's house – however young and naïve that black man was – and deliberately rip a hole in his rectum to transmit HIV, out of revenge, perhaps, for someone who looked like Jesse, maybe, who might have hurt him in the past. Perhaps, then, *that man* was simply lacking in self-consciousness, and had no idea of his strength. Perhaps, as Jesse often did, he had simply forgotten to trim his nails.

Jesse settled the remaining half a spliff in the ashtray. He didn't want to get any more stoned. He felt inspired. A breakdown sounded like fireworks, or an intergalactic war. Owen interlocked his fingers across his belly, closed his eyes and smiled, like a hospital patient on morphine. In between songs he would wake up and top up the champagne. Jesse could almost see blue and pink lasers flash before his eyes. He came from a place that remembered the sounds of steel and iron being hammered into shape, carried on air stifled by black smoke pouring from chimneys.

Owen silently got up to turn the disc over, and still, Jesse asked no questions, just rolled another spliff. The first song on the other side he could imagine Beyoncé dancing to, in a Josephine Baker banana skirt, shaking her wild corkscrew curls. It almost sounded like maracas at the start of each bar, but of course, was too smooth and refined to actually be. Jesse imagined stopping by a chainmaking forge, the men in oily dungarees and boiler suits all dropping their hammers at once as they stopped work for their eleven o'clock blow-jobs. He started to feel paranoid that this would be the music of his death, that this would be the last album he would ever hear before he died.

He closed his eyes and allowed the music to print images on the back of his eyelids. Derelict foundries; shopping trolleys in the algae-covered canals; the gas tank; the disused railway lines choked with stinging nettles, a dustbin for screwed-up, spunked-in porn; the fences with signs up saying DANGER OF DEATH ELECTRICITY KEEP OUT. Nobody on those planes, when they boarded, knew that they were going to die in a terrorist attack. None of them knew that they were going to die together that morning. He imagined what it might have been like inside the South Tower, on impact, to stand and watch a whole aircraft approach the window, and the unbelievable explosion of fire and glass, though there was no time to convey the experience for posterity. *Unknown Pleasures* ended with the echoed sound of broken glass.

Owen lifted off the needle when its circling at the end of the record became unbearable, and switched off the turntable. No other music known to Jesse could follow it; time needed to pass while its energy dissipated. There was only a dribble of champagne left, which he tipped into his flute before crunching the bottle back into the ice bucket upside down. Jesse still had most of a glass left. Owen retook his seat heavily.

'So, what did you think?'

Jesse had nothing to say about it. He thought that what he wanted to say about it, about the silly little Black Country and its crushed industries, would be of no interest to Owen at all. So he looked for other references. 'I've never heard anything like it.'

'What's the closest thing?'

Jesse thought of those afternoons listening to albums with Fraser in his bedroom, when he was supposed to be on the ministry. 'Reminds me a bit of Blur's *13*.'

'My wife and I met at a Blur gig,' Owen said. Jesse thought Owen was laughing at him. Owen spoke to the ceiling, as if he was on a psychiatrist's couch, and Jesse watched his Adam's apple bobbing up and down with each syllable. He had never noticed how long Owen's eyelashes were, before. 'They played at the Corn Exchange in the summer of '94. We'd both just broken up with other people and were near each other in the crowd, dancing with our friends, one of whom was mutual and introduced us. And then they played "Girls and Boys" and the whole place went crazy.'

Jesse didn't mind Owen talking, but he wished he hadn't mentioned Blur when Joy Division were still in his head. Blur reminded him too much of Fraser and his brothers; of the boys at school during the Britpop craze. Of being fifteen, and wanting to be like them, wanting to be considered one of them, but not being one of them. Of his fear of getting an erection in the changing rooms as the few boys who did have big dicks walked around swinging. Of going to the barber and being given a trim that made him look like his hair had been sprayed on with a stencil. He feared he'd be bullied at school for looking like Frank Sidebottom, the big-eyed, brown, sphere-headed comedy character, so when he got home he scalped his head bloodily in the shower with one of his father's razors. He hated himself that much, already – not himself, but his blackness. As he stood on the stairs, the sight of his scalp sprung tears to his mother's eyes; she shut the front room door in his face. He had to take two weeks off school while all the chunks he'd dug out from his scalp pussed up and scabbed over. She considered sending him to see a doctor. He wished now that she had. They might have taken him away from her and sent him to live with people who knew how to raise children with unconditional love.

'She was so gorgeous. Clever. She looked like a model and was reading law. Sorry, I'm stoned. I don't know why I'm telling you all this.' Owen had been talking all the while Jesse had drifted away.

'It's alright,' said Jesse.

Owen, still resting his head on the back of the sofa, turned to look at him, tenderly, in the eyes, then down at his mouth, then back into his eyes, and smiled. Jesse thought that if he didn't cry, he would be downplaying his own feelings, his personal trauma, in front of someone who seemed to possess empathy, in a world devoid of this quality, but that if he did, he would betray himself for being weak and effeminate and unable to look after himself, or to live without his parents.

'Did you always know, when you were younger, that you were gay?' he asked Owen, unexpectedly even to himself, after a silence. Owen nodded, gravely.

'I always knew I liked boys, yeah,' he said, in a low, quiet, confidential voice that vibrated in the settee back. 'Someone's sexuality doesn't change halfway through their life. Everyone's born at some point on the continuum, and it's up to them how truthful they want to be to themselves.'

'So you're bisexual, then?'

Owen got up – before Jesse could ask him not to – to pluck down a slim volume, which he handed to Jesse. 'Thom Gunn, *The Passages of Joy*. This was the first book of poetry I ever bought myself, when I was fifteen,' Owen said. 'He and this young fella …' – he took down another, this time Wilfred Owen's *Collected Poems* – 'are the reasons I became a poet.' He sat back down, facing Jesse, with a foot up under the other thigh.

'Anything to do with the name?' Jesse asked, of Wilfred Owen.

'He was born on the Wirral as well, just like me. Also coincidental is the fact that my surname's Gunning,' he said, proudly tapping a finger on the name Thom Gunn.

'Mine's McCarthy.' Jesse held out a hand, which Owen shook solidly.

'There's already at least one McCarthy in poetry,' Owen winked. 'You'll have to come up with another name.'

Hearing it from someone else's – an actual writer's – mouth, made Jesse realise how silly the idea of him leaving a name in literature sounded. 'So what about this made you a poet?' he asked of the Thom Gunn.

'"Elegy", *Passages of Joy*'s opening poem, was published before the AIDS crisis, but as so much of his later work lamented the consequent loss of gay life, it smelled of prophecy, to me, especially after my English teacher died.' He took a long puff of the spliff, took it down, breathed out through his nostrils and gave it back to Jesse, whose mouth had drained at the mention of AIDS; he took a gulp of champagne. 'It didn't seem possible someone we knew could ever get it; glamorous gays in London or New York or San Francisco – where Thom still lives – got AIDS, not us lads whose dads worked for Unilever and whose granddads fought at the Somme. It wasn't supposed to come to the Wirral, but my English teacher, who I sort of idolised and who'd encouraged me to write, got sick that summer.'

Jesse thought Owen might tear up, and the first thing he thought of was how privileged he would feel.

'There was no one like him,' Owen said. 'He cropped his hair like a skinhead from the docks, but was a grammar school teacher into fin-de-siècle poetry and painting. He took us to the Lady Lever Gallery and contextualised the work there in a way that blew our minds. He wore leather trousers to work, with a regular shirt, tie and suit jacket. Being frowned upon by other teachers made him the ultimate hero to us. He was the first teacher I ever thought might have a sexual life outside – and maybe even inside – work. But as I was studying for my O-Levels, trying to spend as much time with him as possible, something in his constitution changed. He replaced the leather trousers with those that came with the suit jacket – sort of desexualising himself. He grew his hair, started wearing glasses, and was always slim, but he lost some weight, and developed this dreadful cough. I think I was the only student he told that he was HIV-positive.' Here, he turned to look at Jesse, which made Jesse in turn wonder whether Owen knew, whether it was obvious to him, what he was going through. 'Very few people went to see him in hospital. I did, in secret, because rumours spread amongst the parents. He was being branded a paedophile, though no one could prove that he'd actually been involved with any of the students. My dad told me that if I kept contact with him I wouldn't be allowed back in the house.' Owen seemed as if he was deconstructing a recent event, not something that happened sixteen years ago. 'There was nothing the doctors could do except prescribe those reactive early drugs, and run countless degrading tests. Those guys were guinea pigs. He got pneumonia, and Kaposi's sarcoma. Classic case.' Turning his head, he saw Jesse's questioning expression. 'It was a terrifying skin condition. You came out in lesions. Some guys tried to hide it with make-up, which only made them more conspicuous. I tried not to show him how upsetting I found his appearance. He told me it was alright, that he knew how bad he looked. I think he *wanted* me to cry out, for someone to just be honest with him.' Owen paused, perhaps to swallow back tears. Jesse relit and handed him back the spliff, which he seemed cheered by, as if he had forgotten about it, and he took a deep pull, that made a burning sound as if the lit end had been pressed into someone's flesh. 'Because of what I witnessed, I convinced myself that that death would be inevitable if I had sex with men. But I knew I couldn't die of poetry.' He laughed unconvincingly at his own joke. Jesse indulged him. 'Have you ever known anyone die of AIDS?' Owen asked him.

Jesse kept his composure, swallowed, kept eye contact with Owen and shook his head. Owen turned his gaze back to the ceiling, then after a silence, suddenly sat up.

'Are you hungry?'

Jesse didn't suffer from the munchies after smoking weed like other people did, but he had gone to bed without dinner the night before, and hadn't eaten anything more than a couple of heavily buttered slices of toast at a time for several days. He nodded.

'You can peel the spuds,' Owen said, implying that he was going to share his food with Jesse. 'I'll open another bottle of champagne.'

'Alright,' said Jesse, shyly. He felt a little heavy-eyed, but truly happy with it being just the two of them, sharing a rare day in which time meant nothing. 'I like hearing you talk,' he told Owen.

'You'll let me know if I'm too depressing,' said Owen, getting up and leaving with the ice bucket and his flute. 'Let's do it, then.'

As Owen left the room, Jesse read the second verse of 'Elegy': *Even the terror / of leaving life like that / better than the terror / of being unable to handle it.*

Chapter 2

He had refused to work as a kitchen porter at Gilbert's, and walked out without taking the gloves. He hadn't moved to London for that, and showed how he felt by ripping his apron off in front of the customers and throwing it over the bar as he left the restaurant. The room went quiet and everyone saw. He didn't look back. Left his uniform on the locker room floor; washed and ironed his trousers back at the hostel, took them and the shoes back to Topman, who gave him a credit voucher with a year to spend. He didn't care that he wouldn't be paid for the shift-and-a-half he'd worked.

He regretted that he left without saying goodbye to Ginika. It frustrated him that an institution, if Gilbert's could be so called, stood between him and a potential friendship in a new city. He wished her all the best, in his heart, and hoped they would see each other again one day. He thought she had every chance of becoming an actress, or whatever she wanted. Her family were not holding her back for the sake of some shady religious principle. Nowhere in the Bible did it say that God's people should not better themselves academically or arm themselves with secular knowledge. The *Awake!* magazine was wide-ranging in its grasp of science, technology and modern examples of faith under persecution, but was no substitute for an English degree. He told himself he would look up the Ndukwe family in the phone book. It was hardly Smith or Jones.

His route was to be different from Ginika's; he followed his dick. He hung around Old Compton Street, in pint-drinking white-man pubs where he had no trouble picking up fat fifty-five-year-olds with big, bouncy arses, who bought weed for him to smoke, lay still on their stomachs and let him fuck them as hard as he could. He stood out among young men of his kind because he maintained that Witness doorstep charm. Teenage boys threw themselves at him on the dance floor at GAY, but he wasn't interested; his polite friendliness was lost on them. He was into older men, who didn't care if they looked ugly because they already were, and who gave their strong, workhorse bodies over to sex. One of them took some pictures of him nude on their digital camera and uploaded them to the Gaydar website for him.

He picked up men walking down residential streets, on Tube trains, on buses, in hotel lobbies, in clothing stores. Midweek afternoons were the best time to find horny partnered men working from home with their flats to themselves. The best gave him money out of generosity, without him asking, just to help him on his way because they liked him; the more uptight left money out conspicuously for him to steal, which he never did. His schedule filled up. He learned the Tube map, from Acton to Woodside Park, and started to picture the city above ground, catching buses just to look out of the window. The men he chatted to online, expecting him to be a closet-case from Peckham or Croydon fucking on the down-low, paid his travel, so he wore his jeans low and amended his accent to fit their fantasy, and they either let him leave with the weed or promised it would be there for him when he returned. He almost never did, because there was always someone new round the corner.

The most memorable was a fifty-one-year-old he picked up on a Hackney street one hot June afternoon, having just said goodbye to another guy. Jesse was in a bouncy mood, having been given £100 by the fuck as a gift, and walked past a white van whose owner gave him a wide, solicitous smile Jesse wasn't initially sure was supposed to be for him. They got into the back of the van. It was the first time Jesse had touched and tasted a black man, short and stout, with a muscular chest and arse, his body covered with tight curly hair. His dick was thick and his balls heavy, but he was passive, and didn't mind a quickie. He was perfectly prepared, with condoms and lube. Their thick lips mushed together. He told Jesse to call him *Daddy*, and even offered him a job. He was born in Antigua, had lived in the UK since the age of four, and ran his own building company. Jesse might have accepted but he was enjoying his freedom too much. They never got to meet again. Jesse wished Brother Thomas Woodall had offered him a job, working with him as a painter and decorator. Jesse had watched him from across the road, once, on a beautiful sunny day in Great Bridge, working alone on a shopfront, the space behind him empty and white, while he painted the inside window frames, the sun shining right onto him. The outer frames were already finished, blue and white; the lines were straight and the corners were true. The blue and white matched what Brother Woodall was wearing that day, a blue T-shirt under his white dungarees. His eyes were blue, his skin was white, his hair was blond and curly, the golden hairs on his forearms fine. He had a bit of a belly, a bit of an arse. Jesse saw Brother Woodall at the next meeting, shook his hand and complimented him on his job. *I'm saving up so that I can afford you in my room*, Jesse told him. Completely innocently, Brother Woodall said, *Well, I'm sure I can do you mates' rates.*

Jesse could admit that he had always been in love with Brother Woodall – Uncle Tom, as Jesse had been encouraged to call him – maybe since that very first knock on his mother's door with Graham and the *Watchtower* and *Awake!*, when Jesse was far too young to know what he was feeling; far too young to feel anything at all. He should've touched him. He had lost everything anyway. He had censored himself, punished himself, boxed in emotions that can't just have been sinful, being so strong and apparent in one so young, but must have been natural, there since birth; he'd held himself back and *still* been disfellowshipped. The credit he'd built up working all those hours on the ministry, and spending all those long years, just to save the family's face, living in the home of someone who had cut him off in her mind, had gone in an instant. The reputation that had been bestowed upon him as an example to the youth and a refreshment to the old, disappeared with a knock of Brother Grimes's biblical gavel.

Even when Jesse was a sinless child, aged eight or nine, he craved to sit in Uncle Tom's lap and lay his hands wherever he wanted, to be the centre of his attention. Uncle Tom had been in his life from so long ago he was like a father, the father he wished he had, and Jesse would not stop until he found another who made him feel as if he was the most perfect, important person in the universe, by *being* the most perfect, important person in the universe and putting Jesse alone on a pedestal. If only his mother had married Uncle Tom instead; if the whole universe was different, Jesse would've grown up in *his* care; he would've watched *him* standing at the sink, shaving, with just his towel sitting low on his hips.

The commercial listings on Gaydar intrigued Jesse all the more as his funds decreased; it wasn't difficult for him to attract men, and he'd established a connection with those of a certain age and status. He visited apartments with double-height ceilings, in wealthy parts of town, and left with his balls and pockets empty. It made sense that he should use his body, while he could, to earn money. Len was in his sixties and not looking for the sex Jesse would've happily given him, but was nevertheless the most polite and genteel of all the men who contacted him. He seemed to be impressed by the fact that Jesse looked the way he did, yet could spell, and formulate whole sentences – correct use of apostrophes and all – which Jesse found patronising but laughed off. When he went to the Internet café and logged on there was always a message from Len, asking how he'd been, reminding him to stay safe, wanting to hear the latest episode in Jesse's story, who he'd had sex with, whether he'd been looking for a job, which book he was reading. *Why don't you become an escort*, he said in his river-deep voice. *You might as well be paid for what you are doing already. You'll be successful. It's a viable career choice in the twenty-first century.* Len even invited Jesse to move in with him rent-free while he was finding his feet, in exchange for a few errands. He was a filmmaker, he said, and lived in a tower block in Camberwell with his old friend Billy and *a bunch of waifs and strays*, but they were *one big happy family*, and there was always room for one more, especially someone nice, he said.

The hostel scene had grown stale. With all the confidence his growing list of conquests had given him, Jesse had made a move on Jeff – the big Aussie who liked to share a *mull on the stips* – which hadn't gone down well. Not that Jeff kicked off about it; Jesse felt Jeff rather enjoyed the attention. A lawyer in Shoreditch he had been fucking gave him lots of coke, and high as a terrorist, Jesse crashed back through the hostel front door ready to devour any man who crossed his path.

'I want to suck your dick,' Jesse had told Jeff, his thoughts running even faster than his mouth. 'I'll do a better job than your no-lips girlfriend. You'll be able to teach her after having me, and if she dunt do it right you'll know where to come. Look a'these lips. These are dick-worship lips.' Jeff, himself drunk and his girlfriend out at work, kept laughing. Jesse could tell Jeff was running it over in his mind, and every time he laughed, Jesse said something filthier. In between laughs Jeff said something like, *I can't, I have a girlfriend. I'm straight. I would, if you had a pussy, but I'm straight!*

Of course, the next day, Jesse could barely show his face. Having paid a week in advance, he packed his belongings. He was glad not to see anyone he knew on the way out – it was an odd time of day when a lot of the residents, being hospitality staff, were either on their way to work or about to leave. In Camberwell, Len helped Jesse to set up his commercial profile on Gaydar, using some fresh black and white images they shot. As soon as he paid the subscription he started to receive messages, and that very same night, saw his first client – a passive, hairy Welshman who lived in a ninth-floor flat overlooking Soho – for a hundred and fifty pounds.

Chapter 3

'At this point we'd pray,' said Jesse, eyes closed, as the steam from the mushroom ragù, served as a gravy, condensed on his chin and lips.

'Okay, then,' said Owen, expectantly.

Jesse's eyes opened as if the fear of God had been put into him, making Owen smile. A bold shaft of orange-yellow light shone across the back wall. 'What, you want me to say a prayer?' Jesse said.

'Quick, before the food gets cold.' Owen closed his eyes tight, like a child's, then opened one slightly to watch him. Jesse laughed.

'Alright,' said Jesse. He wasn't going to ruin his appetite, before his first Christmas dinner, by traipsing guiltily back to Jehovah. He had never prayed, anyway, not really. He said words in his head but could not believe he was speaking to a real being, who was actively listening. As far as he was concerned, a conversation had to be between at least two voices; otherwise he was talking to himself, and he was not mad. He had been telling himself a lot, recently, that he was not mad.

'Oh, we're saying them silently to ourselves, are we?' Owen asked, a lightly teasing smile on his face, the sort Jesse normally found flirtatious and appealing, but now experienced as aggressive, as if Owen didn't know what he was making Jesse do.

'No, sorry, okay. It's just, I'm out of practice,' Jesse said, keeping a smile on his face so as not to push Owen away. 'I can't involve God in my life any more.'

'It doesn't have to be a long one,' said Owen, more caressingly. 'I just want the privilege of hearing how you would put it. I know little about Jehovah's Witnesses and what they do. It's fascinating to me.'

'Okay,' said Jesse, and he closed his eyes, then opened them again. He was ready to admit he would do anything for Owen. A potential client had said to Jesse, once: *I bet you don't let anyone near you.* If there was anyone Jesse would want to let in, if there was anyone he would trust with his past, his tears, his laughter, his problems, his body, it was Owen.

'You don't have to if you don't want to,' said Owen. 'Not if it traumatises you.'

Jesse closed his eyes, cleared his throat and took a deep breath.

'Dear Heavenly Father Jehovah God. Thank You for the delicious food we're about to receive. Thank You for the sunny, mild day, the beasts of the Earth, the flying creatures of the heavens and the fish of the sea. Thank You for every day of our lives, and for letting us live with freedom of choice, when the rules You set mean the choice to live by truth is still punishable by death in some countries, even in ours. Thank You for bringing Owen and me into each other's lives so we can at least spend this day suffering together, when really, we should be with our families who should love us unconditionally, but don't, because of the rules You set, and because we don't wish to live our lives by the lies You would rather we told. Anyway, before this fatty and bloody joint of beef on my plate gets cold, I will ask You to wake up from your slumber, come to understand that we all just want to love each other and be happy, and stop letting people be taken advantage of, raped, killed, starved, made homeless, impoverished, bullied, scourged, and all the other things You let Your creations suffer. I hope You are actually there so that I didn't spend the first nineteen years of my life talking to myself, but I also hope You're not there, so I don't have to hold You to account for all the evil that's happening, caused by people who think they're the good ones and have got You on their side. I ask this prayer in the name of Your Son and Reigning King Christ Jesus, whose birthday You don't even allow Your supposed true followers to celebrate. *Merry Christmas*. And thank You very, *very* much for champagne and weed. And for Owen. And Joy Division. And Sugababes. And Destiny's Child. Amen!'

Owen's eyes were already open when Jesse opened his. So was his mouth.

'Cheers,' said Jesse, triumphantly, holding up his glass. Owen took his as if unsure, and they clinked.

'Merry Christmas,' said Owen, who had paled slightly. 'That was certainly from the heart!'

'Were you expecting the Lord's Prayer?'

'Or a version of it?'

Perhaps, Jesse thought, Owen had not experienced such honesty at his gilded Cambridge chapels. 'The Witnesses believe in personal prayer. It's another way of ours to distance ourselves from false Christianity.'

Owen shook his head. He was smiling at Jesse in a blushing, high-cheekboned way nobody had ever regarded him with before. If Jesse hadn't been so hungry, he might have become nauseous with infatuation.

'Alright. Well,' Owen said. 'Let's eat.'

The thinly carved pink beef came apart like ham. It would have felt like hacking through a loaf of stale bread were he eating it at home, or at Graham's parents' house, where they used to cook the meat so long it turned grey. Owen had asked Jesse, when searing it, how he liked it cooked, and because Jesse had never thought about it, he'd said, *Well done, please*. The kitchen was L-shaped, with the dining table behind Jesse; Owen stood at the hob with his back to the window. Jesse was picking parsley leaves from their stalks and collecting them in a bowl, playing the Bad Boy Remix of 'He Loves U Not' by Dream in his head, despite the shuffle of songs Owen played from his iPod. Jesse hated parsley, growing up. It dominated the disgusting pre-made gloopy white sauce that accompanied those dry and stringy fillets of cod his mother pictured herself as a fine middle-class housewife for serving.

'Well, then there we have a problem,' Owen had said, as the rich beef smell went straight up Jesse's nose and taunted his empty stomach. 'I eat mine rare.'

He was not allowed to eat bloody meat. From as early as he could remember, Jesse and other Witness children had been made to carry an Identity Card with them, refreshed each January. It was signed by their parents, and an elder, and said that if Jesse were to be taken into hospital care, as a minor with none of his guardians present, doctors could be sued if they decided to treat him with blood-based products. When he became a baptised Brother, he was given a more explicit 'No Blood' card that did not have to be signed by his parents, showing that it was his own decision to disallow doctors from treating him with blood.

'Fuck it. I'll take it just like you do,' he said. He'd been sucking dicks for seven months and here he was worried about a juicy steak.

'Are you sure?' Owen said, as if he was knowingly leading Jesse into temptation.

'I worked in a restaurant for a couple of days when I first moved to London and couldn't believe so many people were ordering steaks with blood circling round the plate.'

'Of course, yeah. "The Blood Issue". Anya deals a lot with that sort of thing,' Owen said. The sizzling got louder as he pressed down the fatty rind on the surface of the pan. 'Did I tell you she was a barrister in child protection? Jehovah's Witness parents have been happier to let their child die than allow them to receive blood.' Jesse thought about Fraser's family tragedy but decided not to ruin his day with Owen by talking about him. 'I didn't know their abstinence extends to the consumption of blood as a food product as well.'

'That's the word the Bible uses. *Abstain* from blood. Acts fifteen verses twenty-eight and twenty-nine,' Jesse said, as if preaching once again from the rostrum at his Kingdom Hall. 'Everything we eat has to be well done, to the point of being barely edible. Burnt to a crisp. Otherwise, it's unclean and unfit for consumption.'

'And is it halal?' Owen said the latter word with a throaty non-English intonation, giving equal stress to both syllables.

'What's halal?' Jesse copied.

'In Muslim communities, only meat that has been bled in a certain way, and prayed over, can be eaten. Permitted food is called halal.'

'No, nothing like that. We just buy any old shit from the supermarket like everybody else does and cook it till it could be anything.'

'What about black pudding?' said Owen, smiling.

Jesse tensed his stomach and pulled a heaving face.

'Isn't that pig's blood?'

'Congealed with groats, dried onion and spices.'

Jesse shook his head. 'I don't know how anyone could eat that, religious or not.'

'But it's supposed to be a delicacy in the Black Country. We used to eat Black Country sausage at home, when I was a kid, on a Saturday, with the grill. Tasty stuff. It's supposed to have aphrodisiacal properties.'

Jesse caught the little flutter of suggestion in Owen's teasing and internally blushed. 'Some things we're thankful not to be made to eat,' he said, playfully.

'You're still using the present tense,' Owen said, as he transferred the joint to a roasting rack in the hot oven.

'Pardon?'

'You still say *we*, and use the present tense, as if you're still one of them.'

It wouldn't take at all long to get used to this new definition of what meat was supposed to be – something to be enjoyed rather than endured. He wanted to see a video of himself eating the meat he used to, resembling a cow chewing grass, turning her jaw blandly. Sometimes, between meals, when he was a child, he would eat the cardboard inner tube of a loo roll, which would act in a similar way, masticated down to a drenched, unswallowable pulp. But not this meat. Not only was it better-quality beef than anything he had ever had before, it was richly charred on the outside and practically raw in the middle. The roast potatoes were crunchy on the outside and soft within. In no time at all Owen had simmered a mushroom ragù, frying diced carrots, onion and celery in a pan with oil and butter before adding the sliced mushrooms and some herbs, bringing it up slowly with beef stock and red wine, and adding quartered cherry tomatoes towards the end. Jesse's own spinach was served, not boiled or raw, but sautéed with butter, garlic and black pepper. Owen had bought sprouts, but the spinach was nearing its *best before* date so they used that instead; Owen said they could eat the sprouts with toasted walnuts and ricotta the next day, or maybe as a snack if they were hungry later. Jesse wondered what sort of meals they could have in six months, a year, *ten* years.

'There's more if you want it,' Owen said, wiping his mouth with the sheet of kitchen roll they were using as napkins, watching Jesse wolf his plate. The sun was weakening, and it was starting to get chilly. Jesse tucked his colder foot behind the other, but didn't want to shut the back door. He didn't want to change anything.

'What about you?' he asked Owen. 'Did you grow up religious?'

Owen shook his head while he was still chewing. 'We went to our local village church but we weren't particularly religious.'

'Was it Church of England or something?' Jesse asked.

'It's a United Reformed Church now, but was originally non-denominational with a Wesleyan minister at the time of its consecration. To be honest, I was more interested in the architecture than the services.'

'What was it like?'

For the first time, he looked serious. 'I grew up in a place called Port Sunlight, on the Wirral, near Liverpool. Have you heard of it?'

'No,' said Jesse.

'It's a very peaceful and utopian model village built by William Lever at the end of the nineteenth century, to house and enrich his workforce. Everyone who worked for Lever Brothers got a house, whether they were a managing director, a machinist or a packer, and these weren't the sorts of cheap, identikit two-up-two-downs that pass today, but high quality, unique designs by impressive and often local architects. Lever believed that if he provided a comfortable and dignified lifestyle for his workers, they would reward him with productivity and loyalty, so I grew up, I suppose, with more of a sense of holism and possibility than your average working-class kid from Merseyside. I lived, and my mum still lives, in a Grade II-listed building surrounded by gorgeous parkland, five minutes' walk from a world-class gallery with an incredible collection of Pre-Raphaelite paintings, Chinese ceramics and Wedgwood Jasper, a beautiful church, a school, a sports ground and a well-stocked library. I had everything on my doorstep.'

'Sounds like paradise,' Jesse said. As Owen spoke, all Jesse could think of was how beautiful he looked, and how much he wanted to see and touch his naked body. He tried not to be seen appraising the hints of musculature, and of nipple, within Owen's T-shirt, or to be caught drifting into thoughts of what they might do together in bed. But he was also thinking about the 'New System', and what Owen was describing sounded quite like what the Witnesses believed their future held.

'I'll have to take you someday,' Owen said, and smiled, brutally. Their eyes met, for the nth time, of course. Jesse couldn't bear it and looked away.

'I saw that,' said Owen.

'Saw what?'

'You just blushed.'

Jesse broke out a smile so broad he covered his mouth. It was as if he was being tickled.

'No, I didn't! 'Ow can *ar* blush?'

'Just because you didn't physically redden doesn't mean you didn't visibly blush and that sounded *very* Brummie.'

'Whatever, Scouser.'

'It's cute. There it goes again.'

'Stop thinkin' you can switch me on and off like a light!'

'Can I not?'

Jesse put his cutlery down and giggled, coughed, composed himself and sipped his champagne. He thought about how lucky he would be if he was able to continue this conversation HIV-negative. The Christmas pudding smelt rich and rummy in the oven. Jesse wondered how any organisation could deprive its subjects of such harmless fun as the singing of Christmas songs, a child's participation in school Christmas plays, the consumption of delicious Christmas dinners. The wilful self-exclusion.

'Do you believe in God?' Jesse asked, and realised he'd never answered Ginika's interrupted question at Gilbert's.

'No, I'm an atheist,' Owen said, which shocked Jesse. Ignoring God was not the same as denying his existence. He didn't know where he stood if there wasn't a Jehovah at the top of the hierarchy. Who was, then, at the top? 'I don't think *belief* helps anyone. If I believed in God, I'd have to ask him a lot of very searching questions, just as you did in your prayer. I don't see why God or any kind of institutionalised faith should encroach upon my life choices, and I understand the privilege I have, as a white Western man, to be able to live like that.'

Jesse had a lump in his throat, and as delicious as the food was, he was now struggling to eat. They both sipped their champagne and Owen topped them up.

'I thought that might change, on becoming a father. We want our daughters to have knowledge, and to be able to do with that as they wish. Anya's Catholic, so if they choose to become nuns, because we raised them as Catholics, fine. If they choose to become whores because we raised them as Catholics, equally fine.' Jesse had looked away. 'Of course, I don't want my children to become whores.'

'I wouldn't recommend it either,' said Jesse.

'I didn't mean to sound like a twat,' said Owen. Jesse found he enjoyed every expression on Owen's face, whether it was mischief, sadness or, as now, apology.

'I know what you mean,' he said. 'Of course no parent would want their child to become a whore.'

'Do your parents know?'

'Of course not.'

'Do they know you're gay, even?'

Jesse nodded, weakly. He felt Owen suspected there was depth to his story, and saw his brow tighten.

'I don't suppose they're the most supportive, are they?'

Jesse shook his head.

'Do you want to talk about it?'

Jesse had often wondered, when he was a child, what Armageddon would be like, and hoped that he would sleep so deeply he would wake up only when it was over. He'd slept through many a shout up the stairs meant to wake him, and Graham had even told him once: *Yo'd sleep through Armageddon yo would.* The tremors would have to shake the world so hard all the evildoers would die. Every building would crumble like the walls of Jericho, or the World Trade Center, and crush the little humans who didn't worship God – not just any old god, but Jehovah alone – to death. How would those tremors begin? Would they start slowly and build to a universally destructive crescendo? Jesse thought of Owen's pretty little model village and how it would be shaken to dust. There would be nothing anyone could do about it; Armageddon would be beyond the control of any human being or organisation. No Richter scale would survive to tell the tale. Nothing could stop God's work if indeed it was God's work. Whatever happened now, it was too late. He was going to die. *You're gonna die at Armageddon.*

He burst into tears so powerfully Owen flinched. He choked, and coughed, and tears ran down into his mouth and mixed with his saliva. Owen stood up and carefully came around the table to put his hands on Jesse's shoulders, then his arms around his neck.

'I'm sorry, I'm sorry,' he kept saying, cuddling him tightly. 'I'm so sorry. Now, now. I've got you.'

For all he couldn't think, Jesse felt that maybe he *had* died, or at least the old version of himself. The Jesse he had been for the first twenty years of his life had died, and this new impostor was carrying on in Jesse's old body as if nothing had happened. He missed him, the old Jesse, the favourite boy of his congregation. Young Brother Jesse McCarthy, who was supposed to one day become an elder and take a Witness wife and have perfect Witness children, on the cover of *Awake!* magazine as the perfect Witness family, whom God would shelter and shepherd through the Great Tribulation. But would he have become an elder? The elders were ten white men. Would they have ever trusted him to lead, or would he have found himself a disenfranchised ministerial servant always knocking on the door but never being allowed in? What would've happened if he was still a Witness? Would he still have pursued his sexual desires? This was a Great Tribulation of his own doing. *Brother*

Jesse McCarthy. He seemed so far away, now. Why had he killed him? He missed his family. Life with them couldn't have been *that* bad, couldn't have been worse than what he was putting himself through, this moment with Owen apart. He missed his Jehovah, his fake prayers addressed to someone who would never speak back, whom he would never see. He was angry with his family for not calling the police and reporting him missing. He was angry with himself for being a hundred and twenty miles away from them and not telling them where, when or if he was coming home. He was angry because he'd made it impossible to go home. He was angry with himself for getting found out.

'I'm sorry,' he managed to say, as Owen held him close to his chest and belly, where Jesse rather enjoyed being. Owen's hands were warm, despite it being cold now in the kitchen.

'Don't be sorry. Your family should be sorry. It's terrible, the way they've made you feel,' Owen said, as he cradled and settled Jesse, who was aware he was dribbling from the corner of his mouth down Owen's beautiful forearm. 'But the beauty of all this is that you get to build your own family. And there's no place like London for that.'

Jesse gently broke free and excused himself to the downstairs toilet, just off the kitchen, to get some tissue and blow his nose. He'd needed that cry, and was glad it had happened. He allowed himself a couple of minutes, looking at himself in the mirror above the sink, to make himself laugh, because the only thing that could ever stop him crying was to see how ugly and ridiculous he looked. (*Stop crying, you look ugly,* his mother had once told him.) He returned to find Owen sitting back in his chair, paler, with his hair gathered back in his hands clasped behind his head. The back door was closed; perhaps Owen was concerned what the neighbours might think of such a fuss being made. The bold shaft of orange-yellow light that had shone across the back wall had gone. It was growing dim in the kitchen. Jesse retook his seat opposite Owen.

'I'm so sorry,' Owen said, again, shaking his head.

'Thank you. I'm okay.'

'Are you sure?' said Owen.

Jesse nodded, and attempted to smile. Owen topped up his champagne, and his own, and they sat quietly for a moment. After one last small mouthful, that tasted like a vaguely remembered waking dream, Jesse pushed his plate slightly away from himself.

'I'll have some more later,' he said.

'Don't worry, whatever you want to do.' Owen sipped from his flute, which was getting grimy with grease, and folded his arms. He got up, switched the lamp on over the dining table, sat down and stretched out his feet between Jesse's, then retracted them as he sat forward again.

'Have you ever sought out counselling?'

Jesse looked at him as if to say, *I'm not mad*.

'I think you should,' said Owen, seriously. 'You've been through a lot, I can tell. You shouldn't have to go through it alone. You can talk to me. Tell me what's happened to you.'

He didn't know where to start. He wanted to forget all that he had been through and start again. He wasn't expecting this to happen. He didn't know whether he could trust what he was thinking and feeling; white men – and it was always white men – had made him feel like this before only to withdraw their love when he was most dependent on it. Sex as fine as he'd experienced with *that man* turned into something that left him hungry, injured, depressed, broke, wondering who he was and where the hell he was going.

As the kitchen got darker and darker, and as the food left on their plates congealed, Jesse told Owen of his disfellowshipping – *But you did nothing wrong!* – how his mother had betrayed him to the elders to suit her own needs, to absolve herself of her own guilt, to have forcibly removed from her the result of her own sin – *It won't make her feel any better, in the long run. What you're going to do is become this really great person and she'll realise what she missed out on. What you're going to do is teach them how to love. How were you able to stay that long after you were . . . what is the word you used, 'disfellowshipped'? Christ.*

In his heart of hearts Jesse wished to keep the door open to return to the organisation, be reinstated. One day he might have been able to say he wasn't gay, actually, that he was prepared to live his life without sex, that Jehovah's love would have been enough. He wasn't automatically willing to break up his family for the sake of his own lack of self-control – *It sounds to me like your family was already broken beyond anything you were responsible for.* – He didn't want to make them look bad for not being in control of their children. That's what it would've looked like if he'd struck out on his own before getting married. And who was he supposed to marry? Why would he do that to someone? Perhaps he could've learned to love a woman that way. To have sex and children with her. Would he always think about men? No woman could ever make him feel the way a man of a certain kind could, just by his presence. No woman could ever smell the way Brother Thomas Woodall did. No woman's voice could ever cloak him in such calm and repose. If he read a book by a woman, it was his mother's voice reading to him in the way, pointing a sharp knife, she'd said 'I wish I could just put this right in you, boy'. – *I wasn't even aware of my neglect of women writers, until I read Angela Carter and Iris Murdoch.* – If he read a book by a white man, it was Brother Thomas Woodall's voice reading to him and he couldn't get enough of it. – *What about when you read a book written by a black man?* – Maybe it was just his own voice, reading Baldwin. – *It's not your fault, you know. It's because you've been taught that God is a white man, and that white men are the earthly embodiment of God. You've been taught to worship white men and to hold everything that they represent, everything they own, as the dearest, most important, most sacred thing in your life. That's why you love their smiles, their skin, their beauty, their voices, their words, their sex. You've been trained to hate yourself and love and desire them.*

After a couple of mouthfuls of the Christmas pudding – Jesse's first ever, and delicious, but too great a challenge, even lubricated with brandy butter, for his nipped appetite – they washed and packed everything up, drank coffee and Jesse told Owen about *that man*. Owen winced when Jesse told him about the scratched wound – contorted his body and smashed his fist on the table as if it was happening to him. He also looked a little offended that Jesse had not told him before, though they had not spoken to each other on such open terms until now. Jesse made Owen understand that he had sought medical advice and was waiting for the incubation period to expire so that he could take a second HIV test. It had been established that he was negative three months before the incident.

Owen told Jesse about a split condom incident of his own, but considered himself to be less at risk because he'd been the one wearing it, though he hadn't been to get tested since he'd become sexually active with men. Still, hearing Jesse's story seemed to change his mood. He didn't say anything, but Jesse thought that perhaps, given what Owen had been through with his English teacher when he was so young, it couldn't have been easy deciding to have the sex he wanted while HIV, though no longer virtually untreatable, was still a chronic illness. He wondered whether Owen and his English teacher ever had sex, but didn't ask.

Chapter 4

Owen replenished the ice bucket, opened a fourth bottle of champagne and they moved into the sitting room, the largest room in the house, directly below his bedroom. It was suddenly eight o'clock in the evening. The sound of Joy Division still resonated in Jesse's head. Owen turned the blinds closed and switched on the two standard lamps either side of the bay window. It was usually quite dark anyway, thanks to it overlooking the front garden, which was small and overgrown, with a wild front hedge that might have been cut back for the winter, except for the privacy it afforded.

Bryan had insisted on a stout, real Christmas tree even though he was not going to be there to enjoy it himself, and had decorated it with fine baubles from Liberty and a vintage ballerina Sindy doll for the angel. The lights were shining and projecting on the walls from the little mirrors on the disco ball hanging from the ceiling. Giant two-seat sofas were backed against three of the walls, around a working fireplace. An oak-and-glass coffee table stacked with back-copies of *World of Interiors* and *Gay Times* lived on an IKEA rug in the middle of the room, unreachable to anyone, so Owen asked Jesse to help him lift it towards where they would be sitting, on the sofa opposite the bay window.

'I understand it might not be the best thing to give you, with what you're going through, but I've got some coke upstairs,' he said. 'Do you want some?'

Jesse nodded and smiled as if he'd like nothing better, so Owen ran up, two stairs at a time.

The folding doors behind them were kept closed, and led to the old dining room, which was currently being repurposed and redecorated for use as another bedroom. Prospective tenants were already being shown around, while Jesse overheard from upstairs phrases like *high ceilings*, *period features* and *original cornicing and rose work*. The doors were going to be removed, and the wall filled in with brick and concrete, so there would be much upheaval, noise and dust in the new year.

Owen came back smiling, with a fat wallet stuffed into his back pocket. He fed five albums into the disc changer and pressed play, then sat down, poured them each a glass of champagne and unwrapped a rock of coke onto one of the empty CD cases – Mary J Blige's *My Life* – edging powder off it with a faded old Visa, hurriedly, as if he'd been waiting a long time for the appropriate hour. Jesse knew how that felt, and he also knew the reward. Mary's was not the album playing. It was bluesy, bassy, dubby.

Getting rid of the albatross. Jesse recalled Coleridge's 'Rime of the Ancient Mariner' from GCSE English.

'What does an albatross look like?'

Owen was surprised by the question and gave a little laugh as he chopped the rock finer and finer.

'Well, there are lots of different subspecies of them, but the wandering albatross sort of looks like a bigger, more aristocratic seagull, with webbed feet and giant gliding wings. They partner for life and can live up to fifty years. They fly enormous distances to get the right food for their young. Coleridge made it a cultural icon in *Rime of the Ancient Mariner.*'

Jesse wasn't expecting this quality of answer, and was slightly resentful of Owen's encyclopaedic knowledge of things, though felt another wave of infatuation at the mention of *partner for life*. He hoped one day to be the sort of person who could confidently answer any question thrown at him, but suspected the versatility of Owen's mind was a result of its Cambridge education. Cambridge. Even the word sounded smug. If it was in the Black Country it would be called *Cam*-bridge, with a hard *a*, not *Came*-bridge.

'What are we listening to?'

'*Metal Box* by Public Image Limited. Do you have a note?'

'No. What year?'

'It's okay, you can use this one,' he said, quickly snatching a pair out of his wallet. 'You're the twenty and I'm the ten. We shouldn't share because of our uncertain statuses.'

'Okay.'

He fondled the note, on one side of which was the Queen, the other, a man with a huge moustache. Uncertain statuses. That made it sound so real. Guilty until proven guilty. He should behave as if he was HIV-positive. He probably was. It cheered him, though, to think that Owen was putting himself in the same boat.

Jesse snorted up the line Owen offered him and sat back, letting the low bassline rumble into him, thinking about his arsehole and the now-dry wound in it, and suddenly, as the coke made him tremble and lick his teeth, feeling it didn't matter. Maybe he shouldn't have told him. Maybe the coke would've made him tell the truth but add, *It's okay, you can still fuck me with a condom and you won't catch anything if I suck your dick.*

'Memories,' Owen said, after sniffing his line. 'Strange things. They come and go. Sometimes it feels like you can remember things from before you were born. I call it borrowed nostalgia. Actually, I won't lie, someone else has called it that before me. What's that about? Is extra-sensory perception at play? Could I have anticipated my own birth? Did someone have to die so that I could be born? I was born in January '71. Jorge Barbosa, the Cape Verdean poet, died on the day I was born. Maybe his poetic soul transferred into mine? I don't write about island nature, but hey, it's an interesting theory. We'll look up who died on your birth date later. This is "Death Disco". Let's have a dance.'

The way he went on, Jesse could listen to Owen's brain shaking out little sweeties forever. He wanted to be spoken to like that while being fucked. He wanted to be hypnotised by someone with a very fine brain and a very large dick, and he could just tell Owen had a very large, jawbreaking dick. He always thought it was those guys who had massive packets, but once he got their pants off it turned out to be almost all fat and swollen balls. Skinny guys with no packet, somehow, seemed to have the biggest dicks. Owen wasn't skinny, but he carried himself with a certain confidence. Jesse knew he would hurt but he'd commit to it. Owen was thirty-two in a month, Jesse thought. A year younger than Jesus was when he died. Fit and strong, and would only get better as he aged. The thought of Owen forever released a second rush of brightness; nice coke. He ground his teeth to the music. His mouth was nice and wet, but he swigged another glass of champagne anyway, mourning, for just a second, the needlessly shit night his family would be having, spitefully shutting themselves in, locking out the world on its one day of peace and unity while their exiled son was having the time of his life.

'It's like our own little club,' Jesse said. They danced in their socks, then Jesse folded back the rug so they could slide around. They spun naturally together in the lights, their bodies touching without awkwardness. Owen allowed himself to feel Jesse's arse, and gave it a squeeze, first with one hand, then two. 'Wow,' he said.

'You ever felt an ass like this before?' Their mouths were close.

'I think I would remember if I did.'

'It's yours,' Jesse told Owen, as other bottoms had said to him.

Owen cleared his throat and released Jesse, then grinned at him. They danced, spun around and held hands. 'They released this as a single without the "Swan Lake" refrain and called it "Death Disco". I prefer this version. You asked the year. Seventy-nine. Same year as *Off the Wall* and *Risqué*, and loads of absolutely great post-punk and industrial I know you'll love. Throbbing Gristle, Wire, The Pop Group, Blondie, Talking Heads. It's extraordinary, your taste in music. Joy Division are an all-time great band nobody listens to any more.'

'It was wicked with a spliff. But I'm not really a fan of Jacko,' said Jesse, and he was immediately reminded of the blonde woman in the pink dress with the little dog in Gilbert's who'd said of him, *Oh, but doesn't he look like a young Michael Jackson!* when he didn't yet have much of an Afro.

'What?' Owen asked, either as if to accuse Jesse of stealing the singer's early look while running him down, or because all black people by definition had to love Michael Jackson, which justified Jesse's distaste for anything after *Off the Wall*, when the negro-nose-mutilation and skin-bleaching started.

'Although *Off the Wall*'s probably his best album. What's *Risqué*?'

'*Risqué*, by Chic? Mate, you've got a lot of listening to do. You can hear the influence of black disco music in this, definitely. Everyone was onto it. White people took what they needed then shut disco down, literally. Have you heard of the "Disco Sucks" movement?'

'No.'

'White Americans disaffected by the lack of guitar music in the charts held a massive rally in a football stadium and basically burned Disco at the stake.' Owen was the sort of man, like Brother Thomas Woodall, who refused to raise his voice whatever the surroundings were doing, expecting his interlocutor to simply listen harder. Only good-looking, successful white men with big dicks ever did that, and everyone else indulged them. 'Not only was it a racially charged movement, it was also homophobic – disco *sucks*' – he made a blowjob gesture – 'as disco was known to be the music of choice among the blacks and gays. Overnight an entire genre, the most popular of the time, disappeared from the charts and legends like Grace Jones and Nile Rodgers had to rewire their sound entirely or face oblivion.'

Jesse's heart was racing. 'I think I know what you mean about borrowed nostalgia. I definitely experienced it really strongly when we were listening to Joy Division earlier. This kind of music just sounds like where I grew up, or at least what those places used to sound like just before I was born.'

'This is the sound of Britain in the disenfranchised, racist, impoverished, hungry, angry late Seventies, where punk meets disco meets funk meets dub, meets art,' Owen said, passionately. 'It brought races together where otherwise there was neo-fascism. You'd see the sort of mix at gigs you'd never see on the street or the football terraces. I was only eight when it was released. There's no way my parents would have allowed me to play this at home. They hated punk, and especially John Lydon.'

'John Lydon?'

'Johnny Rotten from the Sex Pistols. After he left that band, he reinvented himself under his own name and created PiL with Keith Levene. I much prefer this iteration.'

Jesse's shoulders dropped. 'I don't know anything.'

'You're young,' Owen said, cradling Jesse's cheek in his warm hand. 'You've got it all to come.'

Jesse started to feel edgy. He knew that he would need to be topped up with a bump every ten minutes or so to stay in this brave new world, or he would start to retreat back inside himself. His aim, now, whatever the consequences, was to have sex with Owen. He would not reject him. They were men, they could deal with it, and if Jesse wanted him, which he did, they had to face reality and the truth together. But it was still early.

'You were talking about your parents?' Jesse said suddenly.

'My dad died earlier this year.'

'Sorry,' said Jesse.

'You weren't to know.'

It occurred to Jesse that little more than a year ago, he

would've launched straight into a spiel about the Great Hope, that people might welcome their loved ones back to life during the resurrection after Armageddon. He was glad he no longer believed that. Had he ever believed it at all? What *did* he believe in now? He hadn't stopped to think. Could he be an atheist like Owen? He couldn't handle the thought.

'What did he die of?'

'Cancer. It started in his chest and then metastasised. And I chose that as the time to come out, which is why I'm here.'

'I don't understand,' said Jesse. They were standing inches from each other, not really dancing but swishing from hip to hip.

'Have you ever had a close family member die?'

'My dad, but I didn't know him,' said Jesse. 'He died when I was two.'

'So you never knew him. I'm sorry about that,' said Owen. 'But when my dad died, because it was really the first bereavement I'd experienced as an adult, I felt, not necessarily that I could take his place, but that the space his power, morals and control had left would remain vacant, and irreplaceable, so that I didn't have to lie any more. When he was alive I had to do what I could to make him proud of me.'

'You went to Cambridge!' Jesse said. 'And he wasn't proud of you?'

'Of course he was proud of me, but I was supposed to become a teacher, a scientist or a clerk in the company – something professional. My granddad worked on the factory floor, and my dad was a lab technician. He always thought I was a little pansy, with my poetry, my flowers, my Associates records and my little Thom Gunn trace-hoop earring, but he never expected I would stray so far from the family blueprint.'

He no longer wore a trace hoop; Jesse held him by the jaw while he checked both sides, and Owen let him, like a dog; a healed-over piercing dimpled his left earlobe. John Lydon's wailing voice withdrew behind a cloak as the synths flared up around him and the bass guitar served rapidly escalating notes which, altogether with the insistent drums, got stuck in a frantic, claustrophobic groove.

'This is sick, this scratched record bit at the end,' said Jesse, resting his hands on Owen's chest.

'It's great, right? You ever listened to this album before? I thought you'd like this if you liked *Unknown Pleasures*. Same year.'

'What was the singer's name?'

'Of Joy Division? Ian Curtis.'

'And he died?'

'Hanged himself in his kitchen in 1980. He was twenty-three.'

'That's horrible,' Jesse said, thinking of Aaliyah – who died in a plane crash at twenty-two – as the next song, a throbbing, oscillating bassline and wary guitar over cymbals, bass and snare drum, kicked in. 'I like the way this cut straight in from the previous song without them trying to mix the two.'

'"Poptones", one of the greatest songs ever made. About a girl who got kidnapped and driven to a forest but managed to escape, and all she remembered was that it was a Japanese car and they were playing contemporary pop songs on the cassette player, hence "Poptones".'

'It does sound like being lost in the woods.' Jesse was lost in the music, eyes closed, swinging his arms because it wasn't really danceable. He thought maybe he could interpret-dance to it like Aaliyah did Timbaland's staccato beats, but refrained. A twenty-three-year-old singer hung himself in his kitchen in 1980. What a different world it seemed to be, just before Jesse was born. Twenty-two and twenty-three seemed a long way away.

'Shall we have a smoke?' Owen said.

They sat back down and Jesse, already with sweaty, trembling hands, his heart racing, started rolling a spliff.

'So you were talking about your dad.'

'Was I?' Owen said, separating off another couple of lines

on Mary J Blige's blue face, perfect considering the rumoured drug and alcohol issues that accompanied the making of her masterpiece, her no-doubt-vacant eyes shadowed under a low flat cap. 'I don't want to say anything bad about him. He was a good man. Worked hard all his life. His father, grandfather and great-grandfather were all dockers, before Granddad joined Lever Brothers. We got on better as adults, especially after I brought Anya home for the first time, but he was always slightly disdainful of the fact that I was a strong reader and loved reading more than anything in the world. I actually think, now, he'd be diagnosed dyslexic.'

All the while, Owen was fingering his £10 note, rolling it, then unrolling it, then rolling it tighter, staring into the middle distance as if there was a television there. There was a television there, high up in the corner above the Christmas tree, though nobody ever watched it as they all had their own TVs in their rooms.

'I think he thought that I thought that I was better than them, but actually, what he didn't acknowledge was that I was born in the Seventies, not the Forties, and my choices were a lot different from his. My education was a lot better than his. He left school at sixteen having failed his school certificate but straightaway got work for the company. I went to Wirral Grammar School for Boys and excelled. The situation was right, and I got into Cambridge on merit. We hit the sweet spot. He brought me up in this aspirational village but then couldn't handle the fact that I would be different from him, that I wouldn't know or expect the same boundaries he'd grown up with. Anyway, like I said, he was a good man. He married my mother, then they moved into the house she still lives in and had my sister, then me. Mum took night classes and qualified to become a schoolteacher. She didn't get paid that much, neither of them did, but they didn't really spend any money either. My dad kept an allotment and we grew our own vegetables. I had a good childhood, really. My parents took care of us, and in Port Sunlight, we had everything that would benefit a curious and creative child. I can't complain. Sorry, you probably don't wanna hear this happy family shit.'

He finally snorted his line. Jesse felt that Owen probably saw himself as the working-class boy who did well and transcended his birth class and the expectations that were thrust upon him. He thought of Sister Doreen Charles. No education; all conviction. Jesse's was one of the faces she wanted to see again in the New System, she always said, though at not-yet-seventy she had plenty of living time left. John Lydon sang over an exquisitely smooth and bassy synthpop number. That and the song before it comprised a fascinating diptych. *Careering.* There were two ways to interpret that word. Careering, as in dockworking, teaching, prostituting, preaching. But then there was careering, as in running away. Absconding. Perhaps that was what Jesse was doing. When would it stop? When and where would he settle? Was he lost forever? Did he care? He'd suck hard dicks and fuck warm asses until he was dead. With the right weed, he wouldn't stop to eat or drink.

'You alright?' Owen said.

'Perfect,' Jesse said, assimilating one of Owen's stock responses.

'This music too intense for you?'

'No, it's sick.'

'Sick?'

'Fuckin' grand.'

'How fuckin' grand?'

'Smoke some draw.'

'What were you thinking about?'

It was so intense, and erotic, the feeling that someone wanted to know exactly what was on his mind, to be so close to him as to tease out his unvoiced thoughts. Jesse felt that if he could speak his mind truly – if he had Owen's mastery of language, given how he was able to command the attention of an audience at the Kingdom Hall, preaching pure bullshit – he would be able to make Owen fall in love with him immediately. It was Christmas night, and they were sessioning; neither of them was going to go out, or leave. The worst thing would be if one of them yawned off and went to bed. Without the other.

'I'm thinking about death.'

'That'll be the music.'

'I'm thinking about what I used to believe, that everyone who didn't dedicate themselves to the vindication of Jehovah's Will would all die at Armageddon. Like you.' Jesse put a hand on Owen's shoulder and let it drift across his back. 'You're a really nice person and you've been really kind to me. You've shown me more love in one day than my parents have in twenty years, but you're the one who's supposed to die, like everyone else who just so happens not to be a Jehovah's Witness. You're trying to be honest and not to live a lie, and they're doing the exact opposite, strapping themselves down to a hope in a new and better world because they're scared to live their own lives on their own terms.'

Owen sat back, with his arm across the top of the settee, and Jesse leaned in close to him, finding his home. It was wonderful, the feeling of being listened to by someone, when he was speaking from the heart and not from the Bible.

'There's six *billion* people in the world . . .'

'And rising,' said Owen.

'Yeah, and six *million* Jehovah's Witnesses. If Armageddon happened tomorrow, would that mean that six billion people would all die at the same time, blitzed like in a blender?' Owen laughed at the image. 'I don't get it. I can't see it. How will those six million be individually picked out to be saved? I really used to think, as a kid, that one morning I'd wake up and look out my bedroom window and the whole earth'd be rubble, like the aftermath of Hiroshima or something. Like, literally, everything flattened, except because we were Jehovah's Witnesses, Jehovah would've somehow spared us, us and the other Witness family who lived on our estate. Our houses would be the only ones standing, untouched, everything else crushed down to chunks of concrete with rusty bits of metal jutting out, and the odd foot sticking up with a heel on, the odd bloody hand with a wedding ring. The whole earth would look like the landfill site my dad worked on. And for a minute, we'd all be celebrating; we'd all run out our front door and jump up and down and be like yeah! We made it! We're in the New System! Jehovah saved us! We'd be thinking, we're in paradise! And I suppose my family, and everyone I grew up loving, believes that to the death. But then the reality must dawn on us at some point that actually, practically speaking, we're far from being in paradise, cos you know what, we're gonna have to clean all this shit up first, and that includes burying six *billion* dead people, all of them in different states of mash-up, between the six *million* of us spread really thinly all over the globe. That means we'd have to bury a thousand people each. That's not paradise.'

'I buried my dad with a spade, me and a few other blokes. It's fucking back-breaking.'

Jesse rolled up his note. 'And where? I mean, what the fuck? Can you imagine what the smell'd be like? The diseases that'd breed? The fight for food once we've raided all the supermarkets and all the fresh stuff's gone out of date? What would happen when people realised the pangs of distress were greater after than they were before? That the thing they'd waited all their lives for turned out to be harder than their old life? That they'd started dying again, from dust inhalation or food poisoning or blood loss or starvation? Cos their doctor, who wasn't a believer, was dead? That they were starving and freezing cos their central heating didn't work, cos the people at the gas and electricity board are all dead? Most people freak out if they run out of petrol and have to walk half a mile with a can to the garage. What would happen when people realised God actually hadn't been able to wipe every tear from their eyes, and when they realised all the nice people who lived on their street or worked in their office, who just so happened not to be Jehovah's Witnesses, were all dead?'

Feeling emancipated, Jesse sat forward and sniffed up his line.

'I'm glad you're out of there,' said Owen, as he tapped and rubbed Jesse's back. 'It wasn't a good place for someone like you.'

'Thank you. So am I.'

'You know what your story reminds me of? You've lost your centre of gravity, so to survive, you'll need to take steps to create another. I've got a novel upstairs just for you, called *Against Nature*. I'm not sure what you'll make of it. It's an intense read, by a late nineteenth-century French author called J-K Huysmans, who worked full-time for the French civil service whilst writing these brilliant masterpieces of early modernism, on their headed paper, in fine hand. Remind me and I'll lend it to you, if you want.'

Jesse nodded his head, lay back against Owen's body and lit his spliff. The next song, a synth and bass guitar-led instrumental, was again quite different from anything he had heard before, yet somehow familiar, like the incidental music at the end of a sci-fi film shot in a desert with an orange and dark blue sky, representing the dwarfing great beyond, worlds man has yet to discover.

'Of course, I'm not comparing you to the hero of the book, Des Esseintes,' Owen continued. 'You're very different people. He's a fading aristocrat from one of the oldest families in France. But Parisian high society is so integral to his life, just as the Witness doctrine still is to yours, that he needed to do whatever he could within the boundaries of his sanity to disassociate himself from it whilst remaining himself, and it seems like you're in that place, or are about to access that place. I wonder whether that might not have been your principal reason for becoming a sex worker.'

'I suppose so.' Jesse felt as if he was being read to at bedtime by Daddy. He had forgotten that this was the exact reason why he became a sex worker. 'I couldn't survive in this world if I was convinced everyone I walked past in the street was evil and about to be punished with eternal death.'

'Yeah, because the Witnesses don't believe in heaven or hell, do they?'

'No.'

'So what does happen to us when we die?'

'From dust you are and to dust you will return.'

'So our bodies might crumble, but what happens to our souls?'

'Who knows?'

'Do they return to God?'

'I don't know.'

'Do you still believe in God?'

'I don't think so.'

He found he had said that too quickly, and therefore wondered whether it was true or not. They had passed from the world of Public Image Limited into that of Mary J Blige, which, in terms of mood and depth, didn't feel that different, Jesse was surprised to find. With a depressive for a mother, he'd lived with this album since it was released when he was twelve. It was a favourite of hers; it put a voice and words to her pain. God, or at least a belief in God, had given Mary her voice. Jesse was in awe of Owen's taste for Mary. Everything he did, everything he surrounded himself with, deepened his appreciation of him. Jesse wanted to be equally in his orbit. He deserved someone as loyal and open-hearted.

'When's your birthday?' Owen asked.

'May 23,' said Jesse.

'Gemini. Interesting.'

'What are you?'

'January 6. Capricorn.'

'So you're a stubborn goat and I'm a two-faced bitch.'

'Goats believe in what they believe and stick to it. That's not a bad trait.'

'And I'm not actually a two-faced bitch. But I can be one thing and its opposite in the same mouthful.'

'Your eyes are like nothing I've ever seen,' said Owen, surprising Jesse. 'So bright and clear, and endlessly saying different, fascinating things. You might be talking, and I'm listening, but at the same time, it's your eyes that tell me the truth. Like upstairs earlier, when I was sitting on your bed and asked you if you enjoyed sex with your clients, I could tell you did but that something was really missing for you, because you're looking for connection. You're looking for someone who will look at you like they belong to you and you belong to them. You're looking for real love. I can see in your eyes that you are capable of it. Those eyes will never change, unless you change them. Only you have the power to do that. Nothing outside of you can spoil you.'

Jesse wanted to say something corny and absolutely true like, *That's the most beautiful thing anyone's ever said to me*, but instead remained silent and clicked his fingers to the vintage soul beat. Mary's lyrics exposed the intimacy in the room. Jesse suddenly found he couldn't look Owen in the eye. True Gemini behaviour. They shared the spliff and nodded their heads at the class coming out of the speakers. Owen realised what was missing, and tapped Jesse on the shoulder gently. Jesse leaned forward and Owen got up to light the fire, using kindling and logs.

Jesse suddenly felt restless; he was neither hot nor cold, and his palms and the soles of his feet were moist. He got up and shook the life back into his limbs. He thought 'You Bring Me Joy' might be the ultimate Mary song. Floor-stamping drums, bright, so simple, with a dissonant low piano chord played percussively, lyrics sung understatedly – there is melancholy even while she sings of a true love. Age, authority, style. He looked down at Owen's back as he poked the fire. If this was something that was happening between them, Jesse was overjoyed at the thought of where his life might be going. If it was just this night hanging out together, and life would go back to normal the next day, he would still cherish it forever.

The fire was catching, and over the CD sounded a bit like the crackling at the start of a vinyl LP. Jesse wondered what Owen's wife and children were doing. With his freedom of mouth he almost asked, then somehow had the presence of mind not to. Owen would be open with him about such things if and when he wished to be. Jesse carried on smoking the spliff and dancing with his feet together.

When Owen got up, satisfied that the fire was going well, Jesse handed him the spliff. Their eyes locked as Owen approached him, and Jesse almost bent double with the ache. Owen put his hand on Jesse's waist, and they moved together to the vintage soul lick of 'I'm the Only Woman'. I would be your wife, Jesse thought, but still, could hardly look Owen in the eye. He had an erection, but knew he could do nothing about it. He had to pretend he was slow dancing at a Kingdom Hall wedding with one of the elderly sisters to an old Nat King Cole number before he could contain himself, which wasn't easy with a spliff in his hand; weed always made him horny, but since *that man*, what he had realised about himself was that he had to switch off his dick and switch on his brain if he was going to survive in this world.

Owen leaned his cheek against Jesse's, very gently, as if to try it out. Jesse tried his hardest not to tremble. Owen's body warmth was wonderful. Jesse thought he could share everything with him. What was life about other than to find someone with whom you could share everything? Every thought, every success, every drama? Mary, what are you doing to us? Jesse closed his eyes and rested his cheek on Owen's shoulder. That was the moment of trust, of letting go. He didn't mind if he dribbled. He'd found someone who could love him, whom he'd be willingly led by if he was blind. He'd found someone he could love. He'd found someone whose shoulder he could fall asleep on.

'You Gotta Believe'. He'd forgotten how romantic *My Life* was. His mother had bought it on cassette so she could play it in the car. It sounded good in the Sierra Sapphire, but better here, on a proper hi-fi, with the clarity of CD mastering. Back then, Jesse relished the relaxed, happy vibe of the general Nineties R&B landscape. Now he could appreciate it for its musicality. It reminded him of *What's Going On* by Marvin Gaye, *Lady Soul* by Aretha Franklin or *Wild Is the Wind* by Nina Simone. His mother should've gone to prison for getting rid of all her classic soul vinyl.

The lyrics meant little to him as a twelve-year-old boy who had been conditioned to accuse all love songs, particularly sung by black women, of desperate schmaltz, but in this man's arms, now, they meant everything, and Jesse wondered if – hoped, actually that – his mother felt the same love from Graham as he was now feeling from Owen, because then he might even be able to forgive her for choosing him, and their religion, over her son. Here he was, just like her, being loved by a white man. It was a little bit corny of him, to be slow-dancing with him to 'I Never Wanna Live Without You'. Owen held the spliff in front of his face, so Jesse could smoke.

'She's so amazing,' Owen said, as the song entered a coda. 'Like Billie Holiday. Not like other contemporary singers who are all about the precision and power. Mary J's about the emotion and energy, the chiaroscuro, the pain. This is her best work. Every song. Still sounds so good. Don't you think?'

Jesse nodded his head, too content to speak. An escalating blaze of strings and brass immediately retreated to a whimpering guitar phrase like a pining dog's, over which Mary pleaded. Owen sat down and chopped lines again on her face, while Jesse sang along, every word, in his low tone, unintentionally performing for Owen, who sat quietly, watched and listened, smoking the spliff. When the verses were finished, they took it in turns to hoover up their lines. It was good coke.

'That line *Look what you done to me!*' Owen said. 'That's worthy of all the soul greats. Otis, Levi, James Brown ... '

Owen filled their glasses while Mary cried herself to sleep on a bed of shimmering violins, waiting for her man to come home, their dog whining at the door. He stretched his arm back out along the top of the sofa behind Jesse's head, and Jesse rested his hand on Owen's thigh.

He wished he had saved himself for this moment, that he had never been touched by a man in his life. That he hadn't been wounded by *that man*, or breathed the air in 'Dave''s squalid drug den, or fucked that man in the toilets at Compton's, or been picked up by the man in the Bentley, or hired by the stale-smelling elderly man from Southampton who insisted on coming to his room, or the Northern Irishman with the penthouse apartment and the rimming stool, or the Mancunian blue-lipped with poppers, or the policeman in Dorking who called him a nigger and got him to spit on him and beat him up, or the Indian man in Bermondsey who liked him to fuck a line of coke up his arse and asked him to leave at five in the morning when he'd got too high, or fucked mercilessly by the masseur who lived on the Charing Cross Road and refused to pay him just when he'd run out of money, or made love to by the married black man at the sauna who had the biggest dick he'd ever seen, or drunk gin with the handsome, hairy Russian guy whose sweat drops he loved catching in his mouth, or tea with the lawyer in Covent Garden whose skinny little ass took the deepest, hardest fuck he'd ever given, but who had invited round a black boy even younger than him, in school uniform, the next morning while he was still there – Jesse, embarrassed, just left; he should've said, *What the fuck you doing here, boy? Get out!* – or beer with Rufus, whose big daddy arse he had enjoyed so much and come in over and over, but whom he hadn't heard from since. He wondered what had happened to him, with that suspected jewellery theft and suspension, but it didn't matter now. He was with Owen, and if he could wait until January, when he would get tested again and hopefully, hopefully, be negative, then they could have all the sex they wanted, and nobody would need to use a condom because Jesse would never need anyone else and he would make sure Owen never needed anyone else. And they already lived together. He realised it was unlikely, and he couldn't even pray! Besides, what if Owen was just another bad man waiting to reveal his true self as soon as he'd taken from him the sex he wanted? What if he was another Rufus? Were all men the same? Jehovah destroyed Sodom and Gomorrah because the men wanted to fuck the angels he sent. He had heard a Witness say that Jehovah allowed the AIDS virus because he couldn't wait for Armageddon to punish the disgusting, evil gays.

Boxing Day. The 1980s. His mother's family. The men in the sitting room chat cricket and football and drink rum, the women in the kitchen watch soap operas and drink tea. The biggest, oldest men, with the hardest laughs, get a seat; the biggest, oldest women, with the hardest laughs, get a seat. Otherwise standing-room only, and the kids would play in the long hallway trying to work out the old stereogram that hadn't been played since before any of them were born, sometimes getting a little too excited and incurring a wrathful *Tap de naise!* from their grandmother, the meaty contents of whose dutchpot, swaddled in gravy like savoury honey, had gathered a crowd of thirty people at any given time, family or not, to her little stove.

Jesse knew he should be with the men but he always stayed with the women. They were louder, more fun, more exciting. His aunties, girls in their late teens, would laugh and joke and watch the soap with their elders, but when the front curtains were drawn, and Jesse's grandfather was too drunk and merry to do anything about it, they would paint up their faces and dash out clubbing, laughing at their own audacity as the door clapped shut behind them and their heels clicked through the gate into a waiting BMW. How little Jesse wanted to go with them, to cross over into the flashing lights, to drink Babycham and dutty whine to R&B.

Chapter 5

It was morning when he woke up on the settee in the front room. The Christmas tree was on, its lights still flashing inanely, the lamps on, the rug folded and the coffee table drawn up in front of him like they'd been pushed in by a high tide. There were two whisky glasses on the table, with the bottle, Laphroaig, half-empty and topless. The peaty smell had been attractive when they were drinking it but was now odious. A scum of white powder coated the cover of *My Life*, and there was still some coke left in the open second wrap. Owen's laptop lay closed where he had been sitting. Silence.

Jesse reached into his jeans pocket for his phone. It was quarter-past eleven. Where was Owen? He felt horribly lonely. His head ached and his sinuses were swollen. He got up and went into the kitchen to pee in the downstairs toilet, then upstairs to Owen's room. The door was wide open; he wasn't in there. Owen must have needed to go out, and didn't want to wake him. Perhaps he'd driven to Anya's, to surprise his daughters first thing. Perhaps the pain they had gone through together made Owen want to be back with his wife. Perhaps he'd seen sense, and put his marriage before his desires. Owen's car keys, normally at the back of the work surface, were missing. Jesse's bedding was still in the washer-dryer. He couldn't deal with being awake, so he ran upstairs to his clean room, stripped off and got into bed, pulling the top of the duvet over his head.

The doorbell rang obnoxiously, perhaps only fifteen minutes

later. Jesse resentfully got out of bed and put on his dressing-gown, and was at the top of the stairs calling, *Coming!* when he heard a key enter the lock and watched from above a blonde woman let herself into the house. His heart was still racing from the coke. Was she the police? She looked like one of those TV Special Branch officers. But she also looked like she'd been crying. She carefully closed the front door behind herself and stood in the hallway with her back against the radiator and the long front pieces of her hair tumbling over her eyes.

It was Owen's wife. Anya. Must be. She said nothing, just stared down at the floor with her shoulders up near her ears. He knew she had seen him, when coming into the house, as if she expected to, but then she didn't look at him again. He thought he would not speak until she did, because it was too extraordinary that she was there, with Owen's keys. *Owen's not here*, he would say. *I thought he might be with you.* He sat down on the stairs and gathered the skirts of his dressing-gown between his knees, convinced, now, that something bad had happened.

He didn't want to ask her anything stupid, but the tension made him want to scratch himself all over, or laugh, scream, or slap her. Was Owen dead? Why? Why had God taken Owen? He wondered whether Owen's daughters were outside in a car, screaming for their father. He didn't know what had happened, and for some reason, he couldn't ask; it was already his fault; he had known Owen for three months and been in love with him for a day, but this woman, this frigid stranger, had been married to him since the week before Princess Diana died.

He could see she was crying again, silently. He got up and slowly crept down the stairs, and holding the collar of his dressing-gown tight – careful not to touch her because she looked like the sort of person who might lash out – he encouraged her to follow him and sit down at the kitchen table. He asked her if she had come alone or if her children were in a car, and if she needed him to call anyone. He poured her a glass of filtered water from the fridge. She said nothing. Her face was red and as she wiped her eyes, more tears came. Then she spoke, quickly, sweetly, sometimes slurring as she chased and grabbed her tears like children running too close to the road.

'He's crashed his car straight through a shop window. I've no idea where he was going but he was somewhere in South London and they think he fell asleep at the wheel!'

Jesse covered his mouth, as if he was going to be sick, at this unbelievable news. 'Is he dead?' he whispered.

'Why did you let him leave the house and get in his car?' she said, staring right at him, and he straight away blamed himself. 'He must've been out of his mind!'

She got up and fled the kitchen, and her boots sounded hard on the floor as she stomped upstairs. The veins had stood out on her neck as she spoke to him. She had the look of someone who boxed. He heard her check one room, before deciding the second was Owen's. She would have identified it by the clothes over the back of his desk chair. She'd have recognised all the vintage posters, the row upon row of books, the turntable and loose vinyl LPs scattered around, and next to his bed, the school portrait of their smiling daughters.

Jesse flicked on the kettle. They had wanted to have sex, both of them did, but Jesse was sure he was sick, and the last thing he sought was to harm Owen. He couldn't remember going to sleep, and must have passed out, so Owen must've found some-one online, or something, and was driving to them. In Jesse's mind, he'd smashed into a bollard, catapulted through the windscreen – the broken glass at the end of *Unknown Pleasures*. If Jesse hadn't been sick, Owen would not have had to leave the house. They'd be in bed together now, spooning, unbothered by what time or day it was.

Anya was silent upstairs. Tears fell as he made her the cup of tea that he would have drunk to make himself feel better, with semi-skimmed milk and one sugar. He took it up to Owen's room and knocked on the door. She didn't respond so he invited himself in. She was sitting on the end of the bed, staring at the fireplace, folding down a piece of paper into eighths, sixteenths. Perhaps that was why she had come, to get rid of any evidence. He would do so in the living room, when she was gone. Why had Owen gone out? He came to stand near enough to her, and held out the tea for her to take. She ignored it.

'Is he dead?' he repeated, though he wasn't sure how ready he was for an answer. He expected Owen to be dead, though it needn't hurt him too much, because they hadn't known each other for long and everything else was gone as well. He took a deep breath and calmed himself.

'Didn't you have a home to go to?' she said.

'My parents are Jehovah's Witnesses.'

She blinked a nominal apology, and put the paper in her pocket.

'Is he dead?' he asked, more firmly this time.

'No,' she said. She'd stopped crying, and didn't look quite so angry any more.

'Is he going to be okay?' he said.

'He had to be air-lifted to hospital. A miracle that that could even be done on Boxing Day,' she said, perhaps mimicking the tired surgeon who told her this.

'He's the best person I've ever met,' Jesse said, now able to release his tears.

She laughed at him. Owen was the perfect man: intelligent, handsome, strong, masculine, gentle, a listener. She knew all that. She knew the power Owen had to make someone fall in love with him. His grey eyes and long lashes. His charm. His poetry and eloquence; his way of thinking out loud in long, passionately argued paragraphs.

She stood up – making Jesse, expecting a slap, spill the tea he was still holding – and walked round him to the bedroom door. Anya spoke to the dark landing, not to him.

'I'm moving him out of here, and I'll take care of him at home when he leaves hospital. You are not to contact him.' Perhaps now she stopped blaming him, now that she had reinforced the status quo, because she turned round and addressed him more sympathetically. Her face was dry and some of the redness had gone. 'I am his wife and he needs me. I don't want to offend you, but this is a marriage, and only I can fix him. Nothing else matters.'

He waited until he heard the front door close, and a car drive away. He went downstairs and retrieved the few lines-worth of coke left in the wrap. After a long time sitting, staring, thinking of, and doing absolutely nothing, he went back upstairs, put on *Unknown Pleasures*, got under Owen's duvet, pulling it right up to his neck, and stared at the books on their shelves, remembering the one Owen had mentioned, while they were doing coke.

It sounds like you've lost your centre of gravity, he'd said; the memory of his words sounding bright and clear as if delivered through a microphone from the platform at the Kingdom Hall. He imagined Owen with his hair combed back with a centre parting, wearing a suit and a floral tie like the cover of *Power, Corruption & Lies*. Jesse cried alone, until he slept.

A week later, a van came by and workmen packed Owen's things unmethodically into boxes and took them away. In the new year, Jesse settled for a job stacking shelves at the local Safeway supermarket. Bryan came back from Canada and avoided him, convinced Owen's accident was his fault. Jesse tried, a few weeks later when he got his HIV test result back as negative, to call Owen, finding his extension number on the university's website, but they were not allowed to give out his mobile, and he considered sending an email, but knew he wouldn't get it for a long time, if at all. He called around the hospitals, to be told they were only allowed to give out information to the next-of-kin. The old dining room was converted on-schedule to a new bedroom with its own patio door and private terrace. Another man moved into Owen's room and painted his mauve walls off-white.

BRIXTON

Chapter 1

August 12, 2016

The Velux windows are open to birdsong and the west-facing early light, cloudless and mercifully cool. It is a one-bedroom flat in Brixton, with the bed in the old attic of the converted Victorian house. Two nudes, a Keith Vaughan line drawing and an Ajamu print, hang just above their heads. Downstairs, two scuffed mahogany writing desks face one another surrounded by books, and across the room, matching second-hand sofas oppose each other across an original working fireplace. In summer, it is so hot, even with the windows open, that there is nothing for it but to sacrifice themselves to the weather's intentions and wallow in each other's sweat. The leather straps of the bedframe have slackened and cup them together in the middle of the mattress. The arm that is crumpled beneath Jesse has gone to sleep, and the other is around Owen's stomach, their hands held tight. Jesse's dick thickens against the small of Owen's back, on the now-faint, pink scar from the surgeries on his spine.

He frees the arm beneath him and twists onto his front, and as the feeling trickles back, finds his phone under his pillow. When the alarm hasn't gone off, it means he's slept through it, forgotten to activate it, or left it on silent. He congratulates himself with a smile when he discovers he has woken naturally minutes before eight. He's working a double with Georgia and Melania, so twelve and a half hours with two people who despise each other just because they both once went for the same man. Melania won, and she's just lost their baby, so Jesse hopes Georgia, for all their sakes, can finally let it go and sympathise. The two women share the same skin tone and curly brown hair; both are naturally pretty, though one is half-Venezuelan-half-Welsh (nickname: VW) and the other fully Sardinian, so they hate being compared to one another when they could not be more different. The general manager's main job, really, is to write a rota that gives both of them an adequate number of shifts without them ever overlapping, which isn't always possible, especially in the summertime when there are so many absences.

It crosses Jesse's mind, as it does most mornings, to call in sick, but he knows he cannot. Melania's been off work for a week. Everyone else seems to be on holiday. He checks his *Guardian* app; nothing major, only the Republican presidential candidate joking-not-joking about Barack Obama founding Isis. He'd switched off notifications the morning after the EU referendum, so as not to be confronted with shocking news before he was prepared for it. *That* day he called in sick, for the first time in five years. No way was he going to pop corks for braggarts and bigots celebrating the victorious Leave campaign, when its prevailing image was of a river of sun-baked beggars in torn clothes coursing in to overwhelm sloping Albion. *If you do not want to see our England turn into this, Vote Leave.* He often wondered about the number of people, potential customers of his, who would have been involved in it before it went to print, and he hadn't so much as touched a copy of the *Evening Standard* since it ran the campaign full-page in the days before the referendum.

That night, after sprinting out during the break to vote Remain with Owen, he worked a close shift, drank till three in the morning, went home, smoked a really strong spliff and dreamed that he'd worked nine shifts in a row with a cold, then on his first morning off gone for a long lunch at a bistro off Clapham Common with a friend and shared three carafes of Malbec to drown down the gritty oysters and smelly, suspiciously pink chitterling sausage with chips and béarnaise sauce he randomly chose to order. It was a grisly, oddly pungent mess, almost as if he'd slit open a cow's stomach, ripped out its intestine and noshed it off screaming right there in the field. He couldn't send it back, because then he'd look like the black person who didn't know what chitterling sausage was – *chitlins, nigger? You ain't eat chitlins?*

He went to work, in his dream, and worked more hours with the cold. Gruelling shift. Celebrities. A customer, a customer, a customer and a customer, not to mention a customer and a customer, who, having used his newspaper to campaign for Leave from the very start, asked him for some *white* bread without even looking at the basket. Jesse collapsed right in the middle of the restaurant floor, by the till. They sent him in a *white* van to an abattoir to be cleaned out like a suckling pig. Every hair on his body was torched and scraped off leaving his eyes looking a little awake. He still had a mouthful of teeth and his tongue was intact. Delivered back to the kitchen with his entire skin surface oiled up, his abdomen was stuffed with bread, onions and sage. They chopped his legs off at the knee and braised them in chicken stock and *white* wine, garlic and whole shallots. Four hours in the oven was all his slender body needed. A customer waited in the middle of the feasting table, his cutlery stood on ends in his fists, Fernet-Branca having prepared him, the start of a bottle of 2011 Côte Rotie in his wine glass. A customer arrived, followed by a customer, a customer and a customer, not to mention a customer and his customer husband, whom Jesse was never able to look in the eye while alive. His mother, her bleach-job in need of a retouch, carved him wearing a red-wine-stained apron, starting with his head, which sat on a plate in front of the host while everyone took selfies; each meaty haunch, cut from the waist through the natural line into his groin, enough to feed ten with side bowls of stuffing, potatoes and greens, his kidneys a lucky find. Then the abdomen; she plucked out his ribs and separated chunks of steaming flesh with her tongs – *he's a tough one, int he? Maybe he wunt in the oven long enough* – he was close to burnt but it had been hard to judge with his skin, which crisped up nicely. His heart, trimmed, turned up as a Monday lunch special, grilled with a balsamic glaze and served with green beans and a pick-led walnut dressing; his testes, another starter, were poached in milk and deep-fried. His liver came as a main, devilled and pan-roasted in butter with a sherry vinegar deglaze. Delicious, said some customer dining alone, having licked his plate clean and drained his glass of 2011 Cahors dry. I'm not that hungry, explained a customer, having pushed his plate to the side after a mouthful or two. Can we order six financiers, asked a customer, midway through the liver.

He hasn't smoked weed since.

His side of the bed is against the wall, so he has to climb out, but can't do so without disturbing Owen, who squints his eyes twice like a child. Wakefulness rushes to him in a moment as he turns and sits up, his dick hard and flat against his little paunch.

'Morning, love.'

Jesse comes back to him. They kiss. Still a little boozy even though they brushed their teeth before bed.

'Mmm. Morning.'

'Sleep well?' Jesse asks, twisting his shoulder in its socket to get at a back-itch with his thumbnail.

'Not really,' Owen says, rubbing his temples in between fin-gers and thumb. 'Too drunk.'

'Me too,' Jesse says, though he doesn't feel as if he has a head-ache. He's just a little bit hot and furry-tongued. He climbs over Owen to grab the pint glass on the bedside table, swishes the warm water in his mouth, and swallows. He moves down the bed, and Owen lies still and runs his fingers through Jesse's hair, over his ears and down to his shoulders, massaging, flexing his body until his knob slips back over Jesse's soft palate.

Last night they attended a prize-giving ceremony for the year's best novel about contemporary British life; Owen had been one of the judges. The only two black men in the room were Jesse and one of the five shortlisted authors, the Somali-British novelist Liban Warsame. Liban looked sexy in a cream fitted suit tight to his crotch, the patterned shirt beneath open to his hairless solar plexus; Jesse wore a pale blue convertible-collar shirt and dark blue trousers that stood off his body in the heat. He and Liban wear their hair somewhat alike, shaven at the sides and with an inch or two of growth on top, but that is where the resemblance ends. They are as ethnically dissimilar as Georgia and Melania. Liban is dark-skinned, with a smiley disposition, high cheek bones and a crispy little chin beard. He is five years older than Jesse, taller and broader. None of this stopped a successful crime author in a floaty maxi dress approaching Jesse, as soon as the applause had died down from the winner's speech, to wish *him* congratulations.

'Congratulations for what?' Jesse asked her, in all curiosity.

Then she looked at him properly and blushed.

'Oops, sorry! Drunk!'

The winner, for a modern-day comedy of manners set in the Cotswolds, narrated by a biracial married mother of two, is the model-like, pale-skinned, fine-featured daughter of a retired Etonian Oxford don and his Ethiopian-American second (now-ex) wife. As she posed for the cameras in front of a board monoprinted with the logos of the prize and corporate sponsors, everyone drank champagne and fanned themselves over her green eyes and golden curls.

Still, there were some interesting people there, not least

Liban, a former refugee whose novel – about a Somalian family in South London affected by the eldest son's insinuation into a gang and death by stab wounds, driven out of the home by community taboos surrounding his mother's mental illness – had been preferred by Owen, who had been frustrated that the other four judges could not, or would not, see that Liban's novel, even down to its linguistic authenticity, most deserved the greater recognition that the prize would've brought. Jesse saw that they gave the prize to a woman of most faint, pastel-like colour, a nearly white woman from Notting Hill whose story the majority of the judges, being overwhelmingly white, upper-middle-class and highly educated, could use to ask themselves those difficult questions about race without confronting spilled black blood.

He hears the train doors beep and slide shut as he steps off the escalator, so crosses to the empty train waiting at the opposite platform, taking his usual seat against the wall behind the unoccupied one of the two driver's cabins. A heavy, tired-looking black woman jogs on just before the door closes, sits down at the first seat, rests her wrapped head against the Plexiglas panel and closes her eyes, clutching her handbag tight to her stomach. He cringes at himself for assuming she's just finished her early-hours cleaning job. He wonders, indeed, what she is closing her eyes *from*, what she's been allowed to see by people who do not think of her as having an opinion.

He takes out from his tote bag Barack Obama's *Dreams from My Father*, which he's been reading on and off. Obama, half-Kenyan, was raised by an Indonesian stepfather who treated him as his own and taught him what he would need to survive in this world, and a white American mother who stroked his hair, listened to him, and attempted, at least, to answer his questions, most memorably about a photo-essay in *Life* magazine he'd chanced on in a doctor's reception, featuring an African-American man who had bleached his skin into misery and disfiguration, sold on the product's promise of a happy new life in whiteness. Reading, while at college, Conrad's *Heart of Darkness* – a novel Owen keeps urging Jesse to read for literary reasons, setting aside the racial controversies swirling around it – Obama writes of the moment he became aware of the ways whites condition blacks to feel about themselves, about how the qualities ascribed respectively to white and black are internalised by blacks and used then as suicide weapons against blackness.

Obama proved that a black man can be the most powerful person in the world and make the decisions that change the course of history, without being puppeteered. Surely they'll choose Hillary to replace him, Jesse thinks, although he finds it difficult to understand the paucity of suitable candidates. That table of ten Californians he served last week were certain it's going to be Hillary. *All down my Facebook wall's blue*, one of them told him, the same one who, when she asked him where he was from and got him down to Jamaica, said that *she* thought he looked like a young East African boy, and seemed to wait for him to change his mind.

A lot of people get on at Victoria, but the seat next to him is left free. A sweet-looking Japanese girl in a pleated tartan skirt with a Vivienne Westwood shoulder-purse stands over a pair of large Dover Street Market shopping bags, tapping her nail finely on the screen of her panda-eared phone, perhaps a fashion assistant being sent out with returns. A white man with blond hair wearing a shirt without a tie, carrying a small leather briefcase, gets on, sees the seat next to Jesse, makes towards it then stops himself and retreats, holding the other rail in the doorway. He is around forty years old, and looks like the sort of man who went to expensive fee-paying schools, then looked down at Owen, there purely on merit, when he got to Cambridge. He stands and reads the *Metro* newspaper, while Jesse tries to concentrate on Obama's memoir, thinking, maybe he thinks I'm a Muslim.

Maybe white men think black men should not be approached. Maybe he thinks I'm going to stab him in the thigh. Maybe he thinks I'm going to tuck my hand between his legs and cup his balls. A very fat man in dirty jogging bottoms squeezes himself into the seat next to Jesse, finally, at Oxford Circus, just for two stops, and though seats become available at Euston, the blond white man remains standing. Jesse gets off at King's Cross and glances back to the carriage. The white man has taken the seat he vacated and thrown his bag down on the seat next to him, crossing his legs to further discourage anyone from invading what is now *his* space.

He gets to work on time for a pre-shift coffee, feeling relatively alert. The Light Café is a whitewashed former warehouse brightly lit, on sunny days like this, through the narrow Gothic-style windows in its roof, austerely supplemented by simple brass chandeliers. All architectural features are exposed and painted white, except the cast iron stairs to the mezzanine, which are black. The cushionless wooden chairs remain upturned on the square tables; the chessboard floor has been professionally buffed by a contractor. The same core congregation, backed by an evolving parish of food tourists and special-occasioners, has been faithful to this church of cooking for years. He can already identify, by smell, a seasonal menu-in-preparation of fresh fish and shellfish, baked bread, roasting celeriac, tripe steeping in a rich, beefy liquor, and whole bushes of mint and parsley leaves waiting to be picked. The dramatic crashing of bottle bins, full from a busy Thursday night on the bar and now being emptied into a dumpster, can be heard from outside.

Ben, the bearded head chef, is breaking down some unspec-ified carcass with a cleaver on a red board on the pass, the clean chops reverberating in the roof beams; there will be little splashes of blood and gore to swab away before service. He trained as an automotive engineer before his wife's diagnosis with a brain tumour, and had to leave his position at Jaguar to take care of her, during which time he discovered he liked to cook and was very good at it. Because they had no children, when she died he decided he would go to work full-time in a kitchen in Birmingham, then spent two years as a sous-chef in London before coming to the Light Café. The sleeves of his jacket are rolled up, and the top two buttons are open, revealing rugged forearms and an expanse of thick, curly chest hair. He and Jesse nod at each other, and Jesse suppresses a little twitch of arousal as, involuntarily, and not for the first time, his body imagines what Ben's nakedness might feel like close to his own. Various of his clean-cut, youthful chefs de partie, cast as if from a late 2000s Lanvin menswear show, move around in purposeful silence prepping their sections, with quick, hesitant moves, as they reprioritise their mental to-do lists.

The kitchen porter, Oleg, a tightly packed, chain-smoking Ukrainian who looks about fifty but probably isn't, wishes Jesse *good morning*, pausing to bump fists as he carries two armsful of clean utensils across from the main kitchen towards the pastry section, where bread and cakes are on sale to the public. He's been in the country more than ten years yet his English remains limited, understandable given that most of his time is spent alone on the pot-wash, or at best, working in tandem with another KP from Brazil or DR Congo, also speaking their second or third language. Jesse has often wondered what Oleg does about sex. He gets horribly drunk every Friday night and hits on every off-shift female staff member he sees, knowing from the start he is going to be rejected.

Someone from the kitchen has already made themselves coffee, possibly a round for their colleagues, spraying milk everywhere and leaving it to dry into a crust on the steam wand. The grounds inside the portafilter are sloppy and muddy, as left by someone who doesn't know how to extract espressos. Whatever they were drinking, Jesse imagines, was weak, bitter and wishy-washy with too-hot milk and little black grains of

burnt grind on top, the sort you get on train platforms in pro-
vincial towns, identically undrinkable regardless of whether
you order a cappuccino, latte or flat white. The dominion of
bad coffee even in London baffles him. Every café he visits, he
listens out for how the milk is being steamed; if it gargles like
an old Ford diesel, he turns around and walks straight back out.

He bangs out the blackened mess into the coffee-waste drawer
and switches on the grinder (which sounds like a chainsaw in
this space), rinsing out the portafilter in boiling water from the
machine and using it to shake loose any grind left clinging inside
the group head. He hooks the clean portafilter into the housing
beneath the grinder chamber as it comes to a stop, and pulls
the lever twice until it clicks, yielding the perfect amount. He
compacts it with the stamp and wipes off the excess with the
side of his hand, thoughtlessly transferring it to his – luckily,
black – trousers where normally his apron would be, kissing his
teeth and digging out a J-cloth from the nearby drawer to wet
and wipe them clean. He inserts the portafilter into the group
head, takes down a cup from on top of the machine, fills it to
a third with boiling water and positions it, pressing the button
to extract a double espresso. Within a second or two, drips of
golden brown, waxy coffee start to stain the water, steadily gath-
ering into a pour the thickness of a mouse's tail. Within half a
minute, the extraction is complete, topped with a layer of stripy
crema. He takes a sip. He appreciates the slightly chocolatey,
then smoothly apricotty, flavour.

He walks over to the computer and gasps. There are ninety-
one covers on the book. That's more like a December lunch
than August.

'Ninety-one!' he calls out loud, his voice carrying high up
into the beams; then he experiences a moment of panic that he
might be looking at the wrong day, so checks the date in the top
right corner. August 12th.

'Ninety-one?' repeats Ben. Two or three of his underlings

turn their heads and echo him. 'It was seventy-three when I walked in this morning.'

'What's going on? We're supposed to be dead. Everyone's supposed to be away at their other house in Provence or Somerset or something. Fuck's sake.'

'Brexit panic,' shrugs Ben. 'Are you on your own, this morning?'

'Veedub,' says Jesse, and Ben pulls him a commiserative face. 'Melania's in at eleven.'

'Oh that's good news!' Ben says, as he turns to sweep the grim waste off his board into a bin. Jesse has always been rather jealous of Ben and Melania's slow-flirt, the fatherly way he addresses and listens to her.

Think of the money is the usual maxim. Being short-staffed, and so busy, means a greater proportion of the tips and service charge, but only if the quality isn't compromised, resulting in more covers spending less and leaving smaller amounts in gratuities. It is getting on for ten past ten. The chairs should be down and the tablecloths going on by now. The list of things more depressing than having to set up a restaurant by oneself is short, especially to start a twelve-and-a-half-hour slog of a double, and Georgia won't lift a chair or do anything with such commitment as might endanger her nails. She is always late, and no one ever picks her up on it. It is expected, yet she is the first to complain if any of her colleagues turn up after her.

He prints off a list to set up each table with the right number of chairs. The only way he can complete a menial job with a hangover is to plug in his earbuds and just get on with it. Uninspired, having exhausted Beyoncé's *Lemonade* and Kanye West's *The Life of Pablo*, the two masterpieces of the year – and not in the mood for anything else in particular, all his playlists predictable and formulaic – he shuffles his library and straight away comes on 'My Love' from Mary J Blige's *What's the 411? Remix*, one of her earliest hits. *Big tune*, he whisper-shouts, falling into a Mary J-like shoulder-rolling, head-nodding, finger-clicking dance move. For years he didn't even know 'My Love' was Mary, because she sings it in such a cold, dispassionate way.

He wakes up, and it only takes a couple of minutes to athletically pull down and position a hundred chairs, before he runs round with a pile of tablecloths, throwing them on to the tops like boys on BMXs do newspapers on lawns. The external line visibly rings. Even though it's right next to him, someone in the office, probably the manager Terry, picks it up.

Georgia jiggles in presently, wearing a Mary Quant-style red polka-dot button-through summer dress and red patent leather espadrilles – not an outfit anyone expects to shift furniture in – and with her highlights up in a topknot.

'J'arrive,' she says, blandly, flicking on the grinder and throwing her black leather handbag down on the waiter station.

'Morning, Georgia.'

'Morning,' chorus all the chefs, far more brightly than they'd done for Jesse. Oleg, bringing in a delivery of fresh salad vegetables, purses his lips as if to wolf-whistle but thinks better of it.

'You look nice,' Jesse tells her.

'Babes, it's so fucking hot. What's the book like?' she asks him as she clicks two shots of ground beans into the portafilter.

'Ninety-one,' Jesse says, as he billows out and floats down a four-top tablecloth.

'Ninety-one?'

She has her hands on her hips.

'There's nothing we can do about it.'

'Who's on with us?'

'Melania, at eleven.'

That time-slot corresponds to the runner's shift.

'Ninety covers and just two waiters? Who writes this fucking rota, and who made coffee without cleaning the steam wand?'

'Not me, and not me.'

'Morning, Georgia,' says Terry, striding in to finalise the menu with Ben, his pink face and black/grey hair still messy from helmet sweat. 'Morning, Jess, how are you?'

'Morning, I'm good thanks. You?' They shake hands. Jesse's been working there for three years now but Terry's grip only seems to get firmer, as if to reassert his heterosexual masculine distance. He was a promising actor, but his career never took off the way it was supposed to. As a consequence, he could never quite give up his waiting job, and as a family friend of the Somerset-based owners of the Light Café, ended up being their interim general manager before recently accepting the offer on a permanent basis.

'Melania's boyfriend just rang to say she's still ill, and nobody else is answering their phones, so it's just going to be you and Georgia for lunch, though I'll be here to help, and I'll get someone from the bar to run drinks and help keep an eye on food.'

'Oh, I was looking forward to seeing Melania,' says Ben, cleaning down his pass with hot, soapy water. 'Would've made my day.'

'She's still not ready, he said,' says Terry.

Georgia says nothing, just shakes her head while steaming her milk.

Jesse checks his phone, and wonders why Melania didn't text him to say she wasn't coming in. Georgia, having plugged in her earbuds, her phone hanging precariously in a flimsy pocket of her thin cotton dress, struts around the restaurant with a high pile of folded white napkins clutched to her cleavage, and lays them in position in front of the straightened chairs.

After a frosty start to their relationship, when Jesse felt bullied by Georgia and refused to talk to her for three months while having a fantastic time with everyone else, they finally bonded over Beyoncé's self-titled 2013 album and its accompanying music videos for each track, agreeing it was a return to form after the indecisive double LP *I Am . . . Sasha Fierce*.

Then, the following summer, there was an incident. He'd walked in at ten o'clock to find her locked in a furious argument with Terry in the office, presumably over a complaint that had been made by a customer, and knew that he would have to manage her mood for the whole double shift, mainly by staying out of her way. It was the first day of the asparagus season, and Ben had shown him how he wanted it to be served, with a fish knife placed horizontally on the table to tilt the plate so that the melted butter would drain down to the tips in front of the customer. When Jesse set up the *mise en place*, only for her to run the food for that table and throw down the asparagus any old way, storming off in a huff, he took her to one side and asked her if she knew how the asparagus was supposed to be served. She'd been working there for five years by then.

'Bitch, don't fucking talk to me like I came down in the last fucking shower,' she spat, and spun away. 'Just fuck off.'

Jesse hooked his index finger to summon her back.

'*Georgia* . . .'

That led to another three months of enmity, during which Jesse almost left, though as he enjoyed virtually every other aspect of his job, it felt a real shame. A thirty-hour week as a waiter at the Light Café, rather embarrassingly, returns the same average salary as a full-time London nurse, excluding cash tips of on average £70 a week. Melania convinced him to stay. *Don't leave me alone with her, babes, please*, she'd pleaded.

It may not even be a bad thing that Melania's called in sick. Working with the two of them at the same time can be like being in that room where the spiky walls are closing in. Georgia will be forced to actually pull her finger out, even if she'll dispatch her customers as disdainfully as Serena Williams does her early round opponents. On her day, she's a charming, fast waiter who makes fantastic tips for the pot, which is why the management won't sack or even discipline her, and why her colleagues – Melania included – won't push them to. If she's pissed off with the general air of the place everyone will feel it in their pockets, and that is why her histrionics are tolerated. On a good day, her standards are high and her napkins and cutlery will be parallel and perpendicular with those beside and opposite, but today her forks look like they've been laid by a toddler.

Jesse goes round with the knives, straightening the forks at the same time. He follows with wine and water glasses; Georgia with sideplates and salt and pepper pots. There's the toilets to check – three full rolls in each cubicle, all the handsoaps required to be full, the mirrors to be wiped. There's the inevitable remaining cutlery from last night that his darling colleagues won't have bothered to polish, each one of them seeing the thought *Jesse's in first thing* flash subliminally through their minds. After that, the butter pats, the oil-and-vinegar pots, all need to be freshly made up and stored or distributed to tables. The service fridge has to work hard when the weather's like this. Then there are the weekly jobs, a different one for each day, like watering the plants or dusting the chair legs, which often get signed off without being done, though Jesse is always too scared that he'll be the unlucky one who lies and gets caught when Terry randomly pulls the service fridge in the middle of a conversation before checking the clipboard and finding Jesse's initials. So he pulls the fridge, sweeps and sanitises, just as Zac, one of the cute blond chefs de partie, places his huge, steaming cauldron on the staff table. Even Jesse groans at the idea of winter-warmer food on such a hot day, but understands the benefits of its slow-release energy.

'What is it?' calls Georgia, cynically plucking out one of her earbuds. 'Broad bean and black truffle risotto again? Ugh!'

In a restaurant with no music, the pre-service silence can be ominous, and the first chatter of diners meeting in the bar for a gin and tonic or glass of champagne gathers like a murmur of strings beneath the percussive interventions from the kitchen. He doesn't recognise any of the surnames on the booking sheet, but that won't mean he hasn't seen their faces before. It is front-loaded with tables from midday onwards, so there's no chance of being lulled into an inadequate rhythm that it's hard to pick up from, and without a runner, more has to be done from the outset. Giant loaves of sourdough have to be pre-sliced and covered with a dampish cloth so that they won't dry out; it is sensible to prep several baskets before service so that Jesse and Georgia won't be left flat-footed by the early arrivals. In they come, just as Georgia finally emerges from the dressing room in her uniform, white, like Jesse's, but cut for curves. Georgia picks the back of the restaurant, of course, so Jesse is left with the front, where all the niggly little tables of two are, but her choice comes with the caveat of being the auxiliary runner, as her section will be less busy.

That would work in normal circumstances, but Georgia's been walking the boards here for eight years now and knows many of the regular customers, especially the suited guys at lunchtimes who've been coming to the Light Café for twenty years and wish only to be served by girls. So, regardless of whose section she's in and whatever the state of her own, she'll go to those tables, who often don't even bother to book because they feel like they've earned their stripes. As far as they're concerned, Jesse's here today, gone tomorrow like so many waiters in their time, even though he's been here for three years himself.

Ben's already rapping his knuckles on the ticket rail, a beautiful soft clatter that reverberates in the space and furthermore in Jesse's sleep, to get someone's attention to run an order to the bar, but Jesse's in the middle of telling his new two-top the specials and pouring their carafe of house white wine, and Georgia's having a chat with table four, a couple of patronising old peers who toddle around like they own the place but hardly ever spend any money. Terry's answering a call and there seems to be quite a queue of new guests building up at the door. Jesse quickly runs the two salads – kohlrabi and caper-berry; heritage tomato and goat's curd – to the bar, and finds the staff there already busy and running around, asking him if he can also bring them a basket of bread. Georgia's practically foaming at the mouth laughing with the men on four, and Terry keeps on seating tables. Jesse can see there are already bottles of mineral water and jugs of tap waiting for six tables, but has to take an order for his two-top who insisted they were ready but now have questions to ask about all the dishes that he has to describe in full from farm to fork. The dispense bar is rapidly filling up with unserved drinks Terry has put through the till; the bartenders, who can't leave their stations while there are checks running through, are starting to watch the ice melt in their Lillets.

Before putting the order through the till, he has to run food. Ben gives him a knowing look as he runs starters to a table in Georgia's section whose order Terry took, then sees another couple of tables who've sat down and need bread and to be asked for a water-and-apéritifs order. He now has a four, two twos, a three and a five in his section that he hasn't even been to yet. He lowers his chin, furrows his brow and quickens his pace. He's glad he put on his black Air Max 90s rather than his MHL monkey boots. They all get bread thrown down; he interrupts their conversations, whilst apologising for doing so, to tell them the specials and ask them for their apéritif orders.

He runs out to the bar and loads a tray with two gin and tonics, two Lillets, three glasses of house rosé and two halves of lager, whilst squeezing two bottles of sparkling water under the same arm and collecting the handles of four jugs of tap water with his free hand, running them all through to the waiter station without spilling a drop. People look at him then look away and continue their conversations like this is normal, like this is what a waiter should normally be able to do. Sometimes he feels like a whipped servant. The elderly men on four think they've got Georgia all day; she spends longer unscrewing the top off their house Picpoul than Jesse does uncorking bottles of chilled Côte de Brouilly, Sancerre rosé and Pouilly-Fumé, whilst taking a mental note of all three tables' food orders. He is already quite low on patience; there may be complaints today, he thinks.

'Thanks, darling,' says Georgia as she beats him to the till, so he crosses the room to the other, which is engaged by Terry taking ages to find the button to order the prize 2005 Chevalier Montrachet table nine have powerfully ordered to impress their Chinese clients, along with the 2005 Chateau Mouton-Rothschild Jesse would never have recommended for lunch in this heat. Ben raps his knuckles on the ticket rail.

'Excuse me, what's kohlrabi?'

'Excuse me, can we order, please?'

'Where are the toilets, please?'

'What do you recommend?'

'Can we order?'

'Jesse, could you run drinks from the bar, please? They're busy with walk-ins out there.'

'What's . . . kohlrabi?'

Ben raps his knuckles on the ticket rail.

'What's goat's curd?'

'What do you recommend?'

'Hey, there! Nice to see you again! Are we in your part of the restaurant? You gave us such good service last time!'

Ben raps his knuckles on the ticket rail.

'Darling, did you put the order through for twelve? Ben says they're staring at him and he doesn't have a check.'

'What do you recommend?'

'What are heritage tomatoes?'

'It's really hot in here, isn't it! Can you turn the air conditioning up, or something?'

Ben raps his knuckles on the ticket rail.

'Where are the toilets, please?'

'Could you tell us again what the specials are? I could get up and look at the board but I'd rather hear it from you in your lovely British accent.'

'Excuse me, is the mackerel fishy?'

'Tripe? Isn't that supposed to be disgusting?'

'Excuse me. Do you have a kids' menu?'

Ben raps his knuckles on the ticket rail.

'I'm allergic to gluten, dairy, garlic and onions, and I'm vegetarian, but not vegan, so I eat eggs. What do you recommend?'

Ben raps his knuckles on the ticket rail.

'Tell that chef he can fillet my plaice anytime. Is he married?'

'What do you recommend?'

'We're waiting to pay.'

'Where are the toilets, please?'

'Kohlrabi. Fish?'

Ben raps his knuckles on the ticket rail.

'Could you turn the air conditioning down, please? It's blowing a gale in here.'

'Excuse me, more ice, please.'

'Which wine would you recommend to go with the plaice and the devilled kidneys?'

'What do you recommend?'

Ben raps his knuckles on the ticket rail.

'Excuse me, can the chips that come with the tripe be ordered as a side dish?'

'Do you have a colder one of these?'

'Can we have the bill, please?'

'Where are the toilets, please?'

Ben raps his knuckles on the ticket rail.

'Excuse me, can we order some fresh financiers? I know we haven't finished our mains yet but we're in rather a hurry.'

'We're not quite ready yet, sorry . . .'

'What do you recommend?'

'Are you an actor?'

Ben raps his knuckles on the ticket rail.

'Excuse me, can I trouble you for some more bread, please?' (*White* bread.)

'Poor you, being cooped up in here all day in this weather. You must be sweating buckets in that chef's jacket.'

' . . . still not ready, sorry! We definitely promise to look at the menu now . . .'

Ben raps his knuckles on the ticket rail.

'Can we get some more ice, please?'

'Looks like you're not in the same mood as last time, huh.'

'I'm pregnant. Is this cheese pasteurised?'

'What do you recommend?'

Ben raps his knuckles on the ticket rail.

'Bill, please.'

'Darling, there are no more ice buckets. Looks like some of your tables are going to have to share.'

'Sir, do you have another napkin? Mine fell on the floor.'

Ben raps his knuckles on the ticket rail.

'Darling, could you empty the bottle bin? I would but I've got back trouble.'

'Young man, could we please have some more butter, and order another bottle of wine? We're switching to red, so we'll need fresh glasses. Chilled, preferably.'

'Will you get to enjoy the sun at all today?'

'Club soda!'

' . . . erm, erm, erm, okay! Erm . . .'

Ben raps his knuckles on the ticket rail.

'You're doing a brilliant job, Jess. Thank you.'

'I was a waitress in a hotel at weekends when I was seventeen, so I completely understand.'

'Excuse me, we ordered our coffees with the waitress quite

some while ago, but we have to go back to work so can we cancel and just get the bill, if that's okay?'

Ben raps his knuckles on the ticket rail.

'Hi! Do you guys have highchairs?'

'Washroom?'

'Check.'

'Jesse, could you get the door, please?'

Ben raps his knuckles on the ticket rail.

'What's this? Did I order that?'

'What do you recommend?'

'Are you a dancer?'

Ben raps his knuckles on the ticket rail.

' . . . oh no, you sold out of the oysters? Oh, I really wanted some! Can you not just check whether they don't still have some out the back . . . ?'

'I specifically asked for a candle to be brought with my husband's dessert! It was all okayed via email and I even reminded the waitress when we arrived!'

Ben raps his knuckles on the ticket rail.

'You know what, where are you from? Cos you speak really good English, you do!'

The two men on twenty-three seem nice enough, and the old Jesse, before Owen came back into his life, would probably have flirted more with them. They are enjoying a boozy, ties-in-pockets Friday lunch, the two of them taking up a four-top and opening their legs wide under it, slapping their palms on the table as they drink and laugh like West Indians playing dominoes. One is Austrian, and seems rather too elegant and well-maintained, with his thick dark hair, nuanced English and perfect rows of teeth, to be associating with the cocky-looking, stout fiftysomething Essexman opposite him. Their laughs have been filling out the space all afternoon, and while they seem mismatched, Jesse is drawn to their promise of fun among the usual unengaging lunchers.

The service has been less of an ordeal than Jesse had feared; he worked himself into top form and is now feeling more alert and sharper-edged than is necessary – the remaining diners are Friday long-lunchers with nowhere to rush off to. Though the men on twenty-three are in his section, they are close to the door so Terry has been serving them, but the restaurant has started to empty and he's gone back to his important work in the office.

They order more wine – a third bottle of chilled 2011 Moulin à Vent – which, after about 2.30 p.m., annoys the double-shifters because all they want to do is reset for dinner and have as long a break as possible; while there are customers at table someone has to remain *on the floor*. As Jesse opens the wine they begin to involve him in their conversation, asking what his name is and how long he's been working there, then whether he likes football, which team, and speculating about what a smart, good-looking guy like him must be doing apart from working in a restaurant. Talking to drunk people while sober is always a chore, but then comes:

'You know what, where are you from? Cos you speak really good English, you do!'

Jesse's shoulders drop. 'Sorry?'

The Essexman does not alter his cocky facial expression but repeats his question as if Jesse didn't hear.

'Where you from? Where'd you grow up?'

The Austrian doesn't look at all embarrassed, just nods and laughs to fill the space, seemingly aware of some awkwardness, though not of its source.

'Dudley,' says Jesse, as he pours their wine from a height so that it splashes up inside the glass.

The Austrian looks at his fellow diner, who looks confused, for clarification.

'Dudley?'

'A historic town with the ruins of a twelfth-century castle

in the Black Country. Just outside Birmingham. The West Midlands.'

'Dudlaaaay!' laughs the Essexman, as if no one ever has before. 'Where Lenny Henry's from! Oh right, so you were born here, then?'

'You mean, in this country? Yes, I was born in this country, as were my parents,' says Jesse.

'The Black Country?' asks the Austrian of his English friend. 'So that makes you, what, third-generation?'

'I've no idea how it works,' says Jesse, honestly.

'You've lost your accent. What, d'ya get elocution lessons?'

'But you call it the *Black Country*,' says the Austrian, who suddenly looks genuinely interested. 'Like the Deep South?'

It seems his mind has been degraded by his company. *Do not be misled. Bad associations spoil useful habits.* Jesse wonders whether he should tell him that the Black Country is an area on the high planes of the island where, like the Maroons of Jamaica, black World War I veterans seized the land and established a thriving district of farms, shopping precincts and industrial estates run by, operated for and employing black people, where there are black schools, colleges, hospitals and universities all contributing to a buoyant black British economy. That might have been the dream, but instead, he tells him the truth; after all, the Essexman wouldn't have it any other way.

The two men continue to try to make conversation with him as the restaurant empties, even as he takes their payments, seemingly unaware that his mood has changed. There is little he can do other than laugh along, and he shakes the hands they offer him as they leave, the Essexman engaging him in a sort of arm-wrestle and fist-bump mess he's probably been waiting for a black man to hit with for some time.

Jesse and Georgia – who says, *That wasn't actually that bad!* – reset the restaurant for dinner, set up the staff table for the 5.30 meal, count the soiled white napkins and tablecloths from lunch and pack them into orange laundry bags, before heading back to the locker room.

Gini texted him hours ago to say she was organising a picnic in Brockwell Park. It's been a couple of weeks since they last spoke; he hopes her pregnancy is going well and that she isn't still being harassed by her father, who has come to claim her now that he has heard she is a successful playwright. It is still reasonably early: half past three. The Victoria line is as close as the London Underground gets to fast and fuss-free. If he can get there for four he can spend an hour and hit the Tube *just* ahead of the rush hour tidal wave. The last thing he wants to do is go underground in this heat, but the Santander scheme doesn't trust multi-ethnic Brixton with its hire bikes (the nearest station is all the way in Stockwell), and he needs the company of his black people, who also speak *really* good English.

Chapter 2

Gini was offered places at all three of the drama schools she applied to, but chose LAMDA's acting course, starting in September 2002, and stayed on to take their MA in directing, ignoring tacit warnings that nobody would take direction from a black woman. Five years of being passed over for the privilege of directing her favourite plays by Chekhov, Ibsen and Tennessee Williams followed, during which time she and Jesse re-entered each other's lives, working as waiters at a Shoreditch restaurant called Sebastian's. He couldn't believe it when she walked her thin, brown legs in for her three o'clock interview, hair braided up into a vertical phallus, wearing a short pink Duro Olowu tea dress, black Superga Flatforms and a Chanel 2.55.

He walked up to her as she sat at the bar.

'Excuse me, is your name Ginika?'

'Yes,' she smiled, curiously.

'Do you remember me? My name's Jesse. We worked together for two days at Gilbert's on St Martin's Lane.'

It took her a second, but they probably heard her scream in the office. He trained her up and together they pretty much ran the place. They became the best of friends; he called her his oldest in London. Owen came in for dinner one night with his publisher, his old friend from Cambridge, Nicholas St John. Gini was on her honeymoon, and Jesse had never been so pleased to see someone. He had been having a bad day, serving a rude and entitled table of twelve who had chosen that night and that restaurant to host a Robert Mapplethorpe-style death dinner for a charity fundraiser with AIDS; he'd tried to be convivial but they pinched his arm when they wanted something and never said please or thank you. When Jesse recognised Owen, he went straight over to their table, crouched down and cried. Jesse and Owen hugged, laughed, swapped numbers, texted, went on a date, talked, got drunk, kissed, made love, and began their search for lost time.

Owen had got wasted on coke, weed, champagne and whisky that Christmas night – fourteen years ago – and had logged on to Gaydar with Jesse conclusively passed out on the sofa next to him. Both happy in their dark place, they'd been listening to Joy Division's *Closer* and Aaliyah's *One in a Million*. Owen found a shag all the way down in Tooting, some methamphetamised thirtysomething white guy who showed Owen pictures of his spread arsehole and the soles of his feet. Owen thought the roads would be clear enough to drive and that there would be no police around at five o'clock on Boxing Day morning. He got in his car. It was a simple drive, straight down the A10, straight down the A3, straight down the A24, straight to sleep at the wheel, straight into a high kerb, straight through the window of a Costa. His airbag protected his face and head but the momentum of the crash broke his back in two. They had to cut him out and induce a coma. Plagued by a recurring nightmare before the crash, in which his mother shunned him and missed his funeral, then jumped into his grave – next to his father's – as the pallbearers shovelled dirt on top of them, it was a great relief to him when he woke up after his multiple surgeries to find her there by his bedside, reading his first poetry pamphlet with tears in her eyes.

His recovery took two years, during which time UCL, standing by their man despite the drink-drug-drive scandal, kept his post open, filling it, at great expense, with guest lecturers and term-on-term temps. He'd wanted to get in touch, even if he didn't know what quite to say, but didn't have Jesse's number, and Anya had changed his so that the likes of Jesse couldn't contact him. Owen dated other men, warily, but never regained his previous self-confidence, even after fully recovering from his injuries. For years, he lived with his wife – who came to terms with his truth – in a sexless marriage, and helped raise their daughters.

Jesse left Bruce Grove within weeks of the accident, and moved to Kent to live with the dunderheaded son of a retired Tory councillor he met months before on Gaydar, whose front door got smashed in one morning by police carrying out a dawn raid. They arrested the man on suspicion of soliciting a minor (not Jesse) though they were very interested to know who Jesse was – as he appeared young – and demanded to see some identification; perhaps they suspected the man of harbouring a *refugee* minor for his sexual satisfaction. Jesse showed them his provisional driver's licence and overheard them phoning its details down the radio: *Non-white male* . . . He wasn't under suspicion for anything but was still made to feel guilty. They took the man away in cuffs and searched the property, unearthing a large stash of something quickly smuggled out for evidence under puckered lips. Jesse packed his bags and took the first train back to London with £100 out of the man's wallet, all the while panicking that he would be caught and arrested for theft.

After a night in a hostel he found an elderly man on Gaydar called Derrick who was looking for a young man to move in with him rent-free in exchange for occasional sexual favours, so long as he could tolerate living with Derrick's mother, aged ninety-three and suffering from dementia. Enduring Derrick's exhausting attempts at conversation, the odd shit smear on the bathroom wall and awkward interactions with the mother, who called Jesse *Daddy* and constantly tried to force herself into his room, he otherwise spent a restorative two years seeing just one client a week, reading Proust and, as a result, writing self-indulgent-every-thought-in-my-head-matters-and-has-to-be-explored-to-its-furthest-conclusion tripe.

He still didn't know how to live, what to make of the world, who he was, what he was supposed to do, what to think, how to think, but he was grateful for that moment of pause, with a double mattress and two pillows, even if the house hadn't been decorated since the Sixties. After the mother was moved to a home, and Jesse made it clear he no longer wanted to have sex with him (however good his blow jobs were), Derrick introduced a small rent, which he then increased every three months, till eventually Jesse found himself a job in a restaurant. As he got older, worked more and saw clients less, he realised Derrick had rescued him by patiently giving him the space to feel like a normal human being.

The Oscar buzz descended on *12 Years a Slave*, and Gini started to receive scripts featuring Lupita Nyong'o-type characters, as casting agents miraculously began to see the appeal in her dark-skinned, natural-haired, white-toothed appearance. By then, though, she had already started writing her own scripts and was directing pieces written by other black women, such as Winsome Pinnock, debbie tucker green and Joan Anim-Addo, which beat attending endless castings, either for a performer of unspecified race and gender, or for jobs where she'd see the same half-dozen black women forced to compete against each other.

Her first success as a director, at the short-lived Foundlings Theatre pop-up on Old Street (now luxury flats), was a three-act play she'd written the first draft of when she was seventeen called *Cowfoot*, following a West Indian family in London over three generations. Other producers turned it down, saying it was *too niche* because it was written in full patois. She ended up producing it herself while nursing her mother through chemotherapy. She knew the right people and got them on board. *Cowfoot* sold out every night of its run, hit five-star reviews

across the board and turned a profit. Good writing, good directing, good design, good sound and good acting apparently greatly
appealed to black people, to diverse local Silicon Roundabout
techies and their art-PR girlfriends, and furthermore, to white
middle-class demographic theatregoers. Since then, she has had
Soon Come produced at the Royal Court, *Keys to the Shop* at
the Arcola and *Backside!* at the Liverpool Everyman. *Cowfoot*
is being revived at the National next year. She still acts, but has
concentrated on directing since he last saw her playing Emilia
in an *Othello* at the Foundlings.

Jesse was one of the bridesmates at her wedding to Julius
Akinfenwa, also an actor, a dashing prince currently playing
the title role in Biyi Bandele's *Oroonoko* at Stratford. They
went through absolutely everything in preparation except for
the electric slide, so when the DJ played Cameo's 'Candy' –
one of Jesse's favourite songs and music videos of all time – at
the reception and every black person in the whole place from
behatted great-grandmother to popsocked pagebwai got up to
perform the apparently famous line-dance routine (not featured
in the video), Jesse was the only person not to know what he
was doing, and found himself drowning in a vortex of moving
blackness, persistently facing the wrong direction and grazing
the heels of the poor already-suffering stiletto-wearer in front.
Julius pointedly shares the video every anniversary on Facebook.

Such a beautiful day. He comes up out of the Tube at Brixton.
Pret A Manger have recently opened here – a key stage in an
area's journey to gentrification – approximate midpoint between
no-go and Waitrose. He's been in there and seen a homeless man
wearing his jeans belted under his arse walk right in, dragging
the glow back into the end of his foraged rollie, to help himself
to a prosciutto baguette and a can of sparkling apple juice, and
didn't see so much as an eyelash move in protest.

A thin, tacky layer of historic spilt milkshake keeps Jesse's

Lemaire sandals on the ground a millisecond longer than is reasonable. He almost decides to walk to Brockwell to avoid the sweaty bus, and imagines a path in avoidance of the yellows of Amnesty International charity fundraisers – he's already a direct-debit supporter – but finds himself locked behind an elderly woman with a pull-along trolley, then a younger woman with three kids and a buggy; the 35 bus stops to let twenty people off and thirty on, giving him more time to appreciate the smells of the flowers on the truck in front of the station, raw meat from the butcher's on Electric Avenue, southern-fried chicken from KFC and beef patties from the Refill Eaterie on Brighton Terrace. The number 3 is due in one minute. The oft-sighted local woman in a mauve wife-beater, denim miniskirt and slime-green DMs – who looks like a little boy who's had all his teeth knocked out and decided to live the rest of his life as a girl, with Raggy Dolls make-up and a bow tied around her head – is staggering down the opposite pavement in a zigzag, muttering to herself, looking for fag-butts. A boy with a durag on doesn't look at him or address him but he knows that what comes out of his mouth – *battiman* – is directed towards him; then he wonders whether he might not just be a stoned French flâneur in black Nike Huaraches and grey sweatpants dreamily declaiming *bâtiments*. Every Aaliyah-waisted fourteen-year-old girl with long straight hair, a Primark quilted purse, contoured make-up and pristine Vans, he hopes is really listening to Jill Scott and Erykah Badu, and that Bernardine Evaristo and Roxane Gay get to her before the mandem do. Every mother he sees at a bus stop, with her children, he looks her right in the face and hopes she makes them know they're loved. Every man he sees walking down the street with his shirt open, drinking a can out of a paper bag and chatting nonsense, he sympathises with, because he knows that could be him one day.

*

He sees them from a distance, and as he calmly approaches their little spot, even if he can only spend an hour in their company before he has to go back to work, he wonders what people did before they could drop their location pin on WhatsApp. They are gathered under the low-hanging branches of a poplar, its gold and green leaves glittering on the breeze like tinsel. An older-looking man with short dreads, and a young-looking white couple are present. They're playing Mary J Blige's 'Be Happy', the perfect summer park song, through a bassy little Bose pepper-pot speaker.

'I was listening to Mary just this morning!'

'Haaaaaaay!' Gini calls out, wearing big bug-eye shades and a blue and white maternity dress with her corn rows tied at the ends in a scarf. She looks like a little Jamaican girl in the Sixties waiting to have her photo taken professionally, trying on props.

'Don't get up. Oh my God look how big you are already!'

'It's because she's so tiny,' says Surenna, from under her enormous centre-parted afro. Surenna's a Guildhall-trained composer who creates post-industrial soundscapes incorporating dub, synth, experimental and Gospel sounds. She's capable of writing magnificent original pop songs but refuses to sell out like that. Jesse stoops down to kiss her.

'I like your Sade T-shirt,' he tells her.

'Thanks. You're looking good. Melanin's popping.'

'Me? I feel like shit, I've been working.'

She rolls her eyes. 'You look bangin'.'

Jesse recognises the handsome older man with the grey goatee, but can't remember his name. 'Hello,' he ventures, holding out his hand, and they shake in the arm-wrestling way.

'You remember Conroy from the wedding, don't you?' says Gini, who prides herself on knowing, and knowing the schedules of, every 'cool' black person in London. Jesse raises his sunglasses.

'Yes, of course! How are you, sir?'

'You remember Jesse, Conroy?'

'Yes I do, but you had a beard, didn't you, at the wedding?'

'Yeah, I went through that phase.'

'You look better without it. Good to see you, young man.'

'Thank you,' says Jesse, as their smiles linger a second. Good black daddies were so rare, and in Jesse's experience, so worth it.

'And this is my erstwhile intern Mahalia and her boyfriend Ronny,' Gini says of the two young white people sitting together, smiling awkwardly and waiting to be introduced.

'Mahalia?'

Jesse hopes he doesn't sound too incredulous. *Mahalia*. The blackest of black gospel soul singers. Taught Aretha Franklin everything she knew. Now a posh blonde girl with eyes like saucers who looks like she hasn't had a wash yet today, with a ridiculously big and handsome tanned guy next to her falling out of his shorts. Jesse immediately imagines how warm he would feel, spooning. He can't conceive that Gini invited them, so perhaps they were walking through the park on their way home from last night's party and spotted her and Surenna sitting under their tree.

'Nice to meet you. Hi, nice to meet you, Ronny.'

'Is Owen coming?' says Gini.

'I haven't even told him I'm here,' he says, sitting down on the orange kente blanket. 'My phone was in my locker so I got your message at the end of the shift and came straight here. I didn't think it'd be worth dragging him from his desk when I've only got an hour max.'

'But he only lives up there!' she says, pointing in the wrong direction, then correcting herself. 'Surely he'll want to come down and eat some of this beautiful nice organic Jamaican food me spen' nuff time fe cook.'

Gini takes after her mother, being a wizard in the kitchen.

There are Tupperware boxes of various sizes everywhere, containing prettily presented homemade confections.

'What have you got?'

'Do you want me to make you a plate?'

'Yes, please. Is that okra? No okra, thanks.'

Gini bores her eyes into him.

'Okay, I'll try a little bit of the okra.'

'Good! You look like you want feed,' says Surenna. 'A maga y'a maga so. Me shunny able fe see your sum'n deh nuh yuh trowsiz!'

'Thank you! Let's try to maintain the original meaning of the word *maga* by using it as often as possible,' says Jesse. 'But stop looking at my willy.'

'What does *maga* mean?' asks Mahalia.

'Skinny. Like Jesse, the thinnest person I've ever seen who says he works in a restaurant,' Surenna laughs, slapping her thigh.

Gini knows as well as Jesse does that working in a restaurant is a quick route to an eating disorder. Waiters in restaurants such as the Light Café and Sebastian's are too busy – too busy trying to be as thin and beautiful as some of the customers there less to be fed than to be seen – to eat, and when they do get time, cigarettes, alcohol and cocaine suppress the appetite.

Jesse looks upon Gini with love while she serves him her food. She's been like a sister to him, and in some ways, a mother, especially during those times when methedrone, as well as cocaine, was eating through him – giving him tough love, making him see how pathetic he looked, giving him another option that was just as attractive but less reckless; she and Owen combined to make Jesse a morning person. A person who ran around Brockwell Park or Clapham Common; who had vegan smoothies for breakfast; wrote a thousand words before work, nothing special, just who he was, today, and how he was feeling. She and Owen are the only people in his life who have ever met anyone in his family, when his sister Esther found him on Facebook and came down to London for the day. She was shocked at his appearance, that he still looked so boyish, her big brother, six years older than her, but she was impressed with his friends, with the people who had taken him into their hearts. Ruth was still a Witness, and had married. Esther had left the organisation and was living happily with her long-term partner Sean and their two small children Leo and Riley. They found a bond as adults they never quite had as children because their mother kept them so separate. He cried to see how well she was doing, how beautiful she had grown up to be, and they've kept in touch since on a WhatsApp group.

Surenna turns up Kelis's 'Young, Fresh N' New', with its fairground-like synth effect, clicks her fingers and shrugs her shoulders.

'This still sounds so sick,' says Gini. 'No one ever plays this one.'

'Right? Normally when someone bothers to play Kelis it's "Milkshake", "Bossy" or "Trick Me",' says Surenna.

'This is a tune, but "Good Stuff"'s the one,' says Jesse.

'I'm there,' nods Surenna, and they high-five. 'Neptunes for life.'

'You should look out for a new artist from Brixton called JaJa Kisses,' says Conroy. 'My daughter knows her. Really good, sort of understated soul singer in the Sade/Aaliyah way. Watch her blow up, if not this year then next.'

'Yeah, I love her,' says Surenna. 'I wanna work with her. I love how shy she is.'

'How are all your projects going, Surenna?' Jesse asks. Her last gig, at the ICA, was one of the best things he had ever seen, a brilliant projection show, and industrial R&B from another planet. She is also one of the best vocalists he has heard. He cannot believe she doesn't just sign a massive record deal and become the next Missy Elliott.

'Fine. I'm busy,' she says, ever vague-sounding whilst being known to be almost frighteningly productive and driven.

'How's the writing going?' Jesse perseveres. Surenna also happens to be researching a biography of the African-American classical composer Florence Beatrice Price, who was the first black woman to have a symphony performed by a mainstream orchestra. Gini told Jesse a bidding war is brewing among publishers, with Faber in the lead.

'It's going,' Surenna nods, aware of how infuriating she is being.

'How is Owen?' Gini says, as if to keep it between them, then says to the blanket, 'Owen's a poet.'

'What's his surname?' asks Ronny, as if he knows what he wants the answer to be.

'Gunning.'

'What, you're Owen Gunning's partner?' says Ronny.

'Yes,' says Jesse, surprised such a deliberately obscure poet as Owen has been taken in by a horny twenty-year-old with a Cockney accent.

'No way, I love his work! And he lives in Brixton?'

'I don't know him,' says Mahalia, as if she knows lots of other poets.

'I should think Brixton would be the perfect place for a poet to live,' says Conroy. 'All the sounds, the rhythms, the clashes of language and race. Gentrification and halfway houses. I think I've heard of your partner's work, though it's not really my speciality.'

'What *is* your speciality?' asks Jesse.

'Dr Conroy Adam. Lead Curator of Caribbean Diasporic and Black British Collections at the British Library,' says Gini, as she spoons some extra okra onto Jesse's pumpkin and callaloo patty, spinach, fry dumplin and plantain. 'Did I get that right?'

'Precisely,' says Conroy with a shy smile, keeping his eyes to Jesse's with a slightly confused look.

'So mainstream poetry might not be your thing but when it comes to black British . . .'

'Will he get your book in his hands soon?' Gini says.

'You're writing a book?' Conroy asks.

'I wouldn't call it a book,' says Jesse.

Gini shapes as if to serve him a backhand across the face.

'Well, I'm writing, but I've no real thoughts as to form or anything, yet. I'm just collecting material.'

'He's a really good writer,' she tells Conroy, handing Jesse his plate. 'You want some coconut punch?'

'Yes please.'

'Fiction or non-fiction?' asks Conroy.

'Non-fiction, at the moment. Life writing.'

'And what's your surname?' Conroy asks, curiously.

'McCarthy.'

He nods his head. Jesse thinks, why is he looking at me like that?

'Interesting. When do we get to read some?'

'When I get time to finish it. I'm working a lot at the moment.'

'You're gonna have to stop using that as an excuse soon,' says Gini. 'This is supposed to be the quiet time of year yet you're doing more shifts than ever.'

'They're really short-staffed at the moment.'

She and Melania don't really know each other, and he doesn't want to tell Gini, in her present state, about the miscarriage.

'Why's that your problem? Tell them to hire more waiters,' says Surenna, sipping her drink. 'God knows there's nuff people out there a look job an cyah find.'

'Innit,' says Gini.

'Where do you work?' asks Mahalia.

'The Light Café.'

'What, in King's Cross?' says Ronny.

'That's the one.'

'We love it there. The bar's beautiful.'

'Yeah, it's cool.'

'Do you and Owen write in the same space?' asks Ronny.

'Yeah, we have desks opposite each other,' Jesse says, knowing this will impress Ronny, who looks like an absolute playground.

'How many collections has he had published?' asks Conroy.

'This next one will be his . . . fourth?'

'Who publishes him?'

'Endymion.'

'I see. Very small press.'

'He's great. I love him,' says Ronny.

Jesse wonders whether Owen knows he has such fit young fans. 'I'm sure he'd be delighted to hear that.'

'He's working on a new collection, then?' Ronny asks.

'Yes. It's been a long time in the making.'

'What does he write about?' asks Mahalia.

'He writes about working-class men in particular who are kept in a state of low education and expectation while the world changes around them,' says Ronny, impressively.

'But he seems to be expanding his remit with this collection,' Jesse adds, feeling oddly displaced from his rightful position as Owen's gospel-spreader-in-command. 'He's writing a lot about sex and love, all of a sudden.'

'Mmm-hmmmmm . . . ' says Gini.

'He's keen to develop the queer voice in poetry.'

'And I bet you're helping *a lot* with that, aren't you, babe?' says Surenna.

'So exciting!' says Mahalia.

'So he can't come to my picnic?' says Gini.

'He's got an important meeting with his editor tomorrow, so he's preparing for that.'

'What's it like being in the same room as someone writing what's probably going to become a famous collection?' asks Ronny.

'I might ask what it's like interning with the beautiful and amazing Ginika Redmond Ndukwe,' he says to revive Mahalia, who seems to be falling asleep. Gini tells him to shut up. Ronny nudges Mahalia and she reaches for her tobacco.

'How long have you guys known each other?' she asks, a little too loudly.

'Gini was my first friend in London when I'd been living here for three whole days.'

'When did you move here?' asks Ronny.

'Two thousand and two.'

'How old were you?'

'Nineteen.'

'So, wait, that means you're . . .'

'Thirty-four.'

'No! Way! I thought you were, like, twenty-three!'

'Max!' says Ronny. 'What is it about you guys?'

'Black. Don't. Crack!' says Mahalia.

Conroy shakes his head and laughs, despite himself. Surenna sucks her teeth. Gini just looks at Jesse as if to confirm they weren't actually invited.

'Wait, how old are *you*?' Mahalia says to Conroy.

'If you don't mind her asking,' says Surenna.

'This is an even *bigger* tune!' says Jesse, pointing his gun-fingers in the air.

Just in time, Rihanna's 'Man Down'. Jesse puts down his plate, and he, Gini and Surenna all get up and wait for the beat to drop. The amount of times they've been out together and this has come on in the club. They know all the words and sing along. Jesse's phone rings in his pocket. He panics for a second that time has flown and he's already late for work.

'Melania?'

'Bitch, I'm back.'

'So good to hear from you! Are you feeling better? I thought you were still ill?'

'No, but if I stay home I'm just gonna be even more depressed so I thought I'd just come to work and be with normal people instead of my boyfriend who's driving me fucking crazy.'

'Oh?'

Gini has burst out laughing at something – a laugh that fills the sky – so Jesse has to walk away and put a finger in his ear.

'I mean, he's been amazing, actually, I'm being really harsh,' says Melania. 'But I'm still sick of the sight of him. He's literally been absolutely perfect, doing absolutely everything for me. He's taken fucking paternity leave for a dead child, for fuck's sake. I'm like, *Babes, go back to work, I'm fine!* but he's like, *Honey, I wanna take care of you. You've been through something terrible, mentally, emotionally and physically and you're in denial. That's why I have to be here with you.* He's like the Internet this, the Internet that. But sometimes a girl's just got to go through these things by herself, you know? It's my body, and like, you know, I mean, I don't want to shut him out but I just want to smoke like a million cigarette in my pyjama in bed with the blind closed and listen to techno and maybe just go for a fucking shit by myself and yet there he is making sure I'm eating healthy and bringing me remedy and magazine and being like let's go for a fucking walk and wrapping me in scarves and holding my hand too tight and inside I'm like, *Fuck! Off!* but on the outside I'm like baby, thank you, you're being amazing I'm so lucky, and then he's got his fingers in my hair like, *Baby, are you better yet? Do you think it's time to try again cos you know I was reading the other day on this American parenting website about the best way to get over a miscarriage is just to get pregnant again straight away or as soon as your body's recovered* and I'm like, *Yeah, soon babes!* Babes. I'm not letting his dick anywhere near me again. I'm gonna go on the pill and get fitted for a coil. I don't wanna be pregnant. Ever. Again!'

Ronny and Mahalia walk past, waving goodbye. It's like he's holding her up. His ass looks massive in those shorts, and he keeps smiling and looking over his shoulder. Jesse puffs out his cheeks and adjusts himself in his underwear.

'Are you okay, Melania? Do you need somewhere to stay?'

'No, no. I don't know, babes. Maybe?'

'You can stay at mine whenever you want.'

'No, babes, I'm sure it's fine I'll be fine I'll be fine I'll be fine. I don't want to be anyone's trouble.'

'You're not anyone's trouble. Have you spoken to him?'

'No.'

'Are you afraid of him?'

She says nothing.

'Melania, has something happened?'

'Not yet.' There is a breathiness in her voice Jesse's never heard before. 'But he is a little bit too ... how can I say ... forceful, sometimes, you know? He's started working out in the bedroom as soon as I'm up and he's given me breakfast like I'm a child, instead of going to the gym, like he used to. He's pumping his body up because I don't know, maybe, weirdly, he blames himself for me losing the baby, that he didn't create a child that was strong enough to cling on. So now he's pumping up, maybe thinking that when we try for a baby again his spunk will be stronger and therefore the baby will have stronger fucking suction pads on its fingers and toes, or whatever. Maybe he thinks that in the past it was too easy to blame women and so now he's gone into hunter-gatherer-protector mode. It's like he's not even thinking. I feel really bad for him, and know he's suffering more than me. I mean it's the longest he's not been able to fuck me since we met. He barely lets me out of the house, and only with him. I feel vulnerable, and yet I've got this huge powerful angry thing who won't leave me alone. He'd never hurt me, I know that, but I've been in abusive relationship before and I just don't feel one hundred per cent safe.'

'Does he know you're there?'

'No. He went shopping and I got dressed and came to work.'

'Has he been in touch?'

'I switched off my phone.'

'Where will he think you are?'

'Maybe here, maybe at the bottom of the Thames, I don't care.'

'Melania, don't say that, please.'

'I'm kidding, babes. Babes, you want the night off?'

'What do you mean?'

'A table of twenty cancelled. Ben's gone fucking mental because they ordered a lamb and everything. But we're dead tonight. Just thirty covers. I think even I can manage that. And guess what, babes?'

'What?'

She lowers her voice.

'I walked in and Veedub gave me a hug and a kiss and said she was sorry and asked me if she could do anything for me.'

'Oh. My. God!'

'It's that kind of day. So I'm a little bit emotional but I think it's going to be okay. I'd actually rather be at work than miserable at home. And I can do your shifts this weekend, if you want. I know you've been doing doubles nearly every day.'

'Melania! If you think you're up to it.'

'I'm fine, babes, the next step will just be to force myself to get back to normal.'

'Oh darling, if you're sure, but if you do take on my shifts you have to be absolutely certain, because Owen's been begging me to go to Suffolk with him to spend the weekend at his publisher's house. You know what he's like. He doesn't want to drive alone. And if you can't work one of the shifts, especially if it's Sunday lunch, it's not going to be easy for me to come back from all the way there.'

'It will be fine. Go. You deserve a break and it'll be gorgeous in this weather. Imagine the wildflower.'

'Shall we see how you go this evening? Do you want to stay at ours? I think, if you get through tonight okay, you'll be better off being at work than going home. At least for the weekend. Just break the stranglehold. Show him you're still the same woman.'

'Oh, babes, I'm being a dick. I don't blame him, I really don't.'

'But it does sound like you need a bit of space. Do you want me to talk to him?'

'No. I don't know, Jess. No. We'll see.'

'The offer's there.'

'Ugh, babes, I just wanna be a bad bitch and go to Berlin and do a fucking pill and dance with no bra and fuck an arrogant German guy with a really big dick in the toilet. I wanna go to Panorama Bar and run around with my tits out for three days. I don't wanna deal with this grown-up shit.'

'I hear you, darling.' Georgia's voice in the background. It's magical they're talking again, after two years.

'Anyway, babes, it's been ages. How are you? I've missed you.'

'I'm fine. Do you remember my friend Gini? She texted me to come down to Brixton for a picnic, so I'm here now.'

'Ah. Perfect. Stay there, babes.'

'Are you sure?'

'Fucking enjoy your weekend. I love you so much.'

'Oh Melania, I love you, too. Keep in touch.'

'Will do. My love to your darling hubby. Bye.'

'Yes! I've got the night off, and the weekend off!' Jesse squeals, making the next group of white people turn round and share the same thought about loud blacks. Mariah Carey's 'The Roof' is playing.

'That's good, bubbie,' Gini says. 'How come?'

'My colleague's just come back from being off sick. Oh my God, what a blessing. I was just thinking, I'm having so much fun here and I don't want to go back to fucking work. I'll text Owen and see if he wants to come down.'

'You know what, I have to say something,' says Conroy. 'You're the spitting image of someone I used to know back in the

Eighties. You have the same ... about here,' he says, gesturing over his eyes and nose. 'That's why I asked your surname.'

'Jesse's adopted,' says Gini.

'I didn't know that,' says Surenna. 'Did I know that?'

'You did. Remember I showed you the pictures of his half-sisters?' says Gini, as Jesse finishes and sends his text.

'I'm only adopted by, well, I still refer to him by his Christian name. I grew up with my mum and she married again when I was four.'

'You ever know your real dad?' asks Conroy.

'No, I don't remember him. Who is this person you're talking about?'

'His name was Robert Alonso. I was dating his sister Glorie around ... 1979, when I was studying art at Wolverhampton Polytechnic, and Robert painted self-portraits. He wasn't a student, but he hung around the scene a little bit from outside. I know from what his sister told me that he'd been in and out of foster care as a teenager. I think their mum had a bit of a breakdown at some point and the dad died when they were still babies.'

'So you were one of the Blk Art Group?'

'You know about that? Not a full member, no. I was involved in one of the group shows but from the beginning of my studies I knew that curation and writing were going to be my thing, and as soon as I finished my degree I moved to London. But he wasn't a bad painter, you know. Nudes, mainly with flowers – usually roses. His sister and I dated for a while, as I say, nothing too serious, but we stayed friends and I'm still in touch with her. She still lives up in Wolverhampton with her daughter.'

'Does any of this sound familiar, Jess?' says Gini.

'I honestly don't know anything about my dad,' Jesse says, though the mention of nudes with roses gives him a jolt. 'My mum always refused to talk about him.'

'Don't you have a birth certificate or anything?'

'It's only got my mum's name on. When was the last time you saw him?'

'I bumped into him one time at the Tate Gallery, maybe around 1990. He looked unwell, like an old man. I didn't recognise him at first. Glorie never mentioned him at all and I didn't ask. He said he was painting again, to document the process of his illness and had sold a couple of pieces.' The pleasant expression on Conroy's face drops as he realises the uncomfortable truth he has inadvertently approached. 'He had AIDS. He had that face they all had. Drawn and grey. But he still had those eyes, that unrelenting life spirit. That beauty, which did not change.'

Jesse feels an urge to hit out at Conroy, but as with a cynical and presumptuous customer, manages to keep his cool. *The fist clenched round the stem, a thorn pricking the palm, blood dripping down the forearm.* 'It can't be him. The only thing my mum has told me is that my real dad died when I was two.'

'*Your* mum,' says Gini. 'I wouldn't put it past her lying. Not for any other reason than to protect you.'

'She wouldn't lie. She's a Jehovah's Witness.'

'But she became a Jehovah's Witness when you were a child. If she lied to you before she became a Witness then maybe it was difficult for her to change her story, after that.'

'I don't know. It doesn't fucking matter now, anyway,' says Jesse. His mouth has gone dry. 'I'm good. I've got Owen, and you, and all my other acquired family. I don't need all that other shit.'

My dad died of AIDS? When? Does that mean he was gay? Bi? Did he inject drugs? That man in the picture? How dare this man sit next to me in front of my friends and tell me over a picnic, as if it wasn't anything to do with me, that my dad died of AIDS? My dad! Is he talking about the right person? People tell me all the time that I remind them of someone, mostly white people, though, not woke black scholars. If Iago was black, this is the sort of shit he would try. Create upset when there is none, through lies and deception. I was so happy – why has this man planted this in my head? The last time they saw each other was at the Tate in 1990. Robert Alonso. Where have I heard that name before? And my own mother? Has she been lying to me all this time? What did she think was going to happen when I found out? Sister Doreen Charles told me once, 'Hi believe in the trut, that the trut halways fine ha way fe come out.' I don't understand. My mother accused me before the elders, all those years ago, of being a liar, a cheat and a thief, and look at her. She is the liar, the cheat, and the thief. Why would this Conroy man lie to me? Why would he try to trick me? He is the one with the fine rep-utation, who has educated himself and is a man of knowledge and culture. She belongs to a sect that has brainwashed her against her own firstborn. She has lied to me, all my life. My father was alive when I was eight. I was alive for at least eight years and I never got to meet him. He must have died thinking his son cared nothing for him. Were they in contact? What did she tell him? Robert Alonso. A painter. A black male painter of nudes. Self-portraits, mainly, with roses, documenting the progress of his illness ... our eyes ... our unrelenting life spirit ... Nude ... Nude with Othello ...

Chapter 3

The bodies of Othello, Desdemona and Emilia lay lifeless. Iago stood centre stage with his hands on his hips and his chest puffed out, watching the audience watching him, and then simply walked free. Darkness. Jubilant applause and three curtains, the actor playing Iago getting the biggest cheer of all.

'What did you think?' asked Thurston as he and Jesse left the auditorium, among the crowds, in baby steps. People were laughing and altogether seemed happy with what they had seen.

Jesse sighed, while he weighed his words.

'Erm, yeah,' he said, doubtfully. 'I didn't love it.'

'Oh,' said Thurston, surprised. 'Why not? I thought it was great. I thought the director brought a lot of fresh nuance out of it. It's not easy to do something new with one of the most-performed plays in the canon. I very much liked how Desdemona was played by a mixed-race girl, and Emilia was played by a black woman, your friend.'

'Of course, I loved all that commentary on colourism and social class,' Jesse said, 'but I didn't like the way the white man was seen to get away with it at the end, just to go off and wreak more havoc somewhere else.'

A white woman, in front of Jesse in the stream of people

leaving, checked her peripherals and ever so subtly moved her handbag around her front.

'Hmm. Well, his punishment wasn't written in the text,' said Thurston, considering Jesse's point. 'Lodovico left Cassio, as the new governor, to decide on it himself. But perhaps that makes it a comment on male accountability.'

Jesse laughed. 'I suppose only very clever and liberal people like yourself will see it like that,' he said, aware he might be coming across as condescending and bratty. 'The rest will witness righteous white males going unpunished for what they alone think is the right thing to do, especially when there are black women involved. And Cassio's just a twerp who Iago knows won't have the authority or imagination to close him down.'

'Oh, okay well, I'm sorry you didn't enjoy it,' said Thurston, as they came out onto the Thursday evening bustle of Old Street, with far too many people around for that time of night. The temperature had dropped further, and Jesse wound his scarf tighter around his neck.

'But thank you for bringing me,' Jesse smiled, and laughed, buffeted by crowds funnelling into the Tube station, their hot breath freezing on the air. 'I'm sorry. I don't want to sound ungrateful. You're right, it was a great production. I loved the animation, and, you know, it was really well acted, and, yeah, the music and everything was great, and very surprising.'

'Yes, I adored the use of Janáček's "The Madonna of Frydek" in the scene where Othello adorned Desdemona with the handkerchief. Exquisitely done, I thought.'

After the Duke ruled in favour of the marriage, Iago alone, with the audience, watched as an animation was projected onto the back wall, in white lines on black, of two crude figures engaged in livid sexual contact, each splash of semen morphing into endless devilish progeny, while Othello took Desdemona gently from behind by the waist and carefully tied a black handkerchief dotted with strawberries around her neck, as they moved together in peace to the piano music – the Janáček – played live by Desdemona's father Brabantio, much to Thurston's delight, Jesse could sense. The stage emptied, Iago, murderously, last of all.

The two black girls who had been sitting in front of Jesse and Thurston came out of the theatre and smiled at them as they walked past, heading west towards Holborn.

'Bye,' said Jesse.

'Look, what are you doing now?' said Thurston.

'Well, Gini said we should wait for her here. She said she won't be able to hang around for long because she has to go and see her mother, who's been unwell.'

'Oh, what's wrong with her?' asked Thurston.

'Breast cancer,' Jesse said, more with his eyes than with his voice, in case anyone who knew Gini and her mother was standing around. 'Don't let on that I told you. She's very sensitive and worried about it.'

'Understood. Well, I'm terribly impressed that she was able to put in such a measured and energetic performance, considering what's going on in her personal life.'

'It probably helped inform her emotional arc,' Jesse said, grandly.

'Did you ever consider acting yourself?' Thurston said, looking at Jesse with a mildly teasing smile.

'Me? Haha. No. Why?'

'You'd be terribly good at it.'

'Really? That's sweet of you, but I know the work Gini and her colleagues put into training and I know I'd just embarrass myself with my ineptitude. Here she is.'

'Hi!' called Gini, jogging towards them, holding her arms out. She looked excited and happy, more so than Jesse had seen her in some time, transformed from the ashy, tired-looking, barefoot Emilia with an all-off-white outfit, black knee-high boots and a strong lick of bright red lipstick.

'Hello, beautiful! Congratulations, you were amazing, of

course!' She held him tight and he kissed her on the cheek, and she laughed. 'You look wonderful,' he told her as they disengaged. 'How are you feeling?'

She nodded her head, quickly and enthusiastically, her smile as sharp as the moon was on that clear night. Surely this was more than just the adrenaline of having finished a show.

'I'm feeling good,' she said. 'Really good! I love this show, I love my fellow actors, I love the production, my agent keeps calling me with new scripts, *Soon Come*'s been taken up by the Royal Court, it's all good!'

Jesse's eyes were brimming.

'So nice to see someone in the family doing well,' he said, turning to Thurston. 'Gini, please meet my friend, Thurston Bradfield. Thurston, meet Ginika Redmond Ndukwe.'

'Pleased to meet you, and thank you for coming to my show!' she said.

'Thank you! You were wonderful!' said Thurston, whose voice, for all his enthusiasm, sounded suddenly muddy and muffled next to Gini's, which had rung superbly as she called out her stage husband's heinous crimes. 'We're really lucky to catch it. Pretty much every performance was sold out.'

'I know. I'm so blessed,' she said, as she tried to be discreet at checking her phone in her bag. 'How's Owen?'

'Good, he's good. He's up north with his mother. She was in Australia for Christmas so they're having a delayed bit of time together. She's moving there for good.'

'No! How does Owen feel about that?'

'Bloody ecstatic, though he'll miss the house,' said Jesse. Gini cackled, then commiserated. 'One less thing for him to worry about. His daughters give him more than enough stress. Chloe's broken up with her girlfriend and apparently is in a bad way so he's coming back tomorrow.'

'Oh no, sorry to hear that,' she said, with half her attention on her phone. 'Wait, how old is she?'

'Sixteen. Oh, don't worry about the girlfriend, they'll be back together again soon. It's not the first time. It's the stress of her exams that's making her like that. Emma's the natural academic. Chloe's bright but it takes a bit more time, with her.'

'Families, eh?' Gini put her phone back in her bag and pursed her lips, smoothing out the shocking red.

'How's your mum?' Jesse asked, gently.

Completely unexpectedly, Gini beamed and started jumping up and down. Her eyes moistened. She grabbed him by the arm.

'Remission!'

They both screamed and jumped up and down as if they'd been holding their breath until the veins started popping in their temples.

'Oh my God, that's incredible news! Oh my God!' They hugged tight again, and were both crying. 'I'm so proud of her!' said Jesse.

'Innit!'

She nodded, like a little girl, and wiped her eyes with a tissue from her Mulberry bag.

'I'm still gonna run and see her, though, cos all the family are gonna be there. I just want to give her a big hug. We only found out today, with the doctor, and I was doing a casting elsewhere when I got the news, then I had to be here at four and it's just been a lot. But hopefully, soon she'll be able to see me on stage herself.'

Jesse liked the way she addressed both him and Thurston, as if Thurston, being close to Jesse, was just as much family to her as Jesse was.

'I'm so happy for you, and proud of you and everything you've achieved and are going to achieve. You're so beautiful and talented, and you've got a heart this big, and I'm really so, so proud of you.'

'Aww, shut up! Very soon you're going to achieve something

huge too,' she said, looking right into his eyes. 'This is just my turn. A you next!'

She kissed him fully on the lips.

'Look, I've gotta run. I love you and let's see each other real soon. Pleased to meet you, Thurston. Bye!' And straight away she flagged down a cab and disappeared.

'Wow, what a force of nature!' said Thurston, who, blinking and grinning stupidly, looked like he'd just had a line of cocaine.

'Yes, people always say that about her. She should be Ginika "Force of Nature" Redmond Ndukwe.'

'People say that all the time about Josette, too,' Thurston said of his best friend, Josette Cunningham, a Labour MP he met at Oxford.

'What do they have in common?'

'They're both black women?'

'Powerful black women. Forces of nature. To be feared.'

'Interesting,' said Thurston.

'Powerful white men don't get called forces of nature. Older women, I note, get called "formidable". White men never get called that. Do you ever wonder why these things are?'

'Never thought about it before, but you're certainly not wrong,' said Thurston. 'So, what *are* you doing now?'

'Nothing. Why? Might just go home, I don't know.'

'You live in Brixton, don't you?'

'Yes. Are you still in Dulwich?'

'I am, so would it be too much of a detour to stop by at mine for a drink?'

'Really?'

'Don't worry, not for . . . anything like that. Just to catch up properly. The company would be nice.'

Jesse checked his iPhone for the time. It was just after ten o'clock. He'd been listening back over Sugababes' first album, playing the last track 'Run for Cover' on repeat. The original line-up had just got back together after eleven years, and he still hadn't forgiven himself for not booking New Year's Eve off work so that he could go to their comeback show at Ponystep, the Hoxton clubnight.

'Okay. I could get the number three bus back from yours, of course.'

'We could go by Tube to Brixton and get the bus, very easily, or we can get a taxi.'

'Let's just get a cab, it's cold,' said Jesse.

He'd forgotten the house. He'd only been there once, of course, but as they got out of the taxi under a spidery naked lime tree, certain memories returned – the bus stop across the road; the red-and-gold chessboard gable. The silver Audi estate had been replaced by an up-to-date smaller model, an A3. A dog started barking as soon as Thurston opened his front door, and he shushed it down; Jesse remembered another dog, barking twice. He was standing in a hallway that, when he first visited it twelve years before, was painted yellow, he was certain. The walls were now a warm grey, though the floor remained black and white mosaic tiles. There were still paintings up the stairs, and Jesse suddenly remembered the one of the black male nude holding a big red flower and with blood dripping down his arm. Every time he'd seen a depiction of Christ on the cross, he thought of Thurston's picture, but as he ducked down to remove his shoes in the hall-way, he noticed that it was gone. In its place was a watercolour of a more demure, lighter-skinned man, naked, viewed from behind.

'Can I get you something to drink?' Thurston said, opening the door to the kitchen and hanging up his coat while a Dulux dog sniffed around his feet.

'Yes, please,' said Jesse, as the dog trotted out to do the same to him. 'Hello!'

'This is Bella,' Thurston said. 'She's very, very friendly.'

'You're gorgeous!' Jesse said, rubbing her under her chin as she looked up at him. 'How old is she?'

'Three and a half,' he said. 'Still only a puppy.'

The dog that lived there when Jesse first visited would have passed away. Bella was looking right at him, almost purring like a cat, and he didn't want her to get too obsessed, or to get too much hair on his jumper, so he followed Thurston into his kitchen, which was countrified and homely, with light beige fascias and black worktops, dusky pink walls and matte apple-green tiles. The slightly bleached-looking parquet floor was warm underfoot.

'It's lovely in here,' Jesse said.

'Yes, I keep the Aga on all through the winter. So, I'm having a whisky. Will you join me? Or would you prefer wine? White or red? I don't think I have any beer.'

'Whisky's good, actually.'

Thurston smiled and nodded, and scrunched his nose up a little bit, as if to say, *It's the best thing, isn't it, whisky, on a night like this*, and took down a bottle of Laphroaig from a high cupboard, and two tumblers from another. Then he stopped for thought.

'Do you like Laphroaig? It's not to everyone's taste.'

'It's perfect.'

It was still Owen's favourite single malt, despite everything, and they always kept a bottle in the cupboard.

'Ice?'

'One cube, please.'

'Like a gentleman,' he said. 'Do sit down.'

The dining table, which had room for eight, was in a small extension at the bottom of the kitchen, overlooking the garden, which was unseen in the dark, though Jesse thought Thurston might switch on some lights, as people who had such things to show off usually would.

He had been covering someone else's shift at the Light Café when an older white man and a black woman had been seated with menus in his section. Jesse's voice had certainly

changed – his accent had grown more neutral – but Thurston
looked up at him with immediate recognition which, when it
fully registered, caused him to blanch. In a few seconds, Jesse
remembered who Thurston was, and thought him different now,
sexless, unlike the lithe fifty-one-year-old he'd met so early in
his London journey. They said *Hello* to each other properly,
without giving anything away, but at the end of their dinner,
throughout which Jesse had given them his most attentive service, Thurston said to Jesse: 'May Josette know how we met?'
If Thurston wasn't embarrassed, thought Jesse, nor should I be;
Josette took it completely in her stride, seeming rather proud
of Thurston, and smiled at Jesse as a friend for the first time.
Thurston left Jesse his card with a tip under the bill plate, in
the hope that they might see each other again as friends, and
Jesse, though he didn't enjoy two wildly different versions of
himself meeting face to face across time, emailed him, just to
say hello and with no expectations, which led to the invitation.
Thurston was curious about the Foundlings Theatre, but didn't
know anyone young and cool enough to visit it with, and Jesse
had been ill with flu when Owen attended the press night
without him.

Thurston now lit a couple of candles and switched on the
floor-standing Anglepoise in the corner, next to the antique
oak dresser, which displayed a collection of blue and white
Wedgwood plates. Bella crawled under their feet as Thurston
put down a bowl of salted cashew nuts. They reminded each
other that they were born in the Black Country – Jesse in
Wordsley, a village near Dudley, Thurston just down the road
in Wolverhampton – which amused Jesse. Thurston was too
elevated and grand; Jesse remembered reading somewhere
about Queen Victoria closing her blind in disgust as she
passed through Brierley Hill – the inspiration for Tolkien's
Mordor – on her train up to Balmoral. Thurston stressed its
first syllable, like a Pathé newsreader: *WULL*-verhampton,

while most people from there say Wull-*VRAM*pton, slightly rolling the *r*. Thurston told Jesse he was the son of a rector, who'd grown up in Tettenhall (Tetten-hall; *TETT*-null), a historic village in what was then Enoch Powell's constituency, attending the private school there; he was seventeen and studying for his Oxford entrance when Powell made his 'Rivers of Blood' speech. Jesse had the thought that his mother would have been just six, attending her Dudley state school amid spiralling immigration and rapidly filling classrooms, while all of this politics was going on over her plaited head. Thurston, growing up five miles away in a pretty village where everyone was white, saw little of the racism Jesse's mother's generation had to endure, though everyone his parents knew sided with Powell.

Thurston drained the last of his drink.

'Would you like to join me for another, more comfortably?'

Jesse was about to say no, but didn't, so Thurston poured another each, and Jesse followed him, and Bella, through.

This must have been where Thurston's partner used to sit watching television, Jesse thought. It was a large room made cosy by the sheer amount of stuff in it, though noticeably colder than the Aga-heated kitchen, with a white-painted open fireplace, two marshmallowy white two-seat sofas opposite each other in front of it, and a leather-topped coffee table between them.

Thurston put on all the lamps and then turned off the overhead light, before starting a quick tinder fire, to which he added logs. It had the feel of one of those preciously maintained rooms at the Soane Museum. The walls were painted emerald and crowded with small framed paintings and drawings, both landscapes and portraits, and above the fireplace was a beautifully ornate, gilt-framed oval mirror. The recesses either side of it were stacked floor to ceiling with books. Everywhere he looked there was something to look at, a fragile ornament, an exquisite decoration or an elegant candle holder. The small television was in the far corner of the room, facing an armchair in front of the bookcase at that end. Jesse sat on the sofa and petted Bella, who wagged her tail and leaned her jaw into his hand.

'Do you live here alone, now?' he asked, as Thurston poked the fire with a brass rod and swept old ash back into the grate with a matching brush.

'Yes, since Charles died,' he said, with no emotion. It had been five years. 'I thought about getting a lodger for all of five minutes, if that.'

'It's hard to know who might be able to fit in a house like this,' said Jesse, looking up at the antique bronze chandelier, surprisingly subtle and minimal compared to the opulence elsewhere in the room.

'That's exactly it,' he said. 'This is the home Charles and I made. I might not find someone who can appreciate it and be comfortable with all these things. Or, if I did, I wouldn't want to live with someone who treated it like a museum; I'd want them to feel as if they lived somewhere homely, which it is, for me, but I can appreciate it might not be for everyone. Then I thought, if I was to live with someone else, then we would have to start again from scratch and build something together, but I'm far too old for all that now.'

'You're not old,' said Jesse.

'Well, darling, that's very sweet of you, but I honestly am.' He looked at Jesse and smiled. 'Though this is a rather big house for an old man to live in by himself, it's true.'

'How long have you lived here?'

He thought about it for a moment. 'We moved here just after the '87 election. I bet you weren't even born, were you?'

'I was five,' said Jesse, who was used to people underestimating his age. 'If I hadn't been born before then, I'd have been underage when we met.'

'When did we meet?'

'The summer of 2002, when I first moved to London.'

'Christ, that long ago? It's a pity we lost touch,' he said, happy to have brought up the fire adequately.

Jesse had never had a client like him again; nobody after Thurston showed him such compassion, or concern for his well-being. If it wasn't for Thurston giving him the name and number for a sexual health clinic for escorts, where he was diagnosed and treated for gonorrhoea, chlamydia and non-specific urethritis, and told firmly that he should use a condom at all times, then it didn't bear thinking about, as far as Jesse was concerned, where he'd be by now. Thurston, having guessed that Jesse wasn't in absolutely perfect health, stopped the session, but instead of throwing him out like a spent rag, cuddled him, listened to him, told him he was charming, and that he hoped he would find someone nice to take care of him. They wanked together until they both came on their bellies, and lay half-asleep until a buzzer went off that meant Thurston had to attend to his partner. Thurston gave Jesse the money that had been agreed, plus a very generous tip, though there was something about the alacrity with which the door shut behind him before he'd even got to the end of the limestone-chipping driveway, that felt final.

'The house has changed quite a bit since then,' said Jesse. 'You've redecorated.'

'You have a terrific memory,' said Thurston. 'You were only here for an hour.'

'It made an impression on me,' said Jesse. 'I'd never been in a house like this before. You used to have a painting at the top of the stairs, that really stuck with me. I still think about it sometimes. A naked black man holding a rose and the thorn pricking his hand, and blood rushing down his forearm.'

'I've still got it,' Thurston said.

Being with Thurston, writing into his past – and listening to Sugababes – was making Jesse nostalgic for his early London life. Everything seemed so much simpler in 2002. He thought of how lucky he was to still be here. How he would shake that nineteen-year-old clueless, reckless boy, now, for the sex he had, the drugs he took. But the first words Thurston said to him when they met up that evening were, *You've hardly aged at all.* 'Can I see it?' Jesse said.

'Of course,' said Thurston, as he sprang up from his seat. Bella, hitherto restful, got under his feet as if in readiness for some unlikely late-evening exercise. 'Out of the way, darling. Astonishing you should remember that,' he said, as he left the room, shadowed by Bella.

This house really is like a museum, Jesse thought, as he heard Thurston rummaging in the under-stairs cupboard. It sounded like he was leafing through old frames. He stacked paintings where others keep their vacuum cleaners, mops and buckets.

'Here it is,' Thurston said. 'I've had it for years. But when I redecorated the stairs it didn't seem to work there any more. It's a pity, because I do love it.'

He came back into the room with a large, heavy-looking mahogany frame, turned it around and showed Jesse. It looked different from how he remembered it, having idealised it over time and given it shapes and tones that it didn't have before, but seeing it afresh, it had the same power over him, the imagined pain of stigmatisation in his hand. The nude's dick lay thick across his groin, almost purple; his body in soft focus, a black male Ophelia. Blood coursed down his forearm from the centre of his palm. His other hand was tensed, clutching at air, yet his face was relaxed, as if in ecstasy, his lips thick and open, his eyebrows thick and naturally arched, his eyes blissfully closed. He looked more at ease than Jesse remembered him. Was he dead or alive? Twelve years before, he'd left without asking about it, having felt, somehow, as if it belonged to him, and he wanted to cover up its nakedness, as Noah's son Ham had his brothers do to their father, only for Ham's own sons to be cursed forever with black skin like the devil's.

'It's wonderful you remember it. I distinctly remember you standing and staring mesmerised at it, while I was trying to get you into my room,' said Thurston, laughing nervously. 'Topically enough, it's called *Nude With Othello*, Othello being the genus of rose, bred, incidentally, by David Austin in Wolverhampton. Charles and I bought it from a small group show at a gallery in Brixton sort of twenty, twenty-five years ago. I've tried to find out more about it but details are sketchy to say the least. It's signed by an otherwise completely unknown artist called Robert Alonso.'

Chapter 4

Owen had brought a few cans down, and they stayed late at the picnic, until Gini began to tire and she and Surenna left in an Uber. Other friends of Gini's had arrived, among them the art dealer Jermaine Porter, owner of the eponymous gallery on Atlantic Road, from whom Owen has bought work in the past. Jesse and Jermaine talked for a little while, Jermaine's smile as wide and white as ever but with a detectable moue behind it, though Owen monopolised him for most of the hour he gave them and Jesse soon began to feel he was surplus to requirements, obliged to leave one conversation to enter the other. Gini and Surenna made enough small talk to shift the conversation into another sphere, even while Conroy's speculation, and Jesse's incredulousness, remained at the forefront of their minds. Jesse couldn't help but feel a little annoyed by the way Owen turned away from him so that he and Jermaine sat mirrored on the kente blanket, with their legs folded into clamshells open to each another, one hand propped behind, the other dangling on their raised knee, both barefoot.

Elegant, black-skinned and angular, Jermaine had walked for Rick Owens as a teenager while studying for his degree in art history at the Courtauld. He is the sort of man who will retain high cheekbones and a twenty-nine-inch waist into his eighties.

His father was a boxer who read law after a chronic back injury caused him to retire; he now works for the same company as Owen's wife Anya, busily, and often thanklessly, advocating for young black men who would otherwise simply be thrown on the prison skip. His mother is the headteacher at the South London secondary school he went to, which could have been a source of bullying but Jermaine was above all that; he was good at football and athletics, never smoked or drank, went out with a posh blonde girl, dressed immaculately, DJed at house parties and cinched all his GCSEs. Nobody jacked Jermaine Porter for his camera, or called Mrs Porter – who transformed the previously failing school's fortunes financially and academically – a black bitch. Jesse had never owned a camera, but his school peers had frequently called his mother a black bitch. When he told Graham, hoping he would throw his arms around him, again he said, for the thousandth time, *Just ignore'em.*

As Owen arrived, Conroy hurried away, saying he had work to do at home. It seemed he was convinced of his argument about Jesse being Robert Alonso's son, and they swapped numbers and email addresses. He said he was going to get in touch with Glorie, Robert's sister in Wolverhampton, to see if she knew anything. She had never mentioned, not that he could remember, Robert having fathered a child, but that did not mean that he hadn't. Conroy, who has one teenage daughter from a previous relationship, pointed out that men of African descent have pranced up and down the land secretly scattering their seed for generations. Another friend of Gini's, Akilah, an artist, grew up with her mother and big sister in a council flat in Streatham and rarely saw their father, who only occasionally invited himself back into their home and into their mother's bed. It was only while he lay dying of prostate cancer at King's College Hospital that he told Akilah – who had dutifully cared for him while her sister, a mother of two, struggled to complete her nursing degree – that they were two of *nine* children he'd fathered with seven women. *Dat me know bout, anyway*, he'd said. Those had been almost his last words. Gini, even, was one of six by three. *Dat me know bout, anyway*, she'd said, sucking her teeth.

Jesse thought back to the moment when he found that photograph hidden in a Kodak folder in a cupboard in the wall unit, a moment every exposure to Massive Attack's 'Unfinished Sympathy' would charm from the depths of his memory, even to the guilty fear in the pit of his stomach of being caught snooping.

He could remember the basic composition of the picture but not the details of the face; the more he tried to see the face in his mind the blurrier it became. It was of an open-shirted man, thin, dark and model-like, not unlike Jermaine, sitting on a floor with his back against a wall and one knee up, barefoot, looking up at a light source. If it was him, then that is all he has, an impressionistic memory of a photograph long since destroyed. If it was not him, then who was it? It wasn't any of his uncles on his mother's side, he knew that. Why else would she have kept a photograph, if it wasn't of a lover? He could understand why she would have told him he had died when Jesse was two. Knowing his mother and her beliefs and attitudes, if this Robert Alonso was his father, then it would have been traumatic to her to discover that he also had sex with men. She might even have enjoyed his diagnosis with AIDS. *Serve him right*, she might have said, thickening her neck. He would have been dead to her. She would have cut him out like a cancer, killed him off, disfellowshipped him, told her son to forget about him, not that he'd ever been old enough to store any memories. He feels like the radio is on but he can't hear BANG!

Smashing my face against the windowpane! Smashing my face against the windowpane! Smashing my face against the window-pane! Smashing my face against the windowpane!

They're driving down a dual carriageway in almost-white

light. There's a car a little distance in front. He checks the passenger wing mirror. There's a car quite a distance behind. They're cruising quite comfortably in the left-hand lane. The hedges are rolling over Owen's reflective aviators, and their environment is perfectly cool and quiet apart from the music playing. Owen listens mainly to classical, these days.

'Slept okay?'

'Did we hit something?'

They passed a decapitated deer on the roadside last time they drove out into the sticks. Owen laughs.

'Mahler 6.'

'What?'

'The second hammer blow. I've played you this before.'

'You turned it up especially though, didn't you? You're lucky I didn't box you on the jaw.'

'Were you having a bad dream?'

'I'd somehow conflated this with that song by Fad Gadget about a wasp trying to nut its way out of a window.'

'"Insecticide"?'

'That's it.'

Owen laughs.

'You're a strange man.'

They pass a billboard advertising a stately home available for weddings, featuring a smiling white gay male couple.

'Are you alright?'

'I'm perfectly relaxed,' Owen says. 'We're crossing Dedham Vale. Not long now.'

Jesse thinks about the customer he served yesterday, and wonders how this apparently outstandingly beautiful land – Constable Country – could produce such wilful ignorance, but roads are roads. Cars are cars. The land in the country, as in the town, as in the city, is spoiled by cables, electricity pylons, STOP markings, road signs, brightened nevertheless by the yellows of wild cowslip. Hedges, where the last of the red campion and honeysuckle grow, block the views of the landscape – the occasional gap shows a field of dry hay bales or cleared ground through which lilac teasels have sprung. The hedges are in place so that the people who live there and get to enjoy the beauty every day don't have to be subjected to a procession of random traffic.

He wonders what it might have been like for his Jamaican grandparents' generation, coming to England for the first time, taking trains from Tilbury through England's greenest hills, unaware that most of the people in the chocolate-box villages they were passing through would rather non-whites turned round and got the fuck back on their banana boat. How times change. On the day after the referendum, the first beautiful sunny day in London in what felt like weeks – regardless of the news – Surenna Chalise Bailey was told to *go back to the jungle, you fat nigger bitch* by some guy in a dirty white vest coming off the Tube train she was boarding at Stockwell on her way to the Barbican Library. She only heard him because she was listening to the quiet phase of Florence Beatrice Price's *Concerto for Piano in One Movement* through her noise-cancelling Bose cans. She just got on the train, sat her arse down good in the end seat and dissolved him in her inner acid as she read Claudia Rankine's *Citizen*. But she hasn't forgotten. She expects it, now, from people who present themselves a certain way.

Would their grandparents' generation have fallen in love with England right away? If so, how long would it have taken for the honeymoon to end? He's read Andrea Levy's *Small Island* and Sam Selvon's *The Lonely Londoners*, which told him more than any documentary ever could or any family member ever had. He knows they've forced themselves to forget those early days. He misses his grandmother, his family on his mother's side. He misses her dutchpot, her ackee and saltfish with fry dumplin, her currygoat and rice, her Saturday oxtail soup. The smells of the gravies, the oil she cooked the saltfish in with bacon, salt, pepper, onion and garlic. Gini's food's great but she's vegan. Her child will never know.

He reaches over to squeeze Owen's thigh, and Owen folds his hand over Jesse's, soft and warm, a writer's hand. Perhaps, after all this time, he couldn't feel safer, in a stately old BMW 523i SE – the classic, complete with roulette-dish alloys – on a country road, with the man he loves. He would love to have a mother he could introduce his everything to, as other people take for granted.

That photograph was the end between them. He wishes he had kept his nose out of her business; maybe, eventually, she would have shared it with him, if he'd given her the time she needed. Perhaps that would never have happened, and if so, that would have been her prerogative. They had fought over the photograph, and it had been torn in half. It is gone forever. All he has now are maybes, speculations, and he can't even ask her. They have not spoken one word to each other since he left home at nineteen. Fifteen years. She has not tried to call him once. He'd called the house. Hannah, the littlest sister who probably didn't remember him at all, answered and she went to fetch her dad. Graham came on the phone and said, *Allo*, like it was the gas board or something. *Oh*, he said when Jesse said, *Hello, Graham. Dad. It's Jesse*. A silence passed and Jesse asked him how he was. *Fine. We'm all fine*. He waited for a *how are you* in return, which didn't come. He should've waited longer. It had been ten years. Shamed the motherfucker – ha! – into caring, even fakely. 'Is Mum there?' *No, she's out on field service. Maybe give her a ring in the week if you wanna talk to her*. Another silence passed. *Alright* ... Graham said. Not *alright* as in, 'are you alright?', but *alright* ... in a downward-inflecting tone, in the sense Brummies and people from the Black Country use it, to say 'are we done here?' or 'fuck off, then'. *Jehovah's Witnesses*. 'I just thought I'd call to see how you were,' Jesse said. *Right*, came the response. *Well, I'll tell your Mom you rang, then. Alright, then. Bye now*.

'I need a piss,' Jesse says.

Owen checks the map on his phone, stuck on the windscreen with a suction cup.

'There's a petrol station in a few miles. I could do with a coffee, too. Shouldn't have drunk last night.'

They stop to pee and buy water and black Americanos. Jesse gasps when he reads Melania's blizzard of WhatsApp fragments. She got drunk after work, went back to Ben's flat and he fucked her without a condom all night. *Babes oh my God he's so amazing though*, she says. *I can feel him in my toes.* He's already gone to work, and she's rolling around naked on his sheets, smelling him, until she has to go in for four o'clock.

Nicholas St John grew up in Richmond with his mother and sister. His father Randall was the sort of travel writer who never came home. They descend from old landowning money, and so have always just done whatever they wanted. His mother Daphne was, according to Owen, very much a Joan Crawford type, alcohol-dependent, and emotionally disturbed, having never dealt with the fact that she was raped repeatedly as a child by an uncle. It was a relief to Nick to be sent, at eight, to a boarding school, then public school, before walking into Trinity College, Cambridge; his sister, frequently and indiscreetly described by Nick as *my stupid sister Caroline*, was left to live with her mother's bouts of clinical depression. Nick took Owen under his wing at Cambridge, and they have remained close. Owen always insisted he was straight but Nick always knew Owen wasn't. Nick always had boyfriends, and if anything, Owen saw Nick's sexual recklessness as consistent with his upper-class privilege, which made Owen himself more determined to stay real and responsible, and apparently therefore straight.

Nick is editor of *Endymion* – a small-circulation, preciously produced literary journal; has written several biographies – most famously of Rupert Brooke – and set up his own publishing house, The Endymion Press, to publish poets and short fiction writers, all gay men, whom he believes stand at the very top of the tree. Apart from their house in London, he and his husband Jean-Alain live in a detached, thatched-roof cottage painted a shade somewhere between tangerine and terracotta, with several stained-glass windows and a trained bougainvillea bursting richly with purple flowers. The tiny white blooms of a gypsophila pop stunningly against the muted orange. Owen pulls the BMW onto a grey slate driveway next to a grey and black three-door Range Rover Evoque, and Nick comes out to greet them in a white Polo Ralph Lauren shirt and black Birkenstocks, smiling coyly with his hands in his jeans pockets. He's tall, dark blond, yoga-slim and austerely bronzed.

They get out of the car, and naturally, Nick embraces Owen first. Jesse notices the casual intimacy with which he looks Owen in his eyes, the unguarded freedom of his smile and the tightness of their hug, held so long they begin muttering and breathing together. Owen appears almost short in comparison. Nick marvels at their silver new-old car, and Owen jokes that Jesse's to blame for getting him back on the road. Nick releases Owen and approaches Jesse as if in surprise, narrowing his smile and lowering the tone of his voice slightly as they kiss each other on the cheeks. He pats Jesse on the arm like an old chum before guiding him into the house, almost by the small of his back. They enter through the pale green door – under the distressed frame of which six-four Nick has to duck – into a long hallway of naked dark grey concrete hung with still-life oil paintings, and further into a huge extension scattered with sofas, plants, unique pieces of furniture, bunches of flowers and books. Jean-Alain, looking very brown and bursting out of a white deep V-neck T-shirt, minces in through the patio doors with a big schnauzer grin and a fistful of coriander.

'You remember Jesse, don't you?' says Owen.

'Of course! Hi! Welcome to Suffolk!'

While many of the gay male couples Jesse knows could pass for brothers, Jean-Alain could hardly be more different from his husband. About forty, half-Lebanese but blue-eyed and white-passing, he is the most baroquely hairy person Jesse's ever come across, with a thick, dark beard, almost Nietzschean moustache, thumb-thick eyebrows that meet in the middle and a carpeted chest, back-of-neck and forearms. They've met twice before, but it looks as if Jean-Alain's been to the gym a few hundred times since then. Though less tall, he's much thicker than Nick, and has the sort of glowering sexual presence that makes Jesse glad for his black privilege, in that he cannot be seen to blush. He cuddles and kisses Jesse and Owen muscularly, surprising Jesse by biting his lip. He apologises for the smell of the fish on the barbecue and swings his huge arse into the very high-tech-looking kitchen to finish preparing lunch.

If Owen and Nick are going to be holed up all weekend talking poetry, Jesse thinks, then he'll be more than happy for Jean-Alain, an architect by trade, to give him a tour of the bedrooms.

People must have been much shorter in the sixteenth century, when this cottage was built, than they are now, and Jesse wonders whether Nick might not develop some sort of long-term osteopathic problem living here. The guests opt to put their bags up in their room straight away, and follow Nick through the house while he and Owen natter in that way best friends do when they haven't seen each other for a while.

'So what did you *listen to* on the journey?'

'Mahler 3, Abbado, then 6, Bernstein. Jess was asleep but was woken up by the second hammer blow, quite entertainingly.'

'Only because you turned it up.'

'Ha-ha. Very stirring music for a bracing drive,' says Nick.

'It was perfectly relaxing. Isn't it unbelievable how gold and brown everything is from the sun?' Owen says.

'It's even more dramatic looking down through a plane window,' says Nick.

'Is this a Fantin-Latour? No, of course not,' Jesse interrupts, feeling ignored, to ask about a painting, halfway up the stairs, of brightly coloured and various flowers, immediately swallowing his silly mistake.

'No, no,' Nick laughs. They stop to contemplate it. 'It's a roughly contemporaneous copy of a work by an obscure seventeenth-century Flemish painter called Osias Beert. It doesn't quite demonstrate the natural command Fantin-Latour had, sort of three centuries later.'

'Fantin-Latour didn't feel the need to smash you over the head with the fact that these are *beautiful luxury flowers*, did he,' Owen says, turning to Jesse. 'He often toned down colours and shapes and chose roses which were well past their best, such as you might find on someone's grave.'

'They painted in very different times. Fin-de-siècle artists of all disciplines were pretty nihilistic. Just look at these bonny little spring butterflies,' says Nick.

'Paintings like this always remind me of that Henri Rousseau school of "I've never been to the tropics in my life but here's live footage of an actual tiger bounding through the rainforest",' says Owen. Nick laughs, showing all his perfect white teeth, and doesn't look offended at all. 'Pretty, though. Love the leopard-print vase.'

'Ha! Why have I never seen it like that?' says Nick. 'No wonder poor Jean-Alain bought it. Overpaid horribly. Thanks for noticing it though, Jesse. I thought it might disappear, unlit, on the stairs, among all these other, authentic, exquisite, Dutch, Flemish and Spanish still lifes.'

They laugh and come up on to a landing papered in dark blue with a vine pattern, hung with oil portraits and decorated with antique furniture. There are temperature control panels at each doorway. Nick takes them into a pink bedroom facing the rear garden, with a four-poster bed and two walls stacked from floor to ceiling with serious-looking hardbacks. A bunch of fresh roses blooms fragrantly in a black-and-white jasper vase, depicting what seems to be a homoerotic Greek scene, on the walnut art deco dressing table in front of the window. The floor appears to be black leather. Nick suggestively opens the door to an antique rosewood wardrobe chiming with empty hangers.

'Drinks in the garden in fifteen minutes?' he says.

'Sounds good,' Jesse and Owen reply at once, and Nick leaves them to it.

'I always forget the way I end up feeling like I live in a complete shithole every time I come here,' says Owen, ripping off his clammy T-shirt and taking their toiletries into the en suite bathroom.

'Are those the original Scott Moncrieff translations of Proust?'

Jesse crosses the room to pluck out the first volume of *Swann's Way*, blowing the dust off the top as Owen always does.

'It wouldn't surprise me in the slightest,' Owen calls from the bathroom whilst washing his face and hands.

'Have you seen them before?'

By the smell, they haven't been opened and read for some time. They belonged to Howard St John, dated January 1923.

'We had those exact same full first editions at my college library,' says Owen, coming back out still topless and pushing back his hair.

'Who was Howard St John?'

'Nick's great-grandfather. Very eccentric and odd, reclusive man. Left London to escape the Great War, then when it ended, sent his wife and sons back while he stayed here alone to write until he died. Completed a couple of *quite* good novels, but wasn't nearly productive enough to account for several decades of voluntary exile. His huge stacks of poetry though, discovered after his death, reveal him to have delighted in the company of young, hung, full-of-cum farm lads, some of whom he might even have had on this very bed,' he says, pushing Jesse down onto it.

They eat a delicious lunch of barbecued sea bream and fattoush salad, mostly listening to Nick and Owen bitch on about various of their Trinity contemporaries while racing to the bottom of a 2015 Pfalz labelled IF YOU ARE RACIST, A TERRORIST OR JUST AN ASSHOLE, DON'T DRINK MY SAUVIGNON BLANC, after which the poet and his editor, without a word, retire to their literary business in Nick's study.

'There's a market on this weekend, about a half-hour drive away,' Jean-Alain suggests to Jesse while they clean up in the ultra-modern, white-clean kitchen, like a set from a sci-fi film. 'It'll be mostly all shit but there's a good organic store in the village I wouldn't mind picking a few things up from for dinner. Do you collect anything?'

'Books? Records?'

'Then we could go there, if you want. On the way back we could stop off at the pond. Did you bring any swimwear?'

'I didn't.'

'Ha-ha, you might not need any; the boring bastards here hardly use it. The pond, I mean. Just in case, I've probably got some old ones that don't fit me any more from when I was a skinny bitch like you. You wanna see my wardrobe?'

Nick and Jean-Alain's bedroom is also floored with black leather. The walls are rendered in polished light grey concrete with a hint of pink, so the room looks like a luxury version of a Genet prison cell, with roses cut from the garden on the mahogany chest, and in one corner, a giant chandelier of crystals draping down to the floor and pooling. That corner is also given to books. The light shining through the fragments of old stained glass casts coloured panels on the walls and the very large four-poster bed, which Jesse for a moment imagines himself being allowed to enter through its white lace curtains, like a groom handling the layered skirts of his new wife's wedding dress. He imagines Jean-Alain ready and waiting within, naked and showing his arse, watching over his shoulder as he climbs in. Jean-Alain throws open the mirrored doors to a whole scene of leather, kilts, harnesses and the studs and straps of bondagewear.

'None of this fits any more,' he says, rifling through and picking out the odd skinny trouser leg, the odd leopard-print mankini. 'Can you believe my husband and I almost never have sex, now? Well, we did last night, but . . .'

'Why do you have so little sex?' Jesse laughs.

'Babes. Marriage. Don't. It will be the *death* of your sex life.' He is speaking at a volume, with the window open, as if Nick isn't just the other side of the house having a quiet and serious work discussion. 'You're lucky to catch me here, I only do one weekend a month. This place?' He rolls his eyes. 'Babes. You ever been to our house in London?'

'No, where is it again?'

'De Beauvoir. It's on four floors. Dungeon in the basement all the builders fucked me in when they were finished. Amazing. I usually spend weekends alone there. Well, not alone, exactly.'

'So I guess you guys are in an open relationship?'

'Babes, 24/7/3-65! Aren't you? I would die!'

'We talked about it at the beginning and said it would be fine. Are you on PrEP?'

'Of course, babes! I was first in the queue! So you both see other guys?'

'Well, I do.'

'And him?'

'I don't actually know.' Jean-Alain must have seen that Jesse was lying when he said, 'Or care.'

'How long have you guys been together now?'

'Coming up for four years.'

'Babes, wait until you've been together for twenty. Like, Nick won't even fist me, for fuck's sake. I'm like, you're my husband, fist me now! And he's like, do you mind, I'm reading this poem by Ezra Pound for like the one million eight hundred and ninety-six thousand four hundred and forty-fourth time go to sleep and I'm like, fuck Ezra Pound! Pound me! Anyway, it's a gorgeous afternoon so let's get the fuck out of here. I've got like fifteen thousand pairs of swimwear in here. Let's see. No. Uh-uh. Ooh! Try these. Yay, perfect! Do you ever go to the men's pond at the Heath? There's a nudist beach in Suffolk but it's a bit of a drive and I have to be back to cook dinner for that lazy bastard and his guests coming this evening – and for you and Owen obviously! Actually it's a naturist beach so it's full of elderly people and kids so, I don't know if that floats your boat or not but I'll pass thanks.'

The English countryside is beautiful. Everyone knows that. Suffolk is no different. The narrow lanes. The quietness, encroached on only by the soap opera wittering of tiny unseen bird families. The sense that people live a good life, eat well from their own land and are strong and healthy. The clean air the children spend their whole lives breathing. The colours and gradients of fields growing different crops. The cutesy little road signs. The proliferation of buildings more than three hundred years old. The castles and stately homes. The vast numbers of churches for such a lightly sprinkled populace. The wildflowers filling every crevice with colour. But it is also quite oppressive. It is hard to find another black face, any face of colour. A white person can go to Suffolk and blend in. A black person from the same place as that white person is assumed not to be local. If not a local, then an alien. If an alien, then someone not versed in local customs, a potential contaminant, someone to take umbrage with or else completely ignore.

From what Owen has told him, Jean-Alain's father is a Lebanese doctor who fled the civil war in 1975 to work in France, where he met Jean-Alain's mother, a fashion journalist.

Jean-Alain and his sister went to international school in Paris, before he trained with the Architectural Association in London, while she studied languages at Columbia and now works for Unicef. Their parents have retired in Greece. Jean-Alain is as foreign as most folk in Suffolk are used to.

Jesse has never found the countryside relaxing. It makes him anxious. He feels he has to explain his presence to everyone he meets. He has to smile at everyone extra broadly so that people smile back. He has to speak extra clearly and with cut-glass diction so that he doesn't have to repeat himself. It's not *cum on, buzz* but *do you not also wish, dear Cuthbert, that the advertised 88 route might appear with marginally increased regularity on such brisk winter mornings*? And still people look at him like he's got three heads, and laugh.

'You okay, babes? You're really quiet.'

Jean-Alain is swinging the Range Rover around corners like it's a go-kart, playing the sort of unmentionably dull, overplayed, copycat early 2000s R&B that made Jesse lose interest in the genre for a decade.

'Yeah, I'm okay.'

'Tired? Babe, you're on holiday. You should relax.'

'No, no, it's cool.'

'What's going on? Is everything okay with you and Owen?'

'Yeah, everything's perfect.'

'Are you sure? You can tell me, babes. I know what it's like, obviously, being a person of colour in a relationship with a white man. Especially like a proper upper-class, English white man. If we didn't hate each other so comfortably I would've left him a long time ago. We wouldn't be married, because I don't for a minute believe he thinks of us as genuine equals. I'm a trained architect. I'm part of the furniture at Foster & Partners. My salary is more than he will make in ten years, not that he wouldn't have greater earning potential than me if he pulled his fucking finger out. You know how an upper-class white man can just put on a suit and tie and walk into any bank and back out with a million pounds? You and I could never do that, even with the same or greater qualifications.

'If I left him, babes, I'd be fine. He'd make a million in a second, but would he be happy? Babes, no. His personal life would fall to pieces until he could find another boyfriend-stroke-servant to move in with him, cook his food and make it okay for him to go retire to his horrible, toxic, racist, complacent, inbred, white supremacist homosexual world of high poetry. His imprint is the ultimate white gay vanity project; he only publishes white gays he thinks are too good for Faber. I'm telling you, once white gay men have automated the world so that robots do absolutely everything for them, found out how to make their own little white male babies and made it legal to fuck each other's teenage sons à la ancient Greece, they won't need anyone else. They're gonna kill us all, babes. When the water runs out and the place is cooking because of the climate they're gonna look round and be like, *Who's got all the money? Oh well, let's just round up all the brown people, the women and non-white gays and push the fucking button.* That's why even in this whole post-post-postmodern age you've got the fucking KKK back, I mean, look at the thing they're about to nominate! They make us fall in love with them and subjugate ourselves to their legend, but they will never allow us to share in that unless it suits them, unless it massages their salvation. We will always be something other, something inferior.'

'Wow, you really needed to say that,' Jesse says, agreeing with most of it but noticing the flaw in his argument that straight white men might have something to say about.

'I really fucking did!' He bangs the steering wheel, and laughs. 'You know when you don't realise what you think until you've said it?'

'But I genuinely don't feel that way about Owen. I know exactly what you're saying, not that I think someone like you could be trapped unless you wanted to be, but that's not what

I'm going through, because my boyfriend has that awareness. There's nothing he can do about being white, but he knows he has to be absolutely aware of his privileges at all times. He knows he is part of a group that has to give up some of its privileges, and he knows that having the choice to be able to give up some of his privileges is also a privilege. I mean, he recently turned down the Head of Department job at his university and nominated someone else highly qualified who is a woman of colour, and she got the job, which was as much as he could've done for her, because he understands it's about voices being heard in the right places. I know exactly where you're coming from, though. I had this Tumblr account that I had to delete. I was following all these Black Lives Matter blogs, all these African-American black history blogs, and the stuff I was learning was the real truth. From top to bottom. How white people have turned everything to their favour. How they have written and rewritten and reedited history to put themselves in the place of God, using the Bible . . . '

'When there isn't even a single white person *in* the Bible!'

Jesse, who grew up being suffocated with the Bible as if it was a pair of used Y-fronts, had never even thought of that.

'Right? You're right. You're absolutely right. But I just got so caught up in all these blogs and all this discussion, and it explained exactly why my life was the way it was, exactly why my mother was such a bitch to me, exactly why she was such a bitch full stop, exactly why Trayvon Martin died and the killer got away with it, exactly why Stephen Lawrence got murdered and my dad, my white adoptive dad, said, *Oh well, he must've done summat to piss 'em off*, exactly why it's taken twenty fucking years to bring those callous motherfuckers to justice, exactly why black people get overlooked for a white person for most jobs, exactly why the prisons are full of black people who get punished ten times harder than a white person. White supremacy permeates every aspect of our society.

'Obviously, I was learning a hell of a lot about black history and black thought, and having the way plotted out for me to read further, Frantz Fanon, the non-fiction of James Baldwin, CLR James, Audre Lorde, etc, etc. *12 Years a Slave* came out and I burst into tears the second that poor mother got separated from her babies and they were all sold off like fucking actual cattle, and I knew that it was true, and I knew that my ancestors, albeit in a different part of the world, went through something similar, and I realised what a fucking miracle it was that I could be alive because, *white fucking men*, not God, had decided who worked where and who fucking bred with who and my line survived.

'But do you know why I deleted my Tumblr? Because for every one of those brilliant blogs I was following, for every long and sensationally enlightening essay someone posted, I was also following a blog featuring white American daddies showing their assholes, because I just couldn't fucking not, and very quickly I was scrolling past the brilliant essays just to see that next pussy, and I just couldn't deal with what I was feeding into my brain, the dichotomy of wokeness and the attraction to lick, suck and fuck white male ass, because I was literally still licking the oppressor's ass or worse still *dreaming* of licking the oppressor's ass at the very same time as being fed the truth about the long history of his terrorism. I was basically saying to my phone screen, *You can kill my body, you can tear me to pieces and you'll get away with the whole damn lot but can I rim and fuck you first?*

'It was so fucked up. So it all just had to go. But if I blame individual men for all or any of that, I can't live. I wouldn't be able to cope. I'd been seeing Owen for less than a year when all that happened. He didn't know what was the matter with me. I actually almost came to the conclusion that I was never going to speak to a white man again as long as I lived, or at least not have sex with one. But how can that be? If I write a book, who's gonna buy it? White people. If I try to borrow money from the bank, who's gonna sanction it? White people. They have us by the fucking everything, never mind the balls.'

'Babes, I don't even fuck white men outside my relationship any more. I don't give them the satisfaction,' Jean-Alain says as he parks the Evoque somewhere with a pub on the corner and a market on. Several pubescent boys see Jesse and visibly scowl. They cross the road, and Jesse stares down at his own feet. He catches the word 'Dudley' on a drain cover. Better still, it says DUDLEY & DOWELL LTD CRADLEY HEATH STAFFS. Made up the road from where he was born. Cradley Heath, which for a couple of hundred years made sixty-pound chain links for the world's ship anchors (and much smaller ones to bind slaves). How he missed it. The Black Country. Home.

Owen and Jesse walked back to their flat after the picnic and Owen opened a bottle of red wine. They talked about everything Jesse remembered, everything he had ever been told or had been curious about not having being told. Owen had to stop him from ringing up his parents and screaming. The fact that Robert died of AIDS, and was still alive in at least 1990; perhaps Thurston had *met him* at that group show in '91. It was staggering for him to think that he had been alive for at least eight years while this man – the man Jesse was now giving himself the option to believe was his father, because why not! and how cool! – was living in London painting nude portraits of himself with flowers.

He tried Googling him. He freaked out to find Robert Alonso Twitter handles and Robert Alonso Facebook profiles but they were all white Latin American or Spanish and nothing to do with the Robert Alonso mentioned twice in exhibition catalogues from around 1990 that had been scanned as PDFs and weren't hyperlinked to anything. Images, predictably, brought up nothing at all. He texted Thurston – without telling him why because it would sound so far-fetched – to ask if he could have another look at the painting. Where was the rest of his work? Conroy might know, or at least be able to find out.

He kept saying to himself, *I have a dad and he was a painter I have a dad and he was gay or bi I have a dad who was still alive in the early Nineties I have a dad and his name was Robert and he had eyes just like mine I have a dad.* He had been given no explanation for how his father had died, as his mother had claimed he had, in 1984, when Jesse was two, or of why she had failed to put his name on the birth certificate. Perhaps it had been just a one-night stand. Artists are often itinerant; perhaps she hadn't been able to find him. He imagined her going to take an HIV test, despite the fact that Jesse would've been conceived in the summer of '81, earlier than the first diagnosed case of HIV in Britain.

He took several forgotten books down from the shelves at home and buried himself in them. *Rotimi Fani-Kayode and Alex Hirst*; *By the Rivers of Birminam* by Vanley Burke; *Black Britain – A Photographic History*, with an introduction by Paul Gilroy. He watched Horace Ové's *Pressure* on the BFI Player before bed. He filled his mind with pictures of tall, gangly men in skinny flares and afros under flat-caps, as Robert Alonso might have looked in the Seventies, and the naked or leather-clad bodies of dark-skinned black homosexuals in the Eighties. Owen warned Jesse against getting too excited about an unconfirmed attachment to somebody so long gone. *But he was my dad*, Jesse reminded him. *My name is Jesse Alonso.* He imagined that name on the cover of a book.

He realises all too quickly that he's the only black person among the crowds at the market, his only company being a couple of wistful, straw-chewing negro slave ornaments, a framed photograph of a grinning minstrel in blackface playing a banjo, and several golliwogs. Political correctness has not reached this part of the country. Wokeness is a century away. He wonders about the diversity programmes that increasingly fill every bronchiole of London life but that would be pointless here because there are no people of colour, so people do not get taught – and do not expect to be pulled up on – why it is so offensive, and triggering, like a swastika to a Jew, for black people to be confronted with a giant big-red-lips-white-teeth golliwog sitting on the centre of a mantelpiece.

He wonders what would happen if he tried to steal something, as several times he approaches stalls to pick up an object to examine it, only for the stall-holder to turn his back. His skin burns under the glare of a thousand pairs of eyes that drop away from him as soon as he locates them; people stare, but don't want to be caught doing so in case they might be accused of being racist. They glance at his brown legs and suppress laughs. Haughty, dignified, white gay male couples sitting outside cafés in the sun with their arms folded, looking as if butter wouldn't melt, do stare at him, blatantly, as if to say, *Seriously, what are you doing here, city nigger? We came here to get away from the likes of you.* Then they realise he's with Jean-Alain, the hairy bubble-butt muscle-bear fantasy they anaemically tried and failed with on Scruff because he only likes eight inches or bigger, and Jesse's the one left grinning.

Black people appear in the English countryside on TV, on the national news, either as criminals, sportspeople or readers. Jesse wonders whether they might think the BBC News is overrun by blacks and Muslims, so overrepresented are they compared to the world they know. Each man, woman and child who walks past him sets off another schoolboy taunt in his head. It gets to feel like he can't look anyone in the eye, even when he orders a coffee from the organic food store Jean-Alain is rooting around in the back of. He waits outside until it's ready. He doesn't want to have to deal with people's individual responses. He doesn't want to have to ask himself why one person flinches and another refuses to look, while another is being too polite. His legs are the same colour as his face, and he does not have a physical disability. He doesn't want to scare anyone. He doesn't want to be pressed against or follow someone who might think he'll try to steal from or rape them. In Brixton, he crosses the street, or at least makes himself obvious by pretending to talk on the phone, just so that he doesn't come across as attempting to creep up on people, especially women, at night, when he happens to be walking in the same direction, a couple of seconds behind. He feels like an escapee in plain sight, waiting to be trapped. There's little he can do in a marketplace. He hears a snatch of conversation between two women walking past – *They're everywhere, now, aren't they* – *Yeah, I thought that*, and wonders whether they're talking about him.

The barista calls out, *Flat white and Americano for Jesse.* He collects and mutters a *thank you*, eyes down like he's being questioned by the police.

Everyone turns up impolitely early or on time. Jean-Alain, in a breast-baring unbuttoned short-sleeve shirt and ass-hugging white trousers, has left the kitchen momentarily to introduce Owen and Jesse to Father Alexander Merrick-Shaw and his Canadian husband Patrick, who look almost identical, with gym-toned bodies, perfectly groomed yin/yang beards, double-breasted tailored suits and loafers without socks; 'Please, call me Alex!' is about twenty years the senior.

Quickly behind them Jean-Alain introduces Jesse to the Tory peer and Brexiteer Clive, Lord Groombridge. Jesse recognises him immediately, and hopes to God, with a rising panic, that the recognition is not mutual. He'd know that floppy side-parting and those golden-grey caterpillar eyebrows anywhere, and was sure the rather leering stare and sweaty lingering handshake, that felt like putting his hand into a boxing glove someone else has just vacated, would lead to an alarming change of facial expression, but Clive maintained a lofty sheen of ignorance (which was perhaps even creepier). He imagines Clive's wife,

Lady Pamela, possibly the poshest-looking woman he has ever met, would destroy him if she found out. A nimble sixty, with warm brown hair and full make-up, she's wearing a jade-green tailored satin dress with a patent crocodile-leather Delvaux clutch under her arm, and enough jewellery to bring on back trouble. The soles of her stilettos are as red as her lips. She stares blankly into his eyes, smiles and firmly shakes his hand, quickly moving on to Owen – who insists they've met before but she doesn't remember – as if she were there for twenty minutes to cut a ribbon.

While Owen talks to Father Alex and Patrick, Jesse sneaks himself back into the airy coolness of the kitchen, a blue-white grid of lines, right angles and consistent panel gaps that serve to exaggerate further the male-Kardashian curves of its inhabitant. Jean-Alain pops a garlic sourdough crouton with anchovy and Roquefort straight into Jesse's mouth, encouraging him to suck his finger and thumb; the sourdough is pleasingly crunchy and soft, almost chewy.

'I really enjoyed our little swim,' he says.

The water had been freezing cold at the start but they got used to it. There were other people there so they did wear trunks. They splashed about and wrestled, bit each other, kissed in violent little dabs. Jean-Alain is a man of great physical strength, and Jesse is sure he is quite a handful for his tops. He had the audacity to cup Jesse's dick, hard even in the cold, struggling in the seersucker swim shorts, under the water. *Mmm, nice*, he said. *Naughty*, Jesse said, grabbing handfuls of his ass, finding him with a finger. A family turned up and it was time for them to go. Jesse wonders if Nick and Owen are aware of the flirting. He thinks they probably are, but that it is probably par for the course with Jean-Alain, in particular, and Nick knows all about Jesse's promiscuous past.

They drove back from the pond with the windows down, blazing a playlist on Jean-Alain's iPhone called 'Black Girl Pop'.

Timbaland's drums had never sounded slicker. Wearing their shades, they clicked their fingers and flicked their necks to Missy Elliot and Da Brat's 'Sock It 2 Me', pretending they were in the music video fighting belligerent robots on a faraway planet. They sang along to Brandy & Monica's 'The Boy Is Mine', word-for-word; Jean-Alain began singing Brandy's role in her octave, so Jesse had to test himself singing Monica's in hers, going into falsetto too early and having to stay there. The quality and power of Jean-Alain's voice surprised him; when he asked, he told Jesse that he'd been in choirs in his youth and had been encouraged to train as a countertenor, but his then-chronic shyness prevented him. Jesse remembered experiencing the same with school bullies picking on him for playing the trombone.

They returned to find Nick and Owen still holed up in the study, only emerging to quickly shower before dinner. With the door open, Jesse saw an empty cafetière, empty wine glasses, a plate with the remnants of biscuits, a pile of papers and a stack of other writers' collections, reminding him of the still lifes on the walls up the stairs. Owen told him the meeting went well, that Nick loved the new poems. Now that he's got that load off his shoulders, he's emptying his glass quicker than it can be filled.

Jesse heads out with a tray, and follows it, once empty, with the champagne to top everyone up.

'Never not working,' quips Nick, who, as a host, is doing nothing more physical than watching the barbecuing hake.

The alacrity with which Jesse finds himself taking up a servile role frustrates him. He says, *I'm used to it*, when Patrick compliments him on his style of champagne pouring, and smiles uncertainly when Alex and Lady Pamela size him up with admiration, as he emerges with the second tray of canapés flat on his left palm. Yet he laughs off any suggestions to the negative when Jean-Alain, perhaps spotting a minuscule eye-roll, asks him if he's sure he doesn't mind helping. He throws his lips at Jesse and plants five big smackers on his cheek. *Extra nibbles for you*, he says. He desperately wants to tell Jean-Alain about his history with Lord Groombridge, but feels, for the sake of the evening, that he'll have to keep his mouth shut, difficult when so many varied provocations are making it so slippery wet.

Jean-Alain sits the party down in the air-conditioned dining room; Jesse has not seen this much polished silver, on the table and in the backlit cabinets lining the burgundy William Morris-covered walls, since he last visited the V&A. He's next to Lady Pamela; Nick, at the head of the table; and opposite Lord Groombridge. Nightmare.

'We'll swap before dessert,' Jean-Alain reassures.

The first platters go down – a warm courgette salad with pomegranate, Lebanese tomatoes, radish, cucumber, coriander, molasses, chilli and zahtar, and warm hunks of home-made baguette.

'Doesn't it look delicious!' says Lady Pamela, talking to Jesse for the first time.

'It really does,' he says. 'By the way,' he gestures, so that she's aware of the bit of parsley stuck to a top tooth, which she removes with the tip of a varnished nail.

'Gone?'

'Yes.'

'Should come with a warning, haha,' she says. Everything she does and says is accompanied by a monied laugh, as she shakes her expensively blow-dried hair back from her face. 'Ooh, red, please, haha.'

Nick's going around pouring the wine. 'White, or red?' he says, at Jesse's shoulder, a little too firmly, as if in resentment at serving someone he should be being served by.

'I'll start with some white, please.' Nick pours the 2012 Hermitage Blanc splashing into Jesse's glass. 'I've never tried a white Côte du Rhône before,' he says, trying to impress, but Nick moves on to Clive without responding.

The dining room is a-murmur with the *mmms*, *oohs* and continued chatter of eight salivating mouths, and the tinkles and scrapes of silver on porcelain. Jesse is experiencing something quite different, with Lord Groombridge sitting right opposite, discussing the inner machinations of the House of Lords post-referendum. Jesse might have fun with the red-top press if he was still broke, but then again, if he was still broke, he wouldn't be attending a dinner party sitting in a medieval throne-chair.

He's dared to look Lord Groombridge squarely in the eye. Nothing. Perhaps it's just an act, one that counts on him being just as secretive about his past as Lord Groombridge is about his. Perhaps it's a function of upper-class white male arrogance that he doesn't in a million years think Jesse will have the guts to open his mouth and talk. He's stood with his back to the wall and his hands clasped in front of his dick in so many private dining situations before, as a waiter, while important people have been very indiscreet in front of him. Discretion is a part of both of the careers that have defined him, but he finds it outrageous that people will in front of him discuss damaging personal and political gossip, on the assumption that he, as a server, will not be intelligent or literate enough to do anything with that information.

It's not, Jesse is certain, an issue of recognition. He would only have to look at Lord Groombridge a certain way for his rectum to open involuntarily. *Fuck me with that big black dick.* If the world was like that he would excuse them both from the table to another room the other side of the house, pull his sheepish little pants down and give him a good old thrashing for his impudence. He used to love being spanked. They've both changed in the ten years or so since, but their skins are still stretched over the same skulls, Lord Groombridge's a little more loosely, it has to be said. Jesse looks more like a man now, and so certain men, who once valued his boyishness, will now automatically have turned their backs.

'Mike' used to request Jesse to turn up at his door wearing a tracksuit and a cap; he affected a terrible South London accent over the phone right from the beginning so as to speak to Jesse *on a level*. He required Jesse to wear his sweatpants down low, showing his arse in his boxers, because he liked his boys *saggin'*. Jesse would make his way to 'Mike''s Marylebone pied-à-terre and pull his sweatpants down just as he was about to ring the doorbell. 'Mike' would answer the door wearing his own, and a T-shirt or vest. He wasn't bad-looking at all – he still isn't, really – and Jesse might've fancied him a bit more if he'd just been himself. He used to fuck him in front of his giant Georgian gilt-framed mirror on his drawing-room carpet, smoking the weed Jesse brought and sniffing poppers, and he'd say, *Yeah, you love fucking that big white daddy arse, don't ya, boss*. He saw Jesse practically weekly for a while, then he suddenly vanished after that last time, the best time. There'd been days when Jesse was struggling and texted 'Mike' to remind him he was still around, because he was fond of him, really, and he was generous, but he never replied; Jesse assumed it was because he'd suddenly felt ashamed. He still remembers the smell of him, of his particular cologne that he's never discovered the name of, mixed with poppers; the sense of his body relaxing out in front of him, turning himself into a heavy mound of soft flesh; the slapping sound of their connection, the ripple of fat up his back, the sight of his eyes closed and his mouth squashed open on the towel.

So distanced is he – sitting opposite him and talking to Nick about the inherited Constable he's just had reframed above his drawing-room fireplace – from any notion of that life, that he questions himself: is it really him, or am I just projecting my filthy, immoral past on to an innocent man? His voice is the same, though he's ditched the approximate South London accent for present company. He had no idea that he was married to a woman, and assumed he was gay. Even then, because he was so clearly neither poor nor unattractive, he wouldn't have found it difficult to get a boyfriend, so why did he have to hire an escort? It *is* him. The accent may have changed, but the voice is the same, the mannerisms. The hair's the same, the eyes and the jaw; the smile, the pheromones. Jesse is not going to gaslight himself.

'So, young man, what brings you to Suffolk?' asks Lady Pamela, and Jesse hopes she didn't clock him staring at her husband.

'I'm Owen's boyfriend. He and Nick went to university together.'

'What, Owen went to Cambridge?'

With a little hunk of bread in between her nails she scoops up beautifully dressed little mouthfuls of the salad onto her fork.

'They read English together.'

'How fascinating. And you, do you go to Cambridge?'

'No,' Jesse said, as if he should be embarrassed to have not gone to Cambridge, fearing her next question will be, *So what are you doing here, then?*

'Which university *do* you go to?' She is now assuming he is in his early twenties.

'I haven't been to university.'

'Whyever not? It's so easy these days!'

'I just never found myself in the right life situation. But I may still in future.'

'So what do you do with yourself, then? Are you into sport?'

Owen catches his eye, whilst talking to Father Alex, and winks.

'Not really. I write, a bit.'

She almost chokes.

'Really? And what sort of writing do *you* do?'

'Non-fiction, I guess.'

'How charming,' she says, flatly. 'Have you had anything published?'

Her rings clink as she takes up her goblet, which already has big red lipstick marks on it.

'Not yet,' he says, pathetically.

'Oh well, I suppose there can only be one genius in the family, hahaha, yes please, darling!' she says, as Jean-Alain hovers the red over her shoulder, winks and pops a kiss in the air at Jesse as he tops up his white. Father Alex cuts in to ask Lady Pamela how her banker sons are getting on in their new houses in 'Hackney, is it?'

As the wine gets louder in Jesse, he is ready to butt back in to tell her that he quite cleverly fucked two grand out of her bottom bitch husband, actually, but as if to forestall him:

'Please join me in raising a toast to my beautiful, wonder-ful husband, Jean-Alain. My love, I don't know where I'd be without you.'

If Jesse's been wondering whether Jean-Alain is happy being such a formidable man playing dogsbody to his lordly husband, the brimming look of love across the table quells any doubt. All raise their goblets.

'To Jean-Alain.'

Chapter 5

The Black Country. Wull-*VRAM*pton. He has played Beyoncé's *Lemonade* and Solange's *A Seat at the Table* three times on a loop, preparing himself for how, later today, he will turn up unannounced at his parents' front door. To reprogramme his memories. 'Home' sounds like a Knowles-sister album now. Of his engagement, his friendships, his work-in-progress, his holidays. Not the way it sounded before, of engines burning, of diesel fumes, of the landfill site, of the derelict gas works, of the rickety rackety 644 West Bromwich-Great Bridge shuttle bus. Of *Oi, Jovo!* Of uPVC windows shutting. Of *Not today, thank you*, or even of people not coming to their door because they know the Witnesses are working their street. Of rubbish cluttering up the drains, of supermarket trolleys blocking the canal lock, of the belt coming down across his arse across his back across his thighs, or porn strewn through the stinging nettles along the overgrown old rail line. Of the sound of his parents' front door slamming. Of his mother, holding a sharp knife, saying, *I wish I could just put this in you*.

He has come armed with the truth. *I break chains all by myself; won't let my freedom rot in hell*, Beyoncé sings as he rings the doorbell.

Conroy put him in touch with Glorie. A neatly trimmed

front garden. Hanging baskets either side of the front door. Creeping wisteria that will look gorgeous in spring but for now, it's raining. She recognises him straight away. She gives him a strong hug, a loving, motherly hug. *He's ever so posh*, she says to her daughter. There is a true family resemblance. The shape of the eyes. Their eyebrows, thick and shrewd, naturally arched, no need to pluck or shape. He has them, Aunty Glorie has them, her daughter Mareka has them, her grandson Rashan has them. Robert had them. Owen, in a different way, has them.

His father, Robert Alonso. Aunty Glorie Williams, his cousin Mareka Williams, and – he supposes – his second cousin, Rashan Powell. His future husband, Owen Gunning. A whole new family.

Now he has three nephews, a niece, and a godson, Bilal. Gini said there could be no other choice than Jesse as godfather, even though he's no longer a Christian.

He tells Aunty Glorie and his cousin Mareka everything. Stays for three hours. They drink lots of tea, eat red snapper and hard-dough bread, and too much bun and cheese. Certain ornaments all Jamaican people of a certain generation have in their house, like that wooden block shaped like the island with a red, black and yellow ackee berry painted on it.

She shows him lots of pictures she has scanned, on an iPad. His father was *such* a handsome man. There he is playing football, aged fourteen. There he is, smoking a cigarette with a foot up flat against a wall. There he is, at Christmas. He fixates on all the pictures of the family, adds her on Facebook, gives her his email address so she can share them with him on Dropbox.

'Like father, like son, isn't he!' his Aunty Glorie says.

'Mum, you'll embarrass him,' laughs his beautiful cousin Mareka. He just wishes she wouldn't straighten her hair.

Glorie's mother was a lovely-looking woman called Claudette, who served as a nurse. She is dead now. Cancer. Her father she never knew. His name was Norman. He had the eyes, too. He died even younger, of a massive stroke caused by a brain aneurysm. On a summer's day, when he was just thirty-three, he went into the kitchen and dropped like he'd been shot in the head. Robert wasn't even three at the time. Glorie herself was only just over a year old. They both screamed and screamed, climbing on their father's body until the neighbour came round. Luckily, everyone left their doors open, then.

'I don't think Mum ever recovered from that,' Glorie says. 'She tried her best to raise the two of us by herself but it was hard for any black woman in those days. She sold the house and moved here, where it was cheaper.'

'It's hard now,' says Mareka.

'But the racism in those days.'

'Nothing's changed in that respect,' says Mareka.

'It was extra hard for your grandmother, in the late Fifties, with two children to raise, a dead husband to bury, two jobs just to pay the rent, the shame – being from Jamaica where everyone works hard and if you don't work hard you stay on the street – of having to claim benefits if she didn't work those two jobs. And your grandfather was such a good man. She had men at the door asking for her hand in marriage but *None a them fit to lace yuh Daddy shoe*, she used to say. She carried on, carried on, carried on, worked herself into the ground, almost literally. But she came back, and became a matron. And she was able to make this house a home, which you're not getting if that's what you've come for, son-of-Robert.'

She scares him for a second, pointing her green-nailed finger, but she knows that's not at all why he's there, and they all laugh. 'Haha, me a joke. Seriously, the house is nothing special, but it came at a price because she couldn't always keep us together. Robert found life difficult sometimes, and for a while he went into foster care. He lived with one white family for a couple of years and they nearly adopted him. But he came back, and became a painter. All us idiots were telling him to get a real job, and now look at us, talking about his work! What do you know about it?'

'Only what Conroy's managed to find out from the archives. Some of his paintings he sold and are untraceable. But there may – must – be someone somewhere who owns or knows where his studio was and where he kept his canvases, his drawings. I just hope it hasn't been destroyed, because it's good, and maybe, one day, if we do find more of it, we might be able to exhibit it and raise awareness of his existence, as a black artist, as an artist who lived with AIDS, because he's potentially important to both those narratives.' His aunt and cousin watch him so intently, Jesse has the thought they might not be listening to what he's saying, so impressed do they seem by his presence, his existence, his maturity. They giggle like teenage girls at times. 'As it happens, I met someone when I first moved to London, someone from Wolverhampton – of all places – who owned a painting called *Nude With Othello*. I went to visit him to look at it again. I was extremely lucky, because he's retired now, his partner's passed away and he's about to sell his house and retire to the south of France, because of Brexit. It was definitely a self-portrait by Robert. He bought it at a group show in Brixton in 1991, though unfortunately he doesn't remember meeting him. Othello was the name of the rose in his hand, bred right here in Wolverhampton by David Austin.'

'Never!' says Aunty Glorie.

'I've got a picture of it. Do you want to see it?'

'Do I want to see it?' she says, pulling her head back and looking at him through her side-eye.

'It is a bit rude.'

'Then I'll take your word for it, thanks,' she laughs, then drops it quickly from her face. 'I did see him once, before he died. I went down to London and visited him in the hospital.

I couldn't stay long; I couldn't bear to see him like that, and I had Mareka with me.'

'I don't remember that,' says Mareka.

'You were three, or summat. You shouldn't have been there, really, but I took you just to have an excuse not to stay if I got too upset. I left you in the creche. There was no way in a million years I'd ever have taken you onto an AIDS ward.'

'I do have one memory of him,' says Jesse. 'I was at this horrible dinner party, during the summer, in the countryside, the day after I spoke to Conroy. Ugh, it was horrible, this dusty old Brexiteer and his disgusting bejewelled Louboutin-wearing wife who ground her bottom up against me when "Jenny From the Block" came on because I was the only black person there.' They both grimace and laugh as if they know exactly the sort of person Jesse is talking about, though they could never have met someone like Lady Pamela. 'It was vile, and I couldn't help it, I got drunk and shouted my mouth off about the arrogance and ignorance of people who put their own needs before those of the greater number, trust me, I was provoked. But then, do you remember Wham!?'

Aunty Glorie glares at him as if in wonder at the strange turns his thoughts take. 'Of course!'

'Well, their song "Freedom" came on – *doo … doo … doo! Doo … doo … doooo!* – and I had the instant – they call it involuntary memory – recall of being, I must have only been two or three years old, just like *he* was when *he* last saw *his* dad …' His voice breaks.

'Oh, darling, it's alright,' Glorie says, and squeezes his forearm tight. 'You got any tissue, Marie?' She shuffles around in her bag and plucks out a pack of Paloma.

' … And I was in a kitchen, with a tall black man in his pyjamas, and he was making me Weetabix for breakfast, and that song came on the radio, the horns, so distinctive, and I just knew straight away that it was him, and it was all I had of him, so my mother must've known about him, and he must've known about me, and she let him see me. But then she told me he was dead, and he was lost to me, until now.'

'I'm so sorry, Jesse,' says Aunty Glorie. 'But your mom'll have that on her conscience until she is dead.'

'I'm trying not to blame her for everything. The Eighties were a different time, especially when it came to sex being so mixed up with death, and Section 28 coming in and all that. All our favourite pop stars and Hollywood actors dropping like flies. I never for a million years thought my dad would be part of that world, but I'm proud of him. He's like a king, to me.'

'Oh, Jesse. And I'm sure he'd be proud of you.'

'I wish he could come to my wedding,' he says.

'You're getting married!' says Mareka, clapping her son's hands together.

He shows her his phone screensaver.

'Owen,' he says.

'Ooh, he's handsome,' Glorie says, without missing a beat. 'Good for you. I mean what I say when I say Robert would be proud of you, you know, Jesse. You're smart, a good person, I only just met you but I can tell. You didn't deserve to grow up with pain, and look at the person you've still grown up to be anyway. With what's going in the world, it's best to be with someone who makes you feel loved. Nuh waste your time with people who don't.'

He hopes his Aunty Glorie, cousin Mareka and second cousin Rashan will attend. Rashan can play with Bilal. Mareka will meet Jesse's sister Esther, almost her cousin, and their children can play together. Ruth and Hannah, as Witnesses, won't let themselves be there. Of course, their parents are out of the question. They belong to the past. This isn't the past. This is now, and the future.

ACKNOWLEDGEMENTS

With thanks to Sharmaine Lovegrove, Dominic Wakeford, Millie Seaward, Emily Moran, Thalia Proctor, David Bamford, Alan Hollinghurst, Emma Paterson, Monica MacSwan ... and all my friends and family.

CREDITS

In memory of Isoline Vassell – my grandmother – and
Alejandro Mendez (no relation)

Bringing a book from manuscript to what you are reading is a team effort.

Dialogue Books would like to thank everyone at Little, Brown who helped to publish *Rainbow Milk* in the UK.

Editorial
Sharmaine Lovegrove
Dominic Wakeford
Thalia Proctor
Sophia Schoepfer

Contracts
Anniina Vuori

Sales
Andrew Cattanach
Ben Goddard
Hannah Methuen
Caitriona Row

Design
Bekki Guyatt
Jo Taylor

Production
Marie Hrynczak
Narges Nojoumi
Nick Ross

Publicity
Millie Seaward

Marketing
Emily Moran

Copy Editor
Jon Appleton

Proof Readers
Maya Berger
Charlotte Chapman